TEXAS STALKER

BARB HAN

STAY HIDDEN

JULIE ANNE LINDSEY

MILLS & BOON

First Published in Great Britain 2021
by Mills & Boon, an imprint of HarperCollins*Publishers* Ltd
1 London Bridge Street, London, SE1 9GF

www.harpercollins.co.uk

HarperCollins*Publishers*
1st Floor, Watermarque Building,
Ringsend Road, Dublin 4, Ireland

ISBN: 978-0-263-28356-3

1021

FSC
www.fsc.org

MIX
Paper from responsible sources
FSC™ C007454

This book is produced from independently certified FSC™ paper to ensure responsible forest management.

For more information visit: www.harpercollins.co.uk/green

Printed and Bound in Spain using 100% Renewable Electricity at CPI Blackprint (Barcelona)

TEXAS STALKER

BARB HAN

All my love to Brandon, Jacob and Tori,
the three great loves of my life.

To Babe, my hero, for being my best friend,
greatest love and my place to call home.

I love you all with everything that I am.

Chapter One

"Thanks for walking me to my car again, Hammer." Brianna Adair waved at Jeff Hamm, a.k.a. Hammer, for his work as a bouncer at the club where she bartended, before sliding into the driver's seat of her Jeep.

"You got it, Brianna. Be careful and remember what we talked about," Hammer said with a wag of his finger. He might be six feet eleven inches of stacked muscle, but on the inside, he was all teddy bear. Unless someone crossed a line. Then, the Hammer dropped and he earned his nickname.

She adjusted the rearview mirror, checking for any signs the pickup truck from a couple of nights ago was around anywhere.

"If the jerk comes back, I go straight to the cops just like before." Cranking the engine, she blew out a slow breath. Since she hadn't been able to get a good look at the driver and there was no plate, the police report she'd filed had been pretty slim. She shook off the fear rising inside her, trying to convince herself that the mystery guy would not return for another round of stressful late-night bumper cars.

Adjusting the mirror again, all she could see as she pulled away was Hammer. The hulk of a man stood in the parking lot with his arms crossed, watching as she safely pulled away from work.

Her nerves were fried, and her pulse kicked up a few notches just thinking about the ordeal. *Determined* was her middle name. Actually it was Jayne but there was no time for reality. Point being, she'd been working at Cowboy Roundup for two years now and there was no way she was letting a drunk cowboy run her off a job that paid better than any other she'd had up until this point. Not that she planned to bartend for tips the rest of her life. Or even the rest of her twenties. If she was still mixing drinks next year, she'd consider the past two years a colossal waste of time. Working late nights in a skintight shirt and Daisy Dukes was a means to an end. And the end was coming soon. Thirty-seven more days. She'd be hanging up her bandanna for a laptop as soon as she finished her associate degree in website design.

She was so close that she could almost feel the nine-to-five. She'd be trading in white tennis shoes for heels and work lunches. So, yeah, she kept on slinging drinks and ignoring comments about her "perfect" backside and the sizable chest genetics had forced on her. Speaking of genetics… She took one hand off the wheel long enough to touch the necklace that had been a gift from her mother, a lucky charm in the form of a four leaf clover. Maybe some of the luck would rub off on her.

With wheat-colored hair and cobalt-blue eyes, Brianna was the spitting image of her mother, save for her mother's bright red hair. Brianna could only hope her physical features were the only things she'd inherited from the woman. After her parents finally landed jobs at a ranch, so the family could be together after her father had spent most of her childhood working an oil rig, her mother had blown the new sense of security by having an affair.

To make a long story short, her parents had divorced but not before a move and a third attempt to "save" the family. So, the small Texas town where she'd tried to finally put down roots had ended up in the rearview faster than a cowboy could say *tequila shot*.

Her parents had given it a good go in San Antonio. The move had been meant to bring the three of them closer together and, if she was being honest, save her parents' marriage. Going into her sophomore year of high school, the tension at home and the stress of the move finally caught up to Brianna. Her grades fell apart faster than her parents' marriage.

At least they'd tried. Now her mother lived in Nashville with the lead singer of a country band. Not long after news of her mother's remarriage circulated, Brianna's father had an accident on the job and, for the next decade and counting, mostly drank while collecting disability checks and basically swearing off women.

So, yeah, her family was rocking it out. Christmases were awesome. And she realized the lucky charm hanging around her neck might not be so lucky after all. A literal sigh tore from her mouth at the bad memories. She loved her parents, don't get her wrong. And she couldn't blame them for trying to hold it together or how badly it fell apart. Many nights, she'd heard them arguing they needed to stay together for her. Marriage. Family. Commitment. Those words caused her to shiver involuntarily in general and made her a little bit nauseous to boot.

She brought her fingers up to trace the charm. The necklace—a sweet gesture from her mother to bring her daughter better luck than her own—reminded Brianna to stay the course in school and at her workplace after bouncing around from job to job. It reminded her that she didn't have to take a traditional route in life and was probably better off if she didn't as long as she didn't crush anyone else's feelings in the process. It reminded her of the love that could so quickly turn to misery.

Brianna had graduated high school. Barely. Not that she wasn't smart, she'd just refused to get good grades. Looking back, she was trying to punish her parents but ended up hurting her own chances of getting into college. Oh, and she'd refused to take college entrance exams, too. So, you know, she was a real rebel. The only person who seemed to be hurting from her acts of defiance was her. She blamed it on the teenage brain, which, in her defense, hadn't been fully developed at the time.

She'd been too stubborn to ask for help, even when she realized she needed it. Besides, her parents had had enough on their plates fighting day and night while getting divorced. That took a lot of time and energy.

Even though her mother had cheated on Brianna's father, it was impossible not to feel like the woman had cheated on the whole family. At the very least, her actions had had a ripple effect. And wasn't that so true in every area of life?

But, hey, Brianna wasn't about to start feeling sorry for herself when graduation was around the corner. She'd managed to get through midterms and then straight through to working on big final projects caffeinated and on very little sleep because she'd had to take extra shifts at the bar recently. Good for her bank account and bad for the bags under her eyes.

A little concealer later, and she was ready for another

night. The bartending phase of her life was winding down and she couldn't be happier.

Except that lightning just flashed out of practically nowhere and storm clouds started rolling in. She hadn't checked the forecast in a few days—mistake number one in a place like Texas—but she didn't remember there being any rain in it. The zipper was broken on the door of her secondhand Jeep, Code Blue, named for how many times a month it flatlined on her. Not exactly vintage enough to be classified as a jalopy, her vehicle was so old that it didn't have Bluetooth technology or a USB port. It was paid for, though. And that was all that mattered in a vehicle. Comfort was optional. Reliability preferred. But complaining did little good to reverse a situation. Trust her, Dad had done plenty of that when Mom had left.

Real change in someone's life took focus and hard work.

The funny thing was that she would have loved driving this beast in the two years she'd lived in Katy Gulch. She could imagine having her friends pile in and go mudding after a good rain.

That was the old Brianna. The girl who knew how to have fun. The girl who had an easy smile, as her wild hair—hair that she ironed now—flew into the wind carefree.

Code Blue sputtered and she thumped the floating gas gauge. Seemed okay but it was hard to tell. Brianna was looking at buying something more modest now as she socked away new-car funds. If she couldn't get something brand-new, she'd settle for new-to-her. Something more conservative. And something that wouldn't let the rain in while she drove to an office job on a nine-to-five.

And speaking of rain, a couple of droplets hit the

windshield. Of course. Her time at Roundup was coming to a close and these last few weeks were going to take her for a ride. Well, saddle up, baby, because she wasn't going to let a little water bring her down. There'd been enough wet blankets in her life, and she was so done with negativity.

Famous. Last. Words.

The downpour came on like a tsunami. There was so much rain that her canopy literally ripped a little bit more. Of course, the water came in on the driver's side where she sat, dripping on her face and shirt. She put her left hand up, trying to hold the canopy together so she didn't get flooded.

She shook her head, and rain flew everywhere. So, yeah, more of that Adair luck was kicking in. So much for the charm.

Determined not to let a little rain get to her, she refused to give in. She kept smiling, working hard not to let herself get in a mood. She forced her thoughts away from the jerk who'd pinched her bottom when she'd left the relative safety of the bar to clear a table because her busboy hadn't had a break since he'd shown up. Neither had she, but that didn't count. She could handle it. Her busboy was barely legal and there was no way she was going to work that poor kid's fingers to the nubs.

She could sure use a tall glass of wine about now as she flipped on her windshield wipers, which basically sloshed water around. She needed new blades. The next thing to fail her was the antifog mechanism. All of which she'd promised to get fixed once finals were over.

She needed to make a list of things that she'd been putting off. She'd driven past the dealership every day this week, looking at that powder-blue four-door sedan, thinking how nice it would be when she was no longer at the mercy of Mother Nature as she drove to and from class or work.

Out of the corner of her eye, she saw headlights as she passed Maple Road. A pickup truck sailed around a corner, scaring the crap out of her. The vehicle zoomed up to her bumper, pulling up so close she gripped the steering wheel tighter as she readied for impact. *No. No. No. Not this again.*

Brianna managed to swerve into the next lane when he roared up a second time. She strained to get a look at the driver's face. She couldn't make out who was behind the wheel. She had half a mind to pull over or next to him and give him a piece of her mind except that would qualify her as *too stupid to live.*

Road rage was one thing. This guy, if it was the same one, had come back for seconds. A bad sign.

Instead of going head-to-head with Pickup Jerk, she decided to see if she could lose him.

Come on, baby. She could only pray that Code Blue wouldn't fail her now. A fork in the road was coming up and she figured that would be the best time to make a move. She slowed down enough for the jerk to get close to her bumper again, then pushed Blue as fast as she would go.

At the last minute, she cut the wheel right. The maneuver worked. Pickup Jerk veered left just like she'd wanted him to do.

Before she could celebrate, she saw his brake lights in the rearview mirror. He would catch up to her if she stayed on her current path. Dread settled over her, but she knew exactly what to do. Head straight to the cops. She'd mapped out the closest substation after the last encounter.

This time, she was ready.

"Go ahead. Follow me now." Brianna drove the couple of blocks to the substation with the truck on her tail. It tapped her bumper a couple of times, jerking her head forward. Whiplash was not going to be her friend later.

This guy needed to have his license revoked. A night in county lockup might make him question his decision behind the wheel.

Her shift had been long. All she could envision was getting home to a hot bath and a soft bed. She was so done with that job it wasn't even funny. So, picking up a stalker in her last month at the bar wasn't exactly high on her list. And she would take this incident very seriously.

As she pulled into the parking lot of the police station, Pickup Jerk must've realized where she'd just led him because he peeled off in a hurry. Not exactly his smartest move, in her opinion.

At the angle she was sitting, his license plate was just out of sight. She almost turned around and tried to follow him except that Hammer had warned her not to do that. After tonight, she might just grab a shotgun and leave it inside her Jeep.

Okay, bad plan. She couldn't even zip the door shut. There was no way she could leave a shotgun in her vehicle. Knowing her luck, Pickup Jerk would steal it and shoot her with her own gun.

So, yeah, that wasn't happening.

Now, the question was whether or not she should follow through with going inside and filing another report. She was so tired that her bones ached and all she could think about was a hot bath and a warm bed. Nothing sounded better than going facedown on her pillow and it wasn't like she had anything new to tell the officers inside.

Except that this was serious. All her warning bells flared at the fact this man had returned for a second battle. He seemed to know where she worked, and he could follow her home. An involuntary shudder rocked her at the thought.

All right, she decided. She'd go inside and file a report again.

As she sat idling in the parking lot, the hairs on the back of her neck pricked. The feeling of eyes on her caused an uneasy sensation to creep over her. She had the sensation people got when they said a cat walked over their grave.

Trying to shake it off, she glanced around and then checked her mirrors. He might've parked and was on foot because she couldn't see his pickup. Was he watching her? Waiting for her?

With a heavy sigh, she cut off the engine. After zipping up her door the best she could, she checked the back bumper but didn't see any new scrapes or dents. She headed inside the station. Hammer would be proud of her. Actually, he'd be pretty upset that the guy had returned and tried to run her off the road. Creep. Hammer saw himself as guardian of the female bartenders and waitresses at the Roundup. He took their safety personally.

It took half an hour to file a report—for the second time in a week—and fifteen minutes of that was spent waiting to be called to speak to the desk sergeant. He looked to be a few years short of retirement. Stiff back, hard face and mostly bald. He was thin and tall when he stood up to greet her. He stayed behind the counter as he took her statement. She relayed everything that had just happened as he wrote notes, tagging the new information onto her first complaint.

"Any additional damage to the vehicle?" the sergeant asked.

"None that I could see." The parking lot was well lit.

"Be careful on the way home," he urged with a compassionate look.

"Yes, sir." Best as she could tell, *she* wasn't the problem, but she got what he meant by it and gave him a small smile in return.

"Here's my card. Call if he shows back up tonight," the sergeant said.

"I will," Brianna said, taking the card he'd offered, unable to shake the creepy thought there could be a round two.

Chapter Two

This was routine to the officer, and here Brianna was totally out of her comfort zone as she exited the substation. He'd taken her statement and told her to let him know if she saw the truck again. He reminded her not to put herself in vulnerable positions and to stay in well-lit areas if she had to be out at night. He suggested she be aware of her surroundings at all times. She would do all those things. And yet, there wasn't anything comforting about the exchange.

She was still walking away to drive on a near-empty road to an even emptier apartment. Great that she had two incidents on file should this guy come back or do something even worse to her. The cops would be able to lock him away then.

At this point in her life, she had no one at home to make sure she made it there safely. What if she walked into her apartment only to find this guy waiting? The police couldn't exactly arrest every single guy who drove a dark truck to ferret out the jerk who was making her life miserable.

It wasn't like she could call someone this late to come stay with her either. Besides, it wasn't like she had a lot of friends. The past two years had seen her basically keeping her head down and studying. If she wasn't going to class or studying, she was working.

Suddenly, living alone was losing its appeal. She'd always wanted a dog but that was out of the question with her schedule. It would be too cruel to leave an animal home alone most of the day and late into the night. Having a regular nine-to-five where she didn't have to be out on the roads in the wee hours sounded better and better.

Adrenaline had kicked in and it felt like she'd just taken a shot of espresso. So, basically, trying to go to sleep when she got home and settled was going to be fun, if by fun she meant torture. At least she could sleep in tomorrow morning. Thank heaven for small miracles.

At least there was a little activity in the parking lot when she walked to her Jeep. Shift change? Break? She had no idea what a police officer's schedule looked like.

Unzipping the door, she checked the backseat just to be sure. At least the rain had let up. When she saw it was safe, she climbed in the driver's side. The other night when the same thing happened, it had taken hours for adrenaline to wear off. She'd binge-watched Netflix until the sun had come up. By the time she made it to class the next morning, she'd been a zombie.

So, she was none too thrilled for a repeat. Worse yet, this guy really seemed to have it out for her. She started the engine and checked the gas. The floating gauge could be tricky. It didn't move. She thumped the plastic cover over the gauge and it finally moved…all the way to *E*.

Stopping off at a gas station was now her first priority.

Driving, she was keenly aware of anyone else on the road, especially since other vehicles were few and far between at these hours. She kept checking her mirrors, and her stress levels were through the roof by the time she hit the gas station. She picked the largest one she could find that had plenty of lights, figuring it couldn't hurt to be easily seen by the attendant. Not that she could be picky considering how low her tank was.

As she exited her vehicle and opened the tank, Brianna searched her memory for anyone who stood out at the bar lately. After using her credit card and getting the green light, she started pumping. Whoever was making her life difficult had to have come from work. Right? That was the only place she could imagine, especially since she'd been driving home from the bar both times.

The bar had been hopping and there'd been a few regulars, but that was about it. No one stood out.

What about school? Another brain scan turned up empty. She pretty much kept her head down and tried to draw as little attention to herself as possible. No one had tried to speak to her or ask her out on a date.

A truck pulled into the parking lot and her heart sank. Panic caused her chest to squeeze and her hands to shake. And then the fire came back. She refused to live like this. She refused to be a victim. She refused to cower in the face of a bully.

The driver pulled up opposite her at the pump. And the person who stepped out brought a blast from the past along with all kinds of memories.

"Garrett O'Connor? Is that seriously you?" she asked, grateful for a familiar face even if it had been years since she'd seen anyone from that family or that town.

"Brianna?" He tilted his Stetson and his smile sent warmth washing through her. "It's been a long time."

"It sure has," she agreed. And yet not much had changed. Garrett was still tall and gorgeous. He had to be six foot four inches of solid muscle. Working a cattle ranch would do that to a person. He'd never been the workout-at-a-gym type. He was more of a get-his-hands-in-the-earth person. He was also part of one of the wealthiest cattle-ranching families in Texas. "Do you live here in San Antonio?"

"Just passing through," he said, and she realized that his answer was pretty cryptic. Not that it mattered. Why he was in town was none of her business and he was the least creepy man on the planet.

"Wow. I can't believe it's you. How long has it been?" She willed her hand to stop shaking.

Nothing got past Garrett. He studied her with eyes that bored into her, leaving a fiery trail in their wake.

"Everything all right?" he asked, his dark, masculine voice trailing all over her.

There was no use lying to him. And, besides, what were the odds she would run into an O'Connor at a gas station in the middle of the night? And it was Garrett no less. The guy she'd dated who'd also broken her teenage heart. They'd only gone out a couple of times but the minute he'd learned his brother was interested in her, he'd backed off big-time. The man was honor and cowboy code to the gills.

A coincidence like this one couldn't be ignored. It was too random and that made her feel like maybe talking to him again was meant to be. And since she needed to be honest with one person about just how freaked out she was, she said, "No. Actually. It's not."

GARRETT O'CONNOR BLINKED a couple of times just to make sure it really was Brianna Adair on the other side of the gas pump. There she stood in all her glory, basically five feet five inches of beautiful sass and wit. She'd been a real heartbreaker in the past, and it was surprisingly good to see her again. Being a decent person, he couldn't let her comment slip past without offering a hand if she needed one. "Anything I can do to help?"

Garrett and his brother Cash had been born fighting. But Brianna was a huge part of the fallout that Garrett had had with his other brother Colton years ago. Colton was happily married and living in Katy Gulch, Texas, with his new wife and twins. The incident with Brianna was water under the bridge by now.

"Do you mean that, Garrett?" She stared at him with the most beautiful set of serious cobalt-blue eyes. Her straight wheat-colored hair fell past her shoulders and he couldn't help but miss the freewheeling curls that used to be there. The slicked, straight hair still framed her heart-shaped face perfectly. And those pink lips—lips he had no business staring at but sure had enjoyed tasting as a teenager. They'd shared one kiss but it had become the benchmark for all others. And there'd been something about those loose wild curls trailing in the wind that spoke to the heart of her true spirit.

"Wouldn't have said it if I didn't." He had no idea the trouble he was about to get into but for every second she hesitated, he figured the ante went up a few more chips.

"How much time do you have?" She put a balled fist on her right hip.

"I make my own schedule if that's what you're asking." He sized her up as he took a step closer to see if she'd been drinking. He didn't think so based on the person he'd known in high school but people changed and a lot of years had passed since he'd known her.

"Can I ask what you're doing out this late at night?" he asked. Looking into her eyes, ignoring the electrical impulses firing away like stray voltage, he got the impression she was spooked by something or someone. A quick glance around said there weren't many other vehicles on the road. A boyfriend? A husband? An ex?

"I just got off work." She shifted her weight and bit down on the inside of her cheek. That move transported him back to high school. It was also her tell that she was outside her comfort zone.

"And? What's going on, Brianna? I haven't seen you in years and, excuse my saying so, but you look like you've either seen a ghost or done something that's making you scared to go home. Bed is where most folks are this time of night." He'd always been honest to a fault. It was another reason his and Colton's relationship came to a head more often than not. So much so, Garrett had decided a long time ago that it was better he did his own thing rather than work on the family ranch—a cattle ranch that was worth hundreds of millions with associated mineral rights. He was part of a legacy, but he'd always had the need to carve out his own future rather than have it neatly lined up and sorted out for him. Call him unconventional but he had a bone-deep need to create his own life rather than be handed down a fortune for hitting the genetic lotto.

"I could ask you the same question," she fired back after a thoughtful pause.

"What?"

The gas pump clicked in her left hand. She nearly jumped out of her skin. Quickly, she pulled it out of the slot and then replaced it. She leaned her forearm against the tank and said, "Like you said, it's the middle of the night. Why are you here in San Antonio? Plus, don't you live in Katy Gulch?"

"Me? Nah." He noticed how she'd turned the tables. It was easy to see that she needed help, but could he get her to be straightforward enough with him to figure out what that meant?

Chapter Three

"I'm here. Talk to me."

Garrett was right. He was there and it should be easy to talk to him. So, why did the words clog in her throat every time she tried to open her mouth to speak? She knew him. Or, at least she used to be friendly with him.

Friendship wasn't the right word for what had happened between them, though. They'd been close at one time and the chemistry between them sizzled enough to set the gas station on fire even as teenagers. That same draw to him that she'd felt years ago—that same sense of being safe and having someone who would look out for her—had caused her to be honest a few moments ago when he'd asked, when she should've said she was fine and let him be on his way.

"Want to come to my place for a cup of coffee?" she asked, shifting her weight to her other foot. The nervous habit from high school stayed with her to this day.

"Will you tell me what's really bothering you if I do?" He was playing hardball with that devastating show of straight white teeth.

"Yeah, sure."

"Is there someone I should be worried about at your place, Brianna?" he asked. He didn't come across as worried about being able to handle himself so much as mentally preparing in case there was a fight. Garrett had never backed down from a bully and she figured he wasn't about to start. There was a lot of comfort in knowing that some things could be counted on to stay consistent in a world of change. She also realized why he'd seemed so concerned about her.

"Oh, no. It's not like that. I'm not seeing anyone who would do anything like…who would hurt me in any way." The words came out in a rush. What could she say? She didn't want Garrett to think her judgment in people had lapsed to the degree she'd get involved in an abusive relationship. Granted, abusers could be pretty tricky and not reveal themselves until it was too late. But, that wasn't her situation.

Despite the fact her parents had gotten into some pretty heated arguments, there was never any threat of physical violence. Words hurt and there was no excuse for some of the things they'd said. But slaps and bruises had never been part of their deal and she was grateful for that much at least.

"Good." That one word sent a thrill of awareness skittering across her skin. It was more the way he said it. It was the hint of relief that she wasn't in a relationship. Goose bumps prickled her arms. The dark edge to his voice that had a way of washing over her probably caused them. Even at fifteen, he'd had a low timbre to his voice that stirred warmth deep inside and feelings she couldn't begin to know how to handle at a young age.

All of which she didn't need to notice right now, especially after she'd invited him to her place. Of course, she could chalk it up to nostalgia or the fact he had the kind of cowboy code that said he would step in front of a bullet to protect someone he cared about. The fact was probably even more appealing under her present circumstances.

Which actually reminded her that she might be asking him to step into harm's way. He deserved to know the truth so he could make a determination as to whether or not he actually wanted to follow through with going to her place.

His nozzle clicked. He replaced it on the stand and finished his transaction.

"So, Garrett. I should tell you that someone tried to run me off the road earlier. The reason I'm out so late is that I work as a bartender and some creep has followed me from the club twice now." Hearing the words, remembering, brought back the terror of the incidents. Sure, in the moment she'd been reasonably calm, but they had rattled her. She wasn't eager for a three-peat.

"Good to know. Doesn't change the fact I plan to see you home and take you up on that cup of coffee, though."

Relief was a flood to dry plains. "Okay then."

The muscle in his jaw ticked, a sign he was working up to anger. He'd always been a little hotheaded when they were younger, usually around his older brother. The two had been gasoline and fire. She'd always felt a little guilty for choosing one brother over the other when she should've walked away from the attraction to Garrett. It would've made her life a little less painful because he'd broken her teenage-crush heart, ending the relationship before it really got started.

She'd known Colton had liked her. And he was a great guy. Everyone loved Colton. Girls lined up to ask him out. But she only had eyes for his rebellious younger brother. She should've realized she'd been playing with fire. When two brothers liked the same girl, it rarely ever ended well. And since hindsight was twenty-twenty, she also realized she'd been the one to end up hurt.

It was safe to say everyone had moved on from the situation. Her mom's affair had been exposed a few months later and then Brianna's life solidly went downhill from there.

Remembering all that made her realize just how far she'd come since then. She couldn't help but feel a burst of pride at how well she was pulling her life together in the past few years. The sacrifices would be well worth all these late hours at the bar. Plus, this dirtbag making her uncomfortable would move on too.

All she had to do was keep under his radar a few more weeks and she'd be home free. The best scenario would be for him to take a hint and move on.

"Ready when you are," Garrett interrupted her thoughts. "Which way are we headed?"

"Hand me your phone and I'll put in my address in case we get separated." She held out her flat palm.

He fished out his cell, unlocked it and placed it on her opened hand. She took the offering, and then added her cell number and home address into his contacts.

"I'm sending myself a text, so I'll have your number. Okay?" She glanced up and saw the way he was looking at her. His appreciation caused her heart to skip a couple of beats. She was reminded of the popular saying, *old habits die hard.* Falling for him was an old habit. One she didn't need to repeat. Could they be friends? She could use a few of those in her life right now but she'd start with one.

"Sure." His voice came off as nonchalant, but his eyes told a different story. They'd darkened, intensified as he studied her.

She wondered—hoped?—she was having the same effect on him as he was on her. Because being anywhere in the vicinity of Garrett was electric. A small smile upturned the corners of her lips. Even after all this time an attraction still surged. She had to hand it to him, he looked even better than he had before and that was saying a lot.

Handing back his phone, their fingers grazed and more of that electricity sparked. It was good to see Garrett again. A blast from the past, for sure. But also, it reminded her that she could feel like this for someone again.

Was it too good?

GARRETT LOCKED GAZES with Brianna as their fingers touched. Electrical impulses shot up his hand, vibrating through his wrist and leaving a sizzling trail up his forearm. Did she feel the same?

With the way she pulled her hand back, he'd think she just touched a lit campfire. The corners of his mouth turned up the second it dawned on him why. He shouldn't be surprised. They'd had that same mix of attraction and chemistry years ago and the only reason he'd walked away from it then was because of his brother.

The fight the two of them had had when Colton had walked in on Garrett and Brianna midkiss had been epic. The divide that had been growing between them for years became an impassable chasm that day.

Hell, Garrett hadn't known his brother had taken a liking to Brianna. Not that he could blame anyone for noticing her or wanting to be around her. She had one of those magnetic personalities that most people described as lighting up a room. Her smile…forget about that. It had a devastating effect, reminding him that he had a beating heart in his chest. Then and now. Not much had changed there.

Her parents worked and lived on a neighboring ranch until her mother's affair—an affair that had lit the town's grapevine when it was discovered who was involved. A deacon, who was very much still married at the time, and Mrs. Adair, also married, had been exposed when his wife had walked in on them in her home.

The Adair family relocated shortly after, but the two years Brianna had lived in Katy Gulch had breathed life into Garrett. Their breakup had been the right thing to do after finding out Colton had had feelings for her long before she and Garrett had met. It hadn't felt good then to end the relationship despite the circumstances and the memory was still sour.

"The address is there," she said on a shrug. "But you can follow me."

He glanced at his phone, memorizing the address. Despite his reputation in school for being the O'Connor who got mediocre grades, he had a photographic memory. School didn't hold a lot of interest for him, so he did just enough to get by. All he cared about was being outdoors, taking care of the land, and his freedom. Being told what to read and when, or what to study and when, had only turned him off a formal education.

Besides, there was a lot to be learned taking care of the earth and not every smart person lived with their nose in a book all the time. Reading was fine. He enjoyed it. Having someone else's taste pushed down his throat was something else entirely.

Garrett climbed into the driver's seat of his pickup and

navigated onto the roadway behind Brianna's Jeep. The spare tire had a cover that read Code Blue.

What could he say? It made him chuckle. Seeing her again brought up all kinds of dormant memories and feelings. Strange, those weren't normally things he paid much attention to. There wasn't much point in stirring up the past. Tension between him and Colton was usually thick, but that wasn't anything new. The two of them had been on better footing recently, though.

Since their father's murder, all of the O'Connor sons had rallied around their mother, as it should be. She was one strong human and he had nothing but admiration for Margaret O'Connor. She was the rock of the family, always was and always would be. She loved her boys and the feeling was mutual. She also did more for the community of Katy Gulch than any mayor ever could. She ran more charities and spent more time helping others than doing anything for herself. She'd brought up six very strong-willed sons, and she held her own against them.

If he read, it was because of his mother. Countless times he'd discovered her in her personal library where she loved to spend her free hours. Family. Community. Books. Those were the things she held dear. But it was the daughter she'd lost that had marked her, marked the family for sadness. No matter how festive a holiday or how much she smiled, there was always something missing. That something couldn't be filled by her husband or any of her sons. The loss of her little girl, her firstborn, wasn't something Margaret O'Connor had ever gotten over.

A house on KBR, Katy Bull Ranch, had been built for each O'Connor sibling, including Caroline even though their mother knew full well the likelihood Caroline would ever set foot in it was next to nil.

Margaret O'Connor clung to hope of her daughter's eventual return even to this day. Garrett couldn't blame her. He had no idea what becoming a parent was like and didn't have the desire to learn. Kids were great for some people. He'd seen his brother, Colton, fall head over heels for his twin boys from the minute they came home from the hospital.

Kids and Garrett?

He almost choked on the idea. Gripping the steering wheel a little tighter, he also thought about the shame it was that his father had gone to his grave without ever finding out what happened to his only daughter.

With the way both investigations were going, the family might never uncover the truth. He realized that his hold on the steering wheel had caused his knuckles to turn white. No matter what else happened, he couldn't allow his mother to suffer. She deserved to know what happened to her daughter, and her husband's killer belonged behind bars.

Brianna turned into an apartment complex that had three buildings and one large parking lot, about half with covered spots that were numbered. Her hand came out the driver's side window, pointing toward a sign that said Visitor Parking to the left. There were half a dozen empty spaces, so he grabbed the closest one.

Most people wouldn't hesitate to call him misguided for being here on a whim after a chance meetup at a gas station of all places. Since *bad idea* was basically his middle name, he jumped at the opportunity to help Brianna out. She wasn't exactly a stranger.

But then after all these years, did he really know her anymore?

Chapter Four

Brianna parked her vehicle and then waited for Garrett. She leaned her hip against the side and crossed her arms over her chest, in a lame attempt to stave off the goose bumps that rippled up her arms as he walked toward her. His strong, masculine presence was even more difficult to ignore the closer he got to her. The breeze carried his spicy scent, blasting her senses and stirring her heart. Had he smelled this good back in the day?

She cracked a smile at the thought. Yeah, he sure had. But they weren't at her apartment to reminisce about the old days. A cold shiver raced down her spine at the thought someone could be watching them now.

No. No. No. He couldn't have followed her home. She'd been too careful.

Before the thought could take seed, she wrapped her arm around Garrett's and led him up the stairs and to her apartment.

"Mind if I throw on some dry clothes?" Brianna said as they entered. She closed and locked the door behind them just in case. The extra precaution would help her relax a level below panic. Having Garrett here sent conflicting emotions raging through her from excitement to a sense of calm she hadn't felt in far too long.

"Be my guest." He extended his arm toward the hallway. An emotion flashed in his eyes that she couldn't quite put her finger on and decided it was best for both of them to ignore.

"I'll only be a sec. Kitchen's that way." She pointed even though it was obvious in the shotgun-style apartment. "Make yourself at home and feel free to put on a pot of coffee."

"Will do." The amusement in his voice caught her off guard.

She held her ground. "What's that look all about?"

Garrett really laughed now. "You always were a strong woman. Good to see not much has changed."

"I'll take that as a compliment," she quipped, unable to hide how pleased his statement made her.

"Good. Because that's how I intended you to take it." He didn't wait for a response. Instead, he brushed past her toward the kitchen.

Brianna turned on her heel and headed toward her bedroom with a grin. Didn't seem like much had changed with Garrett either. He was still that same tall, gorgeous and strong-willed person as before. She drew a surprising amount of comfort in the thought.

Yoga pants and a T-shirt seemed too dressed down for company. After peeling off her Daisy Dukes and button-down shirt, she threw on a fresh outfit. Standing in front of the mirror gave her a glimpse at black eyeliner that had run down her face.

Nice.

She traded the drowned rat look for a freshly washed face, applied a light coating of lip gloss and ran a brush through her hair. Or, at least she *tried* to. Her kinks were back and she didn't have time to mess with it.

The smell of fresh-brewed coffee convinced her she'd done enough primping. The one-bedroom apartment lacked space and the decor in the bedroom could best be described as exploded laundry basket. This place was nothing more than a temporary stop.

Taking a step into the kitchen where Garrett came into view caused her throat to dry up. She tried to blame her reaction on allergies.

"How do you take your coffee?" Garrett asked, holding up a mug.

"A little cream, but I can get it." She crossed the room in record time but he still managed to beat her to the fridge. Granted, her kitchen was small and he was standing right next to it.

He poured the cream into the mug. "Tell me when to stop."

"That's good." She only liked a tiny bit and he nailed it. The smile he rewarded her with did nothing to calm her racing pulse.

He replaced the milk carton and she got a good look at his backside. Nope. Nothing had changed there either. If anything, he was getting better with age. By the time he turned around, she'd forced her gaze into her coffee mug before taking a sip. The burn in her throat a welcome change from the dryness moments ago.

Brianna reached with her free hand and rubbed her temple. "I've been on my feet all night. Mind if we take a seat?"

"Not at all." Garrett's easygoing nature was another draw to him. Of course, he could snap to fire and frustration in two shakes but she'd rarely seen that side to him. He seemed to reserve that for his older brother, bullies and people who were mean to animals.

She walked to the round table with a pair of chairs off the kitchen, and sat down. The breath she exhaled released some of the day's tension.

"What do you know about the mystery guy from the bar?" Garrett asked, taking the seat across from her.

"Nothing. I have no idea who it could be." She shrugged before taking another sip.

He studied her for a long moment, as if judging whether to press her on this, then said, "I was surprised to find a coffeepot in your kitchen. Seems like everyone's doing pods now," he mused.

"I had one of those contraptions but I missed the smell. There's something about a pot of coffee on the warmer. It fills the whole apartment, which admittedly doesn't take much. Plus, I like to be able to walk over and refill my cup without any hassle, especially when I'm studying." She risked a glance at him. "Weird, right?"

"Not to me." The words came out so casually she believed him.

"Really?" she asked anyway.

"Half the reason I stopped off at a convenience store gas station was to get a cup of coffee tonight from a coffeepot. There is such a thing as too long on the burner, though, and you just saved me from burnt coffee."

"Are you on a road trip?" She could admit to being curious as to why he was driving around so late.

"Kind of. Not really. Chasing down a lead about…" He stopped and shook his head.

"What?" she asked.

"Nothing I want to talk about right now. Besides, I'm here for you not—"

She was already shaking her head before he had a

chance to finish his sentence. "Oh, no you don't. I don't want to talk about me until you tell me what's going on."

Garrett took a slow sip of coffee. He squinted at her like he was trying to analyze whether or not she was bluffing, so she folded her arms across her chest.

"I'm investigating a lead on my father's murder."

Brianna gasped and her chest squeezed.

"I'M SO SORRY."

Garrett had heard those words more times than he could count and not once had they felt like balm to an aching heart. Until now.

He chalked his reaction up to shared history and didn't put too much stock in it. "Someone used my father's credit card in San Antonio and I aim to find out who since it might be connected to the person who killed him."

"What happened to your father? When did he…" She brought her gaze up to meet his and it felt like all the air was suddenly sucked out of the room.

Garrett had to break eye contact and take another sip of coffee to focus on something besides the way her sympathetic gaze reached inside him, touching a place he never left vulnerable.

"He was killed on our ranch and left for the animals to…" Again, he had to stop and take in a deep breath.

"Who would do such a thing to your father? He was a great man, Garrett."

All he could manage was a quick nod of agreement. "We're trying to figure that out as we speak. My brothers have been tracking down information and several have returned to the ranch full-time to devote to the case. Four of my brothers have recently gotten married or engaged. Turns out, Riggs and I are the only two still single."

"Wow." Wide eyes, mouth agape, she didn't bother to hide her shock. "What kind of timeline are we talking about here?"

"It's only been a short time since Dad's murder." He took in a sharp breath. "If I'm honest, I still can't believe he's gone."

"I couldn't be sorrier, Garrett. I mean those words," she said earnestly.

"I know you do and I appreciate you for it." He had no doubt in his mind she was being sincere.

She reached across the table and touched his hand. Electricity jolted through him from the point of contact. He tried to absorb the effects of her touch rather than give away his reaction. And probably did a less than stellar job of it.

"Your mom must be devastated," she continued.

"She is, even though she's trying to put on a brave face when I talk to her," he said.

"She's a strong person but this is a lot for anyone to try to cope with." She gripped her mug a little tighter and he could see the news was impacting her. She'd been around his family years back and probably knew them better than most.

That was a long time ago, a little voice in the back of his mind reminded him. A lot had changed.

"Between Colton's twins and Renee and Cash's daughter she's—"

"Not so fast. Colton is a father?" she asked. Brianna's interest in Garrett's brother shouldn't feel like a knife stab in the center of his chest.

"Yes. As a matter of fact, he has twin boys," Garrett supplied, eyeing her to gauge her reaction.

"That's fantastic news. Is he happy?" She was oblivious to the pinball-machinelike reaction in his gut.

"He's newly married and seems so," he supplied.

"Anyone I know?" She smiled so hard she practically beamed.

"No. Someone from college. No one knew her. She wasn't local. Her name's Makena." He shouldn't care that she was checking on his brother, except that she'd been the reason for the long-standing rift between Colton and him, a feud they'd only recently called a truce to.

"I'm so happy for him." She smacked the flat of her palm on the table. There was a glint in her eyes that hadn't been there earlier. "He deserves all the happiness in the world."

"Agreed." He hadn't meant to come off as curt. Trying to say something to soften it now would only draw more attention to it. He hoped she'd let it slide because he felt stupid trying to explain why he was jealous of his very married brother.

She eyed him a little cautiously as it then seemed to dawn on her why he might be testy. She was the reason for the tension with his brother Colton, and they'd only just begun to repair the rift.

"And your other brothers? How are they doing?" she asked, changing the subject. He took note and appreciated the shift.

"As well as can be expected under the circumstances," he supplied.

"Right." A wall just came up and her smile retreated.

"I'm here to find out more about you and your situation." Redirecting the conversation back to her caused all the spark to dull in her eyes.

"What can I say? I'm working on my degree and the

countdown there on the wall is how many days I have left as a bartender." She pointed to the handwritten number on a torn-out calendar page featuring today's date that had been pinned to a corkboard that hung on the wall.

"You're getting closer," he said.

"Not close enough if you ask me." She issued a sharp sigh. "And now that I've picked up a creep, the day can't get here fast enough."

"Why not quit early?" he asked.

"Not everyone is sitting on a trust fund," she quipped.

He almost laughed out loud. He hadn't touched a penny of his family's money. "I'd be offended if I didn't know you better."

"Yeah, I heard how that sounded as it left my big mouth. Sorry. I know you never planned on leaning into yours. The funny part is that you don't even want it."

"I'd rather make my own way in life," he said, which didn't mean he didn't appreciate everything his parents had been doing for him. Garrett had always needed to prove to himself that he could live on his own if need be. He didn't want to get used to the trappings of always having food on the table and a comfortable bed.

"And I've always admired you for it. But if I was you, I'd take the trust fund in a heartbeat." Brianna laughed and it was musical.

His heart took another hit. One he wasn't sure he could recover from.

Chapter Five

Brianna never thought she'd see the day Garrett O'Connor would be sitting in her tiny apartment. And yet, there he was. It proved whoever was in charge up there in the sky had a sense of humor.

"I'd give you my trust fund in a heartbeat except that you wouldn't take it," Garrett retorted.

Little did he know she'd consider it now that she was older and knew how hard it was to put herself through college. She would have refused when she was young and naive. But all these months of sacrifice were about to pay off and she had no plans to let a scumbag from the bar stand between her and her freedom.

"Try me," she teased, trying to lighten the mood. It had gotten heavy again when the subject of money came up. And, no, she wouldn't let him pay for her college or rent. Despite being tired and a little more than freaked out by the creep, she had a lot of pride in doing this for herself and not depending on anyone else.

Graduation was going to be a big accomplishment. One she'd earned on her own without anyone else's help. And she could almost taste the freedom a real job would bring.

"What are you going to school for?" Garrett nodded

toward the stack of books on the bar-height counter separating the living room from the kitchen.

"Web design," she supplied. "I'm planning to work a nine-to-five job with a cubicle, paid lunches and vacations, and a dress code that doesn't involve showing off the girls."

"Sounds like hell," he quipped. "Except for that last part."

Brianna blushed. It wasn't something she normally did, so it threw her off-balance. Was he jealous? And why did her face heat at the thought?

"It might not be your cup of tea but I'm tired of working all night for tips, slinging drinks. A normal life sounds pretty good to me right now." She motioned toward her feet. "Just ask my dogs how tired they are and how much they bark every night."

"You've never been one to shy away from a tough task." His voice held more than a hint of admiration, and more of that heat crawled up her neck. At this rate, she'd turn into an inferno right before the man's eyes.

"Thanks for saying that, Garrett."

"So, tell me who you *think* is stalking you," he said in more statement than question.

She shrugged her shoulders. "I don't know. That's a tough one. There's a guy in one of my classes who creeps me out. I'll be taking notes furiously in class only to get a weird feeling like I'm being watched and then look up to see him staring at me intensely."

"Has he come around the bar?"

"A time or two," she admitted.

"Is he alone?"

"As far as I can tell. He never has worked up the courage to come talk to me so he takes a table by the dance floor and nurses a beer," she said.

"Any idea what his name is?"

"Derk Waters, I think. I overheard someone say that in a group project when his team was next to mine. By the way, there should be no group projects in college. I end up doing all the work and have to hear complaints from everyone in the process," she said as an aside.

Garrett chuckled. "Maybe you should learn to let others pull their own weight."

She blew out a sharp breath. "And risk a failing grade? No, thanks. Besides, I tried that once and ended up staying up all night to redo someone's work because they slapped their part together."

"Sounds like something you'd do," Garrett said.

"What's that supposed to mean?" She heard the defensiveness in her own voice but it was too late to reel it in.

"You always were the take-charge type. I'm not surprised you'd pull out a win in a terrible situation."

Well, she really had overreacted. She exhaled, trying to release some of the tension she'd been holding in her shoulders. "Thanks for the compliment, Garrett. It means a lot coming from you. I mean, your opinion matters to me."

"No problem." He shrugged off her comment but she could see that it meant something to him too. He picked up his coffee cup and took another sip. "Okay, so we have one creep on the list. What about others?"

"I wouldn't classify this guy as a creep necessarily but he has followed me out to the parking lot at school more than once. He's a TA, so basically a grad student working for one of my professors. He made it known that he'd be willing to help if I fell behind in class," she said.

Again, that jaw muscle clenched.

"Doesn't he take a hint?"

"Honestly, he's harmless. The only reason I brought him up was because we were talking about school and for some reason he popped into my mind. He's working his way through school and I doubt he'd risk his future if he got caught," she surmised. "Plus, this person is trying to run me off the road."

"You rejected him. That could anger a certain personality type," he said. "What's his name?"

"Blaine something. I don't remember his last name." Up to this point, she hadn't really believed the slimeball could be someone she knew. A cold shiver raced down her spine at the thought. "I've been working under the assumption one of the guys at the bar meant to get a little too friendly."

"We have to start somewhere. I believe my brothers would say the most likely culprit is someone you know. I've heard them say a woman's biggest physical threat is from those closest to her. Boyfriend. Spouse. Someone in her circle." He shot a look of apology. "It's an awful truth."

She issued a sharp sigh. "I can't even imagine who would want to hurt me."

GARRETT WAS ABOUT to ask questions he wasn't sure he wanted to hear the answers to but decided to lean on his brothers' experiences in law enforcement. "Is there someone special in your life?"

"Like a boyfriend?" Her face screwed up like she'd just been sprayed with lemon juice.

"Yes." His gaze dropped to the third finger on her left

hand. Relief washed over him when there was no band and no tan line.

"No." She shook her head so hard he laughed. "Wait, it's not funny."

"Your reaction was kind of priceless," he said by way of defense.

She blew out a breath, a move she'd done more than once in the short time they'd been together. She was like a teapot set to boiling over if someone increased the heat on the burner. "Okay, fine. Go ahead and make fun of me."

"Hold on a minute." He put his hands out, palms up, in the surrender position. "That's not at all what is happening here. Don't misunderstand."

"What, Garrett? That I'm alone and haven't dated anyone interesting in longer than I can remember because I also haven't dated in longer than I can recall." Her cheeks flamed and it wasn't like her to get embarrassed. He'd hit on a touchy subject and needed to backpedal.

So, he took in a slow breath before responding, not wanting to fan the flames.

"First off, there's nothing wrong with being alone. I can't tell you how many hours I spend that way, preferring my own company to most." He met her gaze to make sure the flame in her eyes was dimming, not intensifying. Then, he said, "And secondly, you're going to school and working so it sounds like your schedule is too busy for much in the way of free time."

"That's right." Her voice calmed a few notches.

"I didn't mean to insult you and I apologize if I did." Real men said they were sorry when they offended someone. It was a basic tenet for an O'Connor. Finn O'Connor, Garrett's father, had been one of the most stand-up men a person could hope to meet. Garrett wished to be more like his father but that job was reserved for his brothers. In fact, Garrett had always been the one to buck the system. If he could take some of his actions back now…

There was no use going down the road of feeling guilty for something he couldn't take back. His brothers were the "good" O'Connors. Garrett had been the disappointment. *Whoa. Where did that come from?*

Rather than analyze the sentiment, he refocused on Brianna.

"Thank you. Sorry. I'm the one who is being testy." She gave a sincere look.

"Under the circumstances, I'd say you're doing better than you think." He meant it too. Someone had tried to run her off the road twice in a short period of time. "You know, now that I think about it, this has to be someone you know. Or, at least, someone who knows you."

She studied her coffee mug before taking another sip. "What makes you say that?"

"He came back a second time."

A shiver rocked her body. He reached across the table and covered her hand with his in a show of support, but all he did was cause more of that electricity to rocket through his hand and up his arm.

"I feared the same thing." She nodded and then shrugged. "It's just my luck lately." She flashed a glance at him. "I'm not feeling sorry for myself, just frustrated. I'm getting so close to graduating that I can almost taste it. You might not think nine-to-five is heaven, but try slinging drinks for a couple of years in a shirt that's a size too small and shorts I can't wear into the grocery store on my way in to work for fear of a public indecency charge."

He studied her for a long moment without talking.

"This job must mean a whole lot to you for you to be willing to put up with all that."

"It does. And it means a fresh start." This time, when she studied him, he was the one who could feel the heat. "I'd been planning to move back to Katy Gulch."

"Really? Most young folks can't wait to get out so they can be around more people their own age."

"I see that and understand it on some level. Not me. Katy Gulch was the last happy memory I had growing up. I figured I could get a job in Austin and move close to home. Besides, you know me. I've always been a private person who needs her space. If nothing else, living in San Antonio has taught me how much I value distance between me and my neighbors." She pointed to the left. "These guys like to wake up early in the morning and…" A red blush crawled up her neck. "Say *hello* very loudly first thing. I mean, good for them, but their bed is pushed up against that wall."

"Sounds awful." Maybe not for the couple next door but for everyone around them. This was one of many reasons Garrett had to have space. He couldn't imagine sharing a wall with anyone, especially someone he didn't know.

"I wouldn't call it the highlight of my morning," she said with half a smile.

"Not the kind of alarm clock I'd want to hear."

"What about you?" She turned the tables on him. "Do you still live in Katy Gulch?"

"I'm in the process of moving back, but, no, I don't technically live there for the time being," he admitted.

"Why not? You have an amazing family and I just thought by looking at you that you're still a rancher." One of her eyebrows arched.

"I am."

"Then, you're going to have to spell it out for me because I'm not following." Her face twisted up in a confused look.

"I've been working ranches, just not the one I grew up on."

"Really?" There was a whole lot of shock infused in that one word.

"I needed time to figure a few things out for myself." He'd been drifting, searching for something he couldn't quite put his finger on.

"And did you?" Her honesty was refreshing, but also a reality check.

"No. Can't say that I did."

"Then, did you move back home to figure it out?" she pressed. There was something about Brianna that made him want to keep talking. Anyone else and he would have told them to mind their own business after the first question.

"Not really. I came home because my father died, and my sense of time changed. I thought I had all the time in the world to figure out my life and come back home with all the answers. Much to my surprise, I didn't and I don't." He expected to glance up and see judgment in her eyes. Hell, he deserved it. Most looked at him that way once they realized he belonged to one of the wealthiest cattle ranching families in Texas but came to work for someone else.

Brianna set her coffee cup down on the table, stared him in the eyes for a long second and then pushed to standing. "I'd say you need something stronger than coffee after an admission like that."

Before he could say another word, she was at the icebox retrieving two bottles of beer. She walked over and set one down in front of him. She located a bottle opener next and within a few seconds, both caps were off.

"To figuring it all out someday." She held her beer out across the table.

"Or not." Garrett clinked bottles before taking a swig. Despite his bad-boy image, he wasn't a big drinker. He also wasn't a womanizer either but once a reputation took seed he'd learned a long time ago that arguing to change people's minds only embedded the rumors deeper.

Brianna's lip curled on the right side. She tilted her head like she did when she was really thinking. "You know what? I'll drink to that too."

Again, they clinked bottles and then took another sip.

"I have to say, I never thought I'd run into you again, especially not at a random gas station in San Antonio of all places," she said.

"There's one thing I've learned in life. Expect the unexpected, good and bad." Especially bad. Although, tonight was the first stroke of luck that made Garrett believe the whole world wasn't against him.

Brianna took another swig of her beer and then set it down. "It's been a long night. I'm done after a shower."

He didn't think this was the time to tell her not to put naked shower images of her in his thoughts. Instead, he grinned and made a tsk noise. He started to get up but she waved for him to sit back down.

"Stay overnight?" she asked, a hint of pleading in her voice.

"I've got nowhere better to be," he hedged. It was probably a bad idea to sleep over. He'd already compared most of his relationships to the way she'd made him feel years ago. He didn't need to make it worse.

Then again, their brief…*whatever*…happened a long time in the past. He'd most likely built it up in his mind to something grander than it deserved. He'd been a teenager full of hormones back then. They were most likely the reason no one could measure up to Brianna since. And not that they'd shared a brief moment of something truly special.

And even if it was true, spending a little time with her might just dispel the myth. Shatter the pedestal he'd placed her on. A voice in the back of his mind argued he'd placed her there so he could have an excuse to leave a trail of broken hearts.

Was that true?

Chapter Six

Brianna woke to the sounds of movement in her kitchen. She sat ramrod straight and glanced at the clock. Much to her horror, it was barely past seven in the morning. She shot out of bed and grabbed the bathrobe on the hook.

Last night came crashing down on her. The fact that Garrett O'Connor was standing in her kitchen, looking all sizzle and chest hair at an obscene time of day, dawned.

"Morning," she mumbled before disappearing to brush her teeth and splash cold water on her face. The shirtless image of the grown man he'd become stamped her thoughts. Great. She wasn't ever forgetting the image, was she?

At least he was hotness on a stick, and the first kiss she'd compared every other to since she was a teenager. All the poor men she'd dated since didn't have a chance against Garrett. He was just the right amount of rebel and recklessness. His heart was pure gold if he let someone in and she knew that was a rare event. Not like blond-haired Pete who was a software engineer, had already bought the house he planned to bring his bride home to and had asked her to stop by his home on the second date to give decorating tips. She got the feeling almost any woman would do. Like he was filling a position and if someone met the base requirements of being reasonably attractive and intelligent the job was theirs.

There wasn't anything special about dating a guy like Pete.

If Garrett asked a woman out, she could rest assured he saw something in *her.* She didn't fit a certain type or description. He was looking for someone unique and wouldn't fall "in love" with the first decent date who ticked all the boxes.

Walking out of the hallway and into the kitchen, her stomach performed a flip-flop routine. The man was seriously hot and it was so much more than a carved-from-granite chin or those steel-colored eyes. The broken part in him was a magnet to the broken part of her. His sense of humor that bordered on being dark spoke to her, made her laugh. If half of what he said came out of any other person's mouth, she'd be offended and rightfully so. She understood what he meant and how he meant it on a most basic level. His words could touch her like no one else's ever could.

And there was something about a man who never needed anyone else. Garrett had been a loner from the day she first met him. She tried to fit in while he didn't care one bit if he did or not. He wasn't looking for acceptance from anyone.

Untouchable? Even if he stuck around, it wouldn't be for long. He would always need to be on the go, alone. It was just his nature.

"Hey," she said as he studied his cell phone.

"What are you doing up so early?" he asked as she bit back a yawn.

"I'm not used to someone being in my place overnight,

I guess." She tried to shrug it off but noticed the corner of his mouth quirked a smile.

She decided it would be best not to ask what that was about.

"Coffee is fresh. Can I pour a cup for you?" he asked.

"I should get it myself. Don't want to get too used to having someone do things for me," she said before thinking.

He feigned disappointment, clutching his chest in the most dramatic fashion. "Mind if I use your shower?"

"Not at all." Her body reacted with a mind of its own; a dozen butterflies released in her chest and sensual shivers skittered across her skin. But, wait…how? "Do you need me to wash your clothes while you—"

He motioned toward a duffel bag. "I brought it in while you were asleep and didn't want to wake you." He flashed eyes at her. "Sorry about that, by the way."

"Don't worry about it. You were doing me a favor by staying here. I'm a light sleeper but I was out longer than usual."

Again, he couldn't or didn't bother to hide his smirk.

"I won't be long," he said, setting down his coffee mug and walking over to his duffel. He picked it up and motioned toward the bedroom. "This way, I take it?"

"Down the hallway and first door on the right. It connects with the master bedroom," she said, pouring a cup of coffee so she wouldn't be tempted to stare at his strong back.

"I did some thinking last night and I'd like you to make a list of anyone you've been in a fight with lately, male or female. Any disagreements qualify. If you've had words with anyone—" he motioned toward the table

"—jot them down and we can talk about a plan moving forward."

She liked the sound of those last words, especially the *we* part, but she couldn't ask him to stop his investigation into his father's murder on her account. She nodded, though, knowing full well he wouldn't shift course now that his mind was made up. Garrett was a mule when he wanted to be.

Thinking about his father caused her heart to sink. The realization that he was murdered was a physical blow. Finn O'Connor had been such a good man. He was an incredible father and husband. Mr. and Mrs. O'Connor seemed to have the perfect marriage despite the tragedy that struck early and would have torn most relationships apart. The family didn't deserve this.

She fixed her coffee and then moved to the table. She checked her cell phone. Although she wasn't certain why she bothered. It was good for making calls and the occasional message from one of her parents. But that was about it.

Taking a sip of coffee, her curiosity got the best of her. There had to be a news article about Mr. O'Connor's death. He was one of the most famous cattle ranchers around. A family like his made news.

She set her mug down and performed a quick search. Yes, there was an article all right. She skimmed it but there wasn't much more than the details of where he'd been found and that the family would have a private service.

There was mention of their daughter, Caroline, who'd been abducted from her bedroom on the second floor of the O'Connor family home. When Brianna searched for Caroline O'Connor, she saw that a recent attempted kidnapping case had been linked to the family tragedy, but nothing came of it and the case was closed after learning the mother's ex was behind the attempt. The case involved Cash O'Connor, who was now a US marshal.

Brianna hadn't stayed up with O'Connor family news, so it came as a shock to learn Cash had gone into law enforcement. Garrett had mentioned earlier that a couple of his brothers had. She skimmed *related articles* and learned that Colton had become sheriff of Katy Gulch and its surrounding counties. Again, wow.

She shouldn't be surprised that several of Garrett's brothers had joined law enforcement given they were all honorable people. Maybe it was the fact she figured they would all work at the ranch someday. Speaking of which, there had to be a story behind Garrett refusing to work for the family business. One he wasn't telling her.

Lost in thought, she was caught off guard when she looked up to find him standing at the entryway, studying her. She'd been so distracted she forgot to listen for the spigot.

"Everything okay?" he asked.

"Yes." She forced her gaze away from a rivulet of water as it rolled down his muscled chest.

He stood there in not much more than jeans. His T-shirt was slung over one shoulder like a towel. His feet were bare. Awareness caused warmth to ripple through her. Her throat dried up and words escaped her.

She took a sip of coffee to ease the dryness in her throat.

"I was just distracting myself." That part was honest enough. Before he could ask a follow-up question, she steered the conversation back on track. "I thought about this as I fell into bed last night and it's creepy to think someone I know might be responsible for trying to chase me off the road."

"Maybe you don't know them well. It could be someone in passing who is fixated," he said.

The word *fixated* didn't sit well either. "We can't go interrogating every person I come into contact with, so where does that leave us?"

"We start with what we know and interview the names you gave me last night," he admitted. He walked across the room and refilled his coffee mug before joining her at the table. Before he sat down, he spun the chair around and slipped his shirt on. *Shame.*

"And the list we make this morning?"

"We go there too," he said.

"We don't even know if this guy is coming to try again. He might just go away after last night. And if not, this could take days or even weeks to investigate, Garrett. I can't tie up your time like that. You were heading somewhere last night. Somewhere I stopped you from going and you said it had to do with your father's investigation. I don't want to be the one who holds you up from that." She had her elbows on the table and was running her finger along the handle of her coffee mug, too afraid to look up at him while she spoke. She didn't want to see anything there that would convince her to let him stick around.

"I hear what you're saying. I'm basically chasing my tail when it comes to my father's investigation. I need to feel like I'm doing something, keeping busy."

"What about your home? Why not just go back to the ranch?" she asked.

"Because I don't want to face my mother one more time without bringing home some answers. My dad died without ever knowing what happened to my sister. None of us has been able to figure it out. Although, admittedly, I've been a little busy doing something else."

She shot him a look and he put his hands up in the surrender position.

"Okay, I'll admit it. I've been wallowing in my own self-pity just a little bit, but I'm ready to go now. I don't plan to stop until I find something and I can't go home without answers. I can't look my mother in the face and deliver more disappointment." Garrett didn't normally do emotions so the fact he was opening up to her and spilling so much of what he'd been bottling up inside made her sit a little straighter and listen a little more intently.

"I understand." She believed he was being too hard on himself but she understood not wanting to be a disappointment. For very different reasons, she carried the guilt of her parents' divorce for many years before realizing now none of it was her fault. "You're welcome to stay here as long as you like. I'll write down any names that come to mind but I have a lit test later that I have to study for. I have class in—" she glanced at her phone "—a little more than two hours. So, I have to get down to business."

She threw her shoulders back and held her chin up, readying for an argument. Instead, Garrett stood up and asked, "What supplies am I working with in the kitchen?"

He must be hungry.

"I probably have fixins for breakfast tacos if you don't mind using salsa packets from the Taco Shed." She motioned toward a drawer. "There should be plenty in there."

"Breakfast tacos are my specialty."

"I remember," she said quickly, a little too quickly. He didn't need to know just how much detail she remembered about him and the things he was skilled at. The thought of their first kiss caused her face to turn white-hot. She spun around and tucked her chin to her chest to hide her reaction to him—a reaction that was still out of control after all these years and all this time.

"Then, you'll remember how much of a treat you're in for," he quipped without missing a beat. "Why don't you crack open a book and get started while I figure out your kitchen and then feed you?"

"Okay, but I think I'm getting the best part of this deal." Brianna had to admit that it was nice for someone to have her back for a change. She knew better than to get too comfortable in the feeling.

For now, she would do exactly as instructed. Open a book. And marvel that the bad boy of her dreams could cook.

Lit was one of her favorite subjects and she'd wanted to get a degree in English but stopped cold when she looked up salary information. She didn't want to be a teacher and she had no idea what else to do with an English degree. She was handy with computers and could learn anything she put her mind to. Web design seemed like a secure job and she could work for a good-size company.

The paper with two names on it stared up at her. She picked up a pencil and tapped the eraser on the table as she read a dog-eared copy of *Don Quixote*, taking notes along the way.

"You know there's a thing called CliffsNotes, right?" Garrett said from the kitchen.

"Then I won't learn what I'm supposed to from reading the text." She shrugged him off. Even a few hours of sleep had been enough to reset her mood. It had nothing to do with waking up to find Garrett still at her apartment. At least, that's what she tried to convince herself.

The smells wafting in from the next room caused her stomach to growl. Loud.

"Almost ready," he said, dispelling any hope she had that he might not have heard.

Seconds later, he brought over a plate that made her mouth water and a smile to creep across her face. "This is a serious pair of breakfast tacos. I forgot all about the sausage in the fridge. No wonder it smelled so good."

"It's a good thing you didn't point me to flour and ask for biscuits and gravy. Breakfast tacos, I can make." The pride in his voice made her smile even wider.

"Yes, you can." She picked up the fork on the plate and took a bite, mewling with pleasure.

He looked like he was about to say something before thinking better of it. Instead, he whipped up a second plate and joined her at the table.

"*Don Quixote*, huh?"

"Yep," she said.

When he rolled his eyes, she added, "There are people who consider this story the best literary work ever written."

"Then, I'd say they haven't read *The Old Man and the Sea*."

"Not bad, O'Connor. Don't tell me you have a copy in your duffel," she teased.

"As a matter of fact." He made a motion like he was about to get up and prove her right. Then, he sat back down. "Actually, I haven't read it since high school, but I keep it right here." He pointed to his head.

"Oh, yeah? Prove it."

"'No one should be alone in their old age, he thought.'"

Garrett's expression turned serious when he added, "Nor go to their grave not knowing what happened to their only daughter."

Chapter Seven

Truths had a way of leaving lasting scars. Garrett pushed his egg around with his fork before finally stabbing it and then taking a bite. There wasn't much he could do besides wait, so he polished off his meal and then finished his coffee sitting on the small patio.

The walls were closing in on him in Brianna's small space and he needed fresh air. Being indoors much at all had never been his cup of tea. Why would he when he could be out on the land, looking up at a bright open sky that went on for miles?

Seeing Brianna again sure hit him in an unexpected place—a place he'd kept buried underneath years of turmoil. There was something about being with her that made him not care if he'd been locked inside for hours. So, he needed to get a grip before he forgot who he was.

Thinking about her situation made him rethink some of his own mistakes. He had a family who cared about him and a bank account with more zeroes than one person needed. Would Brianna let him help her? Really help her? Like with a scholarship or something? Hell, he didn't know how it worked.

He was a simple man. A good cup of coffee and the great outdoors was all he needed to be happy. Guilt stabbed him when he thought about how hard Brianna was working to make a living and have a future better than her past.

What was his problem?

He'd had a solid childhood. His parents loved him and his brothers were close. Well, maybe not with him. He'd always pulled away from the others and he and Colton were like oil and water. It was probably normal in a large family to have spats but theirs ran deep. There was resentment on both sides. Although, to be fair, Colton seemed real happy the last time Garrett spoke to his brother. Wildly happy. And he'd found what seemed to be real joy with Makena. Garrett was glad for his brother despite a hurt that ran deep.

Their disagreements were habit at this point. Could Garrett change? Be more like the person his family seemed to expect him to be? Not everyone got top grades in school or cared about throwing a ball the farthest.

He'd been compared to his near-perfect brothers for a lifetime. One of the best things about going to work on a ranch and only giving his first name was that no one knew who he was. He didn't come with all the baggage that forced him to try to be perfect all the time.

He realized he was white-knuckling his coffee mug. Forcing his hands to relax, he flexed and released the fingers of his free hand, trying to work out some of the tension that came every time he thought about his brothers. Colton seemed to be the worst. All Garrett had to do was say his brother's name and he could feel his shoulders tense. What was it about the two of them that made it near impossible to be in the same room?

Was it that Colton always thought he was right? Being older didn't necessarily mean being smarter. Although, to be fair, his brother was book smart. He'd been a decent student whereas Garrett had looked for reasons to cut class. Sitting behind a desk had never appealed to him.

He thought about Brianna's plans to get a nine-to-five job and his finger automatically came up to loosen his collar as it suddenly felt a lot tighter. Then, he realized he wasn't wearing a collared shirt. He questioned the appeal of having someone else tell him when to go to work and when to take a break.

The steady paycheck he understood. Those came in handy when rent was due. Working ranches solved the problem of rent for him because the job always came with a spot in the bunkhouse. With all the machines running ranches instead of hands these days, it only took a skeleton crew to handle the labor. It also made him self-sufficient in the cooking department. No one would credit him with being a restaurant-quality chef but he knew his way around a skillet. Meals were usually part of the deal on a ranch too. Not for Garrett. He preferred not to get to know his coworkers or break bread with them.

Did that make him antisocial?

Maybe. But it also made him happy. Or at least it used to. *Happy* might not be the right word so much as less frustrated all the time. A question he'd never once pondered struck while sitting on Brianna's patio, watching the sun make its ascent. Why?

He'd never once questioned why he was so angry all the time, or had been. Losing his father had knocked the wind out of him and he felt nothing but numb until now, until seeing Brianna again.

The alarm he'd set on his cell phone buzzed, indicating she had to be at school soon. He'd lost track of time while sitting outside, the sun warming his face.

With an exhale, he pushed up to standing and then grabbed his coffee mug from the small side table. This was all a person needed to be happy, a little sunshine, a good cup of coffee and a person he…

Never mind the last part. He didn't have to go there mentally about the electricity or bond he felt with Brianna and how it created a feeling that he'd been missing out on something his entire life.

Garrett was a whole person. He didn't need someone else to "complete" him. And yet he couldn't deny the feeling of rightness that came with being around Brianna again. Like the out-of-control world righted itself and time stood still. Like he was exactly where he was supposed to be. Like he would feel an emptiness he'd never known when this was over and he walked away.

Pushing through those thoughts, he opened the slider to the patio and stepped inside. "Ready to go?"

Brianna's face pinched as she checked the time. She glanced over at him and for a split second time warped and he got caught in the wave. He was transported back to high school when a glance at her felt like the sun coming out from behind dark clouds.

Giving himself a mental head shake, he closed the slider, breaking the moment. "Don't want you to be late."

"You're coming with me?" She didn't hide the shock in her voice as her wide eyes blinked up at him.

"That I am."

"Oh. Okay. I guess there's a coffee shop on campus you can sit at while I'm in class," she offered.

"Don't worry about me. I'll be fine. I plan to do a little walking around while I'm there. See who I can talk to." He figured the department secretary would be a good place to start if a TA might be involved. From what he remembered about his brothers going to college the admins knew everything that went on in a department.

As far as starting points went, it wasn't a great one, but it was something.

Brianna packed up her backpack. A couple of minutes later they were heading out the door.

"I know you were driving somewhere when I saw you at the gas station but can I ask a serious question?"

"Yes," he said as he claimed the driver's seat of his truck after opening the door for her. And, yes, she was fully capable of opening her own door. However, her hands were full and he was brought up old-school. Since she smiled and thanked him after, he figured she appreciated the gesture.

"Do you always keep a duffel bag full of clothes and toiletries in your truck?" Her question caught him off guard.

"Yes." He started the engine.

"Can I ask why?"

"I always have to be ready to spend several days out on the land when I'm working a ranch. It's habit to be prepared for anything that can come my way," he explained. "Why? Does it seem odd to you?"

"I was just curious," she said but there was more to it than that. He heard it in her voice—a musical voice that calmed his aches more than was wise to allow.

And he knew right then and there she didn't ask the question she really wanted to. He could hear it in her tone. What she really wanted to know was whether or not there was someone special in his life.

After a short drive and a few directions, Garrett parked on a side street and then walked Brianna to class. He needed to find the arts-and-tech building. The campus was small, so it only took a couple of minutes. It was still early for some, he figured. Days on a cattle ranch started around four thirty, so a nine o'clock class was basically midmorning for him. His late breakfast would hold until Brianna finished at her college. She had one subject this morning, a nine o'clock, which meant she'd be done at noon. He would be ready to chew an arm off by then so he made a mental note to swing by the coffee shop and see if they had any protein for him to snack on to tide him over.

In the meantime, a woman named June was his next mission. According to Brianna, June was the person who kept everyone in check in the department. She was also a student's best advocate, helping sort out schedule conflicts and obtaining the right signature when someone needed to get into a class in order to graduate on time.

The arts-and-tech building was an all white structure looking like something that came out of an alien movie. A hill blocked its view from the main part of campus and when he crested, he was treated to a vision of a modern glass structure surrounded by newly planted trees.

Garrett jogged down the hill and then strode with purpose toward the building. Only a couple of stragglers strolled around.

The office was easy enough to find since it was all glass with large white letters etched in the window, Arts & Technology. He could see June sitting behind a desk with piles of papers on it. As much as the world had gone to tech, some people stood their ground and worked the old-fashioned way. He couldn't fault her. He leaned into tradition when it came to cattle ranching too.

June was tiny behind the massive desk, but her movements were fluid and assured. She had on a camel-colored blazer, a shirt that looked like silk and there was a ladybug pin that could only be described as dainty on her lapel.

She was timeworn and had a short curly hairdo that was probably very popular a couple of decades ago. He liked June without even speaking to her yet.

"Hello," he said after knocking at the door, not wanting to surprise her. Although he seriously doubted anything could rattle her.

She acknowledged him with a wave.

He stepped inside and waited by the door while she studied the paper she had in her hand. She wasn't fast but he figured she was accurate. No rushing. No multitasking with June. She opened a drawer, carefully located a slot and slipped the paper in a folder.

Then she turned toward him, gave him a warm smile and placed her palms flat on her desk, elbows out. "How may I help you?"

"My name is Garrett O'Connor and I was hoping to talk to you about one of the TAs working in the department."

June's eyes widened just enough for him to realize she knew his last name. He shouldn't be surprised. Plenty of folks knew the O'Connor name, especially in Texas. But it still caught him off guard because he didn't really get out much. The glint of recognition came when he talked to someone about a job but most dismissed the notion a real O'Connor would be looking for work at a competing ranch. Little did they know no one truly competed with his family's scale.

June recovered quickly. "Are you a prospective employer?"

He studied her, trying to get a good read on her. Was

she leading him to ask the right questions so she could respond? He hadn't thought about the ethical dilemma she'd be in or the fact there were probably privacy laws covering the kinds of questions he had.

He stared at June for a long moment and caught the slight nod she gave.

"Yes." He could technically interview the guy for a job at the ranch. He was one of the owners. At least on paper. No one would trust his decision-making skills after he'd gone out on a limb years ago to bring a fellow student into the bunkhouse when he himself was barely thirteen, if that. He'd gotten caught up in a new kid's hard luck story at school.

On Garrett's insistence, the family welcomed the kid with open arms. He'd left with full pockets. Full of Garrett's mother's prized earrings. Full of a sterling silver baby rattle that belonged to Caroline and was his mother's most precious treasure. Shame washed over him at the memory.

Was that when Garrett began withdrawing from the family?

Mentally shaking off the fog, he refocused on June. "Can you vouch for Blaine Thompsett?"

June leaned forward and nodded. "He's a good kid."

There were no seats across from her desk. To the left was a hallway with what he presumed would be the professors' offices. To the right was a seating area for students who were waiting to see someone.

"Comes to work on time," she continued. "Of course, I don't know him personally but I've never heard Dr. Stanley complain."

"He reports to Dr. Stanley?"

"Yes, that's his adviser. Blaine transferred in from a

satellite location in East Texas," she continued. "This is his first semester here so I don't know him as well as some of the others but I haven't heard anything that would make him a bad employee so far."

Garrett wasn't sure how much he could push this conversation with June. She seemed loyal and efficient. Someone who prided herself on her work and work ethic. Getting her to give information about anyone under the table didn't seem likely.

He made up a few routine questions employers had asked him during interviews to keep the visit sounding legit.

"Would you like to speak to Dr. Stanley?" She nodded toward the hallway. "I believe he is in his office."

Since the question seemed to come out of the blue in the middle of their conversation, he took it as a sign she couldn't really speak while one of her bosses was nearby. There could be others too. Her space was out in the open in the middle of all the action. From her spot, she could run interference for her bosses.

Brilliant setup for people who didn't want to be available on short notice. There were a few hard walls but a lot of glass on the inside, as well. From his vantage point, he couldn't tell whether professors were in or out.

This was the first time in Garrett's life he wished he had one of his brothers' badges. That would get June talking as much as she was legally allowed to.

Turning on O'Connor charm wouldn't do any good either. Not with June. She was straight as an arrow.

"Oh, here he comes now—Blaine." June motioned behind Garrett. He had no idea what to say to the kid.

This whole conversation was about to get awkward as hell.

A tall, thin guy with a runner's build and a backpack slung over his shoulder walked into the office. His hair was in need of a cut and his clothes seemed like they could use a good washing. On some level, he might be considered good-looking; he flashed a casual smile when he saw June.

"There's someone here checking a reference—"

"I'm Garrett." He turned to face Blaine, cutting June off before she could bust him. Garrett stuck a hand out.

Blaine's handshake was weak at best. He tucked his hair behind his ear and smiled. "What can I help you with?"

"Could I have a few minutes of your time?" Garrett asked.

"Um, yeah, sure, why not?" Blaine gave Garrett a once-over. He probably surmised correctly that Garrett was too young to be a parent who'd come in fighting for a better grade for his kid.

"Outside?" Garrett gestured toward the hallway.

"Yeah. Okay."

"Thank you, June." Garrett used as friendly a voice as he could muster before rushing out the door to preempt June from spilling the beans.

He led Blaine all the way outside and onto the grassy hill. The young guy looked confused. He also looked to be about twenty-three years old and way out of his league with Brianna, but the last part was purely opinion.

Garrett thanked Blaine again for following. "I'd like to ask a few questions if you don't mind."

Blaine pursed his lips together and gave an I-don't-know-why-not look. They were out in plain daylight and that was on purpose so the guy wouldn't be as on edge.

"How well do you know Brianna Adair?" He figured he'd better get straight to it and see how the guy reacted.

"Who?" He shoved his hands in his pockets like a kid being accused of sticking his hand in the cookie jar.

Garrett repeated the name.

"I don't know. Is she a student?" Blaine looked down and to the left, a clear sign he was either lying or nervous. Garrett would double down on both being the case.

"Yes." Garrett crossed his arms over his chest as Blaine rocked back and forth on his heels.

"Let me think." He pulled his hands out of his pockets and used his right to rub the scruff on his chin. He grabbed the strap on his backpack and toyed with the end. "She's in one of my classes?"

"Yes." Garrett waited, giving away nothing of his frustration in his tone.

"Do you mind if I ask why? Did something happen to her?" His forehead creased with concern. The fact that he was stalling didn't sit well with Garrett. There was also the fact that he wasn't admitting to knowing who she was yet. Why?

The simple answer was that he didn't want to be caught hitting on her. That wouldn't exactly look good to his adviser. Self-interest was usually the reason most people dodged answering a question or failed to tell the truth about a situation.

"She's fine. She's in class as we speak," Garrett said.

"Right," Blaine agreed quickly. Too quickly?

"Are you familiar with her schedule?"

Another possibility as to why Garrett would have intimate knowledge of Brianna seemed to dawn on Blaine as he looked Garrett up and down as though sizing him up. Blaine would lose if he threw a punch and he seemed to come to the same conclusion when he surrendered.

"Are you her boyfriend?" Blaine's already white skin paled.

"Let's just say I'm a friend who is concerned about her." Garrett had no plans to budge an inch on giving out any more information about their relationship. Hell, he was having a difficult enough time defining it for himself, especially after that kiss. It wasn't more than a peck on the cheek and yet held more sizzle and promise than any kiss he'd experienced in longer than he cared to remember.

This wasn't the time to think about the kiss.

"But she's okay?" There was a guilty quality to his tone that Garrett didn't like.

"Yes. Why? Is there a reason she shouldn't be?"

"Well, no. I just thought..." He blew out a breath, looking flustered. "If she's okay why are you asking around about her?"

"I'm not asking around. I'm asking you." Garrett caught the guy's gaze and held it, daring him to look away first.

Blaine blinked a couple of times before rubbing the scruff on his chin again. "I know who you're talking about now. Right. Brianna from Design 201. I'm glad to hear she's okay. I don't know how else I can help you, so... I better get to class."

Garrett didn't think this was the time to point out class had started twenty minutes ago. And a question lingered. Why did Blaine suddenly look like a trapped animal trying to escape a cage?

Chapter Eight

Brianna sat in class, tapping the eraser on her notebook. The lecture hall was set up like stadium seating in a movie theater. On most days, they all took notes on their laps. But today was test day. So, tray tables were pulled up and out and notebooks were tucked away inside backpacks.

No matter how hard she tried to focus on the test questions, her mind kept looping back to last night. To the incident on the road and then the strange coincidence of running into Garrett at the gas station. Life was full of surprises. In her experience, they were never this good.

The fact he'd stayed over caused an unsettled feeling to creep over her. Having someone in her corner for the first time in a long time was nice. Too nice? Or just too nice for her? The other problem was getting used to it.

Garrett would walk away later today or tomorrow. He couldn't stay at her place indefinitely. Her small apartment barely accommodated one person. He'd insisted on sleeping on the couch last night even though there was no way a man of his size would come close to fitting, and forget about being comfortable.

And why was she even stressing about any of this when she needed to be focused on taking this test? Failing wasn't an option. She was down to thirty-six days to graduation.

Could she quit her job early? The sleazebag had to be someone at the bar. That was the only logical explanation considering both times she'd been followed by someone after her shift. Code Blue was an obvious ride so there was no confusing her with someone else.

Whoever was after her was *after her*. Another involuntary shiver rocked her. She tried to blame her response on the frigid AC in the building but with the doors opening and closing every fifty minutes or so very little cool air was locked in. The AC would be different at her professional job. She'd been reading everything she could get her hands on about work environments. She would be prepared for the constant air-conditioning in her nine-to-five. Apparently, office temperatures were set to make men comfortable in suits. She wondered if anyone even wore those on a daily basis anymore, except in a handful of positions. The tech revolution made jeans and sweaters *très* chic for office wear. She'd read somewhere that socks were now a big thing in male office wardrobes. Socks?

To each his own.

Any dress code would be better than the outfit she had to wear for the bar. In an office, she could wear clothes. Sweaters. Long pants. Jeans on casual Fridays. The whole "dealing with coworkers" bit wasn't as appealing because she had no idea what to expect. The one thing she was certain of was that she'd already put up with worse. Much worse. At least her current job had prepared her to deal with all walks of life.

The TA at the front of the room checked her watch. "Ten more minutes."

What? No.

Brianna's heart thumped a little louder as the first person stood up, done with her test. She walked it to the front and then set it down on the table. From the back, Brianna couldn't see if the student was smiling or frowning. First one done could mean either she knew every answer and was prepared or she didn't have a clue and gave up. Brianna couldn't take her eyes off the woman.

The nineteen-to twenty-year-old turned toward the door and Brianna got a peek at her face. Smile.

The next person who stood up was a young guy, thick glasses. He'd been sitting in Brianna's row. Done. Smiling. A trail followed as panic engulfed her. She knew the answers to the test. Concentration was her problem.

Since there was nothing like a deadline to kick her brain in gear, she forced her gaze back to the paper and scribbled faster. Her pencil didn't leave the paper until two seconds before time was called.

When she looked up and saw Garrett standing in the doorway, her heart leaped in her throat.

"I WASN'T EXPECTING to see you so early." As Brianna walked toward Garrett, his pulse shot up with every step she took. He'd been leaning against the doorjamb for all of two seconds before class was called.

"Figured I'd walk you to your next class and see if the creep is hanging around." He hoped she'd be able to point the guy out.

"That's a date, um, deal." A hint of red shaded her cheeks with the slip. She dropped her gaze to the floor. "I feel so old in these classes."

He glanced around and guessed the average age of students was probably still in the high teens or early twenties. "You're twenty-six. Not exactly old."

"Not *this* young either," she added without missing a beat.

"No. I hope this doesn't sound like I'm on a high horse but I'm proud of you, Brianna." He could barely look her way for a reaction for fear he'd just frustrated her.

This time when her cheeks flamed red, his chest squeezed.

"That means a lot coming from you, Garrett," she said, her voice low.

"How'd you do on the test?" He needed to change the subject because, for a split second, this felt like one of the most intimate moments of his life.

"I think I passed at the very least. I'm not the best at taking tests but I have a good grade in the class so even if I bombed I'd probably come out okay," she admitted.

"This is a great thing you're doing. Going after your dreams," he said.

"I wouldn't exactly say I'm doing that." She hesitated as they fell in step together.

"Then, why would you torture yourself going through classes, tests and a job you hate?" He didn't mean for all that to come out at once but he was caught off guard by the admission.

"I want a steady job. I'm decent with computers and I have a creative side I thought I could use with web design." She shrugged. "I'm doing this for money, not to follow my dreams."

"Okay then, what would your life be like if you did that?" It wasn't his business to pry and yet he wanted to know more about what made her tick.

"I'd go after an English degree," she said after a long pause.

"English?"

She tapped his arm with her elbow. "Yes, English."

"You want to be a teacher?"

"Not really. That's the part I'm not so sure about. I have no idea what I'd do with an English degree. All I know is that I love reading pretty much anything I can get my hands on. I scribble here and there but, believe me, my writing is nothing to brag about. Web design is a practical choice and maybe not the most exciting one, but I figure it'll pay the bills and then I can do whatever I want with my free time. Maybe take more English classes or just read." She didn't make eye contact and her tongue kept darting across her bottom lip when she paused, a sure sign she was nervous. And then there was the playful elbow jab. Garrett couldn't count the number of times she'd performed that move years ago before they started seeing each other. "I'm probably just selling out."

"Making certain you can take care of yourself financially isn't the same thing as selling out." Was she afraid he'd condemn her decision? He wasn't one to put someone else's life choices down. Her situation was also putting his into perspective—a perspective that was coming on like a kick in the pants but was needed.

"Are you sure about that, Garrett?"

"One hundred percent," he confirmed.

She stopped in front of a building and put her fisted hand on her hip before he could express all his thoughts. He should be proud of himself. That was the most he'd been able to tell someone outside his family in longer than he could remember. Strange as it was, he *wanted* to talk to Brianna. He was downright chatty around her. And that was saying a lot.

"I better go inside." She pushed up to her tiptoes and planted a kiss on his cheek. "I don't want to be late."

All Garrett could do was stand there for a long moment under the spell of that peck. He'd never had a bigger reaction to something so small in his life. So, it caught him off guard that his pulse raced and his heart jackhammered his ribs. Garrett figured a couple of nights at the club sitting in a quiet corner would give him the vantage point he needed to watch her from across the room, see if the jerk showed.

He leaned against the building, scanning each guy who walked past, searching for any sign of the malcontent. A sea of jeans, T-shirts and backpacks flooded the lawn, dispersing in different directions. He had to give it to Brianna; being one of the oldest people in class couldn't be easy.

Her confession sat heavy on his mind as he figured he'd pass the hour-and-a-half class outside her building while he mulled over his thoughts. It wasn't like he had to be anywhere. He was on the way back from investigating a lead that turned out to be a dead end on his father's case. Distracting himself with Brianna's situation was probably for the best. Focusing too much on one subject never helped find answers faster. In fact, the opposite was usually true. The less he thought about a situation or circumstance, the better, the more his mind cleared.

Brianna also gave him a break from the crushing ache in his chest at the thought he would go home to KBR never to find his father there again. He gave himself a mental slap to refocus.

After talking to Blaine, Garrett couldn't exactly cross him off the suspect list. The guy acted pretty dodgy there at the end of the conversation and never really answered Garrett's questions. The whole part about pretending not to know who she was didn't sit right either. Any guy who went to the trouble to follow a woman out to her car to hit on her in a parking lot would definitely remember who she was. Plus, she was in his class. Why was he acting like he didn't know who she was? It didn't make sense. Why not admit that he knew her from class and answer Garrett's questions straight up?

The guy was guilty of something.

Was he frustrated by her rejection? Blaine seemed the nervous type. Was that just grad-school jitters in general or was he hiding something?

Then, there was the creep. Garrett had a good mind to slip into class and have Brianna discreetly point Derk out. A slight nod was all that was needed. Garrett flexed and released his fingers to get rid of some of the strain. Ranch work was all the physical outlet he needed, so not having his usual workout caused stress to build up in his body. Pain caused his shoulder blades to pull taut. He tried to convince himself that lack of a workout was also the reason for the energy that pulsed between him and Brianna every time they were within a few feet of each other, but he could admit his attraction to her was based on more than overwrought nerves with no release. In truth, the teenager who had been a budding beauty had transformed into an incredible woman.

Life had handed her a difficult situation and she was facing it head-on, doing what she could to better her life. Beauty was more than outward appearance. He could admit hers was stunning. And, hey, a nice package could be pretty great to look at. Except that he also knew from eating out of a chocolate box at Valentine's Day back in middle school that not everything in a beautiful wrapper tasted great. For example, what was up with the strawberry-cream one? Seriously. He'd popped one of those in his mouth in seventh grade and nearly gagged. He'd had to run to the trash to spit it out and couldn't get rid of the taste until lunch.

Outward appearance only got a person so far. Real beauty came from the kind of guts and heart it took to work hard and put herself through school in hopes of making a better life for herself. It came in the form of the sacrifice she made and was making.

Garrett couldn't think of her lack without owning up to his abundance. Money he never touched. Why was it so hard for him to take what his family had worked hard to provide for him?

The easy answer? He wanted to make his own way. Now she had him thinking there was more to it. He'd hopped from job to job, never satisfied for long. The changes in employment he made every few months or year only temporarily gave him peace of mind. It never took long for the same problems to surface again. Garrett was a solid worker until he got bored. Things generally spiraled from there. Disagreements about supplies and how to properly tag and record cattle arose. Or how to treat medical conditions in the herd.

Garrett could admit to being stubborn. And he could be a real jerk when he chose to dig his heels in. His temper was legend and something he wasn't proud of.

Being with Brianna again was shedding a whole new light on life, corny as it sounded even to him. But she was. Watching her work for something she wanted so badly, never mind how awful it seemed to Garrett, stirred his admiration.

A part of him wanted to see what she would do with that English degree if given a chance. Hell, the frustrating part was that he could write a check for a scholarship for her without batting an eyelash. He wouldn't miss the money, especially since he never touched it anyway. The idea of finding a way to help others with his money had been on his mind for a while, but he'd never landed on the right way to go about it. Maybe this was it, reaching out to someone he knew personally.

The tricky part would be getting her to accept it. She wouldn't see it that way. She would see it as a handout. And he was fairly certain she'd thank him before rejecting the offer and sending him on his way. No looking back.

The thought felt like a face slap, even though it shouldn't. What should he care if she refused to take his help and then booted him out of her life?

Because losing her would be a real loss, a little voice in the back of his mind pointed out.

Mind wandering, he heard feet shuffling and the sound of chatter filling the hallway through the open door.

Brianna emerged from the crowd with a frown on her face.

"What's wrong?" he asked.

"The creep didn't show today. When I asked the prof if he knew anything about it, he said no. Another student said Derk wasn't coming back. He dropped the class two days ago."

Chapter Nine

"Did he say why?"

Brianna shook her head. "It was my first question, though."

"Any idea where he lives?" Garrett asked. The fact he was still in the exact spot where she'd left him caused all kinds of fireworks to go off inside. Had he waited there the entire time? From the looks of it, he had. This seemed like a good time to remind herself he was never happy in one spot for long. Of all the O'Connors she could have fallen for back in the day, this was the last one she should have picked if she wanted security. Of course, tell that to a reckless teenage heart.

"No. None," she admitted.

"We might be able to convince administration to give it to us. Of course, this process would go a lot smoother if I had one of my brothers' badges," he said.

"There are privacy laws against the school giving out any information. I've heard kids talk about them, being grateful their parents can't log on and check grades at will." Brianna kept to herself mostly. But she'd had to work in a group from time to time and had heard a couple of younger students talking about being close to failing.

"True."

"Plus, if you had a badge, and I think you mean follow in your brothers' footsteps rather than borrow one, you would be bound by some kind of oath not to use it for personal gain," she continued.

He was nodding as he rubbed the day-old scruff on his chin. After sleeping on her couch and then taking less than ten minutes to shower and clean up, he looked too damn good. She had to spend a whole lot more time ironing her hair into submission and applying light makeup. She hardly wore any during the day because she had to wear more than she liked to at night. A little extra eye shadow went a long way toward covering up her real self.

"What about classmates? Did you ever see him speak to anyone?" he asked.

"Rarely. I don't even think he spoke up that much during groups. I never heard anyone complain about him not pulling his weight, though." She searched her memory for any tidbit that could help them figure out who he was and where he lived before coming up empty.

"There has to be a way." Garrett was stubborn. Always had been and always would be. She had to give him that.

"Yeah, sure. We could hack into the system," she quipped.

Her offhanded remark seemed to resonate as his eyes widened.

Brianna put her hands up, palms out. "Whoa. Hold on there. I wasn't suggesting we should—"

"Hacking into the system is a crime." He cut her off, stabbing his fingers through his thick mane and taking a couple of steps in the opposite direction. When he whirled around, her pulse quickened. "I'm not deluded enough to try anything stupid or illegal. Going to jail isn't high on my list of things to do today."

"Okay, good. Because you can be a little…" She stopped when she saw his expression change. Tension pulled his face muscles taut for a split second and he brought his hand down to his side.

But what was that look that had crossed behind his eyes… Expectation? Hurt? Resolve?

What had he expected her to say? Wild? Reckless?

Those words would all be true and yet saying any one of them seemed like it would have a bigger force than a physical punch. Her chest squeezed and it was suddenly hard to breathe, despite being outside where there was plenty of oxygen. It was like someone had punched her in the solar plexus.

Words were powerful, but so were intentions. What she had intended to say seemed to have had just as much impact. Or worse? Because the flash of hurt in his eyes wasn't something that would have happened with physical pain.

Brianna took a step away. She needed air. She needed space.

"Hey, I gotta take a walk," she said when she could finally turn around and face him again.

"What?" His face screwed up with confusion.

"I need a minute. Okay?" The feeling building inside her seemed like it would burst like a volcano if she didn't put a little more distance between them. The kiss, which had been nothing more than a peck, had crept into her thoughts so many times during class she hadn't been able to concentrate.

Without waiting for an answer from Garrett, she took off in the opposite direction. Failing school wasn't an option, which she would do if he was all she could think about. She refused to allow that to happen, not even for a man like Garrett O'Connor. Not when she'd come this far. There was too much riding on her finishing her degree and getting a real job. The thought of waking up one day, bent over from age, still working at the bar and scraping together money to pay for her tiny apartment shocked her to the core. The tips were good now, but for how long? Definitely not forever. When her youth faded would she be relegated to washing dishes or becoming a barback, assisting bartenders for a living? No, definitely not the last one, not when her arm strength faded. She needed a ton of energy to carry boxes of liquor to the bar let alone all the glasses.

Before she realized, she'd made a lap around the building. Garrett stood there, leaning against the bricks with his arms folded across his chest and his legs crossed at the ankles.

This time, she kept a good eight feet of distance between them, taking a step back the second she felt the force field that was Garrett pulling her in, making her want more than she knew better from him, from any man.

As Garrett opened his mouth to speak, Brianna's professor stepped out of the building. He was in his late forties, average height with a stomach that hadn't seen a gym in years if ever, and a bulbous nose. His hair was greasy and near bald on top, which he tried to cover with a comb-over. He had large yellow teeth and a ruddy complexion. He took one look at her and frowned.

"Ms. Adair?" He took a step toward her, oblivious to Garrett.

"Dr. Jenkins." She didn't know exactly what to say except that her gut told her to walk him away from Garrett. Or maybe it was just her needing more space. Either way, she started walking in the opposite direction.

Garrett held back. She didn't have to look to know. She could feel his presence and taking those steps away from him was like walking into the shade on a chilly morning.

"How are you?" Dr. Jenkins, on the other hand, fell in step beside her.

"Fine." She didn't say anything more than necessary, hoping her prof would split off in a different direction so she could get back to Garrett. As much as she didn't want to get too close to him, she could admit being away from him was much worse.

"Are you certain about that?" Dr. Jenkins continued.

"Yes. Why? Don't I seem okay?" Had she really been that transparent? The short answer? Yes. All she'd had to do was take one look at Garrett to confirm. The hurt in his eyes earlier would haunt her. The last thing she wanted to do was let down someone who was helping her. She owed him coffee. Or dinner.

"You've been…distracted lately in class."

In that moment, she realized he wasn't just talking about *this* moment. Hadn't she always been told she wore her emotions on her sleeve? Wasn't that how her mother used to put it when Brianna was sad or lonely as a kid?

Buck up, buttercup. Being a kid is the best time of your life. Her mother's words echoed in her thoughts.

"I promise you that I'm working hard, sir." Her hand came up to touch the necklace and it caused a spark of resolve not to let her mother's words dictate Brianna's life.

Dr. Jenkins crinkled up his nose like someone had just held a bag of dog poo underneath. "When I hear the word *sir*, I turn around and look for my father. Call me Shram."

Why did this conversation make her feel like she was being sold snake oil? She mentally shook off the sensation. She really liked most of her profs. This one had always rubbed her the wrong way, and yet she needed to play the game with him because she needed a good grade.

Dr. Jenkins took a step closer to her and she instinctively drew away from him, elbow out in case he tried to follow. If she'd learned anything at the bar it was to protect her personal space no matter what.

"We can always do more, Brianna," he said so low she almost didn't hear him.

"Excuse me? What did you just say?" She played like she had no idea, but deep down she had no doubt what the "more" meant to him. She could see it in his leering grin, and then he reached out and touched her arm, giving it a little squeeze.

She jerked her arm back so fast he seemed momentarily stunned by her reaction.

His moment of shock was followed by another moment of hesitation. "Keep at it, Ms. Adair. The semester will be over before you know it. If you find yourself in need of extra credit, my office hours are posted."

Was he kidding her right now?

"To be very clear with you, sir." She intentionally used the word he didn't like because it reminded him their relationship was formal not friendly. "I have no intention of needing 'extra credit' because I work hard and deserve to pass."

Last time she checked she had a B minus in his class, which was more than enough to pass the semester.

His body stiffened as though she'd actually thrown that elbow into him like a soccer player gunning toward the goal.

"I appreciate the advice, though. Make no mistake, I'm taking notes." She gripped her cell phone in her hand, pulled it out of her pocket, and held it up.

"With determination like that, I have no doubt you'll pass the course, Ms. Adair." He practically stumbled over his words as he tried to get them out. He seemed very clear on the implication she'd been recording their conversation. "If I or someone on staff can be of any assistance, don't hesitate to reach out."

The man couldn't seem to get away from her fast enough. He practically tripped over his own feet trying to escape.

Garrett jogged up beside her a moment later. "What did he say to you?"

She turned to look at him and his spicy scent filled her senses. The kiss came to mind, how rough his beard felt in contrast to her lips, and she had to fight the urge to do it again for many reasons. Not the least of which was that her recent experience from moments ago had her wanting to reach for comfort.

Brianna almost laughed out loud at the thought. Garrett O'Connor was strength and excitement. He was high-risk, high-reward material. Until the shine wore off and then he would shatter her heart into a million tiny flecks.

The far-fetched part was that he would never want to hurt her on purpose. She realized that on a deep level. They'd known each other for years. Not the facade people put up. The *real*. And the real that was Garrett was too risky for her. She could fall in love with this man. Soul-fulfilling, rock-out-the-sheets love.

And where would that leave her when he got bored and needed to move on? He might not even get bored of her…just bored. He never could stick around in the same place for long.

She whirled around on him, wanting a different reality to be true.

"Can I ask you a question?" she started.

"Okay." He drew out the word, clearly surprised based on his expression.

"How many ranches have you worked at in the past year and a half?" She tucked her cell phone in her pocket and planted her balled fist on her hip. Eyes forward, she kept marching toward the parking lot.

"What does that have to do with anything?" His dark brows knitted together.

"It has everything to do with everything, Garrett." Did he really not see that?

He captured her elbow with his hand, stopping her in her tracks. "Tell me how?"

"Answer the question first." She tapped her toe on the ground, unable to meet his gaze.

He let go of her elbow and issued a sharp breath.

"Let's see." He paused like he was counting. The longer the pause, the quicker her heart beat against her ribs. "Five or six."

"In eighteen months?" She didn't bother to hide her shock.

"Is that important?"

"It is to me." She turned away from him and stalked toward the parking lot, leaving him standing there by himself.

WHAT HAD JUST happened here? Garrett planted his feet on the ground. No way did he plan to give in and give chase. Brianna had to be willing to talk to him about what was going on inside her head. Did she think he was a mind reader?

One minute she gave him a peck on the cheek that left a fiery trail and the next she couldn't stand to be in his presence. She needed to decide which one it was going to be. Hot or cold. There was no room for both.

He fisted his hands as her rejection stung again, stronger this time. Garrett seriously couldn't figure out the opposite sex. If he was being honest, he couldn't figure out Brianna. Maybe he should just walk away and leave her to it. She seemed ready and able to push him away at a moment's notice. Meanwhile, he stood there like a lovesick puppy.

News flash. He wasn't. In fact, he didn't even have to be standing here right now. He narrowed his gaze as he thought about getting in his pickup truck, driving her home and then hitting the highway.

Maybe it was time for him to head back to Katy Gulch and face everyone. He'd avoided it as much as humanly possible so far. *And go back with what?* A little voice in the back of his mind asked.

The lead on his father had turned out to be a dead end. His credit card hadn't been used in San Antonio after all, as Garrett had believed after getting a tip. Garrett had no new information to take back with him. He wasn't any closer to figuring out who murdered his own father. Frustration nipped at him like a determined pit bull.

Garrett could always rent a hotel room nearby. His laptop was tucked in a backpack inside his truck, power cord and all. He wasn't much for computers but he knew the basics. He knew enough to order supplies and perform research. What if the person or persons he was looking for lived in Katy Gulch? The annoying little voice picked that time to remind him about Ms. Hubert, the local who was murdered in her front yard. The investigation into her death prompted questions about Caroline's kidnapping.

With a couple of exhales, Garrett's frustration settled

down a few notches. He seriously needed a good workout. He could go for a run later. He knew full well he wasn't going to leave Brianna defenseless. He caught himself on the last word. She was far from defenseless but she lived alone and had very little in the way of resources.

After watching her deal with her professor, he had no doubt she could handle herself with any rational person. An out of control one? That was a different story altogether. Someone with a gun? Again, that would give someone an unfair advantage over her. Just thinking about it caused Garrett's blood pressure to shoot up. He'd done a lot of things wrong in his life. He'd quit jobs by walking out, sometimes telling his former boss and sometimes not. He'd binged on alcohol over a weekend or two. He'd bet on the wrong horse more times than he could count. But he never let someone he cared about down.

Period.

Even Colton could always count on Garrett if he got the message, as frustrating as their relationship could be at times. If Garrett heard his brother was in trouble, he wouldn't hesitate to track down any SOB who'd threatened him or any of his other brothers.

So, why couldn't he track down what had happened to his sister? Why couldn't he give that peace to their parents? Now that his father was gone, there was no giving Finn O'Connor answers. Garrett's mother, Margaret, had to be sick by now with worry after the past had been dredged up as recycled news. Of course, anything an O'Connor did or didn't do was news. Their family was nothing more than entertainment to some folks. An O'Connor's feelings didn't matter, people thought. They had everything other people wanted. Love. A nice home. Money. Two parents who adored each of them. They had everything except peace of mind when they laid their heads down at night. Garrett had spent half of his childhood wondering if the guy who stole Caroline was going to come back for one of his brothers. Him. He'd spent the other half angry the sonofabitch had taken his sister and not him.

From where he was positioned, he could see Brianna. He could see his truck. He could see her standing there with her arms crossed over her chest, tapping her toe against the earth in a staccato rhythm.

Suddenly, she didn't look quite so fierce. She looked like she was putting up a brave front to cover the fact she was afraid.

After a sharp sigh, Garrett threw his hands down to his sides and closed the distance between them. He marched right past her to open the passenger door before claiming the driver's seat. She stood there as he started the engine.

That woman was the definition of stubborn. She was also the definition of beauty. Confidence. Fire. Intelligence. And other adjectives he didn't want to spend too much time adding to the list.

"You coming?" he said in more of a bark than anything else.

"You leaving?"

"Not until you get your sweet backside in my truck," he said.

"Just go, Garrett." In those three vulnerable words, all his anger melted away. She had her back to him to hide the fact she was crying.

Now he felt like the jerk and he wasn't even sure why.

Chapter Ten

Brianna stood there in the parking lot. Tears brimming. There was no way she was going to cry in front of Garrett. She couldn't remember the last time she'd shed a tear. There were times, in fact, when she wished she could cry just to release all the pent-up frustration inside her. There were days when she felt like she might explode if she didn't find a release valve.

She couldn't remember the last time she'd had sex but her brain screamed *too long*. Forget about good sex or anything that came close to the passion she felt in one little kiss. It wasn't even a real kiss and yet it left her lips tingling for the entire class. She couldn't shake his scent.

"Hey, come on in the truck and let's grab lunch." Garrett's voice normally had the kind of certainty that would make her buy firewood during a Texas summer from him. This time was different. This time, there was none of that usual Garrett swagger. This time, there was none of the confidence that bordered on cockiness. This time, there was a hint of vulnerability.

So, she took in a fortifying breath, plastered on as much of a smile as she could muster and turned toward the passenger seat. Thankfully, the tears welling in her eyes dried up. She wasn't sure if it was pure willpower or a stroke of grace. She'd take either one as she climbed inside the cab and then closed the door behind her. She secured her seat belt without looking at him, tucking her chin to chest to hide her eyes. One glance and she was afraid he'd be able to read right through her.

And she didn't want him to know how thrown she was by what had just happened with him or with Dr. Jenkins. She'd rather put both behind her and focus on who was trying to run her off the road on her way home from work at night.

"We can do this however you want, Brianna. I'm not going anywhere until we see this thing through. But, it would help a whole helluva lot if you talked to me about what was going on. What the professor said that threw you so bad." His words were measured and calm. There was not a hint of accusation or judgment in them. Garrett started up the truck and then put the gearshift in Reverse before backing out of the parking spot.

"I'm pretty sure my teacher just let me know how I could pick up some extra credit, and it made my skin crawl." Her chin quivered but she refused to give in to the emotions pressing heavy on her chest, wrapping around her like a thousand-pound blanket, squeezing the life out of her.

The truck came to a screeching halt. Garrett slammed the gearshift into Drive.

"No. No. No. I don't want you to do anything that could cause me to fail that class, Garrett," she warned, praying he wouldn't impulsively jump out of the truck and find Dr. Jenkins.

"Are you kidding me right now?" Anger caused his voice to shake.

"I know. It's disgusting. Believe me." An involuntary

shiver rocked her body. "I think I threw up in my mouth a little bit when he suggested it."

"Tell me his exact words," Garrett said; more than a little heat radiated from him.

"Why? What does it matter?"

"Because I'm going to make him eat every one of them." With Garrett's size and temper, she had no doubt he could take Dr. Jenkins apart limb by limb.

"And then what?" she asked, needing to find a way to calm Garrett down but also appreciating someone having her back for a change. "He'll press charges. You'll end up in jail. I'll fail the class because there's no way I'd be able to go back in there and face him."

"I can't stand the thought of him getting away with something like this, Brianna."

"He didn't," she quickly countered.

"Not with you. But how many other female students has he pulled this on?" His anger seemed to brim just below the surface, and she had no idea how much or how little it would take to make it bubble over.

"You're right," she conceded. "I can't let him get away with this. But I also have to pass the class. And before that, I have to live long enough to figure out what jerkoff is trying to make sure I end up alone in a ditch in the middle of the night. Right now, Dr. Jenkins is the least of my problems, so you have to let me handle this on my terms."

Garrett issued a sharp sigh.

She turned to face him and saw his jaw muscle clench so hard she thought he might crack his back teeth. "You have to promise me you won't do something…" She searched for the right word.

"Stupid?" There was so much fire in that word, it was as though someone had poured gasoline on a raging fire.

"No." Stupid was the last word she would come up with when it came to Garrett.

"What then?" He turned his face toward her with wild eyes. "Out of control?"

She was shaking her head furiously but it didn't seem to make a difference in the state he was in. "I don't think you are any of those things, Garrett."

"Are you sure about that?" Now he was looking at her like he was murderous Jack from *The Shining* at the moment he lost his mind.

And yet, not a fiber of her being was afraid of him. So, she crossed her arms over her chest and said, "You can look at me like that all day but I know you, Garrett. I don't know what you've been through in the past few years to make you think other people might view you like that from the outside. All I can tell you is that I know personally that you are none of those things. Impulsive? Yes. Stubborn? A mule has nothing on you. But you are not stupid. And you are certainly not out of control."

"If you know me so well then why don't you tell me what I really am?" Some of the fire receded from his voice.

"Give me a minute to think and I'll tell you." She didn't need a minute. It was a stall tactic to force him to slow down. Counting to ten in moments of stress and frustration had gotten her through many a fight.

"Well?" More of his anger faded.

"Incredibly smart, for one. You can make me laugh and it doesn't even seem like you're trying all that hard." She'd keep the part about him being smokin' hot to herself. "I'm not worried about any of those traits while you're this angry."

"What then?"

"Passion. You're a passionate person, Garrett. I've never met someone who goes all in, in quite the same way as you do," she admitted.

"Now, you're just trying to flatter me so I don't take off and teach your professor the right way to speak to a lady," he said.

"You also have a habit of changing the subject any time someone compliments you, which tells me that despite the tough front and sometimes cocky attitude you're actually humble." She stopped there, figuring he would stop her anyway.

"I'm pretty sure you're talking about someone else and I'm about to blush if you keep going, but I'd be honored to buy lunch if you'll allow me to." A smile ghosted his lips despite him trying to let the comments bounce off.

It occurred to her in that moment that he didn't see himself in the same light as she did. It was beyond her how he could *not* know these things about himself. And then, like a ton of bricks, the truth hit her. He didn't know those things because he didn't believe them to be true.

"Deal," she said. Was there a way to help him see himself through her eyes in the short time they would be together? She sure hoped so. It was the least she could do considering how willing he'd been to pitch in and help her.

BRIANNA WAS MISGUIDED. Lack of sleep and too much studying had caused the woman to lose her judgment. Not that he didn't appreciate the compliments. Who wouldn't? But, man, she was so off base there was no guiding her back to the plate.

She seemed to believe what was coming out of her

mouth. So his only recourse to change topics was to feed her.

There was a diner near campus he wanted to check out. He'd looked it up on his phone while she'd been in class and the place was highly rated for its home cooking. He could use a real meal about now. Chicken-fried steak with mashed potatoes and gravy would hit the spot.

He also thought about her professor. The man wasn't getting away with using his position to pressure Brianna into doing who knew what. She was strong and knew how to handle advances like that and hearing her say the words had still been a gut punch. What about a younger student? Would she be as strong? Garrett wanted to get back on campus after lunch to do a little investigating. See if anyone else had a bad experience with this prof.

The diner held true to its online reputation of being one of the most popular food stops in the area. The lot brimmed with cars and trucks.

"I've never heard of this place." Brianna's voice held very little of the lightness he remembered from years ago now. She'd always been a spitfire. Something else was missing too that he couldn't quite put his finger on. Happiness?

If only Garrett could say or do something to give that back to her. She had other qualities now. Qualities worth admiring. Strength. Willpower. And there was still just enough sass to remind him she could kick butt when she needed to.

The image of her rejecting the prof from earlier stuck in his mind. She shouldn't have to be so good at defending herself. A lightning bolt struck. Was that the reason she was so good at pushing people away? Pushing him away?

"Let's see if it's worth all the rave." He parked his truck and then hopped out, coming around to the other side as she opened the door for herself and slipped out. She slammed the door a little harder than she had to but he figured it was her way of working out some of the tension she must be feeling.

Setting his own thoughts aside, he reached for her hand. Instead of pushing him away, she grabbed on tight, linking their fingers as they walked inside the diner.

Eats Diner was a silver tube like a car on a train. The entrance was positioned in the middle of the room and there were an equal number of red vinyl booths to either side. A handwritten sign stood two steps inside the place, asking diners to wait to be seated.

A long bar stretched the length of the space on the opposite wall. Mirrors made the diner look bigger than it was and the smells coming from the kitchen already had his mouth salivating.

A loud growl came from Brianna's stomach, so he figured he'd hit it out of the park with this one and just in time.

"I didn't realize how hungry I was until right now," she said as her cheeks turned a couple shades of red.

"I'm starving." He glanced at his wristwatch. Yes, he still wore one because it wasn't always convenient to take out his phone on a ranch and cell service was always spotty anyway. Much of the time when he was working, he kept his cell in a backpack in his truck or in a sack when he rode his horse. And, yes, he still worked cattle with a horse. A whole lot of ranchers used trucks and ATVs. This was more than a job. It was a way of life. Being on horseback kept him closer to nature. He preferred the sound of hooves to a motor any day of the week and twice on Sunday.

He wasn't kidding either. He was so hungry that he was about to grab a piece of bacon off someone else's plate. Brianna must have read his mind because she gripped his hand even tighter.

"Don't think about it," she warned and at least there was a hint of playfulness in her voice again.

"I wasn't actually going to steal someone else's food," he defended.

"You were thinking about it, though. Weren't you?"

"What makes you think that?" He offered his most innocent look.

"I saw the way you were looking at that guy's plate. And then a little dribble of saliva appeared in the corner of your mouth. Right there." She brought her free hand up to point at his left side.

"Fine. Busted. But I still wasn't going to take anything." He cracked a smile at her observation.

"How many, sweetheart?" A blonde who looked to be in her early thirties bebopped on over as she winked at Garrett. She had on a retro outfit that consisted of neon pink hot pants and a matching shirt with oversize white lapels that looked straight out of the sixties.

"Just the two of us." Brianna held up their linked hands in what he was pretty certain was a show of claiming her territory.

Garrett suppressed a smirk. He and Brianna might not be a thing, but she sure as hell didn't seem to want this waitress flirting with him. To be fair, he was holding Brianna's hand and the wink would qualify as out of line.

The waitress shrugged and said, "This way then."

Brianna stepped in front of Garrett, essentially placing

herself in between him and the waitress, and this time he went all in with the charm.

When the blonde stopped in front of a table and turned, Brianna took a step back, which brought her back against his chest. She reached behind her for his hands and wrapped them around her.

The explosion of heat rocketing through him with the move wiped the smile off his face as he tried not to concentrate on the fact that the action caused her sweet round bottom to press into him.

Blood flew south and what he was hungry for shifted. *Not the time nor the place, O'Connor.* Definitely the right woman, though. An image of the two of them tangled in his sheets, heaving for air after a mind-blowing round of sex took center stage.

Since he was no longer a hormonal teenager, he forced his attention back to lunch. *Chicken-fried steak.* All he needed to do was think about chicken-fried steak instead of…

"Here you go." The waitress, whose name tag read Hailey, presented the booth like she was unveiling a new car. The look on her face was priceless as she gave them a once-over. If Brianna was trying to make Hailey jealous, she nailed it.

He couldn't erase the grin on his face after Hailey walked away.

"What was that all about?" he asked Brianna after claiming their seats.

"No idea." She shrugged like it was no big deal.

"Are you ready to talk?" The woman knew how to drive him mad.

"What do you mean? We're talking right now." Confusion knitted her eyebrows together.

"I'm not talking about idle conversation. If I'm going to be of any help to you, you're going to need to let me in."

She stared at him like they were back in middle school and he'd just dared her to kiss Shawn Fletcher. Then, she folded her arms across her chest and said, "Yes."

Chapter Eleven

"What's his name?"

Brianna was certain her face twisted up at the question based on Garrett's response.

"The professor. You never told me his name and..." He stopped long enough for Hailey to turn over two cups and then pour coffee.

At least Hailey didn't wink at Garrett this time like he was some kind of stud in a bar, eager to be hit on. It was gross and stirred a reaction in Brianna. Hailey needed to take a step back and Brianna had done her best to make certain she did. She didn't plan out the actions she'd taken and she had no regrets.

Hailey clearly got the message because when she took out her pad and pen she looked at Brianna this time instead of pretending she wasn't there. Not that Brianna could blame Hailey for wanting to hit on Garrett. The guy was sex-on-a-stick hotness. But Brianna was standing right next to him and they were holding hands. She refused to be ignored.

"What'll it be today?" Hailey asked.

"I'll have chicken-fried steak with mashed potatoes and gravy. Oh, and the fried okra. Is it any good?" Brianna handed over the menu in time to watch Hailey's eyes light up.

"Ours is the best. I know everyone says that but I'm telling you right now that no one compares to ours." Hailey's demeanor changed. So much so, Brianna was sold.

"Then, I have to try those," she said.

"And you, sir?" Hailey's voice held a whole lot more respect now.

"I'll have the exact same." He handed over his menu and then Hailey scurried away with a smile. He focused on Brianna and his gaze caused her cheeks to burn. "Nice touch, by the way."

"What?" She played like she didn't know what he was talking about.

"I saw what you did there."

"It was nothing." She waved her hand like she was dismissing the idea.

"It was great," was all he said before shaking his head with a slight smile that made her heart free-fall. His chest was puffed out just a little, enough to make her think he was proud of her.

A surprising tear welled up. She coughed and tucked her chin to her chest so she could gain hold of her emotions before looking up at Garrett again.

"I can always figure it out on my own," Garrett's voice broke through the moment. "I'd rather you be the one to tell me."

"What are you going to do to him?" She pulled it together enough to risk a glance at him.

"Nothing until you tell me I can." The tension in his eyes returned and she stared in the face of anger.

"You'll never know how much it means to me that you care...but I need to fight my own battles," she said.

Her words seemed to resonate. After a few seconds, he looked away before taking a sip of coffee.

"Any chance you'd be willing to let me back you up or at the very least be around to watch it happen? I have a feeling you're going to tan his hide when you get around to it," he said with that smirk she was beginning to love.

Whoa, there. Slow down. Love was a strong word. *Like* was better. And she very much liked to see that mischief in his eyes.

"Deal," she said by way of response.

Before they could shake on it, plates arrived. The smell of the chicken-fried steak didn't do justice to how amazing it looked. The batter was caramel colored and crisp. If this dish tasted half as good as it looked, her taste buds were in for a treat. She'd deal with her thighs later. Or not. Running around behind a bar all night kept her in decent enough shape. A few curves didn't bother her.

Hailey's expression was priceless after she set the plates in front of them and scanned their faces. "Y'all go on and enjoy. Holler if you need anything else."

She slid the bill onto the table with a slight curtsy.

"We sure will," Brianna said. She'd served enough couples to realize when a man and woman walked into a bar or anywhere else for that matter together, the server's attention should be on the woman. It was basic etiquette in the service industry. Hailey had taken the hint, though. Her service was better for it too.

"Dr. Jenkins is his name, by the way," she said to Garrett as she picked up her knife and fork.

Not many other sounds were made until the plates were clean other than the occasional moan from sheer pleasure.

"How did I not know about this place? It's so close to

campus," Brianna said when she was so full she thought she might burst. A glance at the bill told her why. The eatery was proud of their dishes and placed value on them. And the food was worth every cent.

She promised she'd come back here after graduation. Speaking of which, she needed to think about the next step of getting a few interviews lined up. She had no plans to stick around the bar a day longer than she had to.

"It was hyped on the internet and I wasn't so sure it would live up." He picked up his coffee and drained his second cup. "Call me a satisfied customer."

"I could use a nap," she said as an image of her curled up in bed with Garrett assaulted her. She shoved it aside, thinking she needed to keep her mind far away from that temptation. She caught his gaze. "Thank you. For helping me last night despite the fact I must've looked like a drowned rat to you. And for this today."

He waved her away like it was nothing. It wasn't. In fact, it was everything to her. She couldn't remember the last time someone volunteered to show up for her like this.

"I know you have a life and—"

His hand came up again to wave her off. "It's nothing you wouldn't do for me if the situation was reversed."

"Why are you so confident about that?" She could tell he was too. There wasn't a hint of doubt in his eyes—eyes that she could stare into all day.

"Because I know you. You might have grown up and so have I. But you're still the same underneath it all and we were close once even though it hurt my relationship with my brother at the time," he admitted.

"I'm sorry about that. I always felt bad about it." The

thought she'd been the one to drive a wedge between brothers hit her square in the chest.

"You couldn't have if Colton and I had been closer," he said without hesitation. "We always had a competitive relationship. I can't even remember how it began or what started it, to be honest. Must have been something when we were kids. Of all the boys, we fought the most. We were the most competitive."

"Then, you must be the most alike deep down," she said.

He stopped for a second and considered her statement. "I'm not sure I follow."

"Think about it. What happens when you put two roosters in a henhouse?" It was the best analogy she could think up on a stomach so full she was afraid the top button of her pants would pop.

"It gets ugly," he conceded.

"Exactly. Two alpha males in close proximity fight. Happens in nature all the time," she said.

"Yeah, but it happened to the two of us. My other brothers are strong-willed, but I don't fight with them."

"Then, you and Colton must possess a quality the other doesn't like in himself. I would definitely say the two of you are more alike when it comes to personality than any of the others," she stated.

"Really?" The news seemed to shock him.

"I think so," she admitted.

All he said was, "Huh."

"Oh, man. I ate way too much." Brianna bit back a yawn.

"Good. Where we're going you'll be able to walk it off."

Garrett's cell buzzed as he walked out of the restaurant. He almost ignored it, figuring it was one of his brothers, but decided to check anyway. Colton's ears were probably burning and that was the reason for the call. He checked the screen and froze. Damiani. Garrett needed to take this one.

"Hey, can you hold on a sec?" he asked.

"Not too long. I got something hot." Damiani's full name was Anthony DeLuca Damiani but he only responded to his last name. He was a private detective.

"No problem." Garrett fished out his truck keys and tossed them to Brianna, who'd taken a couple of steps toward the vehicle. "You go ahead. I'll be right there."

She caught the keys and then cocked her head to one side. "Okay."

He winked at her before returning to the call.

"Hey, man. What did you find?" Damiani was a New York transplant who'd moved to Austin to set up a private investigations shop. He and Garrett dated sisters a couple of years ago. The relationships didn't work out but Damiani and Garrett kept in touch, went out for a beer whenever Garrett was in town.

"There's an alpaca farm that gives tours during the day but also is believed to be a front for a baby ring. I got the San Antonio tip wrong," he hedged. "It wasn't his credit card."

"I know you did." Garrett wasn't trying to make his buddy feel bad about it. "But, seriously, alpacas?"

"Yeah. I know. It's kind of brilliant when you really think about it. Farmland gets a government blessing, and who would think anything sinister was happening there?" Damiani said.

"And why do you think there's something fishy going on?" Garrett asked.

"A tip. I'd rather not say who it came from. I was doing a little fishing of my own and got lucky," he said.

In Garrett's experience, luck happened more often to someone working hard to find answers.

"That's not the tip, though," Damiani said.

"What is?" Garrett asked.

"My guy says someone named Finn O'Connor was asking around about the place." Damiani's voice lowered when he said, "Again, I'd like to express my condolences. I didn't know your father personally, but he sounds like a straight-up guy, you know."

"Yeah. I appreciate it." Garrett needed a second to process what he was hearing, or more important, to steel himself for what he was about to learn. "Where is this place and what's it called?"

"It's off I-35 about a mile north of Killeen," Damiani said before rattling off the address. "Alpaca Rescue is the name of the place. They're a nonprofit but word on the street is that they make their money on what happens inside the house, not so much as in the barn, if you know what I mean."

Killeen was about halfway between Austin and Waco. In no traffic, Waco wasn't much more than a two-hour drive but there was almost always traffic. Tack on another hour to San Antonio. All in all, about five hours round trip under the best circumstances. The loop around Austin was a lifesaver even though it added a couple of miles. Not having to stop every five seconds or move at a crawl was worth any price.

"I respect that you can't give me a name, but I need to know how reliable this source is." If this was true—

and he had no reason to doubt Damiani—someone was willing to kill to keep a secret.

"On a scale of one to ten…he's a twelve." Damiani's voice dropped when he said, "Hey, be careful with this one. You know what I mean? I've got like two friends I actually enjoy meeting up with for a beer and you're one of 'em."

"Thanks, man. I feel the same." Garrett was sincere. He knew a lot of people and called very few of them friends.

"You'll be the first to know should I hear anything else," Damiani said. "In the meantime, watch your back."

"I'll be around for that beer real soon," Garrett said for good measure.

"I'll save you a seat at Dublin's on Sixth."

Garrett thanked Damiani before ending the call and heading toward the truck. He climbed in the driver's seat. "That was news about my dad's case."

He filled her in as he started the engine.

"Listen, Garrett. I totally understand if you need to bail. Your dad's case is way more important and I don't want to keep you any longer than—"

"I'm here. I'm seeing this thing through with you just like I said I would. Believe me, I'd feel a helluva lot worse if I took off to follow up on a lead—and that's all it is at this point—and something happened to you," he admitted. "Plus, there's nothing I can do to bring my dad back at this point."

She was chewing the inside of her cheek, her tell that she was uncomfortable about something. It used to signal she hadn't studied for a test like she believed she should have back in school. He took it as a sign she needed a bit more convincing.

"Besides, I might be able to slip out in the morning while you're asleep and make a run. If I go early enough, I should be able to round trip before..." He stopped right there. "What time is your class tomorrow?"

"Same as this morning but it's an hour and a half," she said. She immediately went back to working the inside of her cheek.

A quick calculation said there was no way he would be back in time. Using his smartphone, he pulled up the internet and searched for the Alpaca Rescue. Much to his surprise, several rescue organizations came up. He had no idea the alpaca population was at risk to this degree. He chalked it up to people getting excited about a pet or even starting a small operation for the fur before realizing how much work it was.

The same thing happened in ranching. Folks got stars in their eyes about living on the open range in an old farmhouse. They pictured the sunsets, which were spectacular. They envisioned having all the fun that came with an animal, which made the work worth it. They got caught up in the romance of it without realizing how hard the day-to-day care could be. First of all, there was a lot of manual labor in a trade like cattle ranching even with machines to make it all easier now.

Most newcomers didn't get past the first year before they were ready to pack up and head back to where they came. Disease could wipe out a herd. Then there were all the financial considerations. Plenty of ranches weren't profitable and if they were, they eked by.

Finn O'Connor had been a pioneer in the industry. He was the first to ensure herds were grass fed and fetched a higher price for organics.

Most folks jumped into owning a ranch with both feet,

never doing all the research upfront. He likened the experience to rehabbing an old house. They were called money pits for a reason.

Brianna was quiet on the way back to campus. Garrett didn't say much either but that didn't mean the wheels weren't spinning in his head. He didn't want to wait too long to check into the alpaca situation. It might be nothing, but it might just crack open the whole case and they'd been waiting too long for answers already. An itch of excitement took hold as he thought about the possibility of finding out who killed his father and what had happened to his sister. What if it was more bad news?

His chest squeezed thinking about the day he would be able to tell his mother what happened to Caroline. Even bad news was better than not knowing.

The next question was whether or not he should bring in his brothers. Too early, he thought. It would be best to wait on it and see if the lead panned out. No one missed him at the ranch. No one expected him to be home. Each of his brothers had reached out recently, some letting him know exactly what they thought about his absence.

But what if he did go home? Then what? Would he get comfortable? Give up the search? Settle?

Did he believe most of his brothers had done the same thing? In truth, Garrett hadn't given it a whole lot of thought. In fact, he'd been so focused on shaming himself for not cracking the case that he didn't really think a whole lot about the others. He hadn't talked to them about it much either. He knew several of his brothers used their jobs to poke around when they could. They had protocols to abide by and oaths to follow.

That was the great thing about Garrett's life. He answered to no one except himself. If he needed to break a law to find out the truth, so be it. He would never hurt an innocent person to get what he wanted, though.

But had he really done all that he could have? The voice in the back of his head chimed in with a resounding *no.* Too often, he'd fallen into the cycle of heading nowhere and then becoming so frustrated that he had to spend some time on the land to rebalance himself. Anger kept him away from people for weeks when he could have pivoted and found a new lead. He'd go off and do something stupid and then the cycle of shame would start over again. He'd condemn his own stupidity and it all spiraled from there.

Recognizing the pattern was all well and good except that he didn't know how to break it. So lotta good it did. Once the cycle started, it was like watching a Mack truck come right at him with no ability to step out of its way.

"Garrett?" The concern in Brianna's voice shocked him out of his revelry.

"Yeah?"

"Are you going to get out of the truck or are we going to sit here all day?" she asked. "Also, you didn't tell me why we came back here."

He looked around, and realized he'd parked in the same spot as earlier at her school.

"Right. I think I know how to find out how to get information about the creep who dropped out of your class."

"Really?" She sounded a little more than shocked.

"It was either this or hack into the mainframe," he teased, trying to lighten the heavy mood that had descended on him. He was certain she'd picked up on it too. "Come on, I'm kidding. I barely know how to work my phone. I'm the last person who would have the skills to break into a computer."

She forced a laugh. At least, it sounded forced anyway. And the smile she gave didn't reach her eyes. Concern, however, was abundant in the tension lines in her face.

"Trust me?" he asked, hoping he'd gained a little of her confidence in the past eighteen or so hours.

"I'm willing to go out on a limb."

They were making progress. Pride shouldn't swell in his chest. It did, though.

"Have you ever thought about having kids?" Brianna asked out of the blue.

"Where'd that question come from?" He didn't bother to mask the shock in his voice. To say she'd caught him off guard was a lot like saying milk came from cows.

"Curious, I guess." She shrugged but he wasn't buying it.

It dawned on him she must be referring to what happened to his sister. He thought about it for a long moment before answering. Not because he didn't know the answer to the question but because he'd never opened up to anyone before about something so personal.

For reasons he couldn't explain and sure as hell didn't want to examine, he decided to go for it.

"To answer your question…yes, I have thought about whether or not I wanted to have kids," he said. "The second part of that answer is a hard no."

The fact she didn't seem surprised or upset shouldn't bother him. So, why did it?

Chapter Twelve

Brianna walked behind Garrett as they entered the Administration Building, thinking about how he'd hesitated before answering her question in the parking lot. She didn't blame him for not wanting kids after what his family had been through. Forget that he wasn't even born yet when the kidnapping had occurred. She couldn't imagine a parent ever truly getting over the loss of a child. Not knowing what happened had to be even worse. Always having a question mark hanging over their heads. Never getting answers. Her heart ached for the O'Connor family and their loss. There were no words to ease that brand of pain.

"Am I too late to drop a class?" Garrett's question seemed to throw the office aide off.

Her face scrunched. "I'm sorry. You'll have to get your prof's permission at this point."

The young brunette in a high ponytail with cheekbones most any woman would kill for scooted her chair to the desk where Brianna stood behind Garrett. From her vantage point, she could see the young adult blushing under Garrett's stare.

The guy could work magic on pretty much any

woman he wanted. Probably men too with his good looks, she mused.

"And what if he doesn't give it to me?" Garrett continued in that smooth-as-silk voice Brianna was certain was meant to butter the brunette up. So, he wasn't against using his considerable charms to get the information they needed. Maybe the lead he got in his father's case had him wanting to speed hers up so he could move on.

As much as she wanted…*needed*…to bust the creep who was freaking her out every few nights on her rides home from work, the thought of Garrett taking off and her old life returning was a gut punch she wasn't expecting.

That *was* the deal. He was kind enough to stick around until the creep either got spooked by his presence and bolted or was locked behind bars where he belonged. She reminded herself that was enough no matter how much her heart protested. If she listened to it, she would be living on a ranch somewhere with this man while chasing after a kiddo or two.

Oh, no. Where did that little news bulletin come from?

Since she didn't want to block any of his mojo, she stayed tucked behind him. His hand occasionally reached back to touch her…reassure her? Any time their skin came in contact a trill of awareness rippled through her. Did he have to be so dang sexy? And caring?

Seriously, though, ever since the call at the diner his demeanor had changed. She had to figure out a way to convince him not to wait to follow up on the lead. What if he waited and the lead dried up? Would he always blame her?

Even if he didn't, she would. She would never forgive herself if he let something slide as important as finding out what happened to his sister or locking behind bars the person who killed his father. Finn O'Connor had been truly one of the most decent and kindest people on earth. Whenever she heard the term *salt-of-the-earth*, she thought of him. He'd welcomed her on the ranch along with anyone else his sons brought home. He worked side by side with his ranch hands and foreman. As far as she could tell, he never took the easy road over doing what was right.

Tears welled in her eyes thinking about his life being cut short. His wife was just as decent and kind as he was. She certainly didn't deserve to lose the love of her life. Losing a daughter, her firstborn, was more than anyone should have to endure. And yet, she'd found a way to keep going despite what had to be a parent's worst nightmare. Brianna hadn't given much thought to having children of her own until the idea popped into her thoughts a few seconds ago. She figured there was plenty of time for that later if she wanted a family, and that was a big *if*. There was no way she could think about kids when she was struggling to take care of herself.

But she was beginning to realize nothing was guaranteed, and later might turn into not at all without her consent. Plus, she never really bought into the whole happily-ever-after lie. People met and fell in love all the time. And then plenty of them fell out of love or, worse yet, fell in love with someone else while they were still married. She could attest to the level of pain that caused.

Her hand instinctively came up to the charm on her necklace. She fingered the lucky piece as more tears welled in her eyes. Refusing to give in to the emotion threatening to suck her under, she glanced around in hopes of finding something else to focus on.

To her left, one of her classmates, who appeared to be working in the office, caught her eye. Oh, what was her name?

Lauren Bishop. She sat next to Brianna most of the time in class and Brianna had seen the name scribbled down on the attendance sign-up sheet enough times for it to stick.

She didn't realize Lauren worked here. Then again, it wasn't like Brianna was in school to make friends. Lauren stood out. One, because she sat next to Brianna most of the time. Two, because she had a string of beads on her backpack that looked like a little kid's preschool art project.

Maybe Brianna could do a little digging of her own. She walked over to Lauren, leaving Garrett to his conversation.

"Hey, Lauren," Brianna said like the two of them were besties rather than two strangers who sat next to each other in class and gave the occasional nod or smile during lectures.

Lauren looked up from the screen she was studying and returned the smile. "Hi. Can I help you?"

Based on the way her left eyebrow arched ever so slightly and her gaze fixed on Brianna, Lauren was trying to place where she knew Brianna from.

Rather than give herself away, Brianna decided to run with it. "I didn't realize you worked in the office."

"Work-study," Lauren corrected. "It's part of my financial aid."

"Oh, nice," Brianna said a little too cheerfully based on Lauren's slight frown. "I'm sure it helps pay the bills."

"It covers my sitter," Lauren said.

"Little girl or little boy?" Brianna might not know

much about kids but she knew how to get people talking from her experience as a bartender. Most people couldn't wait to talk about themselves.

"Girl." Lauren studied Brianna for a long moment. "Do you have kids?"

Brianna excelled at building rapport with her clients and that meant finding common ground. If she was going to do the same with Lauren, she would have to find a different topic.

"Not yet," Brianna said. It wasn't exactly a lie. She didn't have kids *yet.* This wasn't the time or place to go into detail about how she never wanted them either. But then that wasn't exactly true. She'd had a fleeting thought about having Garrett's babies.

"Believe me when I tell you that it's better to wait until you finish school." Lauren gave Brianna a quick once-over and she assumed the woman was trying to figure out an age.

"I hear you," Brianna said, hoping this would lead to the perfect opportunity to get Lauren talking about class. "But now I'm in a spot because..."

She paused mainly for dramatic effect. If Lauren thought she was teasing information out of Brianna she'd be more invested, and that meant more likely to help.

"Never mind. It's nothing." Brianna waved a hand like she was swatting a fly.

"What?" Lauren scooted her chair away from the monitor and toward Brianna. "Go ahead. You can tell me." She glanced around. "Who am I going to tell anyway?"

"Well... I don't know," Brianna hedged.

"It's fine." Lauren leaned over the desk.

"Okay, but it's not really a big deal. I'll figure it out..."

"Figure what out?" Lauren asked.

"A guy from class. We're supposed to partner on a project and he's not here. He gave me his cell number but I can't read his handwriting. Anyway, I can't afford to fail the class. You know? Not with graduation around the corner. I'm so close and so tired of working nights to pay for school." Brianna threw in the last bit for good measure. It was truer than she wanted it to be and about as honest as she'd ever been. The cell phone bit was stretching the truth and she hated doing it. It didn't feel good to deceive someone, but Lauren's fingers were already busy dancing across the keyboard.

"I know the guy you're talking about." Her forehead creased. "Thought he'd been assigned to another group, though."

Brianna wasn't sure what would come up on Lauren's screen. She'd found out the hard way the computer systems at her school did a lousy job of talking to each other. She could only hope Lauren wouldn't see that Derk had dropped the class. Possibly dropped out of school. If the latter was true, Brianna was about to be busted.

Maybe not, she reasoned. She could always say she didn't realize he'd chunked the whole semester.

Her pulse climbed another notch with every second Lauren stared at the screen.

"Got it." Lauren practically beamed. She glanced up and gave Brianna a once-over. "Ready?"

"Yeah." Brianna fumbled for her cell. "This is great. I can't thank you enough. This will be such a huge help."

"I know what it's like to have a partner ditch. Believe me when I say it's no fun. Not everyone here is as focused as some of us." She gave a look of solidarity.

"Right. I got a C on a group project because the person who did all of the graphics decided to stop coming to class," Brianna shared as she palmed her cell. She held it up into the air. "Ready when you are."

Lauren rattled off the number. Then, she leaned over the desk. "Just don't tell anyone it came from me. I can't afford to lose my financial aid." She reached under her desk and pulled out a cell phone. "This is Landy."

The toothless grin on the round-faced angel in the picture tugged at Brianna's heart. Her ovaries cried.

"Your daughter is beautiful." Brianna had never meant those words more. Her chest squeezed at the thought she could end up getting Lauren in trouble or cost that little girl stability. "And I won't tell a soul about this." She held up her cell and used it to cross her heart.

Lauren's eyes widened and her cheeks turned six shades past red. Her gaze fixed on something moving behind Brianna. Or should she say *someone*?

"Are you ready?" Garrett's chest pressed to her back as he said those words in her ear. His warm breath sent a trill of awareness skittering down the delicate skin at the nape of her neck. An image of their babies popped into Brianna's thoughts, a boy who was the spitting image of his father and a little girl who resembled Brianna. Talk about ovaries crying and her heart melting.

How much trouble was she in right now? A helluva lot more than she wanted to acknowledge.

GARRETT FIGURED BRIANNA needed an out. He gave her one. Pretending to be *together* had been as natural as waking in the morning. So, why didn't he want to get out of bed?

Figuratively, of course. But then, literally didn't sound so bad to him right now either.

All that talk about babies earlier should have sleeping with Brianna at the bottom of his list. He suppressed a smile. There wasn't much that could manage that feat.

Brianna cleared her throat. "Yeah. I'm ready when you are."

He reached for her hand and then linked their fingers.

"See you in class," Brianna said to the person she'd been talking to. He'd realized the second she'd disappeared from behind him earlier. Keeping her in his peripheral, he saw her talking to an employee.

"On Thursday." The worker broke off her stare before moving to the monitor and refocusing her attention there.

"Who was that?" he asked as soon as they stepped outside.

"Someone from class," Brianna said. "How'd you do, by the way?"

"Struck out," he admitted.

"Well then I'm glad I saw my classmate." She practically beamed.

"What did you get?"

"A cell phone number," she said. "Which will allow us to do a reverse phone lookup."

He was familiar with a website that offered the service for a small fee. "We can get his address if we're lucky."

"That's right," she said.

"Do I want to know why you know about this?" he asked.

"Probably not," she hedged. "Nothing illegal, if that's what you're wondering."

"Nope. I didn't figure you for the type to break the law," he said.

"Before you nominate me for sainthood, you should

know that I fudged the truth back there. I feel terrible about it too." Her shoulders drooped with the admission.

Her honesty was one of her many admirable traits.

"Don't be too hard on yourself, Bri." He caught himself right there. The term of endearment had no place in their relationship. He used to call her that when they were a couple. "Look, Brianna, you're trying to save your life. This isn't a game. If you had to stretch the truth to get information, it's what you had to do. Doesn't make you a bad person."

"No?" There was a look of hurt in her eyes when she caught his gaze again. She dropped his hand and picked up the pace toward his truck.

He wasn't quite ready to leave yet but by the looks of her, she was done with campus for the day. A question loomed like a heavy cloud. Why did the air between them suddenly turn so cold? He was trying to give her an out, reassure her that she wasn't the worst possible person on the planet like she was trying to convince herself. How had his plan backfired?

"What did I do, Brianna? What did I say that was so wrong?" he asked.

Her hand was on the door handle of the passenger side by the time he caught up to her.

"Seriously. Tell me because I have no idea and the last thing I want to do is hurt you," he said.

She froze for a solid minute before inhaling slowly like she was breathing for the first time.

Gradually, she turned around and then leaned against the truck, eyes closed. She brought her hands up to her temples. "It's what she used to say. The part about lying not making you a bad person."

"She? Who?" And then it dawned on him. "Your mother?"

"Yes." A lone tear streaked her cheek as she dropped one hand down to her side and the other to her chest.

As he approached, he saw that she was fingering the charm on the necklace she wore.

"Nothing was ever anyone's fault with her. But she hurt everyone in her wake." More of those tears streamed down her cheeks.

He reached up and thumbed them away.

"I'm sorry," he said, low and under his breath. "I had no idea."

"It's not your fault," she hurriedly countered. She was too quick to let others off the hook.

"No. It is my fault. I should have known," he argued.

"How would you?" She blinked her eyes open—pure, beautiful eyes that were like looking into a window to her soul. Eyes that held more hurt than any one person should have to bear.

Before debating his next actions, he closed the distance between them, brought his hand up around the base of her neck and pulled her toward him as he brought his lips to hers. Before they touched, he said, "I'm sorry."

She put her hands up against his chest, fists he half expected to pound against him. They didn't. She didn't. Instead, she grabbed fistfuls of his shirt and tugged him closer.

When his mouth touched hers, a thousand fireworks went off inside his chest. He could only imagine how incredible sex with Brianna would be based on the heat in the few kisses they'd shared.

She moaned against his lips, the sweetest, sexiest sound he'd ever heard. Claiming her mouth as his, he dipped his tongue inside those full lips of hers. Honeysuckle never tasted so sweet.

His pulse went from zero to sixty in two seconds flat when she dug her hands into his shirt even more. Her breath was coming out in gasps as tension built inside him, seeking an outlet.

She was the only one who could give him the sweet release he craved.

"Garrett," she moaned against his lips. Hearing his name roll off her tongue was about the most alluring sound. More blood flew south as his own desire mounted.

A stray thought struck that he should probably tone this down in the campus parking lot, but he wasn't about to listen to it. Couldn't even if he tried. Not while those cherry lips of hers moved against his. She bit down on his bottom lip and scraped her teeth across it as she released, and he realized he couldn't let this continue unchecked. Not if he was going to keep his vow to walk away once this was over. And he had every intention of doing just that despite the ache already forming in his chest at the thought.

Much to his surprise, Brianna was the one who pulled back first.

Chapter Thirteen

"We can't do this." Brianna repeated the statement more for her own benefit than Garrett's as her breath came out in gasps. It was true no matter how they looked at it or who was the first to stop. She'd felt the tension in his lips when he had the same thought as she did.

She brought the back of her hand up to her lips, tried to steady her breathing. There was some small measure of satisfaction in the fact he was breathing as hard as she was. In fact, it caused her to crack a smile.

Garrett took one look at her and his face broke into a wide smile, as well. "I know and yet you have no idea how much willpower it's taking right now not to lean forward and claim that beautiful mouth of yours."

"Now I have it on record," she teased.

His dark brow arched.

"You think I'm beautiful," she quipped with a self-satisfied smirk.

"I have no plans to take it back." He referred to the way they used to tease each other years ago.

Brianna laughed, the full-belly kind. She couldn't remember the last time she'd done that, so she didn't fight it. She let laughter roll up and out until her stomach hurt and her cheeks burned from smiling so much.

Gorgeous Garrett O'Connor stood there, one arm resting on his truck, laughing right along with her.

The moment was cut short when a blue hatchback crept by two aisles over. The brakes squeaked and she couldn't shake the feeling that the car's driver was looking for something other than a parking spot. The whole scene was odd enough to remind her they were standing out in broad daylight.

Without a word, they hopped into action. Garrett opened the truck door for her and she immediately thanked him and climbed inside. He quickly closed the door and claimed the driver's seat. Within a minute, they were navigating toward the blue hatchback. Or, at least where it had been. Classes must have been changing because the parking lot was suddenly like an ant farm with cars coming and going, and people flooding the lot.

The hatchback was gone by the time they got to his aisle. Garrett rolled the windows down, no doubt listening for the sound of the brakes to no avail.

Conversation on the ride back to her place was dampened but lighter than it had been.

"I'll be honest with you, Garrett. I can't remember the last time I laughed as hard as we did back there," she finally said as he pulled into a visitor's spot at her apartment.

"If I'm perfectly honest, same here." He leaned his head back on his head rest. "We should laugh more, shouldn't we?"

It was more statement than question.

"Why don't we?" she asked.

"Maybe another question is when did life get so serious?"

She couldn't agree more there. Based on the way his

shoulders slumped and he closed his eyes, she figured he felt that statement in every part of his body.

"Bills started coming due, I guess." She'd had her electricity cut off twice when she was first starting out on her own. Sleeping on a coworker's couch wasn't exactly her idea of fun. Neither was fighting off his drunk roommate when he came home to find her there alone. "But you were always more..."

She stopped right there not wanting to ruin the mood by hurting his feelings.

"Go on," he urged anyway, straightening his neck before turning to look at her. "Say it."

"Nah—"

"You can't stop in the middle of a sentence. What would Mrs. Dooley think?" He'd lightened his voice but there was still a serious undertone.

"Our English teacher probably doesn't care what happened to us," she admitted. They weren't exactly popular with teachers. Well, she took that back. Most O'Connors were, just not Garrett. But he always seemed to go out of his way to separate himself from his brothers.

"Then, finish it for my sake," he countered.

"*You* are the reason I decided to hold my tongue," she said.

"Pretend I'm someone else and come out with it." He was practically begging now. "Never mind."

That sure was a tail whip.

"I thought you wanted to know," she said.

"You're too chicken to say it to my face." Now he really was dragging them back to middle school. She couldn't count the number of times one of them had pulled that line on the other one.

It made her smile.

"All right, but you have to promise not to get mad. Or think I don't appreciate everything you're doing for me." She shot a warning look.

He brought both in a truce.

"Intense. I was going to say that you've always been intense. There. Are you happy now?" she asked, trying to keep the mood light.

"Yes. I kind of am." He laughed out loud.

"It's true. You always had a chip on your shoulder. You know? Like you didn't think you belonged in the O'Connor family or something," she said.

"It's hard to live up to my brothers," he admitted. The hurt returned to his eyes and she hated that she was the one who caused it. "I think I decided early on the only way to stand out in a family like mine was to cause trouble."

"You were never all that bad, Garrett. Just intense, like I said."

"Yeah, that's like the third time you've used that word in the past minute," he mused.

"Sorry. I don't mean it in a bad way. When you set your sights on something, you used that focus for good," she pointed out.

"Most of the time, I've been using it to mess up my life royally," he said.

She caught his gaze and held it. "It's never too late to change, Garrett. Look at me. I'm claiming my future."

"A future that doesn't make you so excited that you're ready to jump out of bed every morning," he said. Again, his hands went up. "I'm not trying to be a jerk here. I'm just trying to better understand what makes you tick."

"My future might not be exciting, but neither is having your electricity cut off because you couldn't pay the bill or living in a cramped apartment for the rest of your life," she said plain as the nose on her face. With Garrett, she didn't feel the need to candy coat her life or what she was trying to do. He'd see right through her if she tried to lie anyway.

"Fair enough." He paused like he was about to say something. Then came, "Ready to go inside and look up that phone number?"

"Yes," she said quickly. A little too quickly?

"How much do you want to bet Derk drives a blue hatchback?" Garrett asked after opening the door for her.

"Wouldn't be against the law if he did." She figured Garrett was on point with that assumption.

"No, it wouldn't."

"Plus, he could be on campus for a whole lot of other reasons," she said. "And remember, the jerk playing bumper cars with me had a truck."

"True again," he said. "And yet..."

"I know. I agree with you. I'm just pointing out what a cop would tell us. Believe me, I have more experience than I ever wanted with local law enforcement." In fact, if she never saw another officer for the rest of her life she'd be thrilled. They were decent enough and she didn't have anything personal against them. Each one had taken down all the facts of her complaints. They seemed interested in hearing all the details. The net result was the same. There wasn't anything they could do about someone trying to run her off the road. Despite a crime being committed against her, she didn't have a license plate or description of the vehicle or perp. There wasn't much they could do.

If she could figure out who was behind the threat, she could file a restraining order. But she was short on proof.

So, each one thanked her and then sent her on her way. The only reason she kept on filing reports was so there would be a history if something bad happened to her and they actually caught the guy. Or, if something happened to her and they needed to look for someone. She figured one small detail might blow the case wide open.

Which reminded her…

"You're forgetting one small fact," she said to Garrett as she opened the door to her apartment.

"Oh, yeah? What's that?" He followed her inside and locked the door behind them. His eyebrows drew together in confusion.

"A large vehicle tried to run me off the road. A small hatchback wouldn't be any match against Code Blue," she said. "And I would have remembered a hatchback."

"Code Blue?" He quirked a brow.

"My Jeep," she said.

He cocked his head to one side. "Good point."

GARRETT SUPPRESSED A LAUGH. Code Blue? As far as vehicle names went, that was right up there with the best of 'em. He remembered smiling when he saw the name on her spare tire cover. The annoying-as-all-get-out voice in the back of his head picked that moment to point out that he hadn't laughed this much in one day in forever. Maybe ever.

Brianna had pinned him correctly when she'd called him intense. Hell, did she think he wanted to be this frustrated all the time? Frustrated with his brothers. Frustrated with himself. Frustrated with the world.

When he thought about it in those terms, it sure seemed like a waste of good energy. He still had a couple of axes to grind, but when Brianna's stalker, his sister's kidnapper and his father's killer were locked up where they belonged, he vowed to figure out a way to laugh more.

He needed more levity in his life because in the few moments he'd experienced it with Brianna, he'd been the happiest he could remember.

Figuring out how to be less intense was the hard part. He could start with knocking the chip off his shoulder when it came to his brother Colton.

Brianna pulled her laptop from her backpack and plugged in the power cord. As far as jalopies went, this computer was a doozie. Would she let him buy her something with a little more zip?

"When is your graduation?" he asked before he could stop himself. It was none of his business because he didn't plan on sticking around once they figured out who the jerk was trying to run her off the road. More of that familiar tension knotted in his shoulder blades.

"Um, thirty-six days," she said. She didn't glance up from the screen that was still loading.

Would she accept a new laptop as a graduation gift? He wanted her to start her new career with something nice. Hell, he could always mail one to her. Buy it off the internet and have it shipped. He made a mental note of her address.

On second thought, he didn't want to insult her. She'd been handling life on her terms and, contrary to her belief, handling it well. Better than well. She was amazing. In fact, she was just the type of person he could see himself settling down for the long haul with if he was the "settling down" type. He wasn't and had no intention of changing his ways. It was enough that he'd decided to work on being less intense. There was no need to go overhauling all of his life.

Besides, hadn't he read something about being careful not to make rash decisions while grieving? And he was grieving. Brianna's case was a distraction. One he needed about now. Because thinking about everything he'd missed out on and would miss out on with his dad for as long as Garrett lived docked a boulder on his chest that made breathing hurt.

Thinking of his dad usually triggered a flight impulse, a need to move on. From painful memories, from sorrow. It was a sentiment he knew well, the desire to be outside, on the go. Being confined in a small space usually made him stir crazy as all get out. But here he was, contented to be in this tiny apartment, not feeling as if he wanted to be anywhere else on earth. He registered the sensation as strange and then tucked it down deep. "Here we go," Brianna said. She turned the screen toward him.

"How far away is that address?" he asked, figuring they needed to get on the road.

"It's close to campus actually. Not too far from where we had lunch, which still makes me want to cry for how good it was," she said.

"We can make the trek back if we—"

"I have to get ready for work. I barely have enough time to pack dinner after driving back and forth to campus." She glanced at the clock on the wall.

"But it's only four-thirty," he said.

"I have twenty minutes to get cleaned up and cram my body into that uniform." She made air quotes with her fingers on the last word. "And then I have to get on the road."

"How far away is the bar?"

"Forty minutes," she said.

"That's a haul," he noted.

"Yep. Exactly. The last thing I wanted was to run into someone from class or, worse yet, one of my professors while tending bar." She involuntarily shuddered.

"Why is that? I mean, wouldn't they come out for the worse in that situation? They are, in fact, the patrons of a bar," he pointed out.

"True. But, I like to keep my worlds separate. At school, I'm a student just like everybody else." She stood. "Right now, I have another 'hat' to wear. Barkeep."

He nodded as she left the room, heading into her adjacent bedroom. He thought back to what had happened with her mother, the affair she'd had with one of the town's prominent men and how that tainted their family name to the point they'd moved to outrun the bad reputation. Brianna's strategy from earlier clicked in his mind and he understood why she would want to be normal after the shame that followed their family.

His chest squeezed remembering the day she'd found him and told him the news her family was moving away. Even though they'd broken up, he'd been crushed. Back then, he'd been head over heels for her. Still was?

But Colton had been too and Garrett hadn't wanted to stand in between the two of them if his brother had had a chance with Brianna.

Did he regret his choice? Considering hindsight was twenty-twenty, the short answer was yes.

Chapter Fourteen

Brianna walked out of the bedroom all done up in her bartending gear and Garrett's heart detonated. He coughed to ease his dry throat, but it did little to help.

"You're beautiful," he managed to say.

She froze, and then caught his gaze. Something stirred in her eyes—an emotion he couldn't quite pinpoint—and the knot in his gut tightened a few more notches. He meant it. She was beautiful. She could be dressed in a potato sack and she would still stun.

There was so much more to her beauty than physical attraction, although she had that in spades. Her intelligence, sharp mind and sense of humor made her darn near irresistible. He almost laughed out loud at that. He was having one helluva time resisting his attraction to her.

"Thank you." The words came out quiet and unsure.

Garrett was floored that she didn't see in herself what was so easy for others to notice. Considering he was having a difficult enough time keeping his thoughts from going down that road again, a road that would be nothing more than a dead end, he decided this wasn't the time for him to convince her.

"Ready?" he asked instead.

"I'll just grab my backpack." She walked past him and her unique citrus-and-fresh-flower scent filled his senses. There was no way he could stand there and allow that to happen so he pushed off the chair, fished out his keys and waited by the door.

"What's the plan?" she asked after shouldering her backpack.

"You'll take Code Blue and I'll follow you from a distance in my truck. That way, I can keep watch for anything unusual."

"I was about to suggest the same thing," she said. It was good they were on the same page. But then, there was a time when he would've sworn they could read each other's thoughts.

The minute she walked over to him, he opened the door and held it.

"Thank you," she said as she ambled by. "Give me a minute head start."

"I don't know where you work." He had to stand too close to her for longer than he cared to while she entered the address on his phone.

She shot him a look before saying, "Will I see you at the bar?"

"Not if I'm doing my job well." Garrett might not work in law enforcement like his brothers but he was one of the best trackers in the county. Hell, probably all of Texas if he listened to other people's opinions of him. But in all fairness, he needed to keep a distance from Brianna in order to stay focused. Because when she stood this close to him and he was breathing in her scent, he could easily get lost.

Garrett didn't do lost. He didn't do the kind of attraction that made him want to be a better person. And he didn't do the whole happily-ever-after lie.

Take his parents, for instance. Through no fault of their own they were dealt a hand that would cause most to shatter. His mother had been affected…no, was *still* being affected to this day by the child who was stolen from her. Would they go back and change their decisions if they'd known what was to come?

Being outdoors, Garrett could keep a clear head. He didn't want for anything. He didn't miss anyone. And he sure as hell didn't stay awake at night like his mother had on Caroline's birthday crying her eyes out.

Garrett stopped himself right there. The revelation came as a shock. He set it aside, figuring he could deal with it later. Brianna needed all his focus now and a minute had passed since she'd headed to her vehicle.

He started for his truck. His pulse kicked up a couple of notches with her being out of sight. He tried to convince himself it was because of the stalker but there was more to it than that. It fell into the category of "more stuff that needed to be kicked aside" for now.

Code Blue exited the parking lot as he cleared the apartment building. Brianna lived on the first floor. He made a mental note to talk to her about that for her next move. She needed to live at minimum on the second floor for safety's sake. Burglars and rapists rarely risked a climb. For one, they could fall. For another, and this was probably the most important reason, they never risked getting seen scaling a building.

Garrett climbed into his truck. His gaze lingered on the empty passenger seat a second longer than he wanted it to. He started the engine and made the drive toward the bar. The ride was easy and there didn't appear to be any stalkers following her to work. Of course, this guy's pattern was to follow her home, which gave Garrett the impression the perp didn't know where she lived.

The blue hatchback could have followed her home from school. Why the bar?

The easy answer was the stalker was one of her customers, not one of her classmates. So, basically, he'd most likely been focused on the wrong thing. Except that didn't exactly feel right in his gut for some odd reason.

Most stalkers knew their victims. Would a customer at the bar know her?

Of course, they could be looking at a psycho she rejected. He should have asked her if she'd had to have anyone thrown out for harassment at the bar. But then, wouldn't she have mentioned that first?

Garrett pulled into a parking spot in the far end of the lot and waited. He would have to walk right past Code Blue to get to his ride later tonight. For now, there weren't many vehicles parked and he didn't want to be obvious that he was following her inside.

He had to take it on faith that once she got inside the building she'd be okay. He positioned his rearview mirror so that he could watch her as she exited her vehicle and walked toward the building. He also had to force his gaze from her sweet backside.

While he waited, he figured he could do a little more digging into the alpaca rescue to see what else he could find out. He fished out his cell phone and pulled up a search engine. He entered the name of the nonprofit. At least, he assumed it was a nonprofit.

Pulling up the website, he got a quick confirmation on the rescue's situation. Apparently, the owners had applied for nonprofit status. He made a note of their names,

Randy and Susan Hanes. Made a quick joke about the underwear empire Randy must have come from.

Garrett cracked a smile at his own joke, bad as it was. Hey, stakeouts were boring. He'd had his fair share of them over the years while tracking poachers on family land, and others. The name was sticking in his craw. Hanes. Was it too obvious?

The thought it could be a fake sat heavy on the back of his mind. He could make a call or two and find out pretty quick but that would mean involving one or more of his brothers. Considering this case was at the forefront of everyone's mind, he'd be figured out in a heartbeat. Would he be putting his brothers in the line of fire? If this lead panned out, a killer could easily put his sights on the family again.

What about Garrett's mother? If anyone made a minor slip and let her in on it, could she handle it? She had to know all her children were investigating their father's murder. Granted, Colton and Cash were the obvious choices, but that was part of the reason Garrett saw it as his duty. His brothers had to follow protocol. They were almost too obvious. Garrett could handle the investigation his own way. No legal limits. No justice system handicapping him. He could get to the truth without the burden of filing paperwork or getting a judge's order.

He could also mete out his own sense of judgment. An eye for an eye?

Hold on right there. Garrett realized he was taking this too far. Maybe it was time to involve his brothers. Do everything by the book. Garrett wasn't worried about his life. It wasn't like he had anyone to come home to at night.

But death was too swift for the person who'd killed

Finn O'Connor. And if Garrett killed someone wouldn't he end up the one in jail? He had to set his white-hot emotions aside on this one and think clearly. He couldn't run off half-cocked and act on impulse no matter how much he wanted to.

Garrett fisted his hands. He fisted and opened his fingers several times to try to ease the tension. His usual outlet of a hard day's work on a ranch wasn't available at the moment. He needed to find another way to blow off steam. And fast. Hopping out of his truck and firing off a few pushups would draw attention he couldn't afford.

A distraction would be nice about now.

Or he could call Colton. His brother might not even answer, especially the way Garrett had been treating the family.

With a deep breath, he pulled up his brother's contact from his list. Before he could talk himself out of it, he touched the screen and the call was in progress.

Colton picked up on the first ring.

"Everything okay?" The alarm in Colton's voice was a stark reminder of how little Garrett called.

"Yes, sure. I'm good," he said as casually as he could. "I had a question and I thought you might be a good resource. It's work related."

There was a beat of silence on the line.

"Okay." Colton drew out the word. "You know I'll do anything in my power to help, but I have to warn you that I'm bound—"

"I won't ask you to violate your oath." Garrett probably sounded a little defensive. His stress levels were rising based on how much more he was white knuckling the steering wheel.

"Then, what can I do for you officially?" Colton asked.

"A little research. I'm checking into a nonprofit for a friend and..." Garrett stopped himself right there. He wanted to tell Colton the truth. "I'm following up on a lead and I came across what I think is a bogus situation. I'd like to vet it out and don't have the first clue how to go about it."

"Is this in my jurisdiction, by chance?" Colton asked.

"Afraid not."

"Then, I have fewer resources and might have to call in a favor. But ask away. I'll do everything in my power to help." The resolve in Colton's voice inspired confidence in Garrett to move forward.

"I'm checking into an alpaca rescue and I think the name on the organization is bogus. The rescue is registered in the names of Randy and Susan Hanes," he said.

"As in the underwear company?" Colton's voice was laced with suspicion.

"My thoughts exactly," Garrett confirmed.

Colton chuckled. "Hanes isn't an uncommon name, though. Could be legit, but I'll check it out. I've come across some strange things in my years as sheriff."

"I bet you have." Garrett could only imagine what his brother had seen and probably done. He met his wife while on an investigation. He literally crashed into her car while in his service vehicle while she was on the run from a tainted cop.

"What's the name of the rescue and where is it located?" Colton asked.

Garrett provided the information along with a warning. "I have to tell you this might not be what it seems, and it could be dangerous to dig further into the details."

"That was a given when you reached out to me." The fact Colton didn't seem shocked or surprised made Garrett realize how often his brother faced dangers every day in his line of work.

The fact he could lose his brother without making amends struck like a lightning bolt on a clear blue sky. At least part of his anger was tied to the same thing happening with his father.

And Garrett had loved the man. He had no idea how to live up to the O'Connor name but that didn't mean he didn't respect it. And now his father had gone to his grave without knowing how much Garrett respected him. The real kicker was that Garrett knew his father loved him. Finn O'Connor left nothing unsaid. He would have found a reason to be proud of Garrett even in the times he didn't give his father one.

So, the thought of that happening with Colton was a gut punch.

"I should be able to do a little digging on this one and come up with some answers for you," Colton said, breaking the silence.

"Much appreciated." Garrett realized how lame that sounded when he wanted to say so much more to his brother. The right words didn't come so he let a few more beats of silence sit between them.

"Is that everything?" Colton finally asked and Garrett could hear the questions in his brother's voice. To his credit, he didn't ask them. He seemed content to let Garrett do the driving on this conversation.

"Yeah, uh, actually, no. I did have something else I wanted to say." More of that cursed silence filled the line. "Since words aren't exactly my favorite thing—"

"They don't have to be. Just spit it out." The fact that Colton seemed to be gearing up to take a punch filled Garrett with regret.

"All I wanted to say was thank you." It was lame but true and covered so much more than just this conversation.

"You're welcome, little brother." Colton hadn't strung that last pair of words in a sentence in far too long.

"I mean it, Colton. You're a great guy and I haven't always been…"

"Don't worry about it, Garrett. Seriously, it's all water under the bridge." Colton was being too nice, letting Garrett off the hook too easily.

Instead of making him feel better, it fired him up. "Hey. I'm not done here."

A beat of silence sat in between them again.

"I'm listening." Colton's voice turned dead serious.

"You've been a great big brother and I've given you nothing but hell. And while I can't promise I won't do the same thing in the future, I can say that I'm sorry about all the times I was a jerk." Garrett hadn't expected those words to roll off his tongue or to feel so freeing. It was suddenly like a chunk of the boulder that had been docked on his chest was lifting, releasing some of the pressure along with it.

"I won't argue the last part. There have been times when you've been a real pain in the backside," Colton said. "However, I will add that I wasn't always Mr. Wonderful on my end either. I goaded you into arguments when I knew better. So, if we're fessing up to the past, I have to take my fair share of the blame."

Garrett chewed on his brother's words for a minute. True enough, there were times when Colton was in the wrong. Why was it so easy to blame himself for every fight?

"Are we good?" Garrett asked.

"Always were on my end," Colton said like he meant it.

"Good. Because I don't want to go to my grave with words left unsaid."

"Whoa there. You need to back that statement up and explain. Does this have something to do with the research project I've taken on?" Colton asked.

"I've just been in my head a whole lot since Dad died. There was a whole lot I could have..." Garrett had to stop himself right there as he got choked up.

"I know what you mean." Colton's voice was low and filled with regret. Regret was something Garrett knew a little too much about. He'd recognize it from a mile away.

"Don't beat yourself up," Garrett said quickly. The irony wasn't lost on him. "I'm pretty good at doing that myself."

"Does it help?" Colton's question caught Garrett off guard.

"Not really. It usually leads to a spiral," Garrett admitted. Full disclosure was starting to release more of that tension balled up inside him.

"Sounds like hell." Colton's honest reaction caused Garrett to chuckle.

"It is." There was no use sugarcoating it.

"Then, why do we do it?" Colton asked.

"Maybe we have more in common than I realized," Garrett said. "I never would have guessed there was a real human underneath that Superman cape of yours."

The statement was only half true. It was meant to be a joke.

"That what you think?" Colton's defensive tone said it fell flat. "I'm some kind of superhero? Because I can promise you the opposite is t—"

"I wasn't saying it to offend you, Colton. But in my book, you always have been."

Colton let a couple of seconds go by before responding.

"When you put it like that, it sounds like a compliment," he said. "One I'd be proud to take."

Garrett ended the call with the promise to do a better job of keeping in touch. Out of the corner of his eye, he spotted a blue hatchback creeping down the side street.

Chapter Fifteen

The bar was prepped and Brianna had spent the past fifteen minutes in the bathroom freshening up before her shift.

Wanda came out of the second stall as Brianna pressed her lips together to even out her lipstick. The popular waitress sidled up to the sink next to Brianna's. The two weren't exactly buds but they worked well together. Meaning, Brianna didn't get in Wanda's way and vice versa. They shared a mutual respect for each other's jobs.

"What are you doing in here?" Wanda's face puckered up with the question.

"What? I'm not allowed to use the bathroom all of a sudden?" Brianna shot the woman her best offended look, even though she wasn't irritated at all. It was fun to tease Wanda.

"No. It's not that. It's just I never seen you in here before a shift, primping." Wanda pulled a tube of lip liner from inside her bra. Nice. She'd have to remember that move.

"Ah, this." Brianna zipped up her mini makeup bag. She'd never kept one in her backpack before tonight, but there was no way she was admitting that to Wanda. Brianna would never hear the end of it. "Figured it would help with tips."

"Ah." Wanda nodded approval. "Here I was thinking you had a man stopping by tonight."

"Me?" Brianna did her level best to pull off that same disgusted look but feared her flushed cheeks gave her away. She wanted to say, *not just any man*, but decided against it. She wasn't ready to share Garrett with anyone. Plus, she had no real designs on him anyway no matter how much her heart protested the thought, traitor that it was. Garrett was a friend who was helping her out. Period.

A quick glance at the mirror revealed that Wanda was studying her. Her cocked eyebrow said she wasn't buying the line. Another fib. Sort of. They were racking up. The little dishonesties would take seed if she wasn't careful. The single piece of advice she'd been given by one of her customers, which had changed the way she thought, was to stand guard at her mind and be as careful of what she let inside as she let out. The tiniest weed could overtake the most beautiful garden.

She couldn't remember the man's name, or it was possible he never told her, but she could pick him out of a lineup to this day if she had to. Because she'd been wallowing in self-pity until that day. She didn't have it all figured out now, but she'd found a direction in life and had gone all in. Before that, she'd been wandering, thinking she wasn't smart enough to go back to school or that she was too much older than her classmates. She had a powerful advantage that she'd noticed was lacking in many of the eighteen-year-olds she'd sat beside, and that was motivation.

"Probably not," Wanda finally said before adding a

layer of ruby-red lipstick. She tucked the tube back inside her bra before shaking the "girls" a few times to let it settle.

"You're seriously going to have to show me how you do that one of these days," Brianna said, changing the subject.

"On last count, I have thirty-six more days," Wanda said wistfully.

Brianna was caught off guard that Wanda would care so much about her last day let alone keep a countdown.

"Yep. I'm almost out of here," Brianna said cheerfully. Too cheerfully. In fact, she was pretty certain it came off as insincere. She didn't want Wanda to feel bad.

"You're a solid bartender," Wanda said by way of compliment.

"Thanks. I like working with you too," Brianna said. She hadn't expected to get emotional about leaving this place. It was always a steppingstone to a better life. Then, she realized this *was* Wanda's life.

"Them classes you take. Are they expensive?"

"A little. Not as much as a four-year college," Brianna said. "I bet you could swing it if you picked up an extra shift here and there."

"You think?" Wanda gave herself a long, hard look in the mirror.

"I do. There's no question in my mind."

Wanda smiled before straightening her blouse to reveal a better look at her cleavage. "Maybe I'll check into it."

"You should." Then, Brianna added, "Or you could work in this castle for the rest of your life."

Wanda laughed. "You've just described hell."

"I guess I did." Brianna laughed too.

"See you out there on the floor," Wanda said walking out the door, but not before an eye roll.

"I'll be right out." Brianna wanted another second to pull herself together. Garrett's lead had been eating away at her all afternoon and evening. She didn't want to hold him up in any way from his father's investigation. Maybe she could convince him to take her along with him. She could get someone to cover her shift at the bar, figure out a way to make up the extra money. Or she could super hustle for tips tonight. She could admit to slowing down a little bit lately. Lack of sleep wasn't always great for the hustle.

She'd find a way to pitch the idea to him after work tonight.

After zipping up her makeup bag, she did a final mirror check before exiting the bathroom. Customers would be allowed inside in a few minutes. She had time to put away her makeup and perform one last check on supplies. Dan the man was her barback tonight. He was usually on point. Starting the night right usually determined how the next nine hours would go.

A great band was playing tonight. Texas Two-Step would be on at nine o'clock and again at midnight. They were good about drawing a crowd. An uneasy feeling toyed with her stomach. The thought of a crowd didn't normally rattle her. Now that she'd picked up a stalker, it made her nervous. The creep could watch her from any corner and she'd be too busy to notice.

She could only hope the guy would move on to someone else. The thought of another woman going through this wasn't exactly reassuring, though. She thought about what Garrett had said about Professor Jenkins. Garrett was right. She couldn't allow the man to get away with trying to use his position to garner favors—and she knew exactly what he meant. A shudder rocked her body thinking about that man touching her; even incidental contact made her skin crawl.

No, she couldn't let him get away with it.

"Smiles on, ladies and gentlemen," Wade Horton said. "One minute till showtime."

Her manager really should work on Broadway. He had a flair for the dramatic and his skills seemed misdirected in a honky-tonk bar, even one as big and reputable as this one. Folks came from all over to boot scoot across the dance floor to a homegrown band. The place was grand with a center bar in a big circle. There were two corner bars on opposite sides of the place, a sawdust dance floor along with a small stage for the band. She'd worked her way up to having her own bar. The center bar was where everyone trained, and shared tips from the jars. Here in the corner, she had her own slice of heaven and she didn't have to share it with anyone.

Brianna wouldn't have it any other way.

Shot ladies walked around, but Brianna had her regulars. Then, there were tourists but they only came this way if the line was too long at the main bar. Everyone who worked here knew the real money was in the corner bars. That, and waitressing. A good waitress like Wanda could bring in a boatload of money on a live band night.

Wade circled the main bar. She waved her arms high in the air to get his attention, smiled when she was successful.

He jogged over.

"Honey, we're about to start the show. What can I help you with?" Wade was in his early forties but he had the energy of a twenty-year-old. Too bad he looked older than his years.

"I need to switch shifts tomorrow night. Personal reasons." She threw in the last couple of words to stem any questions. She wasn't about to tell her boss that she had to check up on an alpaca farm believed to actually be a kidnapping ring.

"Fine. But you need to find someone to trade with." He sounded angry but it was just his way. If he was, he'd get over it fast. She'd never seen him hold a grudge longer than a few minutes.

"Done." She pulled out her cell and fired off a text to Brent. He was always looking for extra shifts and working the corner bar was a bump up from where he normally worked in the center. The response came before Wade had a chance to walk away. "Brent will cover for me."

She held up her cell as proof.

Wade nodded before waving a hand in the air and then moving on.

"Have a good show tonight, Wade," she hollered at his back.

He gave another wave.

Brianna would miss this quirky place, she thought. And then she laughed. No, she wouldn't. She wouldn't miss the cramps in her calves that came with running nonstop for eight-and nine-hour shifts. She wouldn't miss dripping with sweat by the end of the night. And she wouldn't miss having her backside patted as she walked through a crowded room to get more ice or take a break from the bar.

The doors opened and folks started filing in. There were lone cowboys, wannabe cowboys and a fair amount of couples. The women usually came in later in the evening, closer to the band's first set.

Brianna's first customer approached and he was quickly followed by two of her regulars. They each took stools, spreading out enough to leave an empty stool in between them. It was odd to look at each one of them as a potential stalker.

"What can I get you?" she asked customer number one as she pulled two longnecks from the ice bucket, twisted off the caps, and then set each down in front of her regular guys with a smile and a wink.

A thought struck. Was she too friendly? Had she led someone on?

She stopped herself right there. Doing her job meant she was friendly with customers. She never dated anyone from work or led anyone on. There was no way she was going to find a way to blame herself for someone else's actions. Period.

"What do you have on tap?" the newbie asked.

She rattled off the list and then waited for his response as he mulled over his choices. She quickly scanned the room, searching for Garrett. Disappointment caused her shoulders to deflate a little bit when she didn't see him.

The man was good at being a ghost. But then, he'd had reason to be. He used to tell her about trips he went on with his dad and brothers when poachers were on the family's land. It sounded dangerous to her. But he was casual about it. He'd describe it like it was nothing.

"I'll take the first one you said." The newbie settled on an ale.

"All right." Brianna got to work and pretty soon was in a rhythm. The night went by in a blur and she didn't see Garrett one single time. But she did look at everyone differently this evening. So much so, that one of her regulars asked her if everything was okay.

She'd explained that finals were coming up and that she was stressed about all the work she needed to do by the end of the semester. Her true regulars could tell when she was preoccupied.

They were good about it, though. Four of them had asked if they could buy her a drink after work. They'd also said they knew she didn't date from work. A friendly drink was all they were offering.

"You need me to walk you to Code Blue after closing tonight?" Hammer the bouncer asked. She'd seen him twice tonight.

"Nah, I'll be okay. I'm parked close," she said, then added, "Just don't tell Wade on me."

"Wouldn't dare." Hammer crossed his heart.

She hollered a "thank you" mostly to his back as he half jogged, half speed walked in the opposite direction. And then she skimmed the bar again, searching for any sign of Garrett.

A knot formed in her stomach thinking something might have happened to him. Garrett was impulsive. Had he followed a lead and ended up in some kind of trouble? The old Garrett wouldn't hesitate to take off if instinct told him to do so. She'd seen changes in him recently, especially when he talked about his family. Good changes. She could only hope he wouldn't revert back to his old ways for both of their sakes.

A cowboy walked out of the men's room. His hat was low and she didn't get a good look at his face but there was something familiar about him. Was he one of her regulars?

It didn't matter much. He was making a beeline for the door.

Out of the corner of her eye, she saw him try the handle and then knock on the glass. Hammer had to let the guy out. The only door in and out used by the public locked every night at two religiously. No one got in or out but through Hammer.

Hammer. She needed to pick his brain to see if anyone matching Derk's description, or Blaine's for that matter, had come into the bar recently. Why hadn't she thought of asking before?

COWBOYS AND COUPLES were leaving the bar in droves. Garrett wanted to slip inside to check on Brianna. Something told him to stay put. He could do more good here in the parking lot than inside, he reasoned. He surveyed the area, looking for single-occupant trucks or anything that seemed suspicious.

The lot was a sea of F-150s and Dodge Rams. So, yeah, noticing a lone driver in a truck was only a little bit easier than finding a needle in a haystack. He ruled out couples and figured the driver would linger or find a reason to hang around late.

Garrett's interest stirred when a cowboy exited the bar late. He had to be let out by the bouncer, a hefty guy who would give Garrett a run for his money in a fight. Not that Garrett doubted he was the one who would come out on top. But he would know this guy had been there. Very few people caused that reaction in Garrett, so he paid attention to it.

The cowboy kept his head down as he made a beeline to his… Volkswagen?

Garrett mentally crossed this cowboy off the list. Besides, what were the chances he'd go for a repeat this quickly? Slim to none. Garrett was getting antsy because he wanted Brianna out of danger and, if he was being honest, he wanted to follow up on the lead about the alpaca farm.

At least Colton was working behind the scenes to find out if Randy and Susan Hanes were legitimate people and the nonprofit was aboveboard. Those two things would inform him about what he faced. It was a start and he could build from there.

Plus, they had Derk's address now and Garrett wanted to make a stop. The blue hatchback from earlier was a dead ringer for the one in the school parking lot and Garrett wanted to ask the guy a few questions. Being in the school parking lot wasn't exactly against the law. Neither was driving past a bar. Unless this guy had another vehicle at his disposal and used it to torture Brianna.

Speaking of whom, Garrett had been on pins and needles all night. He'd been miserable. And Brianna had everything to do with it. The question was…what did he plan to do about it?

Nothing, he thought, ignoring the little voice in the back of his mind determined to call him a coward.

Chapter Sixteen

Brianna took two steps out of the bar and scanned the parking lot. Garrett couldn't decide if her expression was concern or fear from this distance. He didn't like either. She deserved to be happy. No, more than that, she deserved to have everything she wanted and more. He shouldn't be bothered by the fact she was settling for a nine-to-five life. He shouldn't care one iota.

So, why was he going to lose sleep over it tonight?

He climbed into the driver's seat of his truck, keeping one eye on Brianna when a knock on his passenger window startled him. He cut his gaze over faster than a barrel-racing horse.

None other than the bouncer stood there.

"Could I have a word with you, sir?" A very angry, very determined face stared at Garrett.

"Right now?" Garrett asked before thinking.

"Yes. Now." There was a finiteness to the bouncer's tone that said he'd stand in front of or in back of the truck if Garrett engaged the gearshift.

He had no choice but to step out of his vehicle and meet the bouncer at the back in the dark lot where Garrett could try to keep an eye on Brianna. He could only hope that she would stay put until he settled this matter.

"My name's Garrett O'Connor and I'm a friend of Brianna's." Garrett stuck his hand out.

The bouncer just stared at it, crossing his arms over a massive chest instead. "What business do you have with her?"

The guy oozed protective instinct. His heart seemed in the right place but, man, his actions were misguided.

"Brianna and I go way back," Garrett started but his words were met with a hand.

"I bet you do." His tone said the opposite was true. "What are you doing here?"

"Meeting her after her shift." Garrett was honest enough. He also puffed out his chest a little bit to let the bouncer know he wasn't about to back down. If they needed to fight to figure out who was in charge here, so be it.

No, Garrett thought. That was his old way of thinking. How many times had he gotten into it with one of his brothers, or his boss or a coworker? Dozens. He couldn't think of one time where approaching a situation with anger actually made it better. Sure, there was the momentary rush of winning an argument or a fistfight, of being in the right and proving it. But it never worked out long term. All it ever did was alienate him from the people he cared about and/or the people he worked with.

He took in a deep breath, figuring it might not help but it surely couldn't hurt. Bouncer, on the other hand, fisted his hands at his sides.

Garrett decided to at least try to defuse the situation.

"I think we're getting off on the wrong foot here." Garrett couldn't exactly fault the man for just doing his job and looking out for Brianna. "Brianna and I grew up together and ran into each other last night at the gas station. She'd just left the police station and seemed out of sorts. We hadn't seen each other in years, so it was pretty random. But we were close once and she was shaken up."

Bouncer's eyebrow shot up. His hands relaxed at his sides. "She didn't say anything about being followed home last night."

"No? We can call her over and ask her, if you want. Or, better yet, I can give her a call." He made a move to fish his cell phone out of his front pocket, but Bouncer reacted quickly, moving his hand behind his back where Garrett was certain the man had a gun.

"Whoa there. I'm just reaching for my cell phone so we can give Brianna a call." Garrett held his hands in the peace position, palms up.

Bouncer nodded and said, "Move slow."

"No problem, man." Garrett was careful not to make any sudden movements despite his frustration that Bouncer was drawing attention to them. If someone was watching, he'd be busted. Using two fingers, Garrett eased his phone from his pocket. "See. Just my cell."

Bouncer nodded.

"I didn't catch your name, man," Garrett said as he pulled up her contact.

"My name's Jeff but everyone calls me Hammer on account of my last name being Hamm."

"What do you like to be called?" Garrett asked. Having a nickname and choosing a nickname were often two different things.

"Jeff."

"Okay, cool. Jeff, I can call Brianna right now and settle this or you can take my word and call her yourself. She's pulling out of the parking lot and it's my job to see that she gets home safely. It's your call." Garrett had never tried reasoning with anyone before. He could only hope it worked.

Jeff studied Garrett for a long moment. He glanced over at the empty spot that used to be occupied by Code Blue.

"Go on. And, man, keep our girl safe."

Garrett nodded but he didn't like the thought of sharing Brianna with anyone, not even a decent guy like Jeff. Because if given the chance, Jeff would take a promotion from protector/friend to boyfriend in a heartbeat if the offer was on the table.

Speaking of heartbeats, Garrett's pounded the inside of his rib cage. He rounded the truck in record time and reclaimed the driver's seat. He turned the key in the ignition and got nothing. For a split second he thought Jeff had come over to distract Garrett.

But the guy seemed genuine and that couldn't be faked. Garrett had dealt with more than his fair share of criminals in the poaching world and had worked beside a few on various ranches. He generally knew a bad actor when he saw one. It was always in the eyes.

Garrett bit out a string of curse words as he tried one more time to start the truck. Got nothing but click, click, click. Strange because he'd replaced the battery last month. He darted out of his vehicle after pressing the button that unlocked the hood lever.

"What's going on?" Jeff asked, rounding the front of the vehicle.

"I'm guessing someone unplugged my battery cables while we were talking." Wouldn't have been the easiest ploy, but a smart man could have timed the opening and closing of the hood with the crunch on gravel as cars left the lot, and the lighting out here kept everything in the shadows. It wasn't a tough fix but also gave the jerk an advantage. Garrett palmed the cell he'd tucked in his pocket a few minutes ago. He pulled up Brianna's name from his contacts and touched the screen.

The next two rings were the longest of his life. He fixed his cables while he waited, and slammed the hood shut. She finally picked up before the call rolled into voice mail.

"Hey, you sure are doing a good job of hiding because I haven't seen you all night," she immediately said.

"You are about to have company," he said. "Someone tampered with my vehicle."

Garrett gave a nod toward Jeff, who clenched his jaw so tight it looked like he might crack his back teeth. He'd been used and now someone he cared a lot about was in danger.

"Oh, no. Are you okay?" The fact she was trying to mask the fear in her voice was a gut punch.

"I'm on my way. Did you stick to the route?" he asked.

"Yes." She paused. "I see headlights coming up fast on my bumper."

By the time Garrett heard the *clunk*, he was spewing gravel underneath his tires trying to get out of the parking lot like his truck had wings. Jeff was already jogging toward the bar, or maybe it was his vehicle. He and Garrett hadn't exactly planned their next steps once they realized what had happened.

Someone knew enough about trucks to open Garrett's without drawing attention. He had to be somewhat handy with vehicles.

"I'm going to hang up and call 911 for you," Garrett said calmly. Based on the sound of her voice, she was in shock.

"Okay." She gasped a moment before the second *clunk*.

There was no way she could have gotten very far. They'd mapped out her route beforehand, so he figured she wasn't ahead of him by much.

Then, he heard, as if she were speaking in the distance, "I can't find my phone, Garrett. It got knocked out of my hand when he hit me the second time."

The knot in Garrett's stomach twisted tighter and he struggled to breathe for a second or two. He had to call the cops but he hated getting off the phone with her. Cutting off his lifeline to Brianna was going to be hell.

Then, he realized he could call her back. She could answer through her vehi—never mind. Code Blue was too old-school for Bluetooth. Dammit.

"Call out the street names on the next intersection," he shouted.

No response.

"Garrett. Where are you?" she said before he heard tires squealing.

"I'm hanging up now. If you find your cell, call me back." He had no choice but to end the call with her no matter how much it tightened the knot. He told himself he would call her back and the sound of her phone ringing might help her locate the cell.

He ended the call trying not to focus on the fact he was cutting off his lifeline to her. Then he dialed 911. The conversation with the dispatcher was short and sweet. He made a guess as to where Brianna might be and then got off the phone as quickly as he could after being told the nearest officer was a little more than fifteen minutes away. Jeff had held Garrett up five minutes and then the battery took another three or four. At this rate, Garrett would reach her long before the officer did. And that was only if she stayed on course, which was a fifty-fifty shot at this point. She might have had to veer off course to shake the guy who'd already hit her a couple of times.

Garrett instructed his phone to call Brianna. The phone rang once and his pulse kicked up a few notches. He would give just about anything, including his freedom, to hear her voice on the other end of that line. The second ring caused him to suck in a breath and hold it. The third sent his mind into a downward spiral because one more and his call would go straight to voice mail.

The sound of her voice on the line gave him a split second of hope until he realized he'd just transferred into voice mail.

Garrett issued a sharp sigh. This wasn't a good sign. He white knuckled the steering wheel as he blew through a stop sign. Brianna never took the highway even though it would be faster. She never trusted Code Blue to make it.

The feeling he'd let her down in the worst possible way engulfed him. He couldn't afford to let it take hold. Renewing their friendship, or whatever label worked, was the best thing that had happened to him in far too long.

Garrett gripped the steering wheel a little tighter and made the call again. This time, it went to voice mail on the first ring.

BRIANNA BIT BACK a curse as she wheeled left, practically rolling up on two tires as she made a hard left. She needed to get Code Blue back onto the agreed-upon path home. Garrett would have called the law by now and he would tell them where she was supposed to be.

The truck roaring up to her bumper again was relentless and all this swishing around might empty what little gas was left in her tank. There was a hole the size of a baseball she'd been meaning to have fixed. Car repairs fell behind classes, books, rent and food.

Anger roared through her and she had half a mind to stop her vehicle right there in the middle of the road just to see what this jerk planned to do next. In fact, that's what she did. She knew she couldn't keep going with him bumping her every few minutes. It was inevitable he'd stop her somehow. She'd rather be in control of that action.

She jammed her foot on the brake and prepared for impact. The screech of rubber tires against pavement caused her to tense up. She'd been told by one of her customers that if she was ever in an accident she should relax. How on earth did anyone relax when they were about to be slammed?

The impact never came. She risked a glance in the rearview mirror as the truck slowed down just as quickly.

"Come on, you sonofabitch. Make your move," she bit out. She probably shouldn't play this game but, man, she was so tired of running from this guy. Law enforcement was no help.

Brianna took that back as she fingered the charm hanging from her necklace. She could hear sirens wailing in the night air. They couldn't be too far away, which meant she hadn't gotten too far off track while trying to shake this creep. She took the opportunity to punch the gas pedal as she recited a quick protection prayer she remembered from the few times she'd been taken to church in grade school.

The charm had finally worked. Or maybe Garrett was good luck to have around. Either way, she planned to take advantage of the opportunity to leave this jerk in the dust.

“Eat my gravel,” she said as she mashed the pedal as hard as she could.

Code Blue did its best impression of a race car, which wasn’t much. But she made it around the corner and toward the wailing siren without the truck catching up to her. The truck behind her made the first turn in the opposite direction.

“I thought so,” she said under her breath, not ready to risk him changing his mind. She moved toward the glorious sound of help, wishing she’d gotten a look at the guy. There weren’t a whole lot of streetlights in the small towns surrounding the bar and this was no exception. At least she had a direction and a diversion.

The adrenaline rush started to fade and her hands shook on the wheel. It didn’t take long to find the officer. She flashed her lights and then cut them off. She stood up, waving her arms in the air.

A truck roared up from behind and her heart dropped into her toes as panic gripped her. And then she realized who was behind the wheel. Garrett. She couldn’t get out of Code Blue fast enough as an SUV, lights twirling, barreled toward her.

The look on Garrett’s face would stick in her mind for a long time. Worry lines etched his forehead and bracketed his mouth. The sheer panic in his eyes as he raced toward her nearly cracked her chest in two. A second or two later, she was burying her face in his chest, thinking this was the best spot in the world for her right now.

Chapter Seventeen

Garrett held Brianna as she gave her statement to the officer, giving a description of the truck and pointing to where it took off as he relayed the information. Her body trembled even though it wasn't cold outside and he'd wrapped a blanket around her shoulders. It was most likely from adrenaline, so she wasn't in any real trouble physically. He didn't plan to let her out of his sight moving forward, though.

How stupid had he been? He never should have allowed her to drive home on her own, never should have let her take that risk. He'd been naive to think he could handle this on his own without involving law enforcement or grabbing one of his brothers.

There were situations that required him not running off half-cocked and playing lone wolf. His mistake could have cost Brianna her life. He never would have forgiven himself if anything had happened to her.

When she was finished giving her statement, he gave his. It was short and to the point. He asked for a recommendation for a reputable towing company in the area before the officer retreated to his vehicle. Garrett moved Brianna inside his truck before grabbing her things from Code Blue. He felt around on the floorboard for her cell phone and found it. Then, he used his own to pull up the towing company name before making a quick call to have Code Blue picked up. No way was he risking getting caught behind another vehicle or a red light that would cause them to end up separated. Not again.

He climbed into the driver's seat and then got back on the road to her place, stewing on his mistakes.

"Thank you for thinking so quickly and calling the law." Brianna broke the silence.

"I almost got you killed," he quickly countered. "You shouldn't be thanking me."

She was silent for a beat. Then came, "I know you, Garrett. You can be one intense person. But there's no way you would intentionally put me in harm's way. I doubt you'd let a fly land on me, let alone allow some raving lunatic to cause me any pain."

"And yet look what happened," he ground out. "I failed. You were alone and scared."

"None of which was your fault," she said calmly. There was no reason to rise to his frustration level. He was really only upset with himself and she hated that he blamed himself.

"Not true," he said in a low growl.

"Garrett, I want you to listen here. Okay?" She touched him on the shoulder. "Really listen."

He grunted a yes.

"I probably would be hurt or worse right now if it wasn't for you. Whoever that creep is, one thing is clear. He set his sights on me for one reason or another. We may never know why. It could be my wheat-colored hair—" she flipped a tuft in the air "—so I won't let you take responsibility for some jerk-off's actions. You hear me?"

As much as he appreciated her honesty, he couldn't get past his own failure.

"You are one of the best people I've ever met and I won't let you beat yourself up over this," she contended. Granted, she made a good argument. A logical one. He was burning on pure emotion right now.

He wasn't quite ready to let himself off the hook no matter how much sense she made.

"How many people do you know who would set their own life aside based on running into an old friend at a gas station when she looked like she needed a hand up?" There was a lot more ire in her voice now.

"Probably a few," he countered, but he knew how weak his own argument was.

"Nope. Not even a few. Not even two. In fact, I'd bet the farm that there weren't a whole mess of people *besides* you who would do that for someone who was basically a stranger." Her temper was climbing and he needed to calm her down.

The best way to do that was to make a joke. So, that's exactly what he did, praying it wouldn't fall flat.

"You underestimate how freakin' hot you are," he quipped, hoping she would take the bait.

Brianna burst out laughing. And then so did he.

She reached over and gave him a playful jab in the arm. "I'm going to remember you said that, Garrett O'Connor. You can't take that one back."

Good. Because he had no intention of trying.

When the laughter died down, she said, "I took off work tomorrow so we could visit the alpaca farm together."

"Absolutely not." He was shaking his head no before she even finished her sentence.

"Hear me out before you decide," she hedged.

He took in a sharp breath. Her voice had the tone it always had when she'd made up her mind and was about to win an argument. It was good to know more than a few things hadn't changed about her.

"I'll listen, but that's as far as I'm promising," he said.

"Well good. That's all I asked." She continued before he made a smart-aleck remark they both knew was coming. "If you go there alone, it'll look suspect. Think about it. How many grown men do you see at an alpaca farm on a Friday morning?"

"Probably not many."

"And you don't want to draw attention to yourself. Am I right?" She practically beamed because she knew she had him.

"No, I don't."

"Then, we'll go as a couple. Women fall for that sappy stuff all the time. We can pretend we're on a date and they'll never be the wiser." She sat a little bit straighter, clearly pleased with her argument.

And since he couldn't shoot any holes in it, he agreed.

"One condition," he said.

"Not if it's to tell me I have to stay in the car," she argued.

"Did I say that?" he asked.

"No." She practically sulked and it was about the damned sexiest pout he'd ever put his eyes on.

"But we'll both have to stay in the car," he needled her.

"What?" It seemed to dawn on her when she brought her hands down to slap the seat. "Are you kidding me right now?"

"Would I do that to you?" He wanted to keep the mood light and reduce her stress levels. She'd been in full panic mode before despite keeping her cool.

"It's a drive-through animal encounter, isn't it?" She made air quotes with her fingers when she said the word *encounter*.

"Yes, ma'am."

"So, we really are both staying in the car," she said.

"That about sums it up." He nodded, enjoying the fact he got her to a place where she could kid around again. Brianna deserved a life that made her laugh freely every day. Hands down, her laugh was music to his ears.

Before he got all poetic, he decided to add, "There's a gift shop, though. I'd be happy to buy you a stuffed alpaca."

"And we can snoop around." She wiggled her eyebrows.

"Only if I get the all clear from Colton."

"You told him?" There was straight-up shock in her voice.

"Figured it was time to let him in a little. You know?" He pulled into a visitor's spot near her building.

"Wow. What can I say, Garrett?" She paused for a second. "Would it sound trite if I said I was proud of you?"

"Not at all. In fact, it means a whole lot to hear you say those words." He couldn't help himself. He broke into a wide smile. "He's checking into the background of the so-called owners to see if they are legit. He doesn't know the whole story yet but I plan to fill him in while we're on the way there at first light. Are you certain you can miss class?"

"This once won't tank my grade." She reached over and squeezed his forearm. The move shouldn't send a lightning bolt straight to his heart and it sure as hell shouldn't be so sexy.

Fighting his instincts to pull her close and claim those full lips of hers again, he issued a sharp sigh before exiting the driver's side of the vehicle and jogging over to the passenger door. He opened it and helped her climb out.

"My legs are weak," she said.

"It's all the adrenaline wearing off. It does a real number on your body. Lean on me, Brianna. I won't let you fall."

She didn't look up at him right away, but when she did the tears welling in her eyes were a knife to his heart. From what he gathered so far, there weren't a whole lot of people she could depend on in her life. He'd become one. He wanted to be one.

Inside her apartment, she walked straight to the bedroom and he fought himself once again to keep from following her. The sounds of the spigot turning on didn't help. All that did was put naked images of her in his thoughts.

With some effort he normally didn't have to pull on, he pushed those images aside. It was too late to reach out to Colton now. Garrett would call his brother first thing in the morning. It wouldn't hurt to fill him in on both situations. See what his brothers could do to help.

This whole territory was foreign to Garrett, but he was beginning to see the error of his ways. Shame he had to lose a father before getting the gut punch he'd needed for a few years now. Not that his absence from the family was anyone else's fault. He owned his mistakes. The trick was not letting them own him.

Brianna didn't fall into the same category. She was the most "right" thing that had happened to him in a long while.

BRIANNA FINISHED OFF her shower by making the water as cold as she could stand it. Because one seriously hot man was in the next room and she needed to cool her jets. Plus, she'd watched a show on the nature channel once that said a brush with death kicked in a primal instinct to procreate. So, the fact she wanted to have sex with Garrett more than she wanted to breathe could be chalked up to nature's desire to preserve itself. Or something like that. Or maybe it was replicate itself. Who knew?

Being of sound mind, she had enough sense not to act on the desire. Because on a primal level she knew sex with Garrett would change things for her and she wasn't just talking about their relationship. She knew on instinct it would set the bar so high for all future sex no one could live up to it.

She dressed in her least revealing pajamas, literally her Christmas fleece, and then came out into the living area holding a spare towel.

"Your turn." She handed the towel over ignoring the hungry look in his eyes that made warmth circulate through her. She broke eye contact as fast as she could to stay in neutral territory.

"Thank you." Garrett took the offering and she tried her best not to imagine him naked in her shower. He had the kind of sculpted body normally reserved for athletes who were on top of their game. He came by his through hard work and had the calloused hands to prove it. He had those rough hands she could only dream about against her skin. A thrill of awareness skittered across her body at the thought.

Coffee. She needed caffeine. The long shift was taking its toll and if she crashed now, it would be lights out for half the day. Every muscle in her body ached at this point. A few hours of sleep would only anger her tired bones. She'd learned a long time ago that staying awake after a long and busy shift was the only way to make it to a morning class.

Plus, she wanted to be wide awake for the alpaca farm trip. The two of them had more catching up to do on the drive and she wanted to know what Garrett had been working on in all these years since she'd moved away from Katy Gulch. It might just be the extreme situation or the fact they'd been apart so many years but she could swear she was seeing changes in him. The old Garrett would never have called in his brother, especially not Colton.

Not having siblings of her own, she always thought it was a shame the two of them didn't get along better. All she'd had growing up were her parents. Life had hardened them both in different ways, so basically, she had herself to rely on. There was no extended family to help. Neither of her parents were close with their families. She didn't grow up with large gatherings for the holidays. Which made living in Katy Gulch special to her. There, she'd had friends who she counted as family. The community had been tight-knit. Moving away had been akin to cutting all ties with her world.

Between school and her rebellious years, she'd lost touch with everyone from the small town where she'd spent some of the best years of her childhood. How many times had she dreamed of getting a nine-to-five close enough to town to be able to buy a small place of her own there?

More than she could count. More than she cared to count. More than she knew better to count.

Garrett emerged from the bathroom at almost the exact moment the coffee finished brewing.

"You couldn't have better timing." She chuckled as

she held up the fresh pot. Looking at him while he was wrapped in nothing but the towel she'd given him a few minutes ago was something she knew better than to do. "I'll fix a couple of to-go cups for us."

"Smells like heaven." He retrieved a small toiletries bag from the duffel he'd tucked to one side of the couch. "I'll be done in a sec."

He probably picked up a fresh outfit too but there was no way she was staring at him long enough to find out. He was pure temptation when she needed to keep a clear head. The few kisses they'd shared already occupied too much real estate in her thoughts. Her cheeks flushed just thinking about them.

Coffee. She poured two cups and then took a sip of hers, enjoying the burn on her throat.

Finals would be happening soon and she needed to come up with a plan to get through the next thirty-five days with her sanity intact. She thought about Code Blue. Her Jeep wasn't in great shape but that vehicle was Brianna's lifeline.

The clock read four-thirty in the morning. She needed to change already into something more appropriate for a drive-through animal encounter. Skipping class wasn't ideal but this had to take priority. The place was perfect cover for any kind of kidnapping ring when she really thought about it. It would be off the beaten path but registered. Then, there was the fact people would be coming and going all day. How easy would it be to drive a van full of kids there? Or take them out one by one. Potential adopters could literally drive up and take a child home. No one would question couples coming in or families going out.

The trick would be hiding from the government. But

how many raids were there on alpaca farms? As long as the animals were well cared for there would be no reason to call in the Texas Department of Agriculture, or whatever agency was responsible.

As soon as Garrett exited the bedroom, she set her to-go mug on the counter and then hopped into action.

The sound of the door opening and closing got her legs moving into the living room from the bedroom where her door was closed. Garrett was gone. And so was his coffee mug.

Chapter Eighteen

Movement behind Garrett's truck caught his attention as he started out of the lot. He slammed on his brakes so he wouldn't hit whatever it was that had crept up behind him. A thunk sounded against his tailgate anyway, and he immediately figured out who was responsible.

He hopped out of the driver's seat and left the door open as he walked back to confront a red-faced Brianna, standing in back of his truck.

"What do you think you're doing, Garrett O'Connor? We had a deal and if I can't trust you then—"

He stopped her by claiming her mouth. She put her fists up against his chest but seemed to have forgotten why. The next second, she planted her flat palms against him and pushed. He took a step back to brace himself.

"That's not playing fair and you know it." Her stubborn streak was a mile long.

"Believe it or not, I wasn't planning to take off. I noticed an air station at the front of your apartment and figured I'd check the tires before we hit the road." He quirked a smile.

Her mouth formed an O.

"I wouldn't do that to you, Brianna." He was trying to keep the mood light but he'd seen the look of betrayal in her eyes. It was one she seemed a little too acquainted with. Again, he thought about the situation with her mother's affair, pondering how odd it was how much these traumas stuck in life. No matter how much time passed, the hurt could so easily resurface. "Can you learn to trust me?"

She stood there for a long moment before answering, looking hard into his eyes.

"I'll give it my best shot, Garrett. It's not always easy for me." She issued a sigh. "But I do realize how unfair it is to put all my past pain on you." She grabbed a fistful of his shirt and tugged at it. "I know how you used to be and I figured not much has changed."

He must've worn his hurt on his sleeve because she quickly put her hands up in the surrender position, palms toward him.

"But that's not true. You have changed. You're making amends with your family. You've been nothing but kind to me. And you've held your temper when it would have exploded in the past," she said.

Those words were balm to a damaged heart. Being with her made him want to be a better person—the person reflected in her eyes when she really looked at him.

"So, yes, I'll trust you," she continued. "And I promise not to keep waiting for you to hurt me or desert me."

"Then, I vow to live up to your expectations. This friendship means the world to me, Brianna." There was a flash of emotion across her gaze when he spoke those words—an emotion he couldn't quite put his finger on for how quickly she recovered.

"Friends it is." She stuck her hand out between them.

"We can do better than that." He took it and used it

as leverage to haul her against his chest. He brought his free hand up and then ran his finger along her jawline.

"I'll grab my coffee and lock up." She sucked in a breath before ducking out of his grasp. "Will you wait for me right here?"

"You got it," he said. She'd done the right thing. They kept blurring the line between friendship and…what? Casual sex? Friends with benefits?

He had no doubt having sex with Brianna would be mind-blowing. And yet, he also knew on instinct once wouldn't be nearly enough. Not with her.

Garrett sat on that thought while he reclaimed the driver's seat and waited. A few minutes later, she bounded down the stairs and his chest clenched at the sight of her in a casual outfit of jeans and a cream-colored lacey tank top underneath a cropped sweater. She got to the passenger side before he could exit the vehicle to open her door for her but she didn't seem to mind. She climbed into the cab and then positioned her travel mug in the cup holder. Her fresh-flower-and-citrus scent filled the space, filled his lungs.

What could he say? The woman took his breath away.

"What?" She seemed genuinely confused as to the effect she could have on a person.

Since they were trying to keep their relationship in the friendship zone, he smiled and shook his head as he put the gearshift in Reverse.

It didn't take long to check the tires, fill up the tank and get on the highway.

"I was frazzled last night and didn't think to ask where the tow truck was taking Code Blue," she said as he found a steady speed. Texas highways were notorious for their fast speed limits and this one was no exception.

"I had her towed to the nearest reputable body shop. I hope you don't mind," he said.

"Not at all. An estimate never hurt anyone, right?" she quipped.

"I didn't ask for one. Told them to go ahead and fix her up for you." He knew he was walking a tightrope with this one. Brianna wasn't the kind to take advantage of others and she might see this as charity. She would hate to be considered a charity case.

The silence in the cab ratcheted up his pulse a couple of notches.

"Okay." She drew out the last letter. "I guess I can find a way to stretch my bank account. A little heads-up would have been nice."

"Any chance you'd allow me to cover the charges?" he asked, then quickly added, "Not as some kind of charity but for a graduation gift."

She took her time answering and the suspense was killing him.

"I don't see any harm in accepting a gift for graduation." She raised her eyebrows. "But you do know that I haven't actually graduated yet."

"You will, though. Consider this an early present," he added.

"It's really nice of you, Garrett. And very generous. Let me know how much it is and I can go in halves on it once I get on my feet after my new job," she said.

"Or we could work something else out," he offered.

She tweaked his arm. "Garrett O'Connor—"

"Before you get too upset, I'm only suggesting you can help with my family's website. Do a little pro bono work. What do you think?" he asked.

"That would be all right," she agreed. She pulled out her phone.

He had an ulterior motive with the exchange. It meant he would need to be in contact with her and possibly get to see her again once this was all over.

"It's a good website, though. I'm not real sure you need my help," she stated.

"It's the same website we've had for the past decade. It needs a facelift," he continued. He was determined to pay for the cost of Code Blue's repairs one way or another. This was the easiest way to get her to agree to let him.

"Okay. I'll take a deeper look on my laptop later. The bones of the site are good, though."

Pride filled his chest at the compliment.

"Have you thought about where you'll look for a job once you get out of school?" he asked.

"Anywhere they'll take me." She laughed. "This is probably going to sound stupid to you considering you've spent the last decade trying to get away from Katy Gulch, but I'm hoping to get a job nearby. I'd love to have a small place on the outskirts of town."

"Doesn't sound out of the realm of possibility at all." It was selfish to want her to live close to his home—a home he appreciated more and more with every passing day.

His cell buzzed, cutting into their conversation.

"It's Colton." He hit the button on the steering wheel that answered the call.

"Wow," she said low and under her breath, sounding impressed with the technology in his truck. He'd buy her a brand-new Jeep if she'd let him, but there was no way he'd win that battle. Fixing up Code Blue would have to do for now. Besides, her vehicle had a whole lot of sass and charm, and he sensed she had an emotional attachment to it.

He understood. He still owned his first truck. It was at the ranch, parked at the home his mother had built for him when he was of age.

Recently, his mother had allowed Caroline's place to be used by the occasional guest and it had fired him up, made him think she'd given up on finding her daughter.

"Hey, Colton," Garrett said. "I'm here with Brianna Adair."

"Hi to you both," Colton said before adding, "Brianna, it's been too long."

There wasn't a hint of wistfulness or regret in his brother's voice about Brianna. Water under the bridge? Or was it the fact Colton had a beautiful new wife and a pair of twins most in the family thought hung the moon? Probably all of the above. His brother had found true love with Makena, and Garrett was nothing but happy for them both. Locking down with the right person had made Colton the happiest Garrett had ever seen his brother. Makena had stepped into the role of mother to the twins like they were her own children, which was much needed considering their birth mother had been killed in a tragic car accident not long after their births.

"Thanks, Colton," she said. "It's good to hear your voice again."

"Same," Colton said without a hint of jealousy in his voice. There shouldn't be, but Garrett couldn't deny it made him happy to confirm.

"What's up?" Garrett asked.

"I'm glad you're awake," Colton started. "You were right to question the names on the nonprofit. It turns out Randy and Susan Hanes were an actual couple. They passed away fifteen years ago in the same nursing home within days of each other. Whoever is using their names is pulling off a scam."

"I knew something felt off." Garrett had learned a long time ago to trust his instincts. They were usually backed by experience and he'd come across plenty of folks running from their past in various bunkhouses during his ranching career.

"Which leads me to my next question." Colton hesitated. "Does any of this have to do with Dad?"

"It might. We're heading that way now to check out the place. See if anything else fishy pops up." Garrett could have lied to Colton. What good would it do? His brother wasn't stupid and he had to realize what Garrett was going after. They all were working on the case in some way or another.

"Okay. Keep me posted if you find anything," was all Colton said.

Shock momentarily robbed Garrett's voice.

"Will do, big brother." Garrett coughed to clear his throat.

"Be careful out there. Kidnapping rings are nothing to play around with. I know I don't have to tell you that and you have certainly dealt with vicious criminals before, but..." Colton seemed to get a little choked up. Garrett chalked it up to the emotions that were still raw after losing their father. "We don't know what we're dealing with here yet."

"You know I will." He glanced over at Brianna. "I have a lot to live for and there's no way I'd put Brianna in harm's way. This is solely a fact-finding mission. I plan to get in and then get out."

"If this pans out, it'll be the closest any of us have

come to finding out who killed Dad," Colton stated. "I hope it does."

"Me too."

"Do you need anyone to head that way for backup?" Colton asked.

"Not right now. Like I said, I have no plans to poke the bear if I find trouble here. We'll get in and get out, and then leave the rest to qualified law enforcement personnel. I didn't say anything before because there isn't much to say right now," Garrett explained.

"If you need any one of us, I'll have a chopper on standby," Colton said. "What's the point of all this family money if we don't use it to take care of our own?"

"I'll give you a call as soon as we leave the property," Garrett promised. It was odd to realize someone else had his back. Odd in a good way. Garrett realized just how stubborn he'd been all these years to think he had to go at life alone. But then, maybe he did. How else would he know what he'd been missing?

They ended the call after saying goodbyes. More of those layers of armor encasing Garrett's heart cracked when he thought about how much of a jerk he'd been. All he could say was, experience was the best teacher and he'd had plenty being a lone wolf. What could he say? It was time to play another song.

THE ALPACA FARM would be easy to miss if someone didn't absolutely know where they were going, Brianna thought as Garrett drove down a long, twisty road. A dust cloud kicked up by the tires was so dense that a car could be ten feet behind them and they'd never know.

Sure made it easy for someone to see them coming too.

"We should seem like a couple," Brianna said, taking

off her seat belt to scoot into the middle. Being close to Garrett was always risky, especially when his spicy scent filled her senses. Self-control was her middle name. Brianna held back a grin. It usually was. When it came to being with Garrett, it was more like a goal.

He took his right hand off the wheel and looped his arm around her shoulders. She leaned into it as he pulled up to the front gate.

There was a hut in front of what looked like a ten-to-twelve-foot fence with another foot of barbed wire at the top.

A guy who looked more like a security guard than a ticket seller stepped out of the hut. He had on all khaki-colored clothes and she noticed a holster on his belt.

Garrett rolled down the window, bringing in a dust storm along with it. "Two tickets."

"That'll be sixty-five dollars," the guy said. His face was sun worn and his eyes were shielded by reflective sunglasses.

Garrett reached into his pocket and pulled out a stack of folded-up twenties. He peeled off three and then located a five-dollar bill.

"All right. Follow the signs and don't leave your vehicle or the trail. Keep your speed down below ten miles per hour at all times." He pointed to a camera. "We have several of those around the park. Just because you can't see us doesn't mean we can't see you. If you violate any of the rules, you will be escorted off the premises. Understood?"

This was straight up the strangest welcome Brianna had ever received.

"Got it," Garrett said casually. "Oh, and is there a gift shop for my girlfriend for after the trail?"

"Yep. Straight through that way. They sell food in case she wants to feed the animals. We have a strict policy on no outside food." He pointed to another sign with a big *X* on it across what looked like popcorn and peanut bags.

"Thanks a bunch," Garrett said before driving onto the property as the automatic gate opened. He rolled up his window as the gate immediately closed behind them.

"That guy was creepy," she said.

"I noticed that too. And what kind of park needs an armed guard at the gate?" It was more statement than question.

"I thought the same thing. He probably has a license." She figured that much would be on the up-and-up.

"It would be real difficult to surprise anyone in this operation," he noted. "But just in case they have listening devices planted around, we better hold off speaking any more about it until we're clear of here."

"Okay, good point." She chewed on her thumbnail as her pulse climbed.

He parked and put his hand over hers.

"We can take off if you're not comfortable here," he started.

"Sorry about the nervous habit." She put her hand in her lap. "I haven't done that in years. Guess this is catching me off guard."

"Are you okay with staying?" he asked.

"We didn't come all the way here for nothing, Garrett. I can pull it together."

He leaned in so close she thought he was going to kiss her. Instead, he said, "In case you're ever wondering, I think you're an amazing woman."

Didn't those words send her stomach free-falling?

"You're pretty amazing yourself," she said when she could catch her breath.

"Did you just call me pretty?" He was clearly teasing, and it did the trick.

She laughed.

"How do you do that?" she asked, unable to suppress her grin.

"Do what?" He was acting mighty innocent.

"Make me laugh so much. I swear I haven't laughed this much in years. And it's been a wild ride over the past twenty-plus hours. I don't even know how many anymore. I've lost count," she said.

"Being with someone who makes you laugh makes time fly by," he said. She wasn't sure if he was talking about him or her. Either way, it was a true statement. "We can go inside whenever you're ready."

She also realized he'd gotten this close to her to fill her field of vision. When she looked at him, and only him, her stress levels decreased dramatically.

"Let's go," she said.

He held up a finger before exiting his side of the vehicle and then jogging around to hers. They were supposed to be on a date and he sure was acting the part. The minute she stepped out of the truck, he hauled her against his chest and placed a tender kiss on her lips. Warmth spiraled through her, pooling between her thighs.

He was a little too good at getting her body to react to him. She needed to keep that in mind and close to her heart.

He linked their fingers and shot her a hundred-watt smile in a show of perfectly straight, perfectly white teeth. That smile could melt a glacier. It had already done a number on her heart.

Taking in a breath to bring in something besides his spicy scent, she nodded toward the building. "I hope they have a stuffed sloth in there. I've always wanted one of those."

"You do know this is an alpaca farm, right?" He squeezed her hand.

"That's all? I thought we were going to a ranch or something," she teased.

He pulled her in close, dropped her hand and then looped his arm around her waist. He held the door open for her and she led the way into the small shop filled with stuffed alpacas in various sizes, lava-lamp alpacas, post-cards with alpacas and pretty much every color sweater with alpacas on them.

Garrett followed her around the shop, occasionally standing behind her with his hands on her shoulders. He leaned in for a sweet kiss here and there that smol-dered with the promise of so much more if she let the wildfire rage.

It wasn't difficult to sell a relationship when their chemistry burned hotter than a campfire.

There was a young person working the shop. She looked to be around sixteen or seventeen and stood be-hind the cash register, reading a tattered novel.

"What looks good?" he finally asked.

"How about this one?" She picked up a baby alpaca.

"Looks good to me." He walked over to the cash reg-ister with her beside him. "How much for this one?"

The young girl looked at them with wide eyes. Fear-ful eyes?

Chapter Nineteen

"That one is twenty dollars plus tax." Wide brown eyes stared up at Garrett. This kid was barely old enough to drive and she had a resigned look on her face that would haunt him forever. Walking away from here without taking her with him was going to be one of the most difficult things he'd ever done.

He pulled out a twenty and a couple ones and set them down on the counter as she rang the item up. She glanced over her shoulder like she expected someone to come in from the back any moment. The way she kept checking gave him the impression she was scared.

She counted out his change and set it on the counter. "Can I get you a bag for that?"

"No, thanks," Brianna said, her voice a study in calm. He could almost read what she was thinking because he was mulling over the same thing. This kid didn't want to be here, and not in that bored, I-have-something-better-to-do-with-my-time teenager mode he'd seen too often. She didn't want to be here because she was scared. Forced?

He linked fingers with Brianna again and headed toward the exit, stopping in front of the door. He turned toward the register. "Do you have a map of the property by any chance?"

"It'll cost five dollars," she said, her voice frail.

He walked back over to her. While she turned to reach behind her, he checked her for bruises. The dress she wore was a size too big and she looked underweight for her frame. As she stretched her arm to reach the maps, he saw several purplish marks in various stages of healing. The long-sleeved dress was meant to cover them, just as he'd suspected.

Garrett ground his back teeth. This wasn't the time to act. He needed to think this thing through. Grab her now, and he would be helping her. But how many like her were in the back of this house? Or in a barn? It took everything inside him to walk out the shop door without that young girl. He paid her and thanked her for the map. He couldn't wait to get off the property and call Colton. At the very least, this kid was here against her will and being abused. Colton would know exactly what to do with the information.

Again, Garrett had to force a smile as he walked Brianna to the truck. This time, she squeezed his hand, letting him know she saw it too. He gave a subtle nod. Go about this the wrong way and he'd do more harm than good.

But the stringy-haired little girl would haunt his thoughts until he found a way to get her out of there.

The trail wasn't long, thankfully. Alpacas dotted the landscape. Garrett was ready to get off the property as fast as possible so he could get hold of his brother. Colton would be very interested in what was going on here and he would have connections to dig deeper legally.

There was no way Garrett was going in this place

lone-wolf style. There was too much at stake between his father's case and brown eyes back at the gift shop. Damiani's lead turned out to be hot.

The long windy drive kicked up a dust storm on the way out.

"Those bastards," was all he said, all he could say when he made it back to the highway.

"I couldn't agree more," Brianna conferred. "That poor little girl."

Before he could ask Brianna to, she located his cell and called Colton. They filled his brother in on the scene and Colton promised to get to the bottom of it. He also promised to tread lightly after hearing about security.

"They most likely took a picture of my plates," Garrett said as they rounded out the conversation.

"Why don't you stop by the ranch and pick up a new truck? We can leave that one on the property where no one will be the wiser," Colton said.

"I like the idea, but I better get Brianna back home. She didn't sleep last night after working a long shift," he said.

"Send me her address and we'll send someone out to make the exchange," Colton offered. "That way, you'll have one less thing to worry about."

"I appreciate it," Garrett said. He could get used to this. He thought about Brianna. As an only child, she didn't have anyone who had her back. Well, not until now. Not until him.

"I'll ask one of the guys to swing by. How far are you away from Brianna's house?" Colton asked.

"A few hours, give or take."

"If one of the guys leaves now, he'll be pretty close to meeting you at her apartment," Colton said.

"Sounds like a plan." Garrett ended the call after thanking his brother.

"Any word on Code Blue?" Brianna asked.

"Not yet. We can swing by the shop if you want but I'd rather get you home and in bed," he said before catching himself. "You know what I mean."

She laughed after she suppressed a yawn. She leaned her head back. "I might not make it all the way home."

"Go ahead and close your eyes. I'll be here when you wake up."

"Thank you for saying that." The look she shot him next would stick with him for a long while.

He meant it.

THE NEXT TIME Brianna opened her eyes, she was somehow in her own bed. The shades were drawn and the room dark. How long had she been out?

Her alarm clock had been turned toward the wall, she figured to block any possible light source. She reached over to turn it around as she tried to clear the fog in her brain. This was the first deep sleep she'd had in too long.

The difference? Garrett O'Connor.

This was the first time she'd been able to relax long enough to really sleep. Being shocked awake felt like she was stuck between conscious and unconscious worlds, somewhere in the middle without committing to either side. Moving felt like sludging through quicksand.

She tossed off the covers and then threw her legs over the side of the bed. She sat there for a long moment in an attempt to get her bearings.

The thought of Garrett being in the next room helped to ground her. She listened for any sounds he was still there despite knowing full well he wouldn't leave her.

He'd made a promise and no matter how impulsive he could be, she'd never known him to break his word once given. He might have been a lot of things: rogue, self-centered, misguided, a hothead, but the man's word was as good as gold.

For a moment, she thought about calling out to him for reassurance. Instead, she pushed up to standing, steadied herself and managed to make it to the bathroom without falling over. Coffee would help with the brain fog and she trusted Garrett to be in the next room.

Trust. There was a word. Brianna didn't realize how little she'd grown to trust anyone until recently. Had she shut everyone out? She could say with one hundred percent certainty she kept everyone at arm's length. It was strange because she didn't even realize it had become her habit until Garrett showed up. Even with their history, she was having a difficult time letting him get close. Well, there was physical closeness and the emotional kind. The physical variety didn't seem to be a problem for either one of them. She felt her cheeks flush just thinking about it.

After splashing cold water on her face and then freshening up, she managed to get enough of her bearings to head for the coffee maker. Stepping into the main living area sent her pulse racing. Seeing Garrett sitting at her table, shirtless, was enough to clear the cobwebs.

"Hey there," he said and his voice was low and husky. On a good day, it rippled over her and through her. Now his deep baritone vibrated to her core.

"Hi," was all she could manage as she passed by him. At the very least she managed a smile. Before she stepped into the kitchen area, the aroma of freshly made coffee hit her. "Ah, that smells like heaven."

"Brewed it a couple of minutes ago," he said and she

could hear the smile come through his voice despite having her back turned to him.

"Do you ever sleep?" The man was a machine.

"I dozed off a few minutes here and there," he said.

"You're amazing," she said before realizing she actually said the words out loud.

He laughed.

"Have you taken a look at yourself lately?" he asked. "Not only are you putting yourself through school, but you work a job that would put most people under from the kind of energy it requires. Plus, you make it all look easy. Then, there are your grades."

"How do you know about my grades?" She arched a brow as she filled her favorite mug.

"I know you. Don't deny the fact you're getting all As, Brianna."

"I got a B in history of communication graphics," she admitted, leaning her hip against the counter before taking a sip of coffee. Yes, coffee. The caffeine kicked in almost immediately. Or maybe it was Garrett who had her heart racing.

"Not because you couldn't ace the class, I bet." His confidence in her sent more of that warmth spiraling through her.

"I overslept the test and didn't have enough time to answer all the questions," she said with a shrug. "I realized right then how quickly things could go down the drain. Some professors are hard-core and won't take any excuses or allow for makeups no matter what the situation is. Not that I can blame them. I'm sure they've heard every excuse in the book."

"I can only imagine. Makes it hard when someone makes a legitimate mistake and needs a hand," he said, picking up his own cup of coffee and taking a sip. She remembered the taste of coffee on his tongue. Somehow, it tasted so much better that way.

"I managed to get through it and I learned not to go to sleep after a shift when I have a test the next morning," she mused.

"Life isn't always fair. Doesn't mean we have to repeat the same mistakes over and over," he agreed, smiling. "I'm figuring that one out now, so it's never too late to learn."

She realized he must be talking about his family.

"I'm happy you guys are getting on better footing," she said. "You have a great family, Garrett. It would be a shame not to realize it."

"I realized it a little too late with my dad." The smile faded and she saw hurt in its place. "Don't want the same thing to happen with Colton and the others."

"Speaking of Colton, have you heard from him again today?" She glanced at the clock and most of the day was already gone. It was supper time but her internal clock was a mess. She wasn't hungry yet. Maybe after coffee.

"Only to say the information we gave him will help bust up some kind of ring. The details aren't solidified yet. The law will be able to get a warrant to search the place based on the nonprofit application being in dead-people's names and social security numbers," he said, clenching his back teeth.

"You saved that little girl's life. You know that, don't you?" She sure hoped so.

He shrugged. "Not yet."

"She might still be there for a few more hours or maybe a day but I highly doubt law enforcement is going to move slowly now that they have a warrant to search the premises. That's not exactly easy to get. Plus, we played it cool today. We didn't give anything away." She couldn't stress that enough.

Garrett nodded.

"I'm guessing you would feel better if you personally ripped the people responsible into shreds but we both know it would only feel good for a little while. Knowing they'll end up behind bars for the rest of their lives where they belong is the best possible punishment for those bastards and the only way for justice to be served." She bit back a curse.

"You're right. I know you are." He closed and opened his fingers a few times like he was attempting to work off the stress he felt at thinking about the girl.

"If it makes you feel any better, we can follow up with Colton about her once this is all said and done," she offered.

"I would like that," he said. Some of the tension eased from his face. His shoulders relaxed a little.

"Okay then. What's next? Should we swing by Derk's place?" That reminded her of something else. "Oh, wait. What about Code Blue? Did you get an estimate of when she'd be ready?"

When he smiled this time, it was practically ear to ear.

"She'll be good to go by Monday," he said. "There's a fair amount of work to be done and they have to order a new part, which is the main holdup. But, she'll purr like a kitten—" he flashed eyes at her "—or roar like a mountain lion in your case when they're finished with her."

Brianna beamed.

"I can't thank you enough for your generosity," she said. It still hurt a little bit to accept help of this magnitude but she was determined to get better at it. Because leaning on someone else for a change and being there for them in return made the world feel a whole lot lighter. No matter what else happened and how much her heart begged for more, she hoped she and Garrett would stay close when all this was said and done. She hadn't realized how much she missed having someone in her life until now. She was going out on a limb here but decided Garrett was worth taking the risk.

"You've helped me in so many ways over the past couple of days that it's the least I can do." The sincerity in his words touched her heart.

There wasn't much more to do than smile in return.

"You asked about Derk before we got off on a tangent." He steered the conversation back on course, which was probably for the best. She didn't need to get too caught up in emotions. She made better choices when she used logic and not her heart.

"Right. Should we swing by his place? Maybe talk to him or see what he drives?" she asked.

"Sure. Check out his living situation and see if there even is a way to determine what kind of vehicles he has access to," Garrett said. "But first, we need to get something in your stomach."

"I can grab a quick—"

"Or, I can cook something here." Garrett cut her off midsentence. "I know you're running on *E* most of the time because you have more than a full plate with school and work, but I'd like it if you slowed down."

She was mounting a defense when his hands came up to stop her.

"I think I know what you're about to say and, believe me, I see how you're moving mountains and that means taking advantage of as many hours a day as possible, but you're important to me and I would like to request that you make time to eat," he said in more of a plea than anything else.

The rebuttal died on her tongue. He was right and she could clearly see he was coming from a place of caring. Genuine concern was hard to fight.

"I'm really close to the end of the road with my degree," she said. "I have bills to pay between now and then and a job to find. But, I promise to do my best. Everything you just said is a big part of the reason I've worked my behind off to finish my degree. Believe me when I say that I want to take better care of myself. I realize how much I've been shortchanging that department and I'm so close to the finish line that I can almost taste it."

"I can arrange for a meal service for the next thirty-five days. I heard about it from one of the guys at my last job. He called them divorced-man meals. Said his brother got a delivery every two weeks and the food was good," he said.

She could fight his generosity, or she could take it as a sign the universe wanted to help her out. She chose to see it as the latter.

"Okay," she said.

"Okay?" he parroted. The shock on his face was worth it.

"You heard me," she teased, trying to lighten the mood that had taken a serious turn. "Or do I have to repeat myself?"

Garrett flashed those pearly whites.

"I heard you fine the first time," he quipped. "And now that we've established that, how about you open the fridge and pick out a meal before we head out."

She should probably be frustrated that he'd gone

ahead with his plan while she was asleep. Except that she wouldn't change him even if she could. He would always be a little impulsive and a whole lot of dangerous to her heart.

She sighed. Too bad they couldn't be more than friends.

Chapter Twenty

The drive past campus was filled with easy conversation. They were in a sleek new truck, courtesy of Colton, who'd had it delivered while Brianna rested. Garrett couldn't deny how much he liked being with Brianna. The fact she was willing to let him offer a hand up meant a lot. She wouldn't accept help from just anyone. She could be stubborn when she wanted to be, but he respected her for wanting to do it on her own.

He could relate a little too much to the need for someone to find their own way.

Derk's place was a small duplex. Her classmate's blue hatchback was parked out front. The street was lined with vehicles, some of which were trucks, so it would be impossible to tell if he had access to any one of them.

The only way to find out was to ask.

Garrett parked as close to the white aluminum siding unit as he could manage, which ended up being three duplexes down. He reached for Brianna's hand and linked their fingers without giving it a thought as they walked on the cracked sidewalk.

On the porch, Garrett rapped on the door three times in police-raid fashion. That should get attention. He was used to his physical size being intimidating to most guys and he wasn't afraid to use the advantage on Derk. At the very least, the guy creeped Brianna out. Garrett intended to make certain Derk walked on the opposite side of the street if he saw her coming after tonight.

An annoyed-looking man jerked the door open. Anger caused his eyebrows to look like slashes. Once he got a good look at who was standing on the other side of the door, he chilled considerably.

"What are you doing here?" His gaze bounced from Garrett to Brianna and back. He seemed especially keen to keep an eye on Garrett. Good. The guy knew where his biggest threat came from.

"You're asking the wrong question, Derk," Garrett practically growled. He was intentionally intimidating him.

"What?" Derk was on the tall side but willowy. He had dark circles underneath his eyes and looked like he'd been staring at a screen too long.

"You should be asking how I know where you live," Garrett said to eyes that grew wider by the second.

"How do yo—"

"Who is there?" a male voice called from somewhere behind Derk.

"Don't worry about it. It's for me," Derk yelled back.

"That's a boldface lie and we both know—"

The door cracked open a little bit more and a second young man appeared. He quickly sized Garrett up. His gaze never left once it locked on. "Can I help you, sir?"

This fellow seemed to know when to show respect.

"Yeah, can you tell me which vehicle belongs to this guy? He doesn't seem to want to cooperate," Garrett said.

The man looked at Derk like he was an alien.

"Sure. He owns the blue hatchback." He stepped out

onto the porch and then pointed at the exact vehicle Garrett had seen in the parking lot yesterday. "Why? Did he hit your car and take off or something?"

The guy jabbed Derk in the shoulder. He was clearly a bully and Derk seemed used to taking it.

"Are you two related?" Garrett wondered what kind of man would purposely live with someone who clearly couldn't stand him.

"Not by blood," the guy said. "I'm Everett Fulton, by the way."

Everett stuck out his hand, so Garrett shook it. The fellow had a firm handshake. The kid looked like he worked construction with his jeans and flannel shirt.

"Derk is my stepbrother and our parents cosigned for me to rent this place, so they forced me to take him as a roommate while he's in school up the road," Everett said.

"Which one of these vehicles belongs to you?" Garrett asked.

"I'm the truck right there." He pointed to a late-model Dodge Ram that was practically covered in dents and dirt.

"Does your brother, sorry, stepbrother ever borrow your truck?" Garrett couldn't see Everett handing over the keys, but he had to ask.

"Hell, no. I wouldn't let him drive a go-kart if my life depended on it." Everett scrunched up his face like he'd just bitten into a sour grape.

"Does anyone else live here?" Garrett asked. So far, Everett was an open book.

"No. Just him and me. My girl stays over sometimes but she doesn't live here." His gaze finally slid over to Brianna but quickly snapped back like a soldier at attention.

"You should speak to your brother here about why he

dropped out of school." Garrett had no idea if it was a true statement but he figured this was the best way to find out.

Derk had been a little too quiet up until now and he couldn't seem to look Brianna in the eyes. He'd tucked his hands in his pockets and stared at the cement porch until now.

"I didn't quit school," he quickly defended. "I only dropped one class."

Garrett wasn't sure what to think of Derk. There was something off about the young man. Pinning down exactly what it was turned out to be the difficult part. Was he just a creep? Or something more dangerous? Did he just rub people the wrong way? Was he the result of being bullied for much of his life?

He glared at Garrett while he stood there sulking. He was like a little kid who'd gotten yelled at for not cleaning his room. He lacked maturity, and by the looks of him, self-discipline. None of which made him a criminal exactly.

"What the hell, Derk?" Everett whirled around on Derk. "Your mom and my dad are going to cut you off this time."

"This time?" Garrett figured he might as well ask. Everett seemed more than willing to share information with a stranger.

"He pulled this once before. Claimed he got his heart broken by some chick and had to drop out when in reality he got a restraining order against him." Everett looked disgusted. He fisted his hands at his sides. From the looks of him, he was a real hothead. Would Derk stand up to his stepbrother? It didn't appear so.

"We've taken up enough of your time." Though Garrett couldn't imagine Derk standing up to his stepbrother to ask to use the truck, something clearly was off here. He had a restraining order against him, and access to a truck. They had to pursue this lead further, but right now, he wanted to get Brianna safely away.

"Cool. Thanks for the heads-up about school. I'll let our parents know what he's up to when they think he's in class," Everett said.

Garrett shook the kid's hand one more time before giving Derk a stern look. He looked like he might jump out of his own skin to get away from Garrett if he said boo.

Garrett stared straight into Derk's eyes. "If you happen to be 'borrowing' your stepbrother's truck to follow women who don't want to be followed, your parents won't be the only ones after you. Are we clear?"

Derk diverted his gaze and offered a slight nod.

Brianna had been quiet the whole time and he figured she had a reason. Once they got to the vehicle, she said, "I still don't trust him."

"Can't disagree with you there," he said. "I'm not sure he's bold enough to go for the attacks you've had."

"True. I didn't get that sense either." She climbed into the cab and he closed the door behind her.

Once he claimed the driver's seat, he asked, "What do you think about heading back to your place and then hitting up campus again in the morning?"

"It's a good idea," she said. "I made a decision about Professor Jenkins." She paused for a moment while he navigated off the tight road and onto a major street that led to the highway.

"Oh yeah?"

"I'm turning him in. You were right. Graduation on the line or not, I can't allow him to pull this with others. My silence might enable him to continue preying on women. How could I sleep at night if I knowingly let that happen?" she asked, but it was more statement than question.

"You know I'll support you in any way that I can. If you want legal help, our family attorney will be at your beck and call," he said. "He's on retainer and gets paid no matter what so it would give him something to do."

"Doesn't he specialize in cattle ranches and wills?" She raised an eyebrow when he glanced over at her.

"Probably. Shows you how much I know about the legal system," he admitted. He'd been thrown behind bars a time or two for being rowdy and not knowing when to keep his mouth closed but he had no idea how the family business operated on the office end of the house. There weren't many who could claim to know ranching from a ranch hand's point of view better than him, though.

"I appreciate the offer and I might have to take you up on it if this goes south. I'm hoping it doesn't and I finish out the semester without any hiccups. I can file a formal complaint with the university and I'm guessing with the law," she said.

"You'd be within the statute of limitations, considering the incident only just happened." He parked in a different spot despite driving a different truck. It was good to mix it up. Someone could recognize him. Although, having a dedicated parking spot next to Brianna's was looking better and better to him lately.

The few kisses they'd shared kept cycling back in his thoughts. All he could think was...*more*. He wanted more than an occasional scorching-hot kiss that promised to heat up if they took it a step further. He wanted more than stealing a moment here and there. He wanted more than friendship with her.

But that was probably the best way to ruin what they had, whatever it was that was budding between them. Because it was a helluva lot more than friendship on his end. He'd realized that as soon as she'd uttered the word. He'd been kidding himself thinking he could hit the road after taking care of her problem.

BRIANNA HAD BARELY WALKED inside her apartment when her cell phone started buzzing. Her first thought was her boss. Did her work replacement bail without telling her? The all-too-familiar sinking feeling in the pit of her stomach kicked in.

She located her cell inside her purse as Garrett closed and locked the door behind them. He stood at the door, looking ready for just about anything.

She checked the screen, and then shrugged. "I don't recognize the number."

"Answer it anyway and put it on speaker just in case," he offered.

"Right. Good idea," she said, doing just that. "Hello?"

"Is this Brianna Adair?"

She immediately recognized the voice as Blaine's, the TA.

"Yes, how did you get my phone number?" she asked, not looking at Garrett. She could feel anger coming off him in palpable waves.

"Sorry. Please don't get mad. Or worse yet, get me in trouble," Blaine pleaded.

"You're going to have to tell me what this is about first." There was no way she was making a deal before she knew why he called.

"This isn't about me or your grades," he quickly said. "Don't worry there."

"Then, what?" She risked a glance at Garrett. His arms were folded across his muscled chest. She had no doubt he could snap into position and throw a punch before someone had a chance to register that he'd even moved.

"I just wanted to explain something, but, like it's weird over the phone. You know?" He fell silent, no doubt waiting for a response.

"Since I don't know what you're talking about, I can't say that I do know, Blaine." She glanced up at Garrett, who was nodding for her to go along with it.

"It's sensitive. But there's something I think you should know." He paused a second. "My last class of the night wraps in half an hour. Can you meet me?"

"On campus? Yes. How about your office?" she asked.

"No." He sounded off. Nervous. "What about the parking lot? There's some stuff going on and I think you should know about it."

"Not the parking lot, Blaine," she said.

"You pick a place then. Anywhere but my office," he said.

"How about the lawn by the fountain?" The area was well lit and campus police was never far.

Blaine hesitated for a long moment.

"It's there or your office. Take it or leave it." She wasn't in the mood to play games if he was trying to be cute and ask her out.

"Fine. I'll meet you there." He sounded resigned. "Half an hour."

"I'll be there," she said before ending the call. She immediately caught Garrett's gaze. "We can make it if we hurry."

Chapter Twenty-One

Garrett made it to campus in what Brianna described as record time. He parked the truck and then watched as she bolted toward the lawn. He let her get a solid head start before pulling up the map of campus on his cell and studying the best vantage point.

In a public place, he wasn't worried about Brianna being able to handle herself for a few minutes. She'd explained campus security was good about being visible during class changes. Since this was the last class of the night, there would be plenty of security around. He could use it to his advantage.

In fact, one had just driven behind Garrett and he half expected the vehicle to stop and question him. Class was almost out and he could be picking someone up, so the vehicle kept moving at a snail's pace, winding through the lot. *Good.*

The thought of Brianna walking out to Code Blue every night alone didn't sit well with him. He didn't even want to imagine her driving home in something as unreliable as her Jeep. Come Monday, part of the problem would be solved when she got Code Blue back in tip-top shape. From what the mechanic said, she was lucky it had held out this long.

Garrett had to hand it to her. She didn't give up easily. Most would let the first setback throw them off course. What she was doing was truly heroic in his book. And he was damn proud of the woman she'd become. From a place deep inside him, he wanted to prove he was worthy of her.

He had no idea where the thought came from but, for the first time, he didn't want to shove it aside. He wanted to figure out exactly what it meant and then see if she could possibly feel the same way.

Right now, he had another priority. Keep her alive.

There were four buildings directly on the lawn. One had a coffee shop. It would have been an ideal place to watch from if it was open. A few people started milling toward the parking lot. He was about to be salmon swimming upstream.

Dodging through throngs of young adults, he managed to make it to the Administration Building. He stood with his back against the bricks near the corner. From his peripheral, he could see Brianna sitting on the fountain's edge, waiting.

A nervous-looking guy approached her as Garrett bummed a cigarette off a student walking by. "You have a light?"

"Yeah, sure." The guy pulled out a lighter and flicked it.

Garrett didn't smoke but holding a lit cigarette would provide cover for him standing there rather than heading straight to his vehicle like everyone else. As the sea of students thinned, he leaned his head back against the bricks and faked taking a drag.

Most people weren't all that observant. They noticed

broad strokes, not details. He hoped the same was true for Blaine.

From this distance, he couldn't hear a word being said and he didn't like being in the dark.

Brianna threw her arms up in the air, looking frustrated, and Garrett had to remind himself to stay planted. He needed to play it cool or blow his cover. Was this the guy who'd been stalking her? His thoughts snapped to other possibilities. So far, Derk was his top suspect.

Derk wouldn't *ask* his stepbrother to borrow his truck. He would take it out in the middle of the night without permission knowing full well Everett would rather die than give Derk the keys. The truck already had a few bumps and bruises being a basic work vehicle used in construction.

The way Derk had stood there sulking didn't sit well with Garrett. The blue hatchback at the bar could have been him scoping out the scene, making certain there wasn't extra security or any cops.

There'd been something about the expression on Derk's face that had Garrett thinking. He'd looked like he was doing more than sulking. He'd looked smug. *Dammit.*

It took everything inside Garrett not to shout over to Brianna. He was pretty certain he needed to act fast, and they'd let themselves get distracted with this Blaine fellow. Garrett bit out a few more curses before stubbing the cigarette out on the wall. He cupped the butt in his hand so he could toss it in the trash once it cooled down.

Brianna started to walk away from Blaine. He grabbed her arm. *Wrong move, buddy.*

Garrett didn't even have a chance to move before Brianna snapped her arm down, freeing herself. She spun around and poked her finger in Blaine's chest as she bawled him out. Garrett could hear her voice even though he couldn't quite make out the words.

He pulled on every ounce of self-control to stand there while she finished chewing the guy out. It was clear to see she was fully capable of sticking up for herself. And yet, Garrett still wanted to show Blaine just how uncool it was to put his hands on her without her permission.

This time, when she stalked off Blaine seemed to know better. He stood there, looking dumbfounded. Garrett rolled toward the parking lot and started a slow walk in case he needed to double back. Until recently, he wouldn't have been able to control his temper. This was progress. He had to admit life ran smoother when he took a minute before reacting and he had the added benefit of making better decisions.

Brianna fumed as she approached the truck.

"What happened back there?" he asked.

"Mind if we do this inside the truck?" She didn't wait for an answer. She marched toward the passenger side where he stood. He opened the door, and then made his way over to the driver's seat.

He started the ignition, ready to circle back to Derk's house to talk to Everett a little more, figuring there was no way Derk was still there.

"That jerk just basically begged me not to get his boss Professor Jenkins in trouble by turning him in." Her fisted hands sat on top of her thighs. "Can you believe that garbage?"

Before he could formulate a response, she continued, "The nerve of him. I don't care if Jenkins is in the middle of a messy divorce. If he's hitting on students, his wife *should* leave him."

"How did Blaine know what happened?" Garrett asked.

"Jenkins must have told him. Blaine went on about how Jenkins could come off the wrong way at times, but he didn't mean any harm...*any harm*." She blew out a frustrated-sounding breath as she repeated those last words. "If they think I was born yesterday or that I'm so special I'm the only one he's tried this on, they have another think coming."

"Do you suspect either of them is capable of stalking you with the truck?" Garrett gripped the steering wheel.

"I asked what kind of vehicles they drove," she admitted. "Neither one has a truck. Blaine is driving his mother's old sedan and Jenkins drives a luxury car."

"I believe we need to move faster on Derk," he said. "I couldn't shake the smug look he wore during the visit. Like he was getting something over on all of us."

"He was. He gave me chills." She turned to face Garrett before sucking in a breath. "He's the one who makes the most sense, isn't he?"

"It's looking very much like he had access to a truck," he said.

"Which had quite a few bumps and bruises on it already, not to mention the fact it was covered in dust and dirt."

"Making it easier to hide more scrapes and scratches," Garrett figured.

She smacked the flats of her palms on her thighs. "Before we do anything else, though, I need to report Professor Jenkins."

"A trip to local law enforcement should do the trick after you report him to campus administration," he said. "What are your thoughts on Blaine? Have you ruled him out?"

"I think I have. He's a coward and would do anything Professor Jenkins asked. Blaine hit on me before, but I think he took my rejection seriously and moved on," she said.

"Good. At least the man has some sense. Asking you not to turn in his boss isn't his best move." Garrett twisted the key in the ignition…nothing happened. He cursed as he scanned the area, looking for the hatchback. Derk had to have been the one who'd messed with the battery cables on Garrett's truck at the bar last night. Was he showing off? Proving he could get to Garrett?

"What is it? What's wrong?" Concern brought her voice up a couple of octaves.

"My guess? Derk. He's the reason I was late following you last night. Your friend Hammer held me up and Derk took advantage of the distraction to loosen my battery cables so my truck wouldn't start. It gave him the head start he needed to get to you before I could." Garrett issued a sharp sigh.

"We can always ask for a jump from security," she offered.

"It's not the battery this time. There would be a click, click, click sound. He's doing something else." Garrett held up his phone. "Would you mind texting Colton and letting him in on what's going on while I pop the hood?"

She took the cell with a nod, and then started typing while he exited the truck after unlocking the hood. He figured there had to be a flashlight somewhere in the vehicle. As he rounded the driver's side, his gut clenched.

Brianna was on her way out of the truck with a gun pointed directly at her temple.

"You better stop right there or I'll squeeze this trigger and you'll be picking her brains out of this truck for years to come," Derk said in a high-pitched squeal.

Brianna mouthed, "I'm sorry."

He gave a quick head shake to let her know he didn't for one second believe this was her fault as he put his hands in the air so Derk could see them. If Garrett had his own truck he would know exactly where he kept a backup pistol. He always had a weapon on him while working ever since he was attacked by a coyote at the tender age of nine years old. He still had a scar on his back from turning in the opposite direction and trying to run. If Colton hadn't been nearby and heard Garrett scream, he most likely wouldn't be standing here today.

"Whoa there." Garrett used as calm a voice as possible. Brianna's life depended on it.

"Everyone is always making fun of Derk." The fact he referred to himself in third person wasn't real reassuring as to his mental fitness. "But I'm showing all of you."

"You haven't done anything that can't be undone yet," Garrett said.

"How little you know about me and yet you're talking like you have it all figured out," Derk said. "It's too late now. I'm forced to act much earlier than I'd planned."

He had a plan? Garrett couldn't for the life of him figure out what that meant.

"There's no way he's kicking me out. I won't have it. This had to be done. I won't be taken advantage of again." His gaze narrowed as he used Brianna as a human shield. Even if Garrett had a weapon there was no clean shot.

Derk forced them back a couple of steps, making it difficult for Garrett to see them.

"Don't do this. Whatever you have planned. It's not too late to back out of—"

A wicked-sounding snort tore from Derk's throat. "You have no idea what I'm capable of."

And then it dawned on Garrett.

Everett was probably dead, unconscious, tied up. Something that got him out of the way. The plan. Derk used his stepbrother's truck to harass Brianna and then got him out of the way. But what did he plan to do with…

No. No. No.

The pieces clicked together in Garrett's mind. Murder-suicide.

"But now you're in the way and I have to deal with you too." Derk was almost hysterical as he spoke. "It wasn't supposed to go down like this but what do we do when things don't go our way? We don't scrap the whole plan. We pivot. Ask Mom. She's always talking about making sure we pivot. It's what she did when she married that horrible father of Everett's. Honestly, Everett didn't deserve to live."

Brianna gasped. The terrified look on her face said she'd pieced together the whole plan. Garrett's worst-case scenario was true.

"That's right. I'm the complication. You should probably deal with me first." Garrett would trade his own life to free Brianna. A lightning bolt struck his heart in that moment and he realized how much he couldn't lose her. He had no idea how she felt about him beyond a handful of kisses so hot they could melt metal. But he intended to find out. Because if he had even the slightest chance with her, he had no intention of blowing it this time.

First, he had to find a way to keep her alive.

Derk's face morphed into a scowl.

"You're nothing." He aimed the gun toward Garrett.

In that moment, Brianna made her move. She dropped down, taking his arm with her. The next thing he heard over a few grunts was the sound of metal scraping against concrete. Without hesitation, Garrett barreled around the front of the borrowed truck as the sound of sirens split the air.

Derk threw Brianna aside, his gaze frantic as he searched for the gun. Her head hit the concrete hard, but she bounced right back up and clawed at Derk the second he located the weapon.

Too bad, Garrett was there first anyway. He threw the gun as far as he could before spinning around and diving toward Derk, who was pushing to stand. Garrett dove straight into Derk's knees, and then heard a snap.

Derk cried out in pain as Brianna ran to get the weapon.

"No. No. This can't be happening." Derk bit and scratched and screamed, but he was no match for Garrett. He pinned the kid's arms to his sides and then slammed him on his stomach.

A few seconds later, Brianna stood five feet away, feet spread apart, aiming the gun at Derk.

"You're going to jail for a very long time. I hope you like being locked up with men twice your size and ten times your strength. You thought Everett was bad…just wait until you're locked up in maximum-security prison." Blood trickled down the side of her forehead.

"I got this guy." Garrett tried to soothe. "You can sit down if you want to."

"I'm good, Garrett."

She fainted at the moment a squad car screeched onto the scene.

Chapter Twenty-Two

"What happened?" Brianna came to in Garrett's arms. She blinked up at him as her mind started clicking through the evening's events.

"You decided to take a nap," Garrett teased but worry lines etched his forehead.

"Where am I?"

"The back of an ambulance," he supplied. "Someone has been waiting for you to wake up."

An EMT came into view from around the back of the ambulance. He asked a couple of questions and shone a small light in her eyes. She must have passed his tests because he smiled and nodded at Garrett.

"Everett?" she asked.

"Derk killed him using the gun he intended to shoot you with. There was a suicide note in the duplex that explained how Derk was in love with you and you kept rejecting him. It went on to say that if he couldn't have you no one would." Garrett stopped for a second like he needed a minute before continuing.

Losing a young life was so tragic. Brianna's heart went out to the kid's parents and friends. Based on the look on Garrett's face, he was processing the same way as she was…such a shame.

"Derk had on gloves. I'm not sure if you noticed that," he said.

"If I did, I don't remember," she admitted.

"You took a pretty big blow to the head when you fought him," Garrett said. "I've never been prouder of you, though. And I'm just so relieved you're all right."

He stopped like he needed to catch his breath.

"The timing of this is terrible. I know. But I don't want to wait another minute to know where I stand with you," he said.

Her breath caught and her pulse kicked up a few notches.

"I've realized over the past couple of days what has been missing in my life, which is ironic because I've never believed I needed anyone but myself to be fine. And then I ran into you at that gas station, looking like the sexiest drowned rat I've ever seen." Garrett broke into a small smile at the memory before continuing. "And I've come to know just how much you mean to me." He caught her gaze and held it. "I'm head over heels in love with you, Bri. And I'm asking if there's any chance, no matter how slight, that you might feel the same way."

He closed his eyes and took in a breath.

"Open your eyes, Garrett. I want you to be looking at me when I say this," she said.

He obliged.

"I think I've been in love with you since that first day of middle school when you took the seat next to me and introduced yourself. I know we hit some bumps in the road but seeing you again, being around you again, has only confirmed what I think I always knew down deep. There was never anyone else for me than you. I'm in love with you, Garrett. And I'd like to find a way to build a life together."

"You mean that?" His ear-to-ear smile overtook any hesitation he might have been feeling a few seconds ago.

"With my whole heart."

He bent down and pressed the most tender kiss on her lips she'd ever felt. So tender, it robbed her breath.

He opened his eyes.

"Marry me, Bri. Make me the happiest man in the world."

She was already nodding her answer before he finished his sentence. "Yes, Garrett. I would love to marry you. I think you're the reason I wanted to go back to Katy Gulch all these years. My heart needed to be near you."

Garrett placed a few more tender kisses on her lips before pressing his forehead to hers. "I promise to give you all of me. I promise to always take a few breaths before responding. And I promise to love you for the rest of my life."

"I'll take that vow," she said before reaching up to plant a few of her own kisses.

GARRETT PACKED THE LAST of Brianna's things into box number fifty-four. Her apartment was almost ready to go as she finished her last final. He'd moved in temporarily, but they were both ready to relocate back to the family ranch where he could step into his role in the family business.

The past thirty-some-odd days had gone by in a flash. He was set to claim their life together. Brianna had volunteered to take on the family's website but her heart was in teaching tech to underprivileged kids. She'd signed up to volunteer in Austin once a week and there was a whole lot she wanted to do locally along with some work on the ranch.

Garrett's cell buzzed and he hoped it was the call he'd been waiting for.

A quick glance at the screen said it was Colton.

"Hey, I have good news." Colton started right in.

"Okay." Garrett didn't want to get too worked up before he had confirmation.

"Missy, the abused girl from the alpaca farm, has been placed in your care while they try to locate her parents," Colton said with the kind of pride that made Garrett's chest swell.

"We're official? The foster thing went through even though we're not married yet?"

"I vouched on your behalf as did all of our brothers. We're a compelling team when we decide to get something done," Colton said.

"That we are, brother. That we are." Garrett couldn't wait to tell Brianna the minute she walked through the door. Neither of them had felt right about leaving that little girl in the gift shop that day about a month ago. Now they would care for her while she healed and they launched a proper search for her birth parents.

"Besides, it'll be good practice for both of you," Colton teased.

"Let us tie the knot before we start talking about having a family," he shot back. But with Missy coming into their lives and staying as long as she needed to, and having found Brianna, he knew in his heart that his family was already here. There was plenty of time to discuss having kids of their own someday when they were both ready. As for now, they were home.

* * * * *

[illegible] they were [illegible].

STAY HIDDEN

JULIE ANNE LINDSEY

This one is for Catherine Fisher

Chapter One

Gina Ricci hurried through the cool fall night, pushed by a mounting sense of dread at her core. Normally she enjoyed the short walk home following an evening shift at the animal shelter, but this time something wasn't right. She could feel it in her bones. On the air and in the rain.

She pressed a palm against her gently rounded middle, reminding herself that her deranged ex-boyfriend, Tony, couldn't reach her, or her unborn child, here. "It's okay," she whispered, steeling her nerves and comforting her baby. "I did everything right this time, and there's no way he's here." The words had become a mantra after moving to Great Falls, Kentucky, her fourth stop in two long months of hiding. She'd learned to deal in cash only, and rented an apartment with a building manager willing to forgo the background and credit check. Found work, solitude and a doctor who'd see her without health insurance.

This time, Gina had hope.

She flipped her hood up against the finely misting rain and hurried along the sidewalk toward her building. Around her, the small downtown streets had begun their nightly transition, as quaint shops closed and local honky-tonks opened.

Gina counted her paces, thinking of the cool sheen of water floating on the breeze instead of all the things that could go wrong. Her muscles were tense but fatigued from a long day of work at BFF Rescue, and she could use a nice relaxing shower. Six hours of helping animals and humans find their next best friend forever through photos often left her tired and sweaty, not to mention covered in hair. She loved grooming and outfitting prospective pet adoptees, then uploading their images to the rescue's website. There were no photos of sad animals behind bars on her watch. Gina made sure every picture was dating-app-worthy and showcased the dog's or cat's personality. She even added a nice bio for each animal that included their likes and dislikes. "Loves kids!" for some. "Cranky old lady in search of silence and servitude" for others. If she could, she'd take every pet home with her, but despite her new apartment, Gina was one step away from homeless too.

Her family would be horrified if they knew what she was going through, and she missed them so much it hurt. But it wasn't about her, or them, anymore. Not since the moment a doctor had told her she was pregnant, and she'd known instantly she'd guard the child with her life, to the very end. Especially from its father.

If Tony knew there was a human in the world he could legally control for the better part of the next two decades, he'd stop at nothing to get his hands on that kind of power. Gina had lived under his thumb, and in fear of his fists, for two long years. She wouldn't allow her child to go through that for a second. Even if it meant never seeing her folks or sister again. Though she promised herself that one day, when she was settled and it was safe, she'd find a way to let them know why she'd had to leave. Because they loved her, she knew they'd understand.

Her building was quiet as she approached. No signs of trouble on the sidewalk outside or in the foyer as she darted in and headed for the stairs.

A low rumbling of voices caught her ear before she reached the second floor, and her silent tread faltered midstep. She was accustomed to hearing her neighbors' muffled voices, music and television through the impossibly thin walls, but this particular voice sent a cascade of gooseflesh over her skin. *Tony.*

Gina spun on instinct, fleeing back the way she'd come and sending a stream of continuous prayers into the ether. *Don't let him find us. Don't let Mr. Larkin tell.* Her apartment manager was old but kind, and she suspected he knew she was running from something. There was understanding in his eyes on the day they'd first met, and she was counting on him now.

SHE WOKE HOURS LATER, to the sounds of her phone alarm and a dozen barking dogs. The scent of animals hung in the air. Groggy and stiff from a night on the cot reserved for extralarge breeds, she shook herself back to life and got moving. The receptionist, Heather, would be in soon, along with the volunteers who walked the dogs and cleaned the kitty litter. Sleeping at the shelter wasn't exactly permissible behavior, not that Heather would tattle, but she'd have a ton of questions. And Gina had already told her too much about her past.

She shuffled toward the restroom, rubbing sleep from her eyes, and dragged the go-bag from her locker on the way. Ten minutes later, she was dressed in a change of nondescript clothing, teeth brushed and dark glasses on. A sleek blond wig and gray headscarf added to the completely new look. She grabbed a granola bar from the vending machine to satisfy her grumbling stomach, then headed to the nearby café, desperate for some hot tea and a place to think.

Gina was immediately thankful for the glasses. Gray clouds and rain had given way to a beautiful, clear blue sky and near-blinding sunlight. The crisp mountain air and peaceful smiling faces made it hard to believe she'd really heard what she thought she'd heard the night before.

And hope began to rise in her core.

The café line was long as usual, but always worth it, and Gina fell easily into step at the end. She fished a few ones from her nearly empty wallet and inhaled the sweet aromas wafting through the open door. Four dollars and change would have to cover it today, at least until she got back to her apartment. The bulk of her money was safely hidden in her grandmother's small sewing kit. She'd learned the hard way early on that accessing her bank accounts somehow tipped Tony off to her general location. His money, and his family's influence, had made it nearly impossible to hide this long, but Gina was a quick study, and her baby's future was at stake.

"Chamomile latte," she told the barista when it was finally her turn.

The older woman didn't bother looking up as Gina paid with her crumpled cash, then put the change in an overflowing tip jar.

She could practically taste the warm, foamy drink already. A few sips of her favorite latte would clear her head and bolster her nerve before she made the trip back to her building. Hopefully a chat with Mr. Larkin would put her mind at ease.

"Name?" the woman at the register asked, cup and marker in hand.

"Heather," Gina said, giving the first name that came to mind.

She moved to the other end of the counter to wait on her drink, scanning the busy café for signs of anyone who might be watching. Satisfied she was safe, her gaze rose to a television mounted on the far wall. A breaking-news banner rolled across the screen. The sound was muted, but closed captions were on, and Gina held her breath as she read the gut-clenching words.

Murder in Great Falls… Unknown shooter left one man dead in his home just after 9:00 p.m.

The camera panned wide, bringing her building into view behind the reporter. A body on a gurney was rolled onto the sidewalk, then piloted into a waiting coroner's van.

Her stomach lurched, and she ran to the ladies' room, arriving just in time for her meager breakfast to make a reappearance. Tears welled in her eyes at the possibility it was Mr. Larkin on the gurney. Could it be a coincidence she'd thought Tony was arguing with her building manager last night, and someone was dead this morning? She splashed cold water against her burning face and pressed a wad of damp paper towels to the back of her neck, attempting to pull herself together and stave off the churning in her stomach.

Tony was undeniably a monster, but could he also

be a murderer? The fact that she wasn't sure twisted her unsettled middle even more. She had to let the authorities know it was possible she'd unwittingly led an unstable man to her building, and his visit had resulted in someone's death. It was the right thing to do, even if, hopefully, she was wrong.

To be safe, she'd make the call anonymously. On her way out of town.

Resolve gathered inside her and straightened her spine. She'd collect her tea, find out what happened at her building, then make a call to local police, if needed. From there, she'd gather her things and leave. Her heart broke at the thought, but she shoved the emotion away. She'd prepared for this, knowing the day might come. And if she was lucky, no one in this town's sheriff's department had already been bought by Tony or his family. Maybe then, if he was guilty of murder, he would finally be punished.

Gina willed herself to open the bathroom door, a small, naive part of her clinging to the hope it was all just a coincidence. That she'd overreacted last night. Tony wasn't in town, and whoever had been shot at her building had nothing to do with her.

"Heather," the barista called as she stepped into the narrow hall.

The familiar pang of doom skittered over her skin once more, stopping her short. Paranoia and fear were debilitating some days. Stir in her wildly unpredictable pregnancy hormones, and it was a cocktail for disaster. Clearly this was going to be one of those days.

She shook away the panic and forced her feet forward. She had information to glean and a call to make. Possibly another immediate relocation on her schedule.

A familiar laugh stole the air from her lungs.

Tony appeared at the counter, speaking congenially to the cashier in a smooth, practiced tone. His pressed polo shirt, high-end watch, shoes and jeans screamed of wealth and casual confidence. Everything from his expression to his stance was meant to put the cashier at ease. It was the poison he injected before tying someone to his web.

Gina backed up slowly, ducking into an alcove beside the bathroom door.

"Heather?" the barista called again.

Tony's head snapped up this time, his smile fading slightly as he scanned the room.

The cashier said something, and he returned his attention to her, setting a sheet of paper on the counter between them. He smiled, then reluctantly, after another look around the crowded space, left.

Gina's heart thundered against her ribs and in her ears. Fear clenched her chest and gripped her throat. He'd been so close. The barista had been calling her name. *Not my name*, she remembered, thanking her lucky stars for the habit she'd gotten into weeks ago. *Heather's name.*

She returned to the ladies' room and sat on the filthy floor, knees up and head down, forehead resting on her palms as she struggled to calm herself so she could leave.

She counted to five hundred before her heart rate returned to somewhere near normal and she trusted her legs to hold her again.

"Are you okay, honey?" an older woman asked as Gina pushed onto her feet.

"Yes." She forced a bright smile, bracing herself against the wall for support.

The white-haired woman was, shockingly, the first to enter the ladies' room since Gina had slid to the floor.

"Morning sickness," she said, setting a palm against her middle.

The woman's gaze dropped to Gina's stomach, and a smile erased the concern from her face. "It gets easier, dear," she said. "And one day these moments will seem like little more than a dream."

Gina held on to those words as she exited the restroom, taking her now-tepid tea from the counter with shaking hands. She cut through the waiting crowd of patrons, eyes fixed on the counter where a cashier had spoken to Tony at the front of the café. She craned her neck for a look at whatever he'd left there, then gaped as the flyer came into view.

An image of her in Tony's embrace centered the page above bold text that put a bounty on her head.

Missing Person: Gina Ricci
Age: 26
Height: 5'2"
Weight: 145 pounds
Last seen in West Liberty, Kentucky, on August 8, wearing cutoff jean shorts and a red tank top. $5,000 reward for information leading to her recovery.

Chapter Two

Cruz Winchester put his feet on his desk and kicked back to enjoy the banter flowing between his cousins, Derek and Blaze. Derek, Cruz's business partner and fellow private investigator, had a lifelong love of ruffling his younger brother's feathers, and Blaze, a successful detective, had an equally long running habit of letting him.

Cruz tossed and caught a baseball in the air above his head while the pair battled it out over who had chosen the safer infant car seat for their vehicles. Both Blaze and Derek had recently started families, taking their brotherly competition to new and painfully boring heights.

"All right, all right," Cruz interrupted. "You two are killing me. You're both the World's Best Daddy. Now, can we please move on before all this baby talk gets me ovulating?"

Blaze pulled his gaze, reluctantly, from his older brother and fixed it on Cruz. "I need some help with reconnaissance work on a person of interest in a homicide case in West Liberty."

Derek pressed a palm to his chest, then raised the other, as if he was about to pledge an oath. "I've got this. Whatever you're struggling with, baby brother, I can help."

Blaze cut a droll look in Cruz's direction. "Did you hear that?"

Cruz tossed the ball again, determined to stay out of the drama, but enjoying his front-row seat to the show.

"I could do it myself, if I had more time," Blaze argued. "But I'm working a full caseload right now, and this is important."

Derek waved his raised hand. "I understand," he said, theatrically breaking the second word into syllables. "Some investigative work is better left to a professional."

"Get out of here," Blaze said, laughing at the insinuation. "Just get me the information and bill the precinct." He handed his brother a thin manila folder with the West Liberty Police Department logo printed on the front.

Derek flipped immediately through the papers.

Most of the men in Cruz's family were former military and either current or retired law enforcement. Cruz was proud to be the former, with no interest in being the latter. And he was happy being single, unlike his string of cousins, who'd started getting married off faster than he could accept their fancy invitations.

He dropped his feet to the floor and set the ball aside as a woman shaped like Jessica Rabbit's shorter sister caught his attention outside the office's mirrored storefront windows. His mama would smack him for the mental comparison, rest her soul, but...*damn*, he was only human.

His cousins turned to follow his gaze.

"Who's that?" Blaze asked.

"I have no idea," Cruz said, "but I think I just fell in love."

"That's definitely not love you're feeling, buddy," Blaze returned. "Pull it together."

Cruz counted her steps as she drew closer, willing her to come inside. Her head was down, but she turned her face in the direction of their office several times, stealing furtive glances at the mirrored glass between them. Something in her stride and silhouette said she meant business, and he liked that all the more. "Come on in," he whispered. "Let me help you."

Derek snorted. "In your dreams."

Cruz smirked, but Derek wasn't far from the truth, though Cruz would never admit that out loud. "She's got to be a tourist, right? Maybe visiting a relative or friend for the day." Because he knew most of the women in town, and he didn't recognize her.

She reached for their office door, and pulled it open.

His cousins made equally stupid sounds of shock, then went deadly silent as the woman walked in.

"Hello," Cruz said, popping onto his feet and offering his best ain't-I-handsome? smile. "I'm Cruz Winchester, and this is my partner, Derek. His brother Blaze." He motioned to the other men.

She nodded politely, scanning each of their faces as they were introduced. "Hello," she said, a little unsteadily. Her gaze latched onto the badge at Blaze's hip, and she seemed to shift away by a fraction. She didn't offer her name.

"What can I help you with?" Cruz asked, stepping around to her side of his desk, then leaning casually against it. "Missing pet? Missing loved one? No job is too big or too small," he drawled, putting the full force of his Southern charm behind it.

"If you're having trouble locating loved ones," Derek butted in, "may I suggest the key chains I handed out at Christmas. Show the lady, Blaze," he suggested.

Blaze spun his keys around one finger, the little square tracker spinning with it. "Normal people use them to find lost keys and cell phones. Derek tracks our family."

The woman's brow furrowed, and a cautious smile curved her lips.

Cruz decided instantly that he'd like to see more of that smile, and moving forward, he'd prefer to be the one who caused it.

"You track your loved ones?" she asked, engaging Derek instead of him.

"Because I care," Derek said, with a bow.

"Derek has boundary issues," his brother said, casting a pointed look at the offender in question, before clapping him on the back, then heading for the door. "Now, I'll never be too lost to be found."

"That's right," Derek called after him. "You're welcome."

Cruz smiled despite himself.

The woman's shoulders relaxed. Either at the bizarre icebreaker, or at Blaze's departure, he couldn't be sure.

"I'm going to go see a man about a horse," Derek said, threading his arms into his jacket, then following in his brother's wake. "Holler if you need me."

She watched him leave too, then turned back to Cruz with expectant eyes.

"He's really on his way to see a man about a horse,"

Cruz said. "He keeps a stable on his property. Can I get you something to drink?"

"Water?" she asked, a note of hope in her tone.

Cruz motioned to the chair in front of his desk, then went to get a cold bottle from the refrigerator in back.

To his delight, she was seated when he returned. And she'd removed her dark sunglasses, revealing deep brown eyes and impossibly thick lashes. If she'd been a brunette instead of a blonde, he'd have been lost for good. "I didn't catch your name earlier," he said, half-wondering if she planned to tell him anything at all.

She accepted the water, then drank deeply before replacing the cap. "Gina," she said softly, wetting her lips before going on. "Gina Ricci."

The name sounded familiar, but he couldn't quite place it, or decide why she seemed so painfully nervous.

Her rich olive skin contrasted with the platinum hair she'd tucked beneath a headscarf, and he began to wonder about her appearance as a whole. The big glasses. The way she'd stared at Blaze's badge. Maybe she was on the lam.

He returned to his seat, less impressed than he'd been a moment before. "Are you running from someone?" he asked, in a hurry to move this meeting along.

A beat of shock rocked across her pretty face before she quickly flattened her expression. "I'm looking to start over," she said simply, avoiding any sort of answer, which was essentially a yes. "I'm hoping your line of work puts you in contact with the kinds of people who can create fresh identities."

"Fresh identities," he repeated, unimpressed. "You mean fake IDs. Forged papers, that sort of thing?"

She shifted uncomfortably without answering. Another clear yes.

"I'm afraid you've come to the wrong place. My best advice is that you fess up and turn yourself in."

"What?" She frowned a moment, then bristled. "I haven't done anything wrong."

Cruz leaned forward, elbows on the desk and eyes fixed on hers. "If you aren't running from the law, then what are you running from?"

Her back stiffened, and her shoulders squared. "I think it might've been my fault someone was murdered last night. I want to leave town before anyone else gets hurt, but I'm going to need some help with that."

Cruz did his best to cover the shock that came with that declaration. "You're going to have to elaborate," he said, folding his hands on the desk between them. Surely she was confused, or just plain wrong. But either way, she had his full attention for more than her beauty now.

She pulled in a long, slow breath, then began to talk.

Ten minutes later, Cruz had a new image of Gina Ricci, a name he now recognized from the missing person case in West Liberty a couple months back. He'd heard about her each time he'd visited Blaze and his other cousin, Lucas, at their police department in the next town. Cruz had assumed the worst when she hadn't turned up after a few days. Most folks probably had.

Authorities had looked at her boyfriend, Tony Marino, interviewing him as a suspect in her disappearance. Unfortunately for justice, the guy's family owned half the South thanks to a global chain of rural outfitter stores and a proclivity for sound real estate investments. Their wealth and influence had made him practically untouchable. Regardless, there was never any evidence he'd had a clue where she'd gone.

Now Cruz knew why.

GINA WAITED AS Cruz silently processed her story. "Oh," she said, recalling an important detail she'd nearly forgotten. She pulled the missing person flyer from her purse and unfolded it on the desk between them. "Tony left this at the café this morning. It's a small town, and he's put a bounty on me, so that's another problem."

Cruz examined the paper, then lifted his eyes to hers in a tight expression she couldn't quite read. "You're a brunette?"

"Yes," she said, her inflection making it sound more like a question than she'd intended. But, really, how was that possibly relevant? "Well?" she pressed, resting a hand against her twisting stomach. "What do you think?"

He rubbed a palm across the light stubble on his cheeks and chin. "I think you're brave," he said flatly. "Brave to run. Brave to be here now." He worked his jaw, watching her. "Thank you for trusting me with your story. Who else knows?"

"No one," she said, voice cracking slightly on the two little words. "Will you help me?"

Cruz stretched back in his chair, all lean muscle and confidence. "I can protect you, but I won't help you run. Tony Marino needs to be brought to justice for his crimes. My brother, Knox, is a deputy sheriff here, and my cousins Blaze and Lucas are detectives in your hometown. If you trust me, I can make sure Tony's found and punished to the full extent of the law. Then you can have your old life back, whatever that was before this guy came into it."

Gina's eyes stung and her throat tightened with fresh hope, something she hadn't had in a long while. "Thank you," she said. "I accept." She hadn't dared to ask about his hourly rate or fee, but whatever it was, the cost would be worth it. Even if she needed to take out a massive loan when this was over. Thankfully, she had some savings at her apartment to get him started.

Cruz pulled a packet of paperwork from his drawer and placed it on the desktop beside a pen. "All right. Fill these out, and I'll add you to our client list so we can get started."

She lifted the pen and began to work, hyperaware of his eyes on her, and trying to ignore the jolts of nonsensical attraction flowing through her. She blamed the pregnancy hormones and the fact that she hadn't had any physical contact in months. None. And Gina was a hugger.

It didn't help that Cruz Winchester was unfairly and distractingly attractive. Weren't PIs supposed to be portly, middle-aged drunks? Why did he and his cousins look more like action-movie heroes than actual people? And what must it be like to swim in that gene pool?

The women in Gina's family were short, busty and pear shaped, with thick, unruly hair. She'd learned to work those things to her advantage when she was younger, but even on her best days, she couldn't pull off Cruz's just-stepped-out-of-the-shower look.

"Finished," she said, turning the completed paperwork back to him, and hoping he couldn't somehow read her mind.

He looked through the pages and grinned, then offered her a hand to shake. “Well, Ms. Ricci,” Cruz said, “looks like I’m officially at your service.”

Chapter Three

Gina watched as Cruz looked over her paperwork with a furrowed brow. “You’re a chef?”

“Sous-chef,” she corrected. “I was. Now I work at the animal rescue, matching people with their future furry best friends.” She tried to smile, but couldn’t quite manage the task. Discussing everything she’d been through, and all she’d lost in the process, had raised her anxiety levels to new heights.

He hitched one sandy brow. “Remind me to ask how that works later.”

“It’s on the website,” she said, nervously nibbling her lip. “I’ve enjoyed my work at the rescue as much as working in any restaurant. Maybe more. Cooking came naturally to me, because I grew up in a kitchen,” she rambled. “I’m from this big Italian family, and we’re always gathered in the kitchen. Cooking. Eating. Talking.” A lump rose in her throat at the memories and she stopped. Cruz didn’t care about her past. He was here to fix her future. To do a job. “Sorry.” She cleared her throat, dislodging the lump, then setting her fluttering hands back in her lap, another thing she’d picked up from her family. Her mother loved to swing her hands when she spoke, and her sister had a way of getting her whole body involved when the story was good. They were all a little excitable, and she loved it. She missed it. Blending into the walls was depressing, like wearing a too-tight bodysuit that had constricted her heart, mind and lungs.

Cruz watched her, silently, with sharp, ethereal eyes. Was the color even real? He didn't seem the sort to wear contacts, but she'd never seen anything like them before, a barely there hint of green, practically illuminated by his golden tan. How much time did he spend in the sun? And doing what? "I'm more of a grill man myself," he said, apparently making small talk. "What do you cook?"

"Um…" She pulled herself back to the strange conversation, likely intended to put her at ease. "Everything," she said. "And all the time. At my parents' house, we love one another with food. We're probably all carrying an extra five or ten pounds of pasta and pancetta alone."

His gaze left her face for the briefest of moments, snapping instantly back to meet her eyes. "And you like working with animals?"

"Sometimes more than people," she admitted with a small, but honest, smile.

He nodded again, as if he might understand that concept. "When is your baby due?"

"Five months."

He gave her paperwork another quick look. "Your family doesn't know?"

"No one knows."

"And you were going to have your child on the run?" he asked. "Raise it alone while trusting no one and watching your back every second?"

Her chin tipped up in response. "If that's what it took." She hadn't made clear plans for the birth or childcare yet, but she'd been working on it. Her doctor had assured her she'd do all she could to protect her anonymity during checkups, but Gina would have to give her real name to be admitted for delivery, and labor could take hours. Even in the best situation, she'd be stuck overnight, a virtual sitting duck. Plenty of time for Tony to find her, especially if he had a private detective looking for her, which she suspected he might.

Tony was mean and manipulative, but he was only one person. To keep up the chase on his own, while maintaining the facade of brokenhearted boyfriend and working at his family's company, he'd need help. Paid help that he could control. He'd told her once that people in the worst situations were the most useful to him, because they were money motivated and cash loyal.

Gina scanned the framed photos on Cruz's desk, hoping he couldn't be bought. There was an image of him with Derek on the sidewalk outside their office, pointing at the Now Open sign. Another featured Cruz with a group of strangers in fatigues beside a military helicopter. Pictures of other inexplicably handsome men of every age, holding the hands of their wives and children, or carrying babies in their arms. Her tension loosened at the sight. "Are you close to your family, Detective?"

"Cruz," he corrected. "And you have no idea." His cheek twitched on one side, as if there was a hidden joke in there somewhere. "Here's how this is going to work," he said, seamlessly changing the subject. "We're going to be partners, so we can get the job done faster. Sound good?"

Sooner definitely sounded better than later. It was

the other part that concerned her. "Partners?" Didn't private investigators work alone? And what help could she offer him in return? She'd already told him everything she knew, and she'd written most of it down in the paperwork. Along with half her life story and the complete contact information for her entire family.

"Yep." He stood and stretched his back, before hooking broad palms against the narrow V of his torso. "Now that we've got the contract out of the way, I'm going to need three things from you."

She felt her eyes narrow. "What things?"

"First, never lie to me," he said. "I ask a lot of questions, so if I overstep or ask you something you think is none of my business, say so, but don't lie. I can't help you if you lie, and before we run into this, withholding information is also a lie."

"Okay." She lifted her hands, then dropped them in her lap. Telling the truth was kind of her thing. She was an oversharer by nature and by nurture, usually to a fault.

He worked his jaw, probably thinking she'd agreed too easily, and not quite believing her.

"Seriously," she said, one hand jumping uselessly up again. "I promise. The whole truth, all the time. Whatever I can do to help."

"All right. Second, you have to trust me," he said, crossing his arms and widening his stance. "I can understand why this one will be tough for you, and I saw the way you looked at Blaze's badge earlier, but my family is good to the core, and we're great at what we do. The Winchesters are also deeply woven into law enforcement around here. You might not want to trust them, but you're going to have to trust me. Because we're working with local authorities on this."

Gina bit the insides of her cheeks. He was right: it wouldn't be easy, but she had to trust someone. At least the cocky PI before her was up-front about who he was and what he expected. In those ways, she supposed, he was already being honest with her. "Okay."

"Great." He clapped his hands, then grabbed his coat off the back of his chair. "Let's go see what we can find out at your building."

She stood and followed, a little off-balance by his announcement of their partnership and subsequent demands. "What's the third thing?" she asked, certain she shouldn't go anywhere with him until all his conditions had been stated.

Cruz pushed the door open with one long arm and held it for her to pass. "Try not to fall in love with me," he said smugly as she moved through the narrow frame. His body heat and cologne clogged her brain momentarily, and she arrived on the sidewalk with an awkward laugh.

"I'll do my best."

"That's all I ask." His returning smile made her laugh again. "I'm going to get you your old life back," he promised. "You made a good choice, visiting my office today."

Gina's smile widened, and she hoped more than anything he was right.

Cruz stopped at a new white Jeep with big tires, no top and no doors.

"Your ride is missing half its parts," she said, stalling while she figured out how to climb into it without looking like a child at the playground.

"Are you okay over there?" he asked, sliding onto the driver's seat. "Or do you need a hand?"

"I can get in," she said, reaching reluctantly for the roll bar to haul herself up. "I'm pregnant, not helpless."

"You're also four-foot-ten. I can get you a step ladder if you need one."

"I am five foot two and a half, thank you very much." She pulled herself into the Jeep and reached for the seat belt. "And I'm not some dainty little daisy."

"I doubt anyone would accuse you of that," he said, smiling as he gunned the engine to life.

And she was sure they were going to get along.

CRUZ PARKED BEHIND Gina's building to avoid prying eyes, then waited while she used her key to access the back door.

Crime scene tape stretched across a large section of the first-floor hallway, and he heard Gina gasp at the sight of it.

"We're in luck," he said over his shoulder, leading her toward the deputy surveying the scene inside the open apartment. "Find anything good?"

His little brother, Knox, turned with a frown that bled easily into a smile. He offered Cruz a fist bump in greeting. "How'd you get in here? And why?" he asked. "Derek said you were at the office fawning over some potential client."

Cruz sucked his teeth to stifle a groan, then took a big step to the side. "I'm here helping Ms. Ricci," he said, revealing the pint-size woman behind him. "Daisy, meet my brother, Deputy Winchester. Knox, Daisy."

Gina gave him a dirty look. "My name is Gina," she said. "I specifically told your brother I am not a daisy."

Knox's lips quirked, fighting a smile. "Cruz thinks he's funny."

"I'm hilarious," Cruz corrected.

A moment later, Knox's gaze hardened on Gina, and recognition lit. "Gina Ricci," he said. "You're the woman from the flyers turning up all over town. You went missing in West Liberty three months ago."

"Two," she corrected, setting a protective hand on her barely there bump.

Knox took notice, then raised a confused look to Cruz. "You found her?"

"I found him," Gina corrected, stepping up to Cruz's side. "I'm the client you mentioned earlier, and I was never missing. Not like you think. Was Mr. Larkin the… victim…last night?" Her voice cracked, and she cleared her throat as she turned toward the open door. The answer was obvious, assuming that was Mr. Larkin's apartment, but she waited for Knox's response anyway.

"We aren't releasing the name of the deceased publicly until we've contacted the next of kin," Knox said, in a perfect show of rote memorization and terribly canned speeches.

"She knows whose apartment that is," Cruz said. "Everyone in this building knows who died, which means the whole town does too by now."

Gina batted her eyes, then touched the pads of her fingers to the corners where tears tried to fall. "Mr. Larkin's wife passed away twelve years ago, and his only son is serving in the military. Navy, I think. There's a photo of him on the desk."

Knox nodded. "We're on it, but it will take some time to reach him."

"So it was him," she said breathlessly but resolved.

Cruz cocked his head and smiled at his brother's stunned expression. "I'll let her fill you in," he said. "She tells it better."

Gina gave Knox the wiki version of her situation, including enough details for him to understand why she and Cruz were there, and why she needed his help. She didn't, however, tell him everything she'd shared with Cruz, and the difference felt unreasonably good.

He waved goodbye to his brother as she led the way to her third-floor apartment, planning to collect her things. Slight splintering around the jamb sent his senses on alert, and his arm bobbed up like a parking garage gate. "Hold up."

He listened before drawing his sidearm and toeing the barrier open.

The entire tiny apartment was mostly visible from the threshold, and obviously ransacked.

"Wait here." Cruz moved quickly through the three small rooms, confirming there weren't any hidden bad guys in a closet or behind the shower curtain. "Clear," he said, returning his handgun to its holster.

Gina stood in the doorway where he'd left her, obviously crestfallen as she surveyed the damage. "When I saw him at the café, I told myself he might just be passing through. Going town to town distributing flyers. Maybe chasing leads from people who responded to the older posters. I even let myself hope that last night's shooting was unrelated. A terribly timed coincidence. But I can't ignore this." She kicked a plastic cup out of the way as she trudged through the space. "I really liked it in Great Falls."

Cruz snapped a few photos, then texted them to his

brother. "Knox has already processed the apartment, dusting for prints and looking for evidence."

"Tony wouldn't leave prints." Gina said, opening a cupboard with canned goods and boxed foods. "He's not stupid. And I…" Her voice trailed to a whisper as her gaze snapped briefly to the open door. Likely she was thinking of the murder scene elsewhere in her building. "I need to get out of town."

She rifled through the nonperishables as Cruz took more photos. "I can pay you for your time so far," she said. "Then the police can take it from here. Maybe they'll even slow him enough to give me a head start this time. At least your brother seems like someone who can't be bought. Maybe the authorities will give a damn, now that Tony's finally killed someone."

She dropped her arms to her sides, hands fisted, and she growled.

"Let me help you," Cruz said, snapping on a pair of plastic gloves, then righting a lamp and overturned table. "What can I do?"

"I need to find my grandmother's sewing tin, then I can leave. The apartment came furnished, so I just need my clothes, toiletries and that tin." She searched through a pile of plastic containers on her countertop. "I can repack and be out in an hour. The food and everything else can stay for the next tenant."

Cruz wasn't sure if she was asking him to help her or planning out loud to sort her thoughts, but she definitely wasn't leaving town alone again.

"Tony killed Mr. Larkin, didn't he?" she asked suddenly, turning somber eyes on him. "I know the whole thing is under investigation, but given the things we're certain of, he did it. Didn't he?"

"Probably," Cruz said.

She nodded, expression unreadable. "I keep wondering if Mr. Larkin told him which apartment was mine, then Tony killed him to silence him. Or if Mr. Larkin tried to protect me, and Tony killed him for his refusal to give in. Either way, Tony found me, maybe through the files in Mr. Larkin's office, and either way, it's incredibly sad and unfair that a man lost his life because of me." She pulled in a deep, shuddered breath, and bit her quivering bottom lip.

Cruz piled unbroken plates into the sink, then tossed broken ones into the trash. "You can't do that."

"Do what?" she croaked, looking as if she might like to scream.

"Blame yourself," he said. "You haven't done anything wrong."

She rolled her eyes, then turned away, back to picking through the mess in her tiny kitchen.

"I'm right about this," he said. "Just so you know."

Gina spun on him, cheeks red, and frustration burning in her eyes. "Really? Because Tony is only in this town because I'm here. He only spoke to Mr. Larkin because I live in this building. Do you know what the only common denominator is there?"

Cruz shrugged, and Gina narrowed her eyes like an angry bunny. "Tony," he said. "You ran because of Tony, and he's hunting you because he's unhinged. Unless you're telling me you have some kind of mind control over this guy. If that's true, why not tell him to stop bothering you, so you can get back to your family and friends?"

"Obviously I can't control him," she snapped, digging more wildly through the mess scattered across her floor. "That's the problem."

"Well, it's one or the other," Cruz argued. "Either you control him, and this is your fault, or he does what he wants, and you had nothing to do with it."

Gina dropped onto her hands and knees and looked under the stove.

"What are you doing?" Cruz asked, returning several things to her cupboards.

"I can't find my grandma's sewing tin," she said. "It's small, like the ones mints sometimes come in. It's trimmed in blue and has a flower and ribbon on the front. I kept it up there, with the canned goods, inside an empty mac-and-cheese box."

Cruz finished cleaning the counter, then began lifting things from the floor while Gina moved on to looking under the refrigerator. When the kitchen was cleaned, he moved on to the living room, appraising the details for the first time.

Gina's apartment was officially the emptiest, saddest place he'd ever visited. There weren't any personal effects or keepsakes anywhere. No photos or art on the walls. Only a simple white comforter and sheets on an ancient-looking twin bed. Food in one cupboard. And a set of dishes and hand-me-down furniture that came with the place.

A small whimper turned him around with a jolt. "What's wrong?" he asked, instinctively. *Besides the obvious.*

"It's gone," Gina said, jaw clenched and a single tear on her cheek. "Tony found it, and he took it."

"The tin?" Cruz asked, closing the distance between them on autopilot. Sure, it had belonged to her grandmother, but if that was the worst thing that came from this day, he'd consider it a win.

"All my money was in that tin," she said, face going red, and limbs beginning to tremble. "He didn't need it. He took it so I wouldn't have it. So I'd be trapped." A soft sound bubbled out of her, and she came at Cruz, arms wide and wrapping herself around his middle. She pressed her cheek to his torso and squeezed.

Cruz froze, arms outstretched at his sides like a kid pretending to be an airplane.

"I can't pay you now," she said. "I can't run. I can't even call a car service to take me out of town. I spent the last of the money in my purse on a chamomile latte." She groaned, then pushed away as he curled his arms awkwardly over her. "Sorry," she said, lifting her chin and wiping her cheeks. "I'm okay now. I shouldn't have done that. It won't happen again."

He blinked, caught off guard by her unexpected attack hug, and equally unsettled by her sudden absence. "It's fine," he said, sounding and feeling like an idiot. Typically clients didn't attach themselves to him. Aside from his auntie, no one actually hugged him anymore. And he hadn't realized he missed it.

He frowned at the confusing notion.

"Oh, no," Gina said, winding narrow arms around her middle. "No, no, no, no."

"What?" Could it get worse than a psycho tracking her down, killing her building manager and stealing all her money?

Gina slumped onto the ratty sofa, her beautiful skin going pale. "My ultrasound photo was in that tin."

Chapter Four

Cruz righted the toppled chair and small table, then set the couch back on its feet while Gina pulled herself together. It was evident she hated feeling weak, and probably didn't want his help straightening her apartment, but she also needed time to process. Anyone would. And he needed to get his head around the level of danger that had landed in his lap.

A beautiful woman came to him looking for ways to hide from her ex-boyfriend. The woman turned out to be someone believed missing, not a runaway. Now the ex was possibly a murderer, thief and vandalizer.

If Cruz was upset by all that, how must Gina feel?

He dared a look in her direction.

Her horrified expression had turned to resolve. Her shoulders were squared, and her chin had lifted. One palm lay protectively against her middle. She'd been alone, afraid, on the run and pregnant.

Cruz couldn't begin to imagine what that must be like.

He dragged her mattress and box spring back onto the bed frame, then worked the sheets on top. His gaze flickered back to the woman who'd caught his eye outside the office window, and had needed him more than he could've imagined. The weight of her reality was a steamroller to the chest. Had the monster hurt her? Was that why she'd run?

Cruz hadn't taken the time to wonder why she'd initially left home, at least not in terms of specifics. But now that the possibility Tony had physically abused her occurred to him, Cruz was sure he'd enjoy the opportunity to let Tony see what it felt like to be pushed around, frightened and outmatched.

The thought curled his hands into fists and sent fire through his veins. There were all kinds of low-life people in the world, but men who hurt women and children were the worst. That was another reason Cruz had never considered law enforcement as a career. He didn't have the patience of his brother or cousins, and he wouldn't be able to calmly tend to domestic disputes where someone had been terrifying a loved one. Hunting down adulterers and run-of-the-mill criminals was bad enough. Some days Cruz didn't even want to do that, but it was always worth it when justice was served.

Gina stood and returned to her kitchen, then silently loaded the ancient dishwasher. The movements were stiff and robotic. Her previously astute gaze, distant.

"Hey," he said, making his way to her side.

She raised cautious eyes to his, then closed the appliance door.

Cruz stopped a respectable distance away and opened his arms.

Her eyes glossed, and she came immediately to him. This time, he didn't leave her hanging. She sobbed quietly against his shirt, her small body shaking slightly. "I can't believe Mr. Larkin is dead," she whispered. "He protected me. He gave me someplace to live when no one else would. He didn't care that I couldn't provide him with more than a fake name and cash to cover the rent. He just said, 'Welcome.' In return for his kindness, he's murdered."

Cruz rested his cheek against the top of her head and held her firmly, willing to stay that way as long as she needed. "We're going to find and stop him," Cruz vowed. "I'll keep you safe until we do."

She backed away at that, expression guarded and wary. She wiped a tear from her cheek. "I didn't realize how much I'd missed being hugged." An embarrassed smile played on her lips. "It's been a long time. My family is made of huggers. Talkers. Friends." Her mood elevated slightly at the mention of her family, then she deflated again with a sigh, leaning against the countertop. "I can't believe he found me. I was so careful."

"He didn't find you." Cruz shoved his hands into his back pocket to keep from reaching for her again. "He found your apartment. He can have that."

She rolled her eyes up to meet his. "I'm literally homeless now. I can't even rent a room at a hotel because he took my money. I had to keep it here, because when I opened a bank account in the first town I tried to settle in, he found me within days. Since then, I've relied on cash. Now that's gone. He just keeps taking everything."

"Not anymore," Cruz said. "You did the right thing by coming into my office today. This is where it ends for him. My family's a lot more than just abundant good looks and charm." He winked to ease the tension, then rejoiced when she offered a brief smile.

"He's smart too," she warned. "Conniving and manipulative. Dangerous." She swallowed, then took a moment before going on. "He likes to control people, and when he can't…he can be brutal. And now he knows about the baby."

Cruz's gaze slid to her middle. She hadn't told Tony he was going to be a father. If that didn't tell Cruz everything he needed to know about the kind of monster Tony was, nothing would. He pressed the heel of his hand to his chest, where an uncomfortable shift had taken place. His protective instincts were triggered back at his office, when she'd told her story, but holding her had sent those same feelings into overdrive. The way she'd latched onto him without warning earlier, and the way she'd held him again just now, had knotted everything in his core. And he wasn't sure what that meant.

She rubbed a narrow hand against her forehead. "What am I going to do?"

Cruz shook off the unsettling feeling and moved his hand from his chest to his hip. "For starters, you're coming home with me. My place is safe. You can rest and recuperate while Derek, Blaze and I find this guy."

Her eyes widened, then snapped up to meet his. "I can't do that," she said. "I can't even afford to pay you now. I certainly can't let you give me a place to stay. I'll figure something out."

Cruz crossed his arms. "You're scared, in obvious danger, pregnant and homeless. I know we've just met, but what kind of person do you think I am?"

She shrugged, crestfallen once more. "You seem nice, but people aren't always what they seem."

He wanted to argue that he was much more than nice, but decided to run with it instead. "How nice would I be if I set you loose and wished you luck right now? You're being hunted. I can't turn you away any sooner than you would do that to someone else. Imagine what my auntie would say. You want me to disappoint Auntie?"

She pressed her lips tight, and Cruz could practically see her weighing the impossible options. Keep running, alone, broke and homeless, or stay with a man she'd just met. The last man she'd gone home with had turned out to be a killer. Gina wrapped both arms around her waist, highlighting the weak spot he'd overlooked before.

"Do it for your baby," he said. "Come back to my place with me. Get a good night's sleep for the first time in months. A hot shower. A home-cooked meal. Then you can work on an alternative plan while I help law enforcement find and apprehend Tony. My auntie and sisters-in-law will have anything you need, if anything else is missing here, and they're all a text away."

Her lips parted and her brows rose. "I wouldn't dream of bothering anyone else."

Cruz laughed. "Well, you clearly haven't met my family."

She swallowed, then blushed. "I don't know."

"Gina," he said, enjoying the sound of her name on his tongue, and drawing her eyes back to his. "If you won't come home with me, then let me set you up somewhere. I'll pay, then set up shop outside the place and keep watch. I don't mind that, but it's the weaker option, because if I'm staking out your new digs, I'm not chasing leads on Tony. It puts Derek and the local sheriff's department one man down."

She sunk her teeth into her bottom lip as she considered his offers. "I miss my family."

"Do they know where you are?"

"No." She shook her head. "They know I can't tell them."

"But they know you left intentionally?"

"I think so. I didn't tell them outright, so they couldn't be held accountable for the knowledge, but they should know I'd never leave if I didn't have to. They know how much they mean to me."

Cruz ran a heavy hand over his hair. His family would lose their minds if one of their members vanished, especially one of the women. Statistically speaking, missing women didn't come home, and their reasons for leaving were never good. He made a mental note to get a message safely to Gina's family. They should know she was okay, and that she was with a family who could end this for her. Their contact information was on her paperwork in his office.

"Okay," she said, locking her eyes on his. "I will accept your help, for my baby's sake. I'll stay at your house. I don't want to cause you more work, or do anything to prolong the hunt for Tony. Plus, I intend to see that you're paid for your time on this case. There's no need to add a hotel bill on top of that, and hotels have too many points of entry to monitor with any sort of success."

Cruz chuckled and rubbed his palms together, eager to drop her at his place and get started on tracking Tony. "Very true, and you've made an excellent choice."

"I have one condition," she said.

An unintentional grin spread across his face as he crossed his arms and widened his stance. "All right. Let's hear it."

"I want to help however I can. You have to keep me updated on what you're doing to find him and the progress. I know him. Probably better than anyone, and I can help you if you let me. If you don't, he'll get the best of you. Tony doesn't play by any manual of ethics or honor. You'll underestimate him, and you'll lose."

Cruz clenched his jaw, hating Tony impossibly more every second. "Hey, all I want is to save the day," he said, hoping to sound more cocky than irritated. He dropped his hands to his sides and leaned against the counter with her, trying to look harmless and trustworthy to a woman who had to be scared beyond measure.

"A man with a hero complex," she said, a gentle tease in her tone. "How refreshing."

"You say that like it's a bad thing. What's wrong with a hero complex?" he asked, leaving her side to finish making the bed.

"Well, for starters, it makes me a damsel in distress, and I hate that," she said, folding a dish towel and setting it neatly on the counter. "I know it probably looks that way to you, but I'm doing okay."

"Not a damsel," he said, giving her pillow a playful fluff. "A daisy."

"Oh, shut up." She laughed, and the sound was something he immediately needed to hear again.

They worked in companionable silence until everything had been righted inside her temporary home. It wasn't tough considering the modest quarters.

Eventually, Knox made his way upstairs.

He paused at the open door. "Looks better," he said, turning to face Cruz and Gina.

She offered a small wave. "Cruz helped me straighten up."

Knox nodded. "He's like that. May I come in?"

"Oh," she said. "Of course. Sorry."

He smiled politely, then swept his gaze to Cruz. "She can't stay here."

Cruz returned his most blank expression. "You think?"

"We can call Derek's folks," Knox said, turning

his eyes from Cruz to Gina. "Our aunt and uncle have plenty of room, and they understand these sorts of things. Our uncle is former law enforcement."

Gina looked to Cruz.

He folded his arms. "I offered her a room at my place."

One of Knox's eyebrows rose.

Cruz matched the expression.

"I don't mind staying with your aunt and uncle," Gina said. "I don't want to do anything that's…" She seemed to struggle for the right word, looked to Knox, then Cruz and blushed.

The heat in her cheeks seemed to travel to his pants, along with a variety of inappropriate thoughts about making her blush for far better reasons. Then he gave himself a sharp mental slap. Gina was in trouble. She needed him to help her. Not lust after her. Though he wouldn't mind unpacking the possibility of her returned interest in a few weeks when she was safe once more.

Actually, Tony needed to be cuffed and jailed as soon as possible, because Gina was staying at Cruz's place, and he was only human.

Knox made a loop around the space before returning to Gina. "Is anything missing?"

"My grandmother's tin," she said, stealing an embarrassed look at Cruz. "It had all my money in it, and an ultrasound photo. He wasn't supposed to know about the baby."

Knox rocked back on his heels, head bobbing in understanding. "I see. And your ex has a history of violence?"

Cruz braced himself for the answer.

Gina gave a single stiff dip of her chin, and it broke his heart.

He moved back across the space, drawn to her pain and hating his inability to soothe it. He filled a glass with water, then offered it to her and motioned for her to sit.

She easily accepted the suggestion and the offering. "Thank you."

Knox roamed the apartment, looking at the minute details, examining windows and doing his cop thing. "Keep your eyes out when you leave," he warned. "He could be watching the building, waiting for her to come home."

Gina paled.

Cruz moved into her line of sight, locking his gaze with hers. "You're safe." He took a moment to let the words sink in, then flipped his attention to Knox. "Right?"

Knox nodded at Gina. "You're in good hands."

Cruz returned Gina's empty glass to the sink. "Why don't you pack up? We'll take the rest of your things with us so there's no reason to come back. When you leave my place, it will be to go home to your family."

Her bottom lip quivered at his mention of her family, then her posture straightened. She went to the closet and retrieved a set of luggage.

"Are the books yours?" Cruz asked, eyeballing a small row of tattered paperbacks on the windowsill, several of which he also owned. He couldn't imagine a woman on the run toting books, but neither had he ever heard of a furnished apartment including a collection of classics.

A cell phone rang before Gina answered the question.

She stepped back into view from her bathroom, a pile of shampoos and body wash bottles in one arm, the ringing phone in the other. "It's the animal shelter," she said. "I forgot to call and let them know I'm not coming. What do I do?"

Cruz headed in her direction, then took the bottles from her arm. "Tell them you're sick. You need the rest of the week off. By that time, we'll have a better idea of where things stand with Tony."

She tensed at the sound of his name, then turned away to take the call.

Cruz dragged a hand through his hair as Knox approached. "How's this for a morning?"

Knox smirked. "Murder? Breaking and entering? Abusive stalker? Pregnant woman on the run?" he asked. "I hate that it's happening in my town, but at least I know this guy's going down."

Cruz offered his brother his fist. They locked determined gazes as their knuckles gently collided.

"I've got this," Knox said. "You focus on keeping them safe." He tipped his head to Gina where she spoke softly on the phone, one palm set protectively against her abdomen.

"Divide and conquer," Cruz agreed. And he would take his portion of the duties damn seriously.

Gina pocketed her phone and forced a tight smile in their direction. "I have the flu, and will be in touch as soon as I'm feeling better." She rolled her head over each shoulder and gripped the muscles there. "I hate lying to Heather, but telling the truth puts her in danger."

Cruz's chest pinched again for her. "She doesn't know about your situation?"

"Some." Gina gave a tragic smile. "She's the rescue's receptionist, and my only friend in this town, but I try to say as little as possible. She knows enough to understand why I keep to myself outside work."

Knox made a note on the little pad of paper he kept in his back pocket. "I'll make a call to the animal rescue later today."

A deputy appeared in the doorway, his gaze landing on Knox. "Got a minute?"

"On my way," Knox said, casting his gaze from Cruz, to Gina, then back. "Y'all take care. I'll be in touch."

A few short minutes later, Gina collected the line of paperbacks and added them to a duffel bag in her hand. "This is everything."

Cruz offered his most encouraging smile. "Then I suppose it's time for us to kick stones." He collected her meager belongings and headed for the door, giving her the space and time to say goodbye if needed.

She passed him on the steps to the lobby. "I hope you're sure about this."

He smiled as he watched her go, because he'd never been so sure about anything in his life.

Chapter Five

An hour later, Gina and Cruz were finally on their way out of town. She clutched her purse to her lap as he pulled his Jeep away from the PI office, where he'd stopped to handle a few things and make it known he wouldn't be back for the rest of the day. Gina had stood near the windows, watching the people outside and hoping Tony wouldn't get the same idea she had and come inside to ask how a person on the run might best hide.

Getting back in the Jeep and out of town had been the only thing she could think of as she'd waited. But now, as the city limits sign flew past, and stretches of homes and shops became fields and forest, she'd begun to wonder if her terrible instincts about men had simply moved her from one dangerous situation to another. What if Cruz Winchester was a monster too?

She stole a careful look in his direction. What did Cruz keep hidden under that unbelievable face and playful disposition? She'd been enamored by Tony's looks and confidence in the beginning, and where had that gotten her?

"How much farther?" she asked, taking mental notes of road signs and landmarks in case her instincts were wrong about the man beside her.

"About five miles," he said. His pale green eyes lowered to where she'd unwittingly moved her hand to her middle, guarding the child she hadn't planned, but would do anything to protect.

"Okay," she said, feigning bravery and suspecting Cruz could see right through the false bravado. "I know it's early, but it's been a long day." And she hadn't rested well on the cot at the animal rescue.

She turned her eyes back to the road, imagining Tony shrinking in their dust, and hoping Cruz was the man he presented himself to be. Her cell phone rang, and she started, then stared briefly at the screen. "It's work again," she said, tucking windblown platinum locks behind her ears.

"They're probably just checking in on you," he assured. "Maybe to see if you need anything. It's getting close to lunchtime."

Gina stared at the phone, not ready to tell more half-truths, but also not wanting to worry her boss or friend. She forced herself to answer as the device began its fourth ring. "Hello?"

"Gina?" Heather asked. "Where are you?"

She cringed. The wild rush of wind through her phone's speaker was probably a dead giveaway. Gina wasn't home sick or in bed. "Running to the drug store," she fibbed. "Is everything okay?"

She felt Cruz's eyes on her as she waited for Heather's answer.

"No," her friend said. "Not at all." Her hushed tone set Gina's nerves further on edge.

"What happened?"

"A man was just in here asking about you," Heather whispered.

"Who?" Gina felt her stomach tighten, hoping the

man had been Knox, not Tony. "Wait," she quickly added, then lowered the phone and pressed the speaker button so Cruz could listen too. "Sorry. Go on."

"I don't know. He had a flyer," Heather said. "He said you're a missing person. The flyer's got your picture on it," she said, her voice falling to a frantic whisper. "And you're with him in the photo. Someone in town recognized you and told him you work here. I said that wasn't true, but he wants me to hang the flyer in the window. I don't want to do it. It feels like putting a target on your back. But if I don't do what he asked, I'm afraid he'll wonder why." Heather made a small hiccup sound. "Gina, I'm afraid I screwed up, and I don't know what to do. Is this about that crazy guy you dated? Was that him?"

Gina wet her lips, heart racing and thoughts churning. Knowing Tony had tossed her empty apartment was one thing. Knowing he'd likely killed her building manager, then gone to confront her friend was enough to make her physically ill. She hated the desperation and panic in Heather's voice, and hated knowing she had inadvertently caused it. "You did the right thing by taking the flyer," she said, with as much confidence and comfort as she could manage. "You should hang the flyer and forget everything I told you about my ex. I'm fine. I'm not the one in the photo. Okay?"

"It sure looked like you," she said. The metallic jangling of keys registered through the line. "And that guy said you went missing less than a month before you turned up here. Listen, I'm heading out for lunch. I was going to stop by, but since you're not home, I think we should meet and get our stories straight in case he comes back. And I know this is absolutely ridiculous to say, but please tell me this has nothing to do with what happened at your building. The news is saying someone is dead. What on earth is happening in this town?"

Gina looked to Cruz for strength, then set her resolve to protect Heather's safety, if not her feelings. "I can't meet you," she said, letting her voice go hard and cold. "I'm not feeling well. I'm picking up a prescription, and I'm going home to my mama's house for chicken soup and rest. That wasn't me on the poster," she repeated. "I'll be back at work as soon as I can."

"Oh," Heather said, sounding confused. Hopefully believing Gina's lies. "Hi. Um…is everything okay?" she asked. Her voice was odd, and seemed to be directed to someone else.

Gina slid her eyes to Cruz, who looked to her as well. The fine hairs on her arms and the back of her neck rose to attention. "Who's there? What's wrong?"

"I put the poster up," Heather said. "I hope you find your girlfriend. Is there something else I can help you with?"

The Jeep nosedived as Cruz traded the gas pedal for the brake. He checked his mirror and pulled the steering wheel in one smooth sequence of actions, executing a perfect U-turn on the empty country road. He tapped the phone app on his dashboard and instructed the device to call the Great Falls Sheriff's Department.

"Heather?" Gina pressed. "Say something to let me know you're okay. Are you still at the rescue?"

Heather's scream was brief but bloodcurdling, and followed by the heavy sound of breaths against the speaker.

"Heather?" she repeated, her voice coming small and cracked. "Heather!"

Cruz barked orders in the background against the beating wind and Gina's ringing ears.

A familiar growl lifted through the phone's speaker, refocusing her attention on the device in her hand. "Hello, Gina," Tony said, his voice cruel and self-satisfied.

Emotions welled, then overflowed in her heart and head. The barely pent-up anger unleashed without her bidding. "What did you do?" She screamed the question, body trembling. "I hate you. You know that. Just let me go! Stop following me. Stop haunting me. Stop hurting people!"

"You're angry," he said. "So am I. And you know how this goes. We fight. Then we make up. But you don't get to leave me!" The final words rattled her phone's speaker and released tears from her eyes. She imagined his beet-red face and the strings of spittle that flew from his lips when he was like this. Usually, she was within striking distance, and her muscles tensed in anticipation of the pain that wouldn't come.

In the background, Heather whimpered and pleaded to be released.

Her friend had taken her place.

"Come back here now," Tony ordered, "or I'll fight with her instead. Then she and I can make up too."

Gina's already roiling stomach heaved, and she hung her head over the space where a door should've been as the glass of water she'd consumed made a reappearance. She pushed the length of her cheap wig away from her face and panted as her pulse settled. "Don't," she said, her fire extinguished by fear. "I'm coming," she said. "You can let her go. I'm sorry."

"Good girl," Tony said. "But I'm going to hold on

to your friend until you get here. Then we'll make the exchange. And for the record, it doesn't matter if you want me or not," he said. "You have something of mine now, and I want it back."

The call disconnected and Gina sobbed, wrapping both arms around her torso and her baby.

A hand landed on her shoulder, and she screamed.

"Hey." Cruz's voice boomed in the air. "Gina." He lowered his hand between them, then made a show of opening it, fingers splayed, not fisted, before returning it to the wheel. "I didn't mean to scare you. Knox and another deputy are on their way to the shelter. Your friend won't be alone for long, and Tony will have some explaining to do. You just tell my brother everything you can about that call when we get there, and about any other time he's threatened or hurt you."

Gina bit her lip against a rush of ugly, painful memories, and wondered where she should begin. Then she sent up a silent prayer for Heather's safety and Tony's capture. Maybe he'd finally gone too far, gotten too cocky and would be taken down from his high horse in handcuffs.

Sirens cried in the distance as downtown came back into view.

Gina breathed a little easier, thankful for the perfect storm of luck and timing. The call coming when Cruz was near. Knox moving quickly into action. Heather would be shaken, but at least she would be safe, and Tony would get what was coming to him. Not even his family's money and influence could save him from a murder charge.

The streets were packed with emergency vehicles and lookie-loos as Cruz slid the Jeep into position behind an ambulance. Gina leaped down and met Cruz at the front of the vehicle.

"Doing all right?" he asked.

She nodded, scanning the cluster of men and women in uniform as they spilled in and out of the alley beside the shelter.

Cruz showed her his hand, the way he had in the Jeep, then waited for her to meet his gaze. He moved his arm slowly behind her and set his palm tentatively on her back. "Okay?" he asked, without breaking eye contact. "So you know I'm right here. No matter what's happening over there." He lifted his chin to indicate the alleyway.

She nodded. "Thank you."

Something flashed in his expression at her acceptance, there and gone, too quickly to read. She let him lead her into the mix.

Uniformed deputies nodded as they approached, apparently recognizing Cruz.

Knox hovered near a set of EMTs raising a gurney onto its wheels.

Her heart quickened at the possibility Tony had been shot. Shamefully, she didn't hate the idea if it meant he'd finally been stopped and would be held accountable for his actions when he healed.

Cruz nudged her toward the rough brick wall of the shelter, clearing a path for the EMTs and gurney. But it was Heather's slack face that appeared as they passed. An oxygen mask covered her nose and mouth. Blood-soaked bandages had been applied to her forehead.

Gina's breath caught and her teeth began to chatter as misplaced adrenaline combined with panic in her veins. This was all her fault. She shouldn't have told

Heather about Tony. If she hadn't known the truth, this wouldn't have happened. Gina had known better than to let anyone in, and she'd done it anyway.

Cruz's steadying fingertips pressed against her back. "Let's talk to Knox." He ushered her forward once more, and she craned her neck to watch the EMTs load Heather into the ambulance, eyes closed and body still.

"What happened to her?" she asked Knox, voice cracking. "Will she be okay? Where's Tony? What did he do?"

Knox shifted, keen eyes busily scanning the scene around them before landing on Gina. "She was alone and unconscious when we got here. Blunt force trauma to the head. The assailant probably heard the sirens. Her car's been vandalized, and she hasn't woken up."

Air whooshed from Gina's lungs as she followed his gaze to Heather's car, parked farther down the alley.

Three jagged words had been carved into the paint.

Come Home Gina.

Chapter Six

Cruz turned to face Gina, tipping forward and speaking low and calmly into her ear. "Let's get out of here so Knox and his team can work," he said. He attempted to block as much of the scene around them as possible, but doubted the effort did much to comfort her.

"Okay." She nodded, then raised her hand to clutch on to his elbow.

The warmth of her acceptance tugged at his chest, and he covered her fingers with his.

Together, they moved away, her gaze on the ground, and his seeking Tony Marino in the crowd. He didn't see him there today, but Cruz wouldn't stop searching until he was found.

Back in the Jeep, Cruz took the most roundabout route home he could manage, making sure no one had followed him from town. For the first time since purchasing the Jeep, he wished he'd kept the top and doors on. Suddenly, the full exposure that normally felt so freeing seemed incredibly reckless, and he longed to get Gina indoors and out of sight.

He caught glimpses of her as they rode silently toward his home. She didn't ask about the route, despite the fact that it was completely different than the way they'd gone before. She must've noticed. Little else seemed to escape her. He couldn't help wondering why she didn't question him. In fact, the longer her silence stretched, the more questions he had.

They took the final turn onto his long gravel driveway at a crawl.

"My house is at the back of the property," he said. "It's visible after we round the bend."

She turned a strained expression his way. "You live in the woods?"

"I live beyond the grove of trees," he corrected with a smile. "They're nice for privacy."

Gina didn't smile back. Probably second-guessing her decision to go home with a stranger.

He could hardly blame her, and after what they'd seen in the alley, he wouldn't be surprised if she locked herself in a room once they were inside. Just in case.

He refreshed his smile. "I take it you lived in the city before? Not a country girl?" Suddenly, he wished he'd paid closer attention to the missing person posters and news briefings when she'd first gone underground. He didn't know the first thing about who she was before her life went south, and if he didn't know her, how was he supposed to make her feel comfortable?

"Yes," she said quietly. "I grew up in an older neighborhood near downtown. Lots of houses and people. Always plenty of kids to play with when I was young and hang out with when I got older." Her lips twitched, almost managing a smile. "My family practically absorbs other families. They pull folks into their orbit and keep them there, an ever-expanding family of loved ones. The More The Merrier is practically our family motto."

Cruz snorted. "Sounds like our families would get along. Maybe they could join ranks and take over Kentucky."

She smiled, but didn't respond.

Cruz supposed he must seem like the lesser of two evils to her at the moment. He just needed to convince her to stick with that line of thinking, rather than get the idea to trade him off for the devil she knew. Something told him that if Tony persisted, she'd eventually return to him just to stop him from hurting anyone else. He could only hope the need to protect her baby would erase that notion from her head, if it ever tried taking root.

He parked the Jeep in front of his home, a small, two-bedroom cottage on three acres, complete with a pond and room for expansion.

"This is your house?" Gina asked.

He turned his eyes to the home's exterior and tried to imagine what she saw there.

Weathered gray shakes. Black roof, door and shutters. White trim. Black mulch, lots of flowers, thanks to his aunt, the family's unofficial gardener, and a red rocker on the front porch beside a garden gnome with a hand-painted sign announcing, Welcome Gnome. Courtesy of his neighbor's daughter, who'd thought the little guy was hilarious and brought him to Cruz's place last month. He'd hung the tire swing in his oak tree for his cousins' kids last year, though they were all a little young for it just yet. The place seemed like a normal house to him. "Yeah. Why?"

Gina's smile slowly appeared. Her gaze slid over the porch, flagstone walkway and bushes. "Nothing. It's nice."

He narrowed his eyes. "What's that mean?"

She shrugged, her lips fighting another grin. "It's just that you're..." She waved a hand in front of him. "You know."

"Ruggedly handsome," he said, filling in her blank. "Go on."

She rolled her eyes, but her smile widened. "Plus the Jeep. The PI business. The law enforcement family."

He beamed. "So you do think I'm handsome."

She shook her head. "There's clearly nothing wrong with your self-esteem."

"True," he agreed. "What's that have to do with my house?"

She tipped her head over one shoulder and frowned. "I guess I expected a log cabin or some rustic, manly abode."

"My house is manly."

Her smile widened, but she didn't argue. "Your house looks like a fairytale cottage."

His frown deepened. "No, it doesn't."

She laughed, and his heart gave a sturdy kick. "It's lovely. Just not what I expected."

Cruz climbed the steps and unlocked the door, supposing he might've gone the extra mile in making his house feel like a home, but what was wrong with that? His mama had been too busy making ends meet to bother with the appearance of their home, and he'd intentionally put in the extra effort when it was his turn. "Let me show you around."

Much like her apartment, the bulk of his space was visible from the door. An open-concept living room bled into a nook with small dinette. An island separated the kitchen and living space. A hall led to the bedrooms and bath.

"The house needed to be thoroughly gutted when I bought it," he said. "The price was right, regardless, and I was more interested in the land than the structure. I'd originally decided to renovate a little, just enough so I could live on the property while I built something else. But I got attached." He stole a look at Gina to gauge her response.

She scanned the space around them, seeming to take it all in. Her eyes swept to meet his when he didn't go on.

Cruz ignored the thrumming of his heart, and kept talking. "There were notches on doorjambs, marking a child's growth, and hearts with initials circa the early 1900s, carved into the wooden studs when I replaced the damaged drywall." The restoration work had given him respite when he'd first returned from the military, a place to clear his mind and busy his hands. He'd needed both badly. "I couldn't leave it unfinished, and once it was all redone, I liked it too much to build anything else." As an added bonus, there was enough work to do on the grounds to provide a solid excuse for dodging family invitations anytime he preferred a quiet night alone.

He took her on the two-cent tour, watching her expressions closely and attempting to monitor her comfort level. He wanted to ask her what she thought of his home, and reassure her she was safe there, but he also didn't want to push.

Finally, they stopped outside his spare bedroom door. "You'll be my first guest to stay in here." He waved an arm, encouraging her to go inside. "Make yourself at home. I'll grab your things from the Jeep."

He dawdled outside, allowing her the space and time to get comfortable in his home. He returned several minutes later with everything she owned.

She looked up when he stopped in the doorway to her room. "When you said you've never had an overnight guest in here, you meant in this room specifically?" she asked. Her cheeks pinked, and Cruz smiled at the apparent direction of her thoughts. Gina had been thinking about his overnight guests.

A handful of nice women with excellent taste in men flashed through his mind, and he smiled unintentionally. No, his overnight guests typically didn't stay in the guest room.

Gina sat abruptly on the bed. "I hope my presence won't cramp your style," she teased.

"Not at all." He leaned against the doorjamb and crossed his legs at the ankles. "When my dates get here, we typically go straight to my room, so you can have the rest of the house to yourself."

Her mouth opened and eyes widened. She finally cracked a smile when she noticed his. "You're terrible."

"At least now I know what you think of me," he said. "I plan to prove you wrong, by the way. Now, do you want to lie down for a while, or are you hungry? 'Cause I've got a steak in the fridge that's calling my name."

Gina raised a hand to her platinum hair, then peeled off a wig, using her fingers to let down and comb the dark wavy locks hidden beneath.

Cruz did his best not to moan. Brunettes were his downfall, and Gina had the whole package, from the dark chestnut eyes and olive skin to the curves his dreams were made of.

“Care if I take a shower?” she asked.

His lips parted and he had to work them shut. “No.” He tipped his head to the hallway, then led her to the bathroom. “Towels and washcloths are in here,” he said, opening a built-in cabinet. “Shampoos and soaps are on the edge of the tub. If you need anything else, just holler.”

“Thanks. I brought everything I own,” she said with a sigh and a laugh.

Cruz offered a small smile in return. “I’ll call Knox and try to get an update on your friend while you shower,” he promised.

“Thank you,” she said. “For everything.”

Cruz dipped his chin in answer, his chest tightening as he looked into her eyes. “You’re done running,” he promised. “I’m going to see to that.”

He’d never meant anything more in his life.

Chapter Seven

Cruz gave up on sleep when the first shafts of sunlight climbed his windowpane and the nearest neighbor's rooster crowed in the distance. Cruz had only been under the covers about three hours, and sleep had come in fits and bursts. He'd stayed up researching Tony Marino and his family, then fallen into bed exhausted, only to remember Gina was across the hall.

The fatigue hadn't lasted.

Instead, his thoughts had wandered into the gutter and stayed there, despite his best efforts to be a mental gentleman. In hindsight, all possibilities of sleep had probably gone straight out the window the moment he'd heard his shower kick on shortly after her arrival. He'd known she was naked then, and it had taken a shot of whiskey and stern internal scolding to push the parade of unbidden images from his mind. The efforts had been mostly successful, at least until he'd gotten into bed.

Having Gina in his house made things a lot harder than he'd expected.

He'd initially pulled himself together by going outside to make dinner on the grill, but she'd padded barefoot onto the deck, her long dark hair hanging in damp waves against her shoulders. Her skin had been pink from the heat and steam of the water, then pebbled when the wind blew.

He groaned and scrubbed a hand over his eyes at the memory, trying to unsee the image that had returned to him a dozen times throughout the night. Her cotton sleep shorts rode low on her hips, exposing a tiny ribbon of flesh above them. The T-shirt had clung to her tantalizing curves.

"Nope," he announced to the empty room, pushing onto his feet. "Uh-uh."

Gina needed a protector, and Cruz was determined to be that man for her. To make her feel safe, and to keep her that way as well. Which meant he had to stay focused.

He considered pumping up the AC, then offering her one of his parkas, but hiding her figure wouldn't stop the attraction. If only he was that lucky. Somehow, in the short time since they'd met, he'd become oddly attached to the woman who was short on height and big on everything that mattered, like honor, courage and heart. He admired her bravery and her tenacity, and marveled at the way she'd left everything she loved behind in an effort to protect her baby. She'd given up her home, her family, her support network and her access to money. She'd left with only what she could carry. And she'd survived. On her own and on the run.

Cruz had enjoyed listening to her talk about her parents and sister over dinner. And the way she'd curled onto the couch with him afterward, when he'd grabbed his laptop to do some research on the Marinos. She could've chosen to sit in his recliner or taken a seat closer to the fireplace, but she'd sat beside him, her legs tucked beneath her and the scent of her vanilla body lotion driving him utterly insane. He hadn't been sure if she'd simply craved the company after so many days spent alone, or the security of being near someone who could physically protect her in case Tony showed up unexpectedly. Cruz wanted to think she might be attracted to him the way he was to her, but being pregnant and on the run from a murderous ex was probably all she could think about.

He forced his sluggish limbs to carry him to the shower, then into the kitchen for coffee.

His phone rang as he started a pot of coffee and considered making breakfast. Staying busy helped him think, and making breakfast seemed the most hospitable act he could manage at the awful hour. He raised the phone to his ear. "Winchester."

"Hey," his partner and cousin, Derek, replied. "How's your client?"

"Sleeping," Cruz said, resting his backside against the counter and focusing on whatever news Derek might have to offer. "Learn anything new?"

"Not much," Derek said, sounding almost as tired as Cruz felt. "I'm digging into social media this morning. I spent yesterday flashing a photo of Tony around town, and I plan to get back out there after breakfast."

Cruz smiled. Derek was the king of repetitive, frustrating tasks. He'd keep up the campaign until he had the information they needed, or spoke to every human in Great Falls. "Anyone recognize him?"

"Everyone recognized him," Derek said, breaking the first word into syllables. "Tony was not shy with those flyers, and the locals all bought his story. He's got the whole shopping district on the lookout for her, and missing person posters in half the shop windows.

I had to set at least a hundred people straight. I turned it around and told them Tony's the person of interest. I handed out my business card and directed anyone who saw him again to call me or the sheriff's department immediately. I told them not to confront him because he's believed to be dangerous."

Cruz's smile grew. "Smart. Have you heard anything about the receptionist's condition?" he asked.

"No. I've got a nurse contact at the hospital who's going to text me if Heather wakes or has any visitors."

"Good." Cruz nodded. "I looked into Tony's family last night. Gina said they were connected and influential, and she wasn't kidding. Tony's dad owns a chain of outdoor sportsman shops that are spreading across the Midwest. Apparently the Marinos aren't just rich. They're big-game hunters, trackers and gun enthusiasts, doing regular business with shooting galleries and archery ranges."

Derek made a disapproving noise. "So our guy's likely been raised on a steady diet of testosterone and marksmanship."

"That's what I'm thinking," Cruz said. Not exactly the skill set he preferred in an opponent, and the worst possible for Gina's stalker.

"Thankfully, he's not the only one," Derek said.

Cruz's smile returned. The Winchester men had all been raised by a former lawman, trained by the U.S. military and were completely lethal, though none resorted to any force greater than was absolutely necessary for attaining their goals. Cruz's dad had been aggressive for other reasons, and often without reason, but thankfully, he hadn't stuck around long. His uncle, Derek, Blaze and Lucas's dad, had stepped in to fill the vacant role. Now Cruz and Derek regularly tracked and occasionally apprehended criminals. Their brothers and cousins made arrests. The laws of the state of Kentucky determined the punishments.

"Did you find any previous arrests on file?" Derek asked. "What kind of a record does Tony have?"

Tension gripped Cruz's shoulders, and he pinched the bridge of his nose. "That's another point of concern. There were four previous allegations of domestic violence and stalking against him, but none of them amounted to anything. The first case occurred during his senior year of high school. He was eighteen and the girl was sixteen. Her name was redacted, and the charges were quickly dropped. Three more cases were opened during his stint at a local college. Same results."

"Always makes me wonder how many more victims there were," Derek said. "How many didn't tell?"

Cruz grunted. He'd thought the same thing. Only a small percentage of abused women ever came forward. Probably because the offenders too often got away. And Tony Marino was one of them. "I hate these guys." He poured a cup of coffee from the finished pot and let his thoughts run over the details he'd gained through Tony's file. "He's got a lengthy list of smaller infringements, from traffic violations for excessive speed and running red lights to illegal gambling and shoplifting."

"The richest ones always think they're above the law," Derek said, the sound of a car engine humming to life on his side of the line. "Why is that?"

Cruz smiled. "Don't know. I've never been rich." He opened the fridge, pulled out a carton of eggs and a pile of veggies. "I suppose it's entitlement, or maybe this guy's just a run-of-the-mill sociopath."

What kind of person murdered an old man one night, then waltzed around town the next day intentionally interacting with everyone? All so he could locate his next victim. Cruz cringed as the thought presented itself. Gina would not be Tony's next victim. Not on Cruz's watch.

His second line beeped, and he took a look at the cell phone's screen, checking the caller ID. "Hey, Knox is trying to reach me."

"Take the call. I'll see what I can dig up in town today," Derek said.

The cousins disconnected, and Cruz took his brother's call. "Hey. What do you have?" he asked, skipping the customary greeting.

"I'm not sure," Knox said, sounding mildly optimistic. "Maybe nothing."

"Can you be a little less vague?" Cruz asked, taking another long sip of coffee.

"I've got a drunk guy leaving a bar, about a block from Gina's apartment building, around the time of Larkin's death. He parked in the alley behind the building to avoid paying for valet. I guess the bar's lot was full. Anyway, he claims to have seen a man fitting Tony's general physical description leaving the apartment building. He remembers because the man was wearing gloves and wiping his hands on a cloth. He didn't think that made sense."

"That's great," Cruz said, standing taller and feeling distinctly hopeful for the first time since taking the case. "Bring Tony in. Get him in a lineup. See if this guy can identify him."

Knox snorted, probably thinking he knew how to do his job without Cruz's help, but Cruz didn't care.

Knox needed to move on this. Gina's happiness depended on it. "That's where the problem comes in," Knox said. "This guy laughed through half his statement. He thought he'd imagined it all, and was shocked that I wrote the story down. Especially since he was, and I quote, 'superwasted.' Not my strongest witness, and I don't want to alert Tony and his legal team to start building alibis and a defense case until we've got something more substantial."

Cruz locked his jaw, then cracked a row of eggs into a mixing bowl and beat them until he felt a little better.

"For now," Knox said, "we're collecting facts and leads. There's no way to know what will be important later."

Cruz chopped a trio of mushrooms and a wedge of yellow onion. "Derek's headed back downtown to talk with folks who have Gina's missing person flyer in their shop windows. He's trying to track Tony's movement from the last couple of days." If Cruz was lucky, Derek might even run into Tony. In that case, the jerk would be under arrest by lunchtime.

"Sounds good," Knox agreed. "I'll give Derek a call. I don't want him confronting this guy. Tailing him and letting me know where I can find him is enough."

"Have you had a chance to take a look at Tony's record?" Cruz asked. "The other accusations. The dropped charges."

Knox sighed, long and dramatic. "Sometimes, I think you have the idea I got my badge from one of those claw machines."

"Or a Cracker Jack box," he joked, tossing a bit of pepper into his mouth.

"Of course I looked at his record," Knox said. "I've

got contact information on each of his former accusers, and I plan to reach out to them today. I'm shooting for face-to-face encounters, so I can get a read on their eye contact and body language, but one of the women left the state about three weeks after she dropped her charges. I'm going to have to settle for whatever I can get from that one."

"That sounds good." Cruz nodded. Anything they could use to build a case against Tony would be helpful. He added the chopped veggies to the eggs, then poured them into a heated pan. "Keep me posted on your findings. In real time, please."

"You got it," Knox said, agreeing in his usual easy way. He'd always been great about keeping the lines of communication open, something Cruz had been thankful for on more than one occasion.

The thought tightened something brotherly and protective in his chest. "Knox?"

"Yeah?"

"Be careful."

Chapter Eight

The low murmur of a male voice startled Gina awake. Her muscles tensed, and her breaths halted as she opened her eyes to unfamiliar surroundings. It took a moment, and the slow, easy laugh of Cruz Winchester, to bring her up to speed. She wasn't alone in her dinky, lonely apartment, a chair wedged under the doorknob for added protection. She was in the guest room of the sexiest private investigator in Kentucky. Possibly on Earth.

She stretched beneath the butter-soft sheet and inhaled the faint lavender scent of the pillowcase. Then took a long moment to appreciate her complete situation. The past twenty-four hours had been the scariest of her life. A kind man had died and Heather had been hospitalized, both because of Gina, yet she'd stumbled into Cruz Winchester's life. And he'd kept her safe.

He'd gained her full attention at hello, then he'd taken her under his wing of protection and given her the use of his guest room.

Not to be outdone by the overall adorable appearance of the cottage, her new room was something ripped straight from the pages of a magazine. The curved metal bed frame was dark, as were the wide polished floorboards, but the bedding, curtains and rug were all creamy white. Pale blue designs on an abundance of decorative throw pillows coordinated perfectly with the robin's-egg-blue paint on the walls.

The fluffy down comforter had felt like heaven as she'd pulled it up to her chin the night before, trying hard not to think of her handsome host any more than absolutely necessary. Her emotions were obviously heightened, and her hormones were definitely out of whack. She couldn't afford to get confused about what was happening between her and her protector. She was in danger, and he was doing a job, nothing more. Those deeply interested looks he gave her from time to time, the ones that stole her breath and curled her toes, were probably just him wondering why she was staring at his abs, forearms or lips. A bad habit she'd formed immediately upon meeting him, and one she wasn't sure she could break.

The scents and sounds of breakfast crept under her door, and she climbed eagerly out of bed. If breakfast was half as good as dinner had been, she never wanted to leave this place.

Gina darted into the bathroom to brush her teeth and hair, then hurried down the hall toward the kitchen.

Cruz stood at the stove in pajama pants and bare feet. Shirtless and glorious, brows furrowed as he reached for the phone on his shoulder. "Be careful," he said before disconnecting and setting the device on the counter.

His gaze jerked to her, as if sensing her arrival, and his lips quirked in a cocky half smile. "Good morning. Sleep well?"

"Morning," she said, more shyly than she'd intended. "I did. Thanks. You?"

He gave a soft laugh, then turned back to the skillet before him. "Not even close," he said, giving his head a little shake. "I hope you're hungry and like omelets. I used some chopped veggies and a handful of cheese. If eggs aren't your thing, I also have fruit and yogurt. Steel-cut oats and granola."

"I like eggs," she said, sliding onto a tall stool at the island behind him. "You certainly eat healthy for a bachelor. I thought single men lived on cold pizza and chicken wings."

He grimaced over his shoulder at her. "Not if I can help it."

Gina stared at the T-shirt lying before her on the granite countertop. A puddle of soft gray fabric she was certain would smell like him if she lifted it to her nose.

Cruz returned his attention to the stove, extinguishing the flame beneath the pan and removing it from the heat. The muscles of his back and shoulders flexed visibly with each twist and lift of his arms.

Gina rested her chin in her palms, enjoying the surge of interest and adrenaline. She normally required two cups of coffee to feel so alert.

"I played ball for a while," he said, picking up the conversation she'd nearly forgotten. "Nutrition was a big part of the required fitness for me."

"What kind of ball?" she asked, suddenly visualizing the body before her as that of an athlete. "Were you any good?"

Cruz turned with two plates of eggs and set them on the island between them. "Baseball, and yes. I was very good."

Her cheeks heated. "I'll bet."

He handed her a fork and napkin, then delivered

two glasses with water. "Can I pour you some coffee to go with that?"

"No." She grinned. "I'm good."

"I'll bet," he said, echoing her words, and punctuating them with a wink.

Gina drained half her glass of water before digging into her meal.

Cruz stood across from her while they ate, and she was both thankful and disappointed by the barrier between them.

"Tell me about baseball," she said, genuinely interested in who Cruz had been before he became a private investigator, and trying to imagine the man before her as a high school jock.

His smile grew. "I could hit a home run before I could spell the words," he said, reverence and nostalgia in his tone. "By high school, I was being recruited by a dozen scouts, college and minor league. I had offers for everything from free rides at universities across the country to opportunities other kids in Great Falls, Kentucky, haven't even dreamed of. I thought baseball was my calling. The thing I was destined to do, and something that would change my family's world."

"What happened?" she asked. Obviously, he hadn't become a professional athlete, but why? "An injury?" she guessed.

The wistfulness of Cruz's expression thinned until it looked more painful than positive. "My mom was diagnosed with advanced ovarian cancer. My dad wasn't in the picture, so it was up to Knox and I to keep the lights on when she had to stop working."

"So you gave up the thing you loved most," she said,

feeling the tug of his loss in her chest, along with a swell of misplaced pride. "For her."

Cruz pulled his distant gaze back to Gina, fixing her with those soft green eyes. "There's nothing I wouldn't walk away from for family. It wasn't even a choice to be made."

Her hand crossed the island on instinct, covering his before curling her fingers beneath his palm.

He held her gaze, curiosity and something else playing in his soulful eyes. Slowly, he dropped his attention to their joined hands.

Gina released him immediately, understanding she'd crossed a line. "Sorry."

His arm snaked forward to catch her before she could set her hand onto her lap. Long, gentle fingers circled her wrist and gently pulled her hand back to him.

Her eyes widened, and her breath released in a startled pant. She could've broken free with the lightest of tugs, but she didn't want him to let her go.

When his piercing gaze met hers once more, he wet his lips, then set his big, calloused palm on hers, releasing his hold and allowing her to make the next move.

She parted her fingers, sliding them between his. "Do you ever regret leaving baseball?" she asked, desperate to keep him there and talking. She wanted to know more. Anything and everything about him. And she didn't want the strange, charged moment to end.

"No." His voice was thick but confident. "If I'd chosen baseball over Mama, I would've been on the field instead of at her side when she passed, and that is something I could not live with. I don't let people down," he promised.

Gina's eyes stung as the news of his loss reached across the island to her heart. "I'm sorry about your mama."

His phone rang, and they jumped guiltily apart. His eyes were wild, and his expression stunned.

She imagined she looked the same.

Cruz glanced briefly at the phone, then adjusted the waistband of his pajama pants before tugging the T-shirt over his head. "Hello, Auntie," he said, lifting the device to his ear.

Gina finished her water, willing her heated chest and cheeks to cool.

He spoke kindly but quickly, then ended the call a few short moments later and returned to his breakfast. "That was Derek's mama. She's a second mother to Knox and me. She's also a busybody of epic proportions, and she heard I have a woman staying with me. So she wanted to see if she could bring you something."

"Like what?" Gina asked, warmed by the stranger's offer and by the loving way Cruz spoke about his aunt.

He laughed. "Anything you'd like, as long as she can get a look at you. She wants to be sure you're comfortable, happy and doing as well as humanly possible, given your situation."

"I am," Gina said. Her stomach soured, and she pushed her plate away. It was too easy to get lost in the bubble that was Cruz Winchester. Too easy for her to drop her guard. She cleared her throat and straightened her spine. "I don't need anything else, but I'd like to help with your search for Tony however I can. Maybe you can fill me in on what you know so far. I heard you on the phone when I woke."

Cruz patted the counter and nodded. The same curious look returned to his eyes, but he didn't ask her any questions. Instead, he picked up his fork and finished his probably cold breakfast while filling her in on everything she'd missed while she slept.

Gina listened carefully, determined to help. "I used to keep tabs on him through social media," she said. "The only thing he loves as much as himself is a spotlight." The posts and pictures on his account had given Gina a heads-up on what kind of mood to expect him in most nights. His unpredictable temper had made her thankful for the information on more than one occasion. "I haven't dared log into my accounts since I left home, just in case he has someone watching them. I bought a burner phone and only use the internet at libraries on public terminals." She shook her head and sighed. "I'm sure he can't go long without being the center of attention. Tracking his movements on Instagram would be a good start. Maybe take a look at his parents' Facebook page."

Cruz frowned, an unnatural expression on his typically jovial face. "You can use my laptop whenever you want. I leave it on the coffee table, or my desk if it's charging. I'm always logged in, so you can use my social media accounts to snoop and no one will track you. This is a private network."

She blinked. "Thanks."

Cruz carried their plates and glasses to the sink. "Do you think Tony could be tracking your family online?" he asked.

She considered the answer a moment. "I don't know," Gina admitted. "I'm not sure what he's capable of, which is why I haven't tried to reach out to them. Why?"

"Because I'd like to talk to your family," he said. "I think Tony knows you're close to your family, so he likely went to them first, hoping to find a lead on your whereabouts. Something he said to them might be helpful to us now. Also," he added, a bit more cautiously, "I'd like to give them an update on you."

"You want to talk to my family?" she asked, a thrill whipping across her skin. She'd give just about anything to see them again, or even to hear their voices. To trade text messages. She hadn't even allowed herself to do that, just in case Tony was somehow monitoring their communication. It was unlikely, and she was admittedly paranoid, but she had everything riding on staying away from him. Her baby depended on it. And she had no doubt that Tony's family could find someone willing to bend to their wishes in exchange for enough cash, no matter where she turned for help.

Except, maybe, the Winchesters.

"Your folks should know that you're okay," Cruz said. "Whatever amount of peace that gives them is worth the risk, and I'll make sure it's a very limited risk. If one of my family members was missing, we'd all be consumed with fears of the worst."

She hated that he was right. Her family was probably beside themselves. "My little sister, Kayla, started school at Bellemont University in West Liberty last fall," she said. "She lives on campus. It's a busy place, and it would make sense for my folks to meet her there from time to time. Maybe we can plan to be there the next time they are," she suggested.

Emotion flooded to the surface as she imagined seeing her family again, of holding them and telling them how much she loved them.

"Let me talk to my cousin Lucas," Cruz said. "He's a detective in West Liberty and a graduate of Bellemont.

He might have an idea about where to meet and when. We can send a message to Kayla through him. I'll get dressed and stop by the police station. You can make yourself at home while I'm gone. The security here is better than Camp David. You don't need to worry."

"I won't," Gina said. "Because I'm coming with you."

Chapter Nine

Cruz strode back down the hall toward the living room just after lunch. Lucas had made a morning trip to the Bellemont University campus, something he apparently did on a semiregular basis, and he'd passed a message on to Gina's sister while he was there. The school was within Lucas's jurisdiction, and as a special victims detective, he stayed in contact with campus police. Cruz hadn't given much thought to Lucas's routines before, but he supposed it made perfect sense. Lucas had a deeply personal connection with assault survivors. His wife had been a victim while they'd lived on the Bellemont campus together years ago, before they were married, and her attack was the reason he'd gone into law enforcement. Lucas knew firsthand what attackers took from their victims and their loved ones.

Cruz couldn't imagine working exclusively with those kinds of criminals, but his cousin did it well. "You about ready?" he called to Gina, checking his watch as he arrived in the large open space.

Gina stood near the glass doors in the kitchen, gazing onto the deck, arms wrapped protectively around her middle. This was her most common stance, and it tugged harder at his heart every time he saw it. She probably had no idea she was doing it, or just how often she stood that way, but Cruz had begun to notice everything about her. Knowing she cradled her unborn child as much from fear of a looming monster as from instinctual, maternal love made Cruz tense and anxious. Emotions he'd strictly avoided for years.

She turned to him with a muddled expression of hope and sorrow. "I can't believe I get to see my sister. Are you sure it's really safe?"

Cruz extended an arm in her direction, thankful he could do this for her. "Yeah. I'd hoped to arrange for your folks to be there too, but Lucas thought it was too risky right now. He asked her to hold off on telling your parents for a day or two. If Tony's watching her or them somehow, we don't want to tip our hand. Hopefully you'll see them again soon."

She wiped a tear off her cheek and gave a shaky laugh. "Sorry. Tears of joy, I promise. And I know Kayla will understand. My folks will too, when they eventually find out what's going on."

Cruz smiled, lifted as always by her contagious laugh and beautiful smile. "Don't thank me yet," he said, forcing his cover-up, cocky grin into place. He knew the mask of overt confidence put others at ease. "You're going to need a disguise."

Gina stilled. "Should I grab my wig?"

He pulled a baseball cap from his back pocket and gave it a shake. "I'm not a fan of the wig, and people have seen you in it. Any chance you can get all your hair into this without looking like the gnome my neighbor's kid left on my front porch?"

She laughed. "You have no idea. This is one of my secret skills."

"Wearing a hat?" he asked, smiling sincerely back. "I know infants who can do that."

"You know a lot of infants?" she asked, digging through a handbag she'd dropped near her shoes in the entryway.

"My family is experiencing a baby boom of sorts," he said. "So, yeah. Soon there will be more Winchesters under two than over thirty."

She laughed, then returned the bag to the floor and headed for the hallway. "We haven't had a baby in my family for a decade. Mine will be a total guinea pig for me. I feel a little bad for him or her already."

"I'm sure you'll be great," Cruz said. An image of Gina with a newborn bloomed in his mind, and fresh pressure built in his chest. He shook it off and rolled his shoulders back. He really needed to get a grip, and get his head in the game. Today was a big day, and despite his cousin's assurances about the outing, Cruz was nervous. Potentially putting himself in harm's way wasn't an issue, but unintentionally leading Gina into danger was something he wouldn't soon get over. "How do you feel about wearing one of my jackets?" he asked, projecting his voice in her direction. She could easily blend with the college crowd if she'd stop hugging her middle. Maybe holding her hand would help with that.

"Only if you plan to pin me," she said, returning with a smile. She'd twisted her hair into a tiny knot on top of her head and paused to strike a silly pose.

"How'd you do that?" he asked, genuinely curious as she moved closer. Gina had somehow reduced a mile of thick dark hair into something smaller than his fist and secured it into place.

"About fifteen years of ballet lessons," she said. "I'm the master of the tight bun."

He laughed, brows rising, and her cheeks went red. "Nice."

She laughed again. "Where's the jacket?"

He turned toward the row of hooks on the entryway wall. "Denim or leather?"

She moved to his side and examined her options. Then, she stroked a palm down the sleeve of his favorite brown bomber. "Definitely leather."

Cruz pressed a hand to his chest as she threaded her short arms into his long sleeves. She knew she was killing him, right?

She grinned up at him. "How do I look?"

He groaned and shook his head. She looked like she should be straddling his motorcycle, whipping off that hat and letting her long dark hair fly wild and loose behind her while she wrapped those arms around his waist. "Like you're ready to go," he said, forcing the image out of his head, and telling himself he couldn't actually feel the heat of her hips cradled against his backside, or the weight of her breasts against him, not even her warm breath on his neck.

Yep. She was definitely killing him. Cruz led the way to his Jeep and opened the door for her.

She stopped to look at his freshly reassembled ride. "When did you have time to do this?"

"I took care of it last night," he said, pressing the door shut behind her when she climbed in. There had been no way he was taking her anywhere again without every precaution in place. That included his Jeep's doors and roof. As an added bonus, his windows had a healthy tint to obscure views of her as they drove. He wished he could somehow transport her across campus unseen. His extralarge equipment bag could probably hold her, but he doubted she'd agree to be toted around like a sack of bats and balls. Instead of making the suggestion, he reminded himself that she'd already proved she was tougher than she looked. Whatever happened, she could and would handle it as it came, just as he would. And he'd never been so senselessly proud of someone he had no claim to in his life.

Chapter Ten

Gina held her breath in anticipation as Cruz navigated the pleasant tree-lined roads of Bellemont's beautiful campus. She'd been here once before, when Kayla had come on an official tour as a prospective student. Their dad had been obsessed with security. Their mother fussed over the dining options, and Kayla had been mostly interested in scoping out the student body. Specifically, the guys' bodies. She'd even requested a tour of the gym and pool for this purpose, exactly like the hormone-driven wild card she was. Kayla was everything a little sister should be, carefree, fun loving and generally adored. Gina had always been the dull, quiet, mildly insecure older sister, which, coupled with her comparatively shy nature, had made her the perfect target for Tony's charms and manipulation. If only she had seen that sooner.

"I think this is it," Cruz said, sliding his Jeep into a parking space outside her sister's hall.

She powered her window down by a sliver, enough to let the autumn air seep in without revealing herself to onlookers. Smiling students gathered in groups and clusters on the lawns and walkways between the Jeep and building. Muffled music from portable speakers played beyond the glass. The scene seemed surreal, a view of another world, where Gina's nightmare hadn't yet reached.

"Ready?" Cruz asked.

Gina bit her lip. The thrill of hugging her sister again had been replaced with fear for Kayla's safety on the drive to campus. What if she and Cruz accidentally led Tony to her doorstep? She scanned the smattering of faces in search of him. "What if Tony hired a private investigator like I did?" she asked quietly. "I keep looking for him, but he might have someone else watching Kayla's dorm on his behalf. He has the money, the brains and the motivation. Plus, he can't be everywhere at once."

"I know every PI in the area worth his or her salt," Cruz said. "If one of them sees me with you, they'll call to ask what I was doing here before they report back to him. Professional courtesy." He slid her a confident smile. "Plus, none of us got into this line of work to wind up on the side of the bad guy."

"Okay, well, what if he hired a friend?" she asked, scanning the unfamiliar faces more closely. "Or paid a student? He told me once that everyone has a price, and the lower the price, the more loyal the ally. College kids are broke, right?"

Cruz's door opened and shut. When she turned back in his direction, he was gone.

A knock on her window caused her to gasp.

Cruz leveled her with a pointed look through the tinted glass. "I wouldn't have brought you here if I didn't believe you and your sister would be safe. Trust me."

A silent war erupted inside her. She believed Cruz

was good, honorable and true. She believed he could and would protect her, whatever the personal cost. It seemed to be the very definition of who he was. But the last man she'd trusted…

She growled internally, then jerked open the door, forcing the thought away. Tony was an exception. He was not the rule, and she wouldn't allow him to cause her to fear all men or to believe that he somehow represented the norm. He was a cruel and awful human who would never again control her or her choices.

Cruz jumped clear of the swinging door. "Well, all right." He smiled. "Love the enthusiasm."

She laughed, feeling lighter as one more link in Tony's chains fell away from her.

Cruz offered his hand. "It's probably best if we walk around like two kids in love instead of a private eye protecting a woman on the run. You know. Just in case."

Gina easily accepted the offer. "I thought there wasn't anything to worry about? No prying eyes, remember?"

Cruz used their joined hands to drag her close, then he released her in favor of sliding his long arm across her back and tucking her against his side. "It's basic due diligence. An extra service I provide at no charge." He turned his face toward hers, and she angled her head back for a better look at him. He was handsome in a way she was never prepared for, and looking up at him from this angle, pressed against his lean, muscled side, engulfed by his warm, spicy scent, she felt her toes curl inside her sneakers.

"Good," she said, forcing a casual smile, "because you're working on a commission basis until Tony's caught. I can't access my bank accounts to pay you before then."

He grinned. "All the more reason to keep you close and safe. If anything bad happens, I won't get paid." His eyes flashed with mischief as he flexed his fingers against her side. "Cuddle up. We're in love."

She smiled as they began to move toward the dormitory's set of double doors. "You realize we can't get in without a key card, right?"

"Untrue." He turned her back against the exposed brick near one door, then stepped smoothly into her personal space, curving his tall body over hers, until she felt as if they were the only people around. "Is this okay?" he whispered. "If I'm too close, nudge me back."

She rolled her head against the brick. "No. This is fine." She had no idea what he was doing or why, but she wasn't about to object. Her senses were on fire, and the heat in his eyes was slowly melting her bones.

He searched her face for several long beats, as if he might say something of dire importance.

Gina focused on breathing normally and remaining upright, while her body begged her to pant and collapse.

Cruz's gaze relented suddenly, flicking over her head for the barest of seconds before returning to her. "Here we go," he whispered, a look of deep satisfaction lifting his perfect lips.

The glass door opened beside them, and a pair of guys in hoodies and sweat pants darted out.

Cruz snaked a long arm out to catch the door before it closed, then he straightened with a proud smile. "Ladies first."

Gina released a slow, ragged breath, and a small laugh followed. "You're suspiciously adept at that," she said.

"Not my first rodeo." He winked, then looped his arm around her once more. "Lucas said she'd be in the laundry area. We need a key card to access the elevator or stairwells. That would've taken forever."

Gina spotted a sign directing them to the laundry center, then tugged him in that direction, trying not to think too hard or long about how easy it had been to get into the building. "Not how you wanted to spend the rest of the day?"

Cruz slid a peculiar look in her direction, then barked a rugged laugh.

The distinct and familiar squeal of her sister brought Gina's teasing to an end. Her eyes snapped up to see Kayla running at them, arms out and tears falling. She barreled into Gina, and nearly knocked her over. "I can't believe you're really here."

Cruz tightened his hold on Gina, bracing her against the impact. He cleared his throat when Kayla didn't let go. "We should take this reunion somewhere more private," he suggested quietly.

Kayla pulled back. Her gaze rose over Gina's head and her eyes widened. Her mouth opened.

"Kayla, this is Cruz Winchester, the private investigator who's looking after me."

"Shut. Up." Her little sister released her in favor of extending a hand to Cruz. "Was the cop I talked to your brother?" she asked. "You kind of look alike."

"Cousin," Cruz answered, shaking her hand. "I trust he was nice."

Kayla gave a guttural, appreciative chuckle. "Oh, he was very nice." She turned back to Gina. "Have you seen the cousin?"

"Not that one," Gina said. But she had seen Derek

and Knox. There was little doubt as to what her sister thought of Lucas, given that he looked like Cruz, even vaguely.

"Ladies," Cruz pressed, tipping his chin to a group of students crisscrossing the area.

Kayla led them to the suite she shared with five other students on the third floor. The roommate who shared her bedroom was thankfully in class. The others were nowhere to be seen. "Sit down and tell me everything immediately," she instructed. "Start with why the hell you ran away." Her sister's initial excitement had slowly settled into something angrier, and more like betrayal as they'd made their way upstairs.

Gina didn't blame her. She'd left without an explanation and would feel exactly the same if their roles were reversed. She also knew Kayla would understand once she'd heard the story.

"Do you have any idea how worried we've been?" Kayla went on, tears pooling in her eyes. "How many people we've spoken to? All the flyers we distributed? We went on the local news, begging whoever took you to bring you back. Mama called a psychic to try to find you. Dad hired a private investigator. They thought they'd found you a week after you left because someone used your bank account, but that was the last thread they found to pull. It was hard. Having the hope yanked away again."

Cruz gave Gina a knowing look. She'd thought Tony had found her when she accessed her bank.

"Dad's PI found me?" Gina asked.

"Yeah." Kayla flopped onto her twin bed, and patted the space beside her until Gina sat too. "Tony went crazy from there. He got his own PI and put him on the hunt. Or at least he said he did, but nothing turned up again. We thought you were dead." Her eyes misted with tears once more. "What have you been doing? And why?" She swung her attention to Cruz. "Your cousin wouldn't tell me anything, except that Gina was okay and coming to see me. And that I couldn't tell anyone. Not even Mom and Dad." She turned back to Gina with a flabbergasted huff. "What is happening?"

Cruz leaned against the wall beside the door and waited silently while Gina forced the complicated and heartbreaking story through trembling lips.

Kayla's gaze dropped to her sister's middle when she finished. "You're having a baby?"

Gina's eyes heated with unshed tears. "Yeah."

Kayla lunged for her again, pulling her into the tightest, most sisterly hug that her heart could've asked for. "I love it already. I'm going to be its favorite aunt."

Gina laughed. "Looking forward to knowing the gender so you don't keep calling my baby 'it.'"

Cruz snorted.

Kayla laughed. "Sorry. This is all just…a lot. I knew it had something to do with Tony. I hate that guy."

Cruz shifted, head tilting and curious-investigator expression in place. "Why? Did he ever do or say anything that rubbed you the wrong way? Something specific?"

Kayla looked from Cruz to her sister. "We reached out to your friends after you went missing, and they said you'd pulled away from them months before. I'd had no idea. You came around the house less often, but I didn't realize he was slowly isolating you. I would've shown up at your place every day. Twice if I had to. I realized after talking with your friends that the only time I saw you anymore was when you came over with Tony, and that was when I started to wonder if he was the reason you were gone. I told Mom and Dad, then none of us trusted him. Dad thought Tony might've killed you." She covered her mouth, eyes wide, as if it could've been true.

And it could've.

Gina embraced her little sister once more. The isolation had begun without her even realizing, and the bad experiences with him had escalated from there. "I'm sorry I scared you. I didn't know what else to do. He was angry one night. I don't remember what it was about. Sometimes, I didn't know. I'd just learned about the baby, but hadn't told him, and he choked me." She paused to catch her breath, humiliation scorching her cheeks. Her fingers rose to the tender skin, where she could sometimes still feel his fingers squeezing. The marks had healed weeks ago, but she wasn't over it. She doubted she ever would be. "I panicked," she said. "He'd never done that before, and it hit me. His aggressions were escalating. What would he be like by the time the baby was born? What if he hurt the baby? Or killed me? And my baby would be left in his hands. It was all too much, and I worried that telling anyone would bring his wrath on them too. At first, I only planned to take a couple days to think it over, but he kept calling me. Over and over, straight through the night. Then he somehow tracked me to the Hilton and came into the lobby demanding my room number. I left right after he was thrown out. I learned later that someone pulled the fire alarm and the building was evacuated. I knew he did that to flush me out. Thankfully, I was already gone. So I just kept running. I tried to disappear."

"I heard him yelling at her one night," Kayla said, turning a guilty expression on Cruz. "I told our parents, and they promised to talk to her, but she said it wasn't a big deal. I wondered if I'd been wrong. I thought I was crazy."

Gina gripped her sister's hand. "I'm sorry. I didn't want them to worry. I should've talked to you about it, but I just wanted to forget."

Kayla swung her attention back. "When you disappeared, I blamed myself for not making someone listen when I knew how he'd talked to you."

"This isn't your fault," Gina said, shocked and horrified that Tony's behavior had hurt Kayla too. That she'd shouldered this burden of guilt alone and without cause.

"When Tony came around looking for details, Mom, Dad and I didn't say anything about our suspicions," Kayla said. "We didn't know what to make of him or his potential role in whatever had happened to you. He came over all the time, asking the same questions. When did we last see you? What did you say? Where might you go? His family practically orchestrated a crusade to find you. I think we all wondered if it was for show. If he knew where you were all along because he'd taken you there."

Gina's skin heated with the horror of Tony visiting her family without her as a buffer to his anger. What if he'd lashed out at them? She used to think he kept his internal monster contained, saved only for her displeasure. But after what he'd done to Mr. Larkin and Heather, a new, impossibly scarier image of Tony had taken shape in her mind.

"Hey." Cruz stepped forward, concern on his brow. "Are you okay?" he asked Gina.

She nodded, though it felt a little like an out-of-body experience.

"Do you have any water in there?" he asked Kayla, glancing at her minifridge.

She pulled out two bottles and offered them to him.

He took one, opened it, then passed it to Gina, who accepted on autopilot. "Drink. You look white as a ghost."

Gina put the bottle to her lips out of obligation, trying to be polite, but her thirst came from nowhere. She drank half the bottle without stopping, and came up for air a little breathless.

"Sorry," Kayla said, returning the second bottle to the fridge. "I can't imagine how hard this has been for you. I'm too focused on me. What can I do to help?"

Gina looked at the closed fridge. "Were those Mama's leftover containers I saw in there?"

Kayla frowned, then smiled. "Yeah. Manicotti. Do you want some?" She opened the fridge again and slipped two containers into a bag, then passed it to Cruz. "For later."

His lips quirked and he nodded. "Care if I ask a few questions before we have to go?"

"No," she said. "Please do. I want to help Gina come home. Safely."

"What can you tell me about Tony or his behavior since Gina's been gone?" Cruz asked. "Do you have ideas where I can find him?"

"I don't know where he is now," she said. "But I might have something useful." She turned and opened a drawer in her desk. "I started keeping a log of his behavior on the third day that Gina was gone. Everything I read online said that after three days, the odds of a victim returning are drastically reduced. I kept thinking about his angry voice on the night he yelled at her, and I was sure he'd done something to her. So, I took notes." She passed a folder to Cruz. "I logged every time he showed up at our house, how long he stayed and anything he said or asked that made me uncomfortable. I also clipped newspaper reports with her name and interviews he gave about her."

Cruz flipped through the notebook, head nodding. "This is great. Can I keep it? I'd like to hand it over to my brother. He's the local deputy for the area where Tony's been seen, and where we believe he hurt those people."

"Go for it," she said. "I hope it helps."

Gina squeezed her sister's hand in thanks.

Kayla unhooked a minicanister of pepper spray from her book bag and gave it to Gina. "Before you go." She closed Gina's fingers over the can.

Gina considered telling Kayla she needed the defense spray more than Gina did. She had Cruz after all, but she knew Kayla likely had a drawer full of similar products. Their father would've made sure of that.

Cruz's phone rang a few short minutes later, and the sisters stopped to listen, though it was a brief and mostly one-sided conversation. Cruz smiled as he tucked away his phone.

Hope inflated Gina's heart and goose bumps scattered across her skin. "Good news?"

He nodded. "Knox needs me back in Great Falls," he

said. "My informant, Rex, is at the station, and I want to talk to him."

Gina set her empty water bottle aside and gave her sister one last hug. "I love you. Stay safe. And remember not to tell anyone you've heard from me, okay?"

Kayla nodded quickly, her eyes filled with tears once more. "Love you too."

"Nice to meet you, Kayla," Cruz said, opening the door and setting his palm against Gina's back. "Lucas will be in touch. We'll try to work out another visit again soon. Maybe with your folks next time. Until then, watch yourself. Get another pepper spray in your book bag."

Gina warmed impossibly further to him. His thoughtfulness toward her sister's safety meant everything. She waved over her shoulder, unable to say the word *goodbye.*

Cruz wrapped an arm around her shoulders once they were in the hallway, and pulled her in close.

"Protect her," Kayla called after them, her thin voice cracking on the words.

Cruz cast a confident glance over his shoulder, devilish grin in place. "With my life," he said.

And Gina believed he meant it.

Chapter Eleven

Cruz parked in the visitor lot of the Great Falls Sheriff's Department. His skin tingled and his heart pumped hard with anticipation. Rex was an excellent friend to have in the PI business. He saw and heard everything that went on in their town—good, bad and gruesome. He knew all the worst kinds of people, but Rex was one of the good guys. More or less. And he only sought Cruz out when something big was afoot.

According to the recent call from Knox, Rex had dialed Dispatch and requested to be picked up by a cruiser, for appearances' sake. Smart, because thugs, which was what Rex pretended to be most days, rarely walked willingly into the sheriff's department, and Rex had a reputation to uphold. He'd told the deputy who'd taken the call that he wanted Knox to make his faux arrest, and the entire conversation was so bizarre, the deputy had passed the news on to Knox, assuming it was a joke. Knox had rerouted his cruiser immediately.

Following the flashers-and-handcuffs show, Rex had refused to talk until Cruz was present. The guy had had too many unpleasant, but probably deserved, run-ins with lawmen to believe any of them could see past his rough exterior. So Knox had made the call.

Cruz unbuckled and gave his silent passenger an appraising look.

Gina had been distant since they'd returned to his Jeep. She'd wiped tears discreetly and answered his questions with simple, often one-word answers, and stared out her window without bothering to make eye contact. It was the first time since they'd met that she'd shut him out, and he didn't like it. Even after her friend had been attacked, Gina was open to discussion, ready to be comforted. This was something else completely, and he felt the loss of her communication in his gut.

"Come on," he said, in the most positive tone he could manage. "Maybe Rex has something we can use to speed up the inevitable." He stared at her cheek until she dared a look, then he offered a wink and reassuring smile. "Tony's capture and arrest are inevitable, in case that was unclear."

Her lips quirked in response, but she was fully deflated, and the half-hearted effort didn't reach her eyes. The light and joy that had filled her in her sister's presence was completely extinguished. What remained was heartbreaking, but she persevered, climbing down and moving in the right direction.

Cruz met her at the front of the Jeep, then he set a hand against her back as they moved toward the station. He watched her for signs he'd crossed a line, but her expression gave nothing away. He told himself that Gina was from a family of huggers, so the physical connection would be a comfort to her, and he ignored the part of himself who knew the touch was selfish. He'd wanted an excuse to regain the connection they'd shared on campus, one that had felt so easy and natural, he'd craved another hit. "This okay?" he asked eventually, assuring he hadn't overstepped.

She nodded. "Thank you." The ragged breath following her words sounded like a release of nerves, and he smiled at the possibility his presence and touch had helped her relax.

Before them, a pair of deputies held the door as Cruz and Gina passed through the glass vestibule. The Great Falls Sheriff's Department was a relatively new red-brick building just outside the more populated downtown area, and a place Cruz visited often.

"Hey, Cruz," the deputy greeted him as he held the door. His partner simply nodded.

Cruz returned the greeting, trying not to eyeball the second deputy, whose attention was fixed on Gina.

Inside the lobby, the man at the desk smiled. "Your brother's waiting for you," he said, buzzing the door to the interior offices unlocked as Cruz and Gina headed that way.

"Thanks," Cruz called.

They passed several more uniformed deputies in the long narrow hall. Each greeted Cruz in words, while their eyes trailed over the woman at his side.

Gina made a small, unfamiliar sound, and he slowed his pace to look at her.

Had she noticed all the interested looks too? Had they made her uncomfortable? "What?" he asked finally, needing to know.

She raised her brows along with her grin. "Is there anyone here who doesn't know you?"

Cruz frowned. "Probably not," he said, confused. That was what had made her laugh? "Small town," he reminded her.

"I live in a small town," she said. "I don't know everyone I pass, and I don't know any police officers."

"Maybe you live in the wrong small town," he suggested, returning her smile. "It helps that my little brother is a deputy here. Plus, Derek and I do work for these guys on occasion."

"There you are." Knox's voice stopped Cruz in his tracks, and Gina froze with him. They backed up a few paces and turned toward an open door on the right. Knox stood behind a small table in a viewing room, waving them inside. "Gina." He nodded.

She waved, then took a seat at the table when Knox did.

Cruz preferred to stand.

Knox switched his gaze from his brother to Gina, then back, deadly serious, just the way he was born. "I wanted to brief you on my progress before you speak with Rex," he said. "I've tried to reach Tony through all the usual means. Home visit. Office visit. A trip to his parents' house. So far, I haven't made contact, and no one at those locations is offering any help. In fact," he said, pausing to shift on his seat, "his mother threatened to call her husband and report me." Knox pursed his lips, expression going comically blank. "She was calling a businessman to report a deputy sheriff. If that doesn't tell us everything we need to know about this family's inflated sense of purpose and power, I'm not sure what would."

"That's the Marinos," Gina said. "They run their world and control everyone in it."

Knox frowned, and concern lined his youthful face. "They run sporting goods stores."

"They have a lot of money and no scruples," she

said, voice flat and hard. "They lure you in with appearances, hospitality and pretty views, then they stick you to their web."

Cruz moved close to Gina and leaned a hip against the table, eyes fixed on Knox. "Did you tell his mama or coworkers he's wanted in association with murder and assault?"

"Of course not," Knox said. "I told them I was looking for Gina and hoped he could help."

Gina thunked her elbows on the table and rested her face against her palms.

Cruz's hand landed lightly between her shoulder blades without thought.

Knox tracked the motion with his gaze, curiosity in his keen eyes, then carried on as if nothing was amiss. "We've got to be careful how we approach this," he said. "We don't want to tip our hat to the fact that Gina is in our care and under our protection. He could lash out again. We need a solid case for arrest, and preferably no more innocent victims."

Gina raised her face from her hands, a look of disgust on her pretty face. "'Preferably'?"

Knox nodded. "We can't control Tony until he's in our custody. We can only do our best to find and apprehend him, then hold him on the strongest legs possible. Currently, we don't have any evidence to put him at any of our crime scenes. There's only your testimony to hearing his voice through Heather's phone and behind Larkin's apartment door. That's circumstantial at best. A first-year law student could get him off charges based on that."

Cruz straightened, pulling his hand away from Gina, and stuffed his fingers into the front pocket of his jeans.

Knox stood. "That's all I've got for now. If you're ready for Rex, I'll bring him in." He reached for a remote resting on a ledge in the wall behind him and pointed it at a television mounted in the corner, before walking back into the hall.

The flat-screen illuminated with an image of a room like the one they were in.

"You doing okay?" Cruz asked Gina as the door closed behind Knox.

She took a full breath and nodded. "I'm trying," she said. "But my heart and head are everywhere. If I'm being terrible company, it's me, not you."

Cruz snorted. "It's not you. It's the situation, the uncertainty and a wild card named Tony Marino."

She grimaced. "Who wouldn't be wreaking havoc on this town if not for me."

Cruz groaned, debating the boundaries of his role in her life once more. Giving in to the moment, he crouched at her side, bringing his gaze level with hers. "The way I see it, a lot of people have failed you where Tony is concerned. Not the other way around."

She lifted a sincere but uncertain gaze to him.

"I won't be one of them."

The television drew their attention when the door to the room on-screen opened. Knox led Rex inside and offered him a seat at the small table. Rex sat, and Knox left.

"That's my cue," Cruz said, pushing back onto his feet. "I'm going in there, and Knox will sit with you. You can watch and listen while I talk with Rex."

The door to their room opened, and Knox strode inside. "You're up."

Cruz looked to Gina, who offered a small smile, letting him know she was okay without him, because why wouldn't she be? And he went to see his informant.

Rex looked up when Cruz entered the room. The young man's wary eyes tracked him as he moved. Rex was a good argument for nature over nurture, because no one had ever nurtured Rex as far as Cruz could see, but the kid still knew how to do the right things.

"You rang?" Cruz asked, offering his hand in the familiar shake they shared. Rex had taught Cruz the set of simple motions when he'd rolled into his life three years ago, after stealing a car the insurance company had tasked Cruz with finding.

Rex had planned to sell the car, or its parts, for cash. It was a harsh winter, and Rex was cold and hungry. His girlfriend had pushed him into the crime because she hadn't wanted to stay at the shelter. She'd claimed someone there had sexually harassed her, and Rex couldn't protect her when the men and women were separated at lights out.

Cruz had returned the car and fed the teens, then put the girlfriend up for a few nights at a hotel until the snowstorms had passed and Rex was bailed out. A bond had formed between them that day, when Rex had realized it was Cruz who'd ponied up the dough and kept his girlfriend safe when he couldn't.

Now, at the ripe old age of nineteen, the young man before him rocked his head back in silent greeting. The girlfriend was long gone, and any debt between the men had long ago been paid, but a friendship had taken root in its place. Rex folded his tattooed hands on the table, amusingly at home, despite his dangerous appearance. "'Bout time you showed your pretty all-American face," he said, a reference to Cruz's high school baseball career. It was something Rex had read about online after looking him up three years ago, trying to decipher Cruz's angle for helping him out. Eventually, he'd realized Cruz was just a good guy, but the baseball detail clearly still amused him. "There's only so much free coffee and doughnuts a guy can handle."

Cruz took the seat across from him and smiled. "Sounds like my brother gave you the royal treatment. He usually makes me get my own water from the fountain."

Rex stretched long jean-clad legs beneath the narrow table, a faint smile playing on his pierced lips. "Yeah, well, he pretended to arrest me first. So there's that."

"He's accommodating too," Cruz said. "Why not just call an Uber?"

"I wouldn't have needed the theatrics if you were at your office."

"I've been busy," Cruz said, nerves zigzagging in his unsettled stomach. "You have news?"

"Yeah. I was lifting some dude's wallet when a rich guy stopped me." He lifted his brows in challenge, daring Cruz to scold or reprimand him, per the usual.

Cruz bit down on the insides of his cheeks, forcing himself to let Rex go on.

"The second guy bumped right into me, knocked me away from my mark before I could get the wallet. I thought it was dumb luck, at first. Then the second guy pulls a Benjamin from his wallet and just holds it out to me, stuck between his two fingers like he's about to smoke a cigarette."

Cruz felt his brows rise. "Someone gave you a hundred dollars after catching you trying to steal a wallet?"

Rex dipped his chin in response. "He said he saw

what I was up to, and told me if I needed money, he had a job."

Hair rose on the back of Cruz's neck as he listened, taking in Rex's tone and posture. "What kind of job?"

Rex flicked his gaze to the camera on the wall behind Cruz's head. "He told me to watch the building where that guy was killed, and call this number if I saw the lady from the flyer." Rex rocked onto one hip, extracting Gina's folded missing person flyer from his pocket. A phone number had been scribbled across the top in pen.

Cruz's fingers curled into fists on his lap. "Anything else?"

"I get another hundred every time I call to tell him more about her movement, but I haven't called him," Rex said, leveling Cruz with a pointed stare. "'Cause I saw her with you, which either means you need to know this because you're in the reunion business now, or you need to know this because that guy's no good. Maybe even hunting your lady. She sure didn't look lost when I saw her. So, I don't know what's up with her, but in my experience, a man with money to burn is dangerous."

Heat rushed over Cruz's chest, spreading from his core to his forehead in seconds. "You're right to tell me," he said. "She is in danger, and I'm keeping her safe. That starts with getting my hands on this guy, but so far he's smoke."

Rex nodded solemnly. "I figured. I'll do what I can, but hold on to her tight because I'm not the only one he's paying to find her. And someone else will gladly turn her over for money."

Heat turned to fire on Cruz's skin. "That's not going to happen."

Chapter Twelve

Gina struggled to find her breath as the conversation between Cruz and Rex unfolded on-screen.

"You're okay," Knox said. His deep voice was jarring in the otherwise silent room. "Rex is loyal to Cruz. He's an asset, and the fact that he came here looking for him tells me he's serious about helping us keep you safe."

Her gaze flickered back to the men on camera.

"I've got you," the younger man said, voice low and eyes searching. The deep intention behind the words felt like a pledge of fealty.

The fact that a stranger would willingly insert himself into her mess, based on Cruz's involvement alone, was both humbling and mind-boggling. Gina's family and friends were close, but outside her immediate bloodline, she wasn't sure she knew anyone who'd intentionally put their well-being on the line for her. The relationships she'd been exposed to since meeting the Winchesters gave her an incredible sense of hope.

Knox's desire to help might've stemmed from his badge, but she got the feeling his reasoning ran much deeper. Same for their cousin Derek. And for Cruz. Now Rex. Was it because their world was so much more dangerous than hers used to be? Maybe living in a constant state of emergency caused people to reevaluate priorities and align themselves more steadfastly to doing the right things.

Maybe truly good people simply had a way of finding one another.

"I saw you and her carrying suitcases away from the building, and I heard her apartment was trashed," Rex said. "This guy's going to know she moved on, and if I don't reach out and report that, I'm either hiding something, or I'm not a very good informant. Either way, I lose cred and he'll cut me loose."

Gina's muscles tightened as Cruz nodded. "So you'll call and let him know she's gone," Cruz said. "He already knows that."

"I can tell him I caught sight of a cleaning service hauling boxes down from her apartment. Then I'll give him the number I saw on their van. Your number or your brother's. When he calls you for information, you can arrange to meet him, or do whatever it is you good guys do."

Cruz stood and freed his wallet from one pocket. He handed Rex a folded set of bills. "Get something to eat. Do not buy weed. Take some food home for later."

"Nah." Rex waved him off. "I don't need your money." He rose to his feet, then met Cruz at the end of the table. "I'm working at Allen's Wrench. Folks are nice. The pay is fair, and they don't even mind my ink."

Cruz's smile was wide and proud. "Well, okay, then." He tucked the money back into his wallet. "I'll have to bring the Jeep around sometime. Get a look at you in action."

Rex looked away, fighting a smile and a blush. His head bobbed. "Yeah, all right."

Cruz pulled him into an awkward man-hug. They patted one another's back, then split ways.

"I'm here for you," Rex said. "Whatever you need."

"I know," Cruz agreed, his voice low and rough. "The guy you're dealing with is dangerous. So be careful."

Rex lifted his chin. "Yeah." He offered Cruz a fist to bump, then reached for the door to leave.

Gina felt her lungs strain and realized she'd been holding her breath. More and more people were being pulled into her storm, and she absolutely hated it. How had things gotten so out of control? When would the madness end?

Would someone else be hurt in the wake caused by her escape?

Knox's gaze heated her cheek, causing her to steal a look his way. "How are you doing?" he asked.

"I'll be okay," she answered quickly, willing the words to be true.

"You really are safe with Cruz, but if you'd be more comfortable with our aunt and uncle, the offer stands. I spoke to them on the matter again this morning. It won't hurt Cruz's feelings." Knox grinned, and the sudden resemblance to his brother was profound. "Everyone involved only wants you to feel safe. You've been through enough."

She forced a tight smile. "Thank you."

The door to their room opened, and Cruz appeared in the doorway, pale green gaze moving swiftly from Gina to his brother. "You heard all that."

"We did," Knox answered. "It's a good plan, assuming we can get Tony to meet with us, or at least stay on the call long enough to trace it. It'll be a quick sting."

Gina tried and failed to take on a little of the Winchesters' confidence. It was nice that they looked out for one another, and for Rex. She appreciated the extra step Knox had taken to be sure she was comfortable at Cruz's place too. He was right to ask, because she wouldn't have likely said so if she wasn't happy there, not after Cruz had given her a place to stay when she'd needed it and agreed to take her case, even when she couldn't pay.

An obvious realization settled over her, and she inhaled the freedom that came with it. The time had come for her to stop running and start fighting. She wasn't alone in the battle, and the Winchesters didn't have to be either. Gina needed to switch gears.

Now, if she could just keep her heart and head in line while spending so much time with the man who'd stolen her breath at first sight.

GINA'S STOMACH RUMBLED as she retrieved her mom's manicotti from Cruz's refrigerator. She sent up silent prayers of gratitude for the small portion Kayla had sent home with them. "Mind if I use your oven?" she called to Cruz, giving herself a mental pat on her back for asking. It seemed odd to make herself so comfortable in the home of someone she'd just met, but he'd repeatedly insisted she try. She'd spent so long tiptoeing around Tony's place, even after living there for months, caution had become second nature. Today, however, she was actively reminding herself that Tony was an anomaly, and she couldn't let him darken her view of the world anymore. Despite his every effort to make her feel like something less, she wasn't buying his lies anymore. She wasn't a burden or a hassle. She was Gina Ricci, and she was a dang delight.

"Help yourself to anything you want," Cruz answered from his seat at a desk in his living space. "If you're hungry, I can make dinner."

"I'm heating the manicotti," she said, smiling at her assertion. "Would you like some?"

Cruz stopped typing. He twisted at the waist and hooked an elbow over the back of his chair. "You'd share that with me?"

"You're sharing your entire house with me," she said. "I suppose it's the polite thing to do, but you're getting the smaller piece."

He smiled. "I accept."

Gina transferred their dinner from her mother's plastic containers to a baking dish, then slid the cheese-and-spinach-stuffed pasta sleeves into the preheated oven and set a timer to warm them up. The microwave would've done the work faster, but in Gina's opinion, the oven did a nicer job.

She considered taking a seat at the counter, or returning to her room until the food was ready, but wandered in Cruz's direction instead. He'd been typing diligently on his laptop since they'd returned from the sheriff's department. She'd forced herself to leave him until now, but curiosity had finally gotten the best of her.

He stilled as she approached, as if he'd heard or sensed her arrival.

"What are you up to?" she asked, determined not to feel as if she was intruding.

Cruz gave his keyboard a few dramatic taps, then turned to face her. "I've established a website for the fictional cleaning service Rex is name-dropping to Tony.

I've been texting with Rex, and we decided giving Tony the number was too easy, too suspicious. Instead, Rex will name-drop, then Tony will look for a number on his own. He'll find the number to my unregistered pay-by-month cell phone and give me a call for more information on where I moved the lady in your apartment." He grinned, obviously proud of himself, and clearly not doing something like this for the first time.

"That site looks real," she said, pulling her attention over his shoulder and stooping for a clearer view of the monitor. "You did all that since we got home?"

He shrugged. "I create a lot of cover stories. I'm getting faster with practice. If you ever need a website, I'm your guy."

Gina laughed. "Good to know."

"I also designed a few ads for the company and set them to run immediately in our town's community forums. The extra effort will make it even easier for him to find me, and help legitimize the front."

"Well, aren't you a man of many talents," she mused. Her cheeks burned a moment later as the comment turned extremely dirty in her mind.

Cruz's eyes twinkled with renewed mischief, obviously picking up on the unintended double entendre and likely her blush. "That I am," he agreed.

A smile broke over Gina's face, and she turned away on her toes. "I'd better go check on dinner."

Cruz followed her into the kitchen, then opened a cupboard for plates. "You want to eat at the island or the table?"

"Island," she said breezily, knowing the chairs there were much more closely spaced.

Inside the oven, the manicotti bubbled slightly, letting her know it was ready. She donned the pair of oven mitts hanging from a hook on the side of his nearby refrigerator, then moved the baking dish to a trivet Cruz had placed on the countertop.

She took her seat beside him, and fell easily into conversation about their already very full day. Gina especially enjoyed Cruz's rehashing of time spent with Kayla. He'd noticed everything from their obvious bond to candid photos of her family hung around her sister's vanity mirror and computer monitor. She shared the stories behind the snapshots and smiled at the memories. "I miss them so much," she admitted.

"I can see," he answered warmly. "I'm working on fixing that."

By the time the manicotti was gone, and Gina was stuffed, Cruz had slipped away to take a call. It was the first time he'd left her to talk on the phone, and her curiosity spiked. What was different about this call?

She considered following him and insisting he keep her in the loop. Except she couldn't be sure the call was about her case, and if it wasn't, she had no right to listen in.

Gina busied herself washing the dishes, then wiping countertops, before pacing the width of his living room until a better idea came to mind.

She crossed the space to the desk where Cruz had worked earlier and borrowed a notepad and pen, then took a seat on his couch to think and write. Just because she wasn't on the run anymore didn't mean she should be a complete bystander. After a couple years spent with Tony, she had to know something that would be useful in finding him, at least indirectly.

She tapped the pen against the paper, then began a

list of names. She included everyone she could think of who shared Tony's world, starting with his personal staff. A housekeeper who came weekly. A favorite driver who took him to important events. Friends she'd met at his parties. Frenemies and scorned exes he'd whispered about at galleries and charity dinners. Anyone who might know something more than she did and could be convinced to tell. She considered adding his family members, but Knox was already on that, and the Marinos would never turn on Tony anyway.

Soon, the page before her was full, and the result was a bit of a surprise. Tony was private and guarded, but she'd forgotten how often he was in the spotlight. He might've kept his personal demons tightly under wraps, but a great number of people knew enough about the camera-ready version of Tony to possibly offer local police a little insight. For example, where did the driver and town car take him most often? Where had Tony traveled with the scorned exes? Had he recently requested access to a friend or business cohort's cabin or empty apartment?

She considered the places Tony had taken her, but none were close enough to keep an effective eye on Great Falls. Either he had a new hideout, or he was hiding in plain sight.

Her skin crawled at the thought.

A sharp clap of hands caused her to yip, and nearly leap from the couch.

Cruz parted his clasped hands as he approached, a look of apology on his face. "Sorry." His gaze moved swiftly over her wide-eyed face, to the palm pressed to her chest, then to the borrowed notebook on her lap. "I didn't mean to startle you. I have news, but what's this?"

Gina passed him the notebook while working to regain her composure. "I made a list of everyone I've ever met through Tony. I don't know many last names, but this seemed like it could help. May be a good start for you detective types."

Cruz evaluated the paper, brows raised. "This is more than a start. This is fantastic. Knox and Derek will be thrilled for the added leads." When his gaze returned to hers, something soft and new was there. She wasn't sure, but it seemed a lot like pride.

She averted her eyes a moment before pushing onto her feet and sliding her palms against her middle. "I hope it helps. Now it's your turn. What's the news?"

A slow grin spread over Cruz's face. "I was on the phone with Derek. He's been following your parents all day."

Her muscles stiffened at the mention of her folks. A seed of fear took immediate root. "Why?"

"I asked him to," Cruz said, scanning Gina's stricken face and painfully tense posture. "For you," he clarified. "He's making sure they aren't being watched by anyone else."

"And they aren't?" she asked, feeling her fingers curl against her sides. "Right?"

"No." Delight danced in Cruz's eyes. "Which is why we think it's safe for you to visit them."

Gina's heart leaped. "What?"

"According to you and Kayla, your parents attend mass every week. We thought it would be easiest to slip into the church and meet with them in a private room. They can come and go as usual without drawing any inquiring eyes, in case Derek somehow missed their tail."

Pressure built in Gina's chest, and she threw herself

against Cruz, wrapping him in the energy and appreciation she couldn't yet speak.

His strong arms closed around her on a chuckle. "I hoped this might be your reaction. Remind me to always be the one to deliver your good news," he said. "And to provide it as often as possible."

She laughed, then settled into him for a long moment, enjoying the warmth and comfort of his embrace. His heart beat fast and strong beneath her ear, and she wondered if he felt the zigzagging electricity too. If only she could find reasons to hold on to him like this more often.

"There's one more thing," Cruz said quietly, skimming his palms up her spine. "We've been out in the Jeep a couple times already. We should probably mix it up."

She tipped her head back to ask what he had in mind, and the heat of his breath swept over her, knocking her silent instead.

"How do you feel about taking my motorcycle?" he asked.

And every part of her squealed with joy.

Chapter Thirteen

Gina scooted in close to Cruz on the sleek black motorcycle. Her heart hammered as the machine purred beneath them, rocketing over the ribbon of winding country road in the darkness. Her bulbous helmet and mirrored shield gave her an exhilarating feeling of anonymity when rolling fields and scattered farms gave way to clustered downtown buildings and a sea of taillights.

St. Peter's Cathedral rose above all else in the distance. Its majestic spires gleamed white beneath strategically placed floodlights.

A surge of excitement raced through her, knowing her parents were so near. Her limbs tightened in response.

With one large palm, Cruz covered her clasped hands where they lay on his chest, then curled strong fingers over hers. Her galloping heart moved straight to a sprint at the silent encouragement, and she rested her cheek against his back.

Soon, the motorcycle sailed into a narrow employee parking lot behind St. Peter's, and she followed Cruz's lead in dismounting the bike, but leaving her helmet on as they approached the building. She'd been to church with her family a thousand times, but always parked in the visitors' lot out front. She'd never even seen the black metal door where Cruz stopped to knock.

The barrier opened immediately, and someone in a suit and tie ushered them inside.

Gina's heart swelled as the man's face registered. "Mr. Garcia," she whispered, her happy heart beginning to dance at yet another positive piece of her past.

Mr. Garcia had been a friend of her parents for as long as she could remember. He and his wife had even babysat Gina and Kayla when they were young. "Thank you," she whispered.

He offered a warm smile, then greeted Cruz with a handshake and nod. "I invited the Riccis to wait for me in the multipurpose room," he said softly as the muffled sounds of organ music rose in distant parts of the building. A choir of voices and the ashy smell of incense followed. "I told them I wanted to discuss another fundraiser for our affiliated elementary school. I'm quite sure they'll be thrilled to see that was all a ruse." He grinned, and his dark eyes sparkled with pleasure. "We should hurry so you'll have as much time as possible with them." He turned and hurried down the long, narrow hallway with Cruz and Gina on his heels.

"How do you two know each other?" she asked the men, not caring who answered. Was her world really this small?

Cruz set his palm against the small of her back, matching his pace to hers. "We don't."

Mr. Garcia smiled over his shoulder. "I answered the phone when his partner, Derek, called and explained the situation. I happened to be in the office after a meeting with the school's advisory board. The regular office staff had already gone home for the day. It was a perfect alignment of circumstances, really. I caught your parents as soon as I saw them pull into the lot." He paused at the closed door to a large gathering room usually saved for wedding showers and funeral dinners, then offered Cruz a determined look. "If there's anything else I can do to help, just ask."

"Thank you," Cruz said.

Mr. Garcia stepped aside, pretending to fiddle with his phone, probably standing guard as a lookout.

Cruz opened the door, and motioned Gina inside.

Her mother's gasp and sob propelled her across the room and into the embrace she'd needed for months.

"Baby," her mama cooed. The single word was soaked in relief as she buried her face in Gina's hair. "I can't believe it's you." She pulled back to look into her daughter's eyes, a mix of elation and misery on her round face. "We've been so scared. Where have you been? Are you okay?"

Her father hovered, motionless at their sides before wiping heavy hands over his crumbling features.

Gina reached for him, pulling him into their sweet reunion cocoon.

Long minutes passed before the tears and professions of love began to slow.

Cruz stepped in with a box of tissues when Gina's nose began to run. "Maybe we should all have a seat," he suggested, adding a brief introduction of himself before motioning to the nearest round table, large enough to seat eight. "We don't have a lot of time, but there's plenty to say."

Her dad cleared his throat, then led the women to the table. He pulled chairs out for Gina and her mom, then her parents bookended her. Her dad's arm went around her shoulders, and her mama squeezed Gina's hands.

Cruz nodded, and Gina began to tell her story once more. Just as she had for Kayla, and like her sister, her parents cried. Hurt and betrayal registered in their eyes as she explained the truth about Tony and all the things she'd kept from them. They clung to her and to one another, heartbroken, when she admitted she'd felt as if she'd had no other choice than to run.

"We could've helped you," her dad said, voice heavy with despair. "We will always help you. No matter the fight. I thought you understood that, Gina. Always."

Her mother pulled more tissues from the box and dabbed them to her eyes. "I can't believe he hurt you, and we didn't know. Kayla warned us one night when she heard you arguing, but we couldn't believe it was more than a heated dispute. The Marinos are pillars of the community, and Tony was always so polite. That family made it their full-time job to find you."

Gina rubbed her mama's arm. "I didn't want to upset you by telling you about the early fights with Tony. By the time he'd become dangerous, I was afraid to get you involved. I can see how wrong I was now, but back then, it was hard to see anything clearly. I'm so sorry."

"Oh." Her mama stroked her hair and pulled her close. "We do not blame you," she whispered emphatically. "And we don't judge you. You hear that? We would never."

Her dad shifted, unsettled and antsy now. "Do you think his family knew about this? About the things he did to you? About what he's doing now?"

Gina pulled in a ragged breath. She hadn't even told them the worst of it, only that he'd become abusive, and she'd run. She steadied herself with a glance at Cruz for strength, then pushed ahead before she started to cry all over again. "I don't know how much Tony's family knows about who he really is, behind closed doors, but I know they would never turn him in or aid in his arrest. The family isn't what they seem either. They're dark," Gina said, her voice falling unintentionally to a whisper. "I didn't see it until it was already too late, but they're manipulative, always scheming for influence and power in their circles." She dragged her attention from her dad to her mom, then back. "I know you'll always protect me," she said, needing him to understand he hadn't done anything wrong. "You've made that obvious to Kayla and I all our lives, but the world had gotten muddled to me. I was trying to protect you."

Her dad sighed, then pulled her in for another hug before kissing her head. "Let us help you now. We aren't completely useless, you know?" He forced a humorless smile, then raised his eyes to Cruz in question. "What can we do?"

"Dad," she said carefully, drawing his attention to her once more. There was something else they needed to know right away. "There's another reason I ran." Her eyes stung and blurred as she lowered her attention to her hands, now pressed against her abdomen. "I needed to protect my baby."

Her dad covered his mouth, and his gaze jumped to her mother.

"Gina?" her mother asked, turning her back to face her, then wrapping her in another hug.

When she straightened, her dad's eyes glistened as he looked from her face to her middle. "We're going to be grandparents?"

Gina nodded, and her dad pulled her into a hug.

He held her hand when he released her, then turned doubly determined eyes on Cruz. "And your family is looking for Tony?" her dad asked.

"Yes, sir," Cruz returned, taking over while Gina and her mom stole another long hug. "My brother, Knox, is the deputy sheriff assigned to Gina's case," he said, repeating the information Gina had initially dumped on them. "My cousins are detectives in West Liberty, where Gina was first reported missing. They'll oversee things from your town, while Knox keeps watch from mine. My partner, Derek, and I are working with the sheriff's department to protect Gina and her baby while also tracking Tony. So far there hasn't been any word on where he's staying, but the hunt is happening covertly. He's got enough money to run and stay hidden if he knows we're after him. We don't want to tip all our cards yet."

Her dad grunted. "You have enough evidence to arrest him, then? Will Gina need to stand trial? Do convicted domestic assault criminals even get any jail time?"

Gina's heart seized, and she straightened in her seat, locking gazes briefly with Cruz.

"Not often enough," Cruz said. "But murderers do."

"What?" her mother cried.

Cruz pressed onward, providing the ugly details of Mr. Larkin's murder and Heather's attack.

Her dad swore.

Cruz stood, then fished a pair of cell phones from his pocket and handed one to her dad, the other to Gina. "These are unregistered. I've added my name and number in the contacts, as well as all the information you need to reach my brother and cousins. Also, a number for reaching Gina."

Gina clutched the device against her chest, her heart swelling with joy. When had he done this? How long had he been arranging this reunion with her folks? How had she missed it?

Her mother made a small sound of excitement. "Kayla is going to be so jealous."

A little laugh bubbled from Gina's lips. "Thank you," she told Cruz.

He tipped his head forward slightly, in one small but magnanimous move. "You'll be able to keep in touch now, but you can't let anyone else know." He fixed her with his piercing gaze, then shared the look with each of her parents. "Only answer if the incoming number belongs to one of the contacts I've programmed. Unknown numbers get ignored. Always. Understand?"

Her dad's lips parted as he looked from the phone to Cruz. "Yes."

Her mom sighed deeply, audibly relieved. "But we can talk to her?"

"Yeah." Cruz smiled. "A little, and as needed. Otherwise don't deviate from your usual routines. It's evident that you're happier now than when you arrived here tonight. Try not to let that show when you leave this room," he continued. "Given all that's happened with Gina's case in the last few days, we don't want anyone to suspect you know where she is or how to find her."

The door to the room opened, and Mr. Garcia stepped inside, a palm raised in apology. "Sorry," he said. "I didn't want to interrupt, but mass is ending."

Gina's heart sank as her mom's arms wound around her once more.

"I love you, Mama," she whispered, before standing and turning to her dad.

Her father wrapped her tight in the most fatherly of hugs, then kissed the top of her head. He cupped her face in his hands when she started to pull away. "I love you, baby girl."

Suddenly, the hero of her youth seemed more gray and fragile than she'd ever thought him before. "I love you too," she said.

"We'll do everything we can to bring you home safely and soon," he vowed.

"I know." She nodded. "I'm going to be okay," she assured them, meaning it in her marrow.

Her mother moved to her father's side as Gina went to Cruz.

"Protect our little girl," her mom pleaded to Cruz, echoing Kayla's parting words as they headed for the door.

"And our grandbaby," her dad said.

"With my life," Cruz vowed once again.

Then he clutched her hand and towed her away.

Chapter Fourteen

The sprint to his motorcycle gave Gina time to collect herself emotionally. The helmet's mirrored visor hid her puffy eyes as they climbed aboard, and the night enveloped her wholly as they rocketed back through town.

Her mind raced with thanks for the day's reunions and for the phone in her pocket, provided by Cruz. The sexy private investigator was becoming more of a hero with every action. His quiet confidence and easy smile had done more for her in a few days than any love interest ever had, and he probably didn't have a clue. Because he wasn't playing games. He didn't have a side agenda or ulterior motive. Cruz Winchester was sincere and honorable in ways she'd forgotten men could be, and he'd irrevocably changed her ideas about what was acceptable. Never again would she accept any relationship that didn't make her feel secure, seen and valued. Because if a man she'd just met could make her feel like this, then anyone seeking a position in her life permanently would have to bring a serious A game. Not just for her benefit, but for the life she would soon bring into this world.

The bike slowed at the final stoplight at the edge of town. Behind them, the area's nightlife was in full swing. Before them, a quiet country road reached out to carry them home.

A shrill ringing rose from her pocket, barely audible through her helmet and over the sound of the motorcycle's engine. Gina felt Cruz's chest rumble as he chuckled in response.

"We didn't get far," he called.

Gina grinned as she liberated the new phone, then called back to Cruz. "Can I answer?" Her heart leaped, eager to hear her mom's voice again, though it hadn't been more than ten minutes since she'd last said goodbye.

Cruz pulled forward as the light changed and guided the motorcycle into an empty parking lot. He circled away from the security lights and traffic, then settled the engine so she could speak, unfettered by the sound.

She tugged her helmet off and pressed the phone to her ear. "Hello, Mama," she said, brightly. "Everything okay?"

"We're fine," her mama said firmly, sounding as if she wasn't actually sure. "It's probably nothing..." The following pause stretched across their line, hollowing Gina with each impossibly long beat.

"Mama?" she pressed. "What's wrong? Just say it."

"The company monitoring our home security system called. We've had a break-in."

CRUZ PACED HIS living room an hour later, hating the pained expression on Gina's face. The only thing worse than seeing her misery was knowing he'd contributed to it, even a little, by insisting they go back to his place, rather than to her parents' home. She'd wanted to see them after learning about the break-in, but he couldn't allow it, even if it hurt her not to be with them.

Her priority was her family, but his priority was her safety.

So he'd driven her to his place as planned, and though she understood, logically, why she couldn't be with her parents, the pain of not going to them was etched on her face.

His phone buzzed against his palm as he fielded the texts from his cousins Blaze and Lucas. Neither of the detectives typically covered break-ins or missing persons, but they'd had no trouble getting involved when Cruz asked.

The newest text was from his partner. "Derek just arrived," he told Gina, moving to join her on the couch. "Blaze and Lucas have spoken with your folks and confirmed that they are fine. The intruder was long gone when they arrived, and police were already on the scene. I'm sure your mom and dad will call as soon as they can. They're probably just waiting until they're alone again. They know how important it is to keep your reunion a secret."

Gina fixed him with an angry and exasperated stare, cheeks pink from emotion and eyes narrowed. "I hate this so much. I know this happened to them because of me, and it makes me crazy. I left town to keep Tony away from them. I hurt and worried them for months, but I told myself that was okay, because at least they were safe. Now he's closer to finding me than he's ever been, and he circled back to where he started. I haven't protected them at all. I worried them for nothing. Who knows what he'll do next? And there's nothing I can do to help."

Cruz rubbed his palms over the thighs of his jeans, willing himself not to reach for her, and deciding silently that if she reached out to him, the only right thing to do would be to hold her. But it had to be her choice. Her decision. Her move. "You're doing exactly what you should be doing right now," he said.

She nodded, but didn't look convinced. Her gaze slid to the floor, then to her twined fingers, where they rested on her lap.

He hated the waves of guilt and conflict rolling off her, and wished she could see how strong she was. She'd made a brave and selfless choice, despite unthinkable circumstances, and there was honor in that risk, not shame. "You've consistently done the right things, since the day you ran away, and you've made it abundantly clear to Tony that he cannot control you any longer," Cruz said. "He's apparently not accustomed to that, and he's mad."

Gina's frown deepened. "So it was definitely him? No chance of a coincidence?"

"No." Cruz pursed his lips, realizing she'd still held some hope that they were wrong. "According to Blaze, the front door was kicked in. The hutch in the dining room was overturned, and all the dishes inside were destroyed, along with several porcelain figures and an oil painting above the fireplace in the living room." He paused to swallow against the itchy dryness of his throat, when she sucked in an audible breath. "A message was spray-painted in red across the carpet." He waited for her gaze to meet his before adding the final detail. "'Keep hiding. Keep paying.'"

Gina's hands curled into fists. Her jaw locked and her cheeks darkened. "That was absolutely Tony," she seethed. "Who else would it be? He went straight for my family's most cherished possessions. He wanted to hit us where it hurt."

"The items in the dining room were important?" Cruz guessed, aligning the new information with what he knew about Tony Marino. He was a manipulator and a world-class jerk.

"Everything he destroyed was an heirloom," she said. "The china and figurines came from Italy with my father's family at the turn of the last century. The painting was a portrait of my great-great-grandmother and every bit as old and irreplaceable. What he did was cruel. This wasn't a burglary. It was a punishment."

Cruz stretched onto his feet, then went to the kitchen for two bottles of water. "It sounds counterintuitive, but it wouldn't be all bad news if Tony lost a little control. A plotting, self-poised sociopath is a lot harder to catch and build a case against than one who's lashing out and acting on impulse." He returned to the couch and offered Gina one of the bottles, then opened the other for himself. "But I'm not convinced that's what's happening. More likely, breaking into your parents' place was intended to either draw you out or to produce some details on your location. He went while the house was empty for a reason. He might've sorted through their things, their papers, their computers, if they leave them unlocked."

Gina sipped the water, appearing to consider Cruz's words. She set the bottle aside a moment later, then pulled her feet onto the cushion beneath her. Her eyes rounded and her gaze darted, an indication of rapid, probably unpleasant, thoughts. "What if you're wrong and my family was his target—they just weren't home?"

"I don't think so." Cruz set his nearly empty bottle aside, and sorted through the mash-up of thoughts in his mind. He wanted to console her so desperately, it was complicating his ability to remain strictly logical, and this was new and scary territory.

One of the things that made Cruz an excellent private investigator was his ability to compartmentalize. He separated himself emotionally from the cases, because keeping a clear and objective mind was key. Working with Gina had blown all that out the window, and it was a continuous struggle to keep his eyes on the end goal instead of on her.

"Why?" she asked, forcing him back to the conversation at hand.

"You have to remember that he still doesn't know you're with me, or that the lawmen in two towns are after him. He thinks he's going to get what he wants. So hurting your family isn't in his best interest, because that would ensure you'd never come back," Cruz said. "I think he's still trying to manipulate you, and the break-in at your parents' house was designed to intimidate and motivate you to return to him, if you're still in touch with your family. It's probably also a test to see if you're in contact with them. And I'm sure he did some snooping while he was in there wrecking things. Thankfully, you hadn't spoken to them before that point, so there wasn't anything to find."

Cruz didn't bother to add the other, more gruesome, truth. If Tony had wanted to hurt the Riccis, he could've done that at any time. Instead, he'd waited to make his move while they were away, at their weekly mass.

She nodded slowly, looking slightly comforted by the awful conversation. "So he's throwing a tantrum."

Cruz smiled. "I guess that's one way to look at it. But here's the thing. The louder he yells, the easier it will be to find him."

Gina inched closer to Cruz, tucking herself against his side and pulling his arm around her shoulders. "Is this okay?"

"Yeah," Cruz answered, careful not to let his shock register in his voice. He brushed locks of dark hair off her shoulder, letting the silky strands slide between his fingers, half-mesmerized by the heavenly feel and scent.

"What do we do now?" she asked.

It took a moment for the question to make sense in Cruz's mind, and for his wandering thoughts to return to the moment at hand.

"We stay here, safe and together, while Derek and local law enforcement keep looking for him," he said, liking the notion more by the second. "Tony can't stay off the grid much longer without making himself look suspicious. People get busy, go on trips, take a few days to be alone, but they come back. They move on with their lives. So my family will watch for signs of his return home or to his office, while I keep you out of sight."

"What happens when they locate him?" Gina asked.

"If he shows up at his home or office, a West Liberty officer will invite him to the station for questioning in your disappearance. Even if his lawyers get him out before charges can be pressed, at least we can follow him from there. Just being called out at this point should be enough to shake him."

Gina yawned.

Cruz turned his lips toward her head. "You should probably get some sleep," he said softly. "Derek is spending the night outside your folks' place, keeping a quiet watch from several houses away. You can give them a call in the morning if they don't call you before then."

"I won't be able to sleep," she said. "And I don't want to be alone. Do you mind if I stay with you a little longer?"

His heart gave a heavy kick and he fumbled for how best to respond. Gina was soft and warm against him. Her heat registered through the material of both their shirts and seared him in wholly perfect ways. The sweet scent of her erased any need to check in with his cousins right away.

"All right," he agreed, adjusting her in his arms so her head rested against his chest. Then he let himself relax and enjoy the moment, delighted that she wanted to be there with him too, even if it was only to avoid being alone. And he wished, self-indulgently, that one day soon, he could tell her exactly how little he minded her choosing him over an empty room and bed. And how much he'd like her to choose him again every night.

Chapter Fifteen

Cruz woke to the blessed scent of fresh coffee. He'd stayed up long after Gina had fallen asleep on the couch, tucked sweetly against him as if she belonged there. He'd done some research on the Marino family, Tony and his father in particular, then talked to Derek off and on until nearly dawn, sorting his complicated thoughts on the case and keeping Derek company while he watched over the Riccis.

He hadn't dared to move Gina to her bed, fearing the trip would wake her, and knowing she needed her sleep. So he'd tipped her over where she sat, slid a pillow under her head in his absence and covered her with a blanket before sneaking away to catch a few hours of sleep for himself. He'd briefly entertained the thought of carrying her to his bed, but that seemed like a bad idea for multiple reasons, not the least of which was that every time he touched Gina a little, he longed to touch her more.

The thought of touching her more had kept him from falling asleep immediately when he'd finally crawled into bed, despite the hour. Now he was groggy and that made him cranky. So he padded on autopilot toward the scent of freshly brewed coffee, like a sailor following his siren song. He placed mental wagers on how many cups it would take to truly wake him and doubted anything could do the job after roughly three hours of sleep.

Until Gina came into view, standing near the glass deck doors again, staring at something beyond. His gaze trailed over her long dark hair, hanging in waves over her shoulders and across the crisp white cotton of her T-shirt. The reflection of her pretty face was visible in the glass, and her wide brown eyes seemed fixed on a pair of red birds in the apple tree out back.

Cruz let his greedy gaze travel down her back to the pink plaid sleep shorts and bare legs beneath. A surge of adrenaline coursed through him, doing more to wake him than any amount of caffeine ever could. And a low groan escaped his lips.

Gina spun, eyes bright and smile wide. She had a white mug clasped between her small hands.

Cruz feigned a stretch and yawn to cover the less appropriate sound he'd made a moment before. "Good morning."

"Good morning," Gina echoed.

He headed for the coffeepot, then poured a mug to the brim. "Thanks for this," he said, turning back to her before taking a hearty sip.

Gina bit her lip. "Of course." She moved to the island then, claiming a seat on the stool across from where he stood. "Tell me when you're more awake, because I have an idea I want to run by you," she said.

He hoped idly that her idea aligned with any number of the ideas he'd fallen asleep enjoying, but assumed he wasn't that lucky. "What is it?"

"I've been avoiding social media all this time, trying to stop Tony from somehow finding me, but websites like Facebook are great resources for us too. Even if Tony hasn't updated his feed, his mom or someone else who's seen him might have." She fidgeted, then bit her lip again. "Sorry. I've been limiting my caffeine intake since finding out about the baby, but I've had two cups in the last hour, and I think I've reached my limit."

He laughed, buoyed by her smile and envious of the caffeine rush. "I'm working on catching up with you," he said, lifting his mug in evidence. "Meanwhile, keep going."

She folded her hands on the island and took a deep breath. "What if I reach out to a few people online, only two or three, and only the ones I'm certain will be willing to help me build a case against Tony? I can make a new account and keep the exchanges private."

Cruz sucked down the rest of his coffee, scorching his tongue and burning his throat in the process, needing the caffeine to take hold before discussing anything that could wind up putting Gina in harm's way. "Care if we have breakfast while we talk this through?" he asked. He grabbed the English muffins and a jar of peanut butter from his pantry, then raised them in Gina's direction.

"Sure." She smiled. "Thanks."

Cruz set the items on the counter.

Gina left her seat and met him at his side. "Do you have an apple? I can slice one to go with the muffins."

He pointed to the fridge, and Gina retrieved an apple.

She went to work on that, while he split two muffins and dropped the pieces into his toaster.

"I like the overall concept you've got going," he said, "but I don't like the risk." He waited for her to argue. When she didn't, he went on, "You'd be putting a lot of trust in people from a very untrustworthy guy's world, in order for this to work. And that makes me nervous," he admitted. He took another sip of coffee and reminded himself to think about her proposal logically and cautiously, but not so overprotectively. He felt, belatedly, a little like Captain Obvious, since Gina knew better than most people exactly what she could be getting into.

"That's true," she agreed, "but people as awful as Tony inevitably make a few enemies along the way. They just aren't outwardly vocal about it, so we need to find them."

"I take it you have some ideas about who to contact first," he said, pouring a second mug of black coffee and trying to accurately weigh the risk against the potential reward.

"I think so," Gina said. She leaned against the counter. "I know you're worried about me, but you don't need to do that. You can oversee all the online exchanges, and if anyone is willing to meet in person, you can choose the place, come with me or go alone. I don't care, as long as the end result is Tony behind bars."

He couldn't argue with that. The plan was sensible and smart. Plus, it kept her out of harm's way. The worst thing that could happen was if one of the people she reached out to snitched to Tony. But even then, Gina would still be safe with Cruz. "Seems like you've thought it all through," he said. "I don't hate it."

"Good," she answered, dividing the apple slices between two plates with a grin.

Cruz finished his new cup of coffee, then added peanut butter to the toasted muffin halves and placed two beside the apples on each plate.

He carried their breakfasts to the small dinette near

his sliding glass doors, and Gina followed. They ate companionably for several minutes before he spoke again. Stomach full and caffeine working, he had more questions. "Who do you have in mind for your targets?"

Gina leaned forward, hands folded beneath her chin. "Tony has a sister he doesn't speak to, and a secretary he treats like trash. Actually, I think he fired her a few months ago. There's also an ex-girlfriend who avoids him like he's contagious at every gala and fundraiser. She even left once, immediately after seeing us arrive."

"Let's skip the sister," Cruz said. "Families are complicated, but I like the others as potential resources." A recently fired employee and ex-girlfriend who wouldn't share the same room with Tony were compelling witnesses. Both would also have access to information Cruz's family might potentially use to build their case.

Gina finished her apple slices with a thoughtful expression. "I was also friends with the girlfriend of Tony's friend Ben," she said. "Her name's Celia, and Ben works at Tony's company. I think Celia would help me get into contact with the secretary and old girlfriend. She might even have information on what Tony's been up to lately, if he's spoken with Ben."

Cruz stretched back in his seat, feeling more like himself by the minute. "The friend's girlfriend is unlikely to feel obligated to tell Tony you contacted her. She might tell her boyfriend, though. What's he like?"

"Nice," Gina said. "He seemed like a good guy. I could always tell when he thought Tony was being awful to me. He didn't speak up like he should've, but he also never behaved like Tony. They've been friends a long time. I sometimes got the feeling a shared history, more than actual affection, was what kept them in one another's circle."

"If Ben works at Tony's family's company, he might've also worried about losing his job," Cruz added.

Gina chewed the edge of her lip as she nodded, lost in thought once more.

Cruz longed to soothe her tortured lip, but tried not to stare.

Gina never seemed to stop thinking, planning or troubleshooting. It was no wonder she'd stayed off Tony's radar for as long as she had. She was too smart for him, and he must've hated that.

Cruz smiled at the thought.

"What?" she asked, freeing her lip and drawing his eyes up to hers.

He lifted his palms, pleading the Fifth.

Her phone rang, and she released him from her gaze. "It's my parents."

"Take it," he said. "I've got this."

Gina carried her phone to the couch, folding herself onto the cushions with a warm, anticipating smile. "Hello?"

Cruz allowed himself a moment to wonder what it might be like to keep her in his life after her danger had passed. Would she be interested in him if she no longer needed his protection? Was the attraction he felt between them born of heightened emotions alone? Did she feel it too?

He carried their plates to the sink and turned the water on. How great would it be to see her baby born? To be asked to stick around and be a part of their lives?

He shook his head and scrubbed the plates a little harder. Clearly, the coffee hadn't given his muddled brain as much clarity as he'd thought. There wasn't any reason to think Gina would want to see him after this was over, let alone want him hanging around to watch her raise her baby.

Or be part of both their lives in a permanent way.

He finished the dishes, then wiped the counters as he thought about the plan she'd proposed over breakfast. It was a good plan.

Gina made her way back to the kitchen a few moments later, the cell phone no longer at her ear.

"How's your mama?" he asked.

"Good." Gina smiled. "They're getting new carpet, and she promised to call me every morning at this time, so we'll always have that to look forward to." Her lip quivered, whether in sadness or joy, he wasn't sure.

Cruz opened his arms to her, and she fell easily against his chest, wrapping him in a tight squeeze. "You really are a hugger," he said, tightening his grip when she tried to escape.

She laughed against his chest. "And you aren't?"

"Only for you," he admitted, and she seemed to melt against him.

"Thank you," she whispered. Her cheeks were pink when she stepped away from him.

He would've given everything he owned to know what she was thinking.

"I gave my obstetrician the number of my burner phone. I hope that's okay. You were very specific about who I could talk to on it, but I don't know how long I'll be living here, and it'll be time for me to see her again in about ten days. I didn't want to cancel the appointment if I didn't have to."

"Sounds good," he said. "I wasn't thinking about

your doctor when I set up the phones. I didn't know you saw a doctor regularly. Is that normal? You're both okay?" He tried to look less clueless than he suddenly felt.

"Yeah." Gina smiled. "We're fine. Pregnant women usually see their doctors monthly until the last month or two. Then I'll see her, or someone else, more often."

He nodded, making a mental note to look into her doctor's background and office location. "I can take you to your appointments if you want. Just let me know."

"I will. Thanks."

Cruz pushed his hands into his pockets. "I guess we should see about putting your plan into motion."

"Really?" she asked, brightening at the word. "Now?"

"Sooner is probably better, right?" he asked. "For what it's worth, you should know I think you're brave for wanting to help. Knox was thrilled to get that list of people in Tony's circle last night, and I know this will help too." He grinned, feeling misplaced pride bloom in his chest. Gina wasn't his to take pride in, but he couldn't help the wave of good vibes. "You might wind up bringing Tony down all by yourself," he said, punctuating the words with a wink.

"Sure." She laughed. "Just me and my handsome bodyguard." Her gaze drifted over his chest, then up to his lips, stealing the air from his lungs in a long delicious burn.

When her eyes met his, he took a step closer, enjoying the crackle of energy around them.

The doorbell interrupted like a wet blanket on a fire, and he cursed whoever waited outside.

"Be right back," he said. His steps were light as he went to see who had the world's worst timing.

Gina had been flirting with him. She was looking at his lips, and someone had the nerve to visit? At that moment?

He swallowed a groan as he checked the porch through his front window.

Derek waved, already watching the window. "Derek's here," he announced, opening the door with a less than welcoming expression.

His cousin strode inside, casting a curious look at Cruz on his way to the kitchen. "I've been awake for twenty hours, and in a car for nine. I'm stiff, tired and sore. I need coffee and a lengthy massage."

Cruz pushed the door shut and locked it behind him. "You can have my coffee, but I'm not giving you a massage."

Derek waved a greeting to Gina as he poured, then gulped from a mug.

"What brings you by?" Cruz asked, joining them in the kitchen and hoping there was a quality reason for the interruption.

Derek took his time on the coffee, eyes closed and apparently two blinks away from dropping asleep on the floor.

"Are you okay?" Gina asked, sincere concern on her pretty brow.

His eyes peeled open, and he seemed to struggle with focus for a moment. "Yes. Tired."

She looked to Cruz.

He shrugged. "Go on," he urged. "Tell me what you know, then you can black out on the couch and I'll give Allison a call so she doesn't worry."

Derek finished the coffee, then set his empty mug on the counter. "A doorbell camera on a home at the end of the Riccis' block caught Tony's car turning onto the street around the time of the break-in. It's not a smoking gun, but considering everything else, it's going to strengthen the case. Knox is working on that now."

Gina covered her mouth, and her eyes went wide.

Cruz moved to her side, eyes trained on his partner. "That's incredible. Nice work, man."

Derek's smile widened as he stumbled clumsily toward the couch. "It gets better. Knox went out to shake some trees about an hour ago, and ran into Tony arriving at work, as if it was just another day at the office. He didn't know about the doorbell camera yet, so he invited him downtown for a chat about the missing Ricci girl." He waved at Gina as he collapsed onto the couch. "Now Knox is waiting on the Marino family attorney to arrive so Tony can be questioned."

Cruz felt Gina's eyes on him, and he turned to meet her gaze. "How do you feel about a trip to the station?"

Chapter Sixteen

Gina hurried into the room Knox indicated, then started at the sight of Tony and an older man on the television. Her heart pumped and ached as she struggled for breath. The sight of him induced a powerful need to run.

"It's okay," Cruz said. "Do you want to sit?"

Gina shook her head, at a complete loss for words and willing the ringing in her ears to subside. She crept carefully toward the screen, her muscles tense and chest tight.

Tony looked bored as Knox entered the room.

The older man beside Tony, presumably his attorney, shifted forward on his seat. "Deputy Winchester, I trust you've returned to apologize to my client and me for wasting our time."

Knox stared, blank faced. "No, sir."

"Then I hope you were able to come up with something more substantial than a list of unrelated crimes, the victims of which, excluding Gina Ricci, my client has never even heard of," he said.

Knox opened the file folder he'd carried back into the room, then fanned a set of photos onto the table.

Cruz moved to Gina's side and set his hand against her back for support.

"What's this?" The attorney dragged the images closer, then dared a look at Tony's unchanged expression.

"Those are the photos of Mr. Marino's car on the street where a break-in occurred last night." Knox took the seat across from the other men.

The attorney shoved the photos away. "Another crime? Do you plan to pin every broken law in Kentucky on my client before we leave here today? Which will be soon," he added, a note of threat in his tone. "Furthermore, what are you attempting to make of a grainy surveillance photo of a car resembling my client's Volvo, on a public street at a decent hour?" He released a dramatic labored sigh.

Tony alternated between examining his nails, smirking at Knox and glaring at the camera, never speaking a word.

"How can he be so cocky?" she whispered. She'd seen him behave this way before, superior and untouchable, but never when faced with a deputy sheriff for crimes he obviously committed. Wasn't he nervous at all? "He killed a man, brutally attacked a woman and broke into my parents' home. Still he sits there as if this is all a game. As if people don't matter, their possessions and lives don't matter." Gina wrapped her arms around her middle, terrified once more by the possibility of what he might do to her baby given the chance.

The attorney stretched upright, buttoning his suit jacket and glowering at Knox. The arrogance and condescension in his expression were thick and intimidating, even through the shared wall. "We're done here. I suggest you get your act together before approaching my client again, unless you'd like me to file harassment charges. I'll be reaching out to your superior this afternoon, so we don't have to get that far." He moved toward the door and Knox opened it. The attorney jerked his head in the direction of the hall, directing Tony to leave, then he followed Knox out.

Tony stood slowly, eyes fixed on the camera, then slunk in that direction, like the lethal predator he was.

Gina's stomach clenched and her breath caught as Tony grew larger on-screen.

He lifted a hand and wiggled his fingers while staring angrily back at her.

"Anthony," the attorney called, poking his head back through the open door.

Tony's lip curled in a feral mix of distaste and amusement. As if he knew she was there, knew she was shaking. And could see her spiraling.

As if he was going to make her pay, and she knew it.

She closed her eyes and felt Cruz shift positions. When she opened her lids, it was the protector, not the monster, looking back.

Cruz had moved into the space between her and the television. He raised his brows, then widened his stance, lowering himself by several inches, bringing his face closer to hers. "You're with me now," he said. "And Tony Marino is never getting near you again."

She released a shuddered breath as she stepped against him and pressed her cheek to his chest, the way she had earlier that day. There was so much to hope for in his words, and she needed every one of them to be true.

GINA WOKE EARLY the next morning after her worst night's sleep in weeks. Seeing Tony sneer, knowing he was close enough to punch a hole through the wall and grab her, had been more upsetting than she'd realized at the time. The effects of his stare, combined with memories of his wrath, had kept her awake long after her body and mind had begged for rest.

Then, before she'd realized she finally drifted off, the sounds and scents of breakfast had filtered images of Cruz into her mind. She'd opened her eyes to a powerful sense of relief, and smiled at her current situation. Tony couldn't hurt her anymore, but her heart would surely break when it was time to walk away from Cruz.

She'd become unreasonably attached to her new protector and friend. At first, she'd been drawn to his face and attitude, but later, as they'd talked and spent time together, she'd become even more interested in his steadfast sincerity, kind heart and sense of honor. Cruz made her laugh, and he seemed to connect with her on some unexplainable level, in ways she'd never experienced. Life with him over the last few days, despite the peripheral awfulness, had been easy and natural. It was as if they'd known one another for years instead of days. The results were peaceful and pleasant, things she didn't want to let go. And the more he told her about himself and his family, the more she wanted to learn. She hoped to meet his big family, see where he'd come from and hear stories about him as a kid.

When she thought of leaving his life, after it was safe for her to go, she knew a piece of her heart would surely chip off and stay with him.

But for now, she'd take the moments as they came.

She and Cruz parted ways after breakfast. Gina took her mom's call, and he went to take a shower. She curled on his couch to think after saying goodbye to her folks.

She still needed to reach out to Tony's friend's girlfriend, Celia. She just hadn't decided how to start the complicated conversation. It wouldn't come as a surprise to the other woman that Gina had run away. Celia had been around long enough to know Tony was controlling and temperamental. She'd heard the way he spoke to Gina when they were together. She'd seen the bruises Gina always claimed were a result of her clumsiness, rather than Tony's hands. The complicated part for Gina now was determining the right way to ask for help and possibly relevant dirt on a dangerous and powerful man.

"Yeah." Cruz's voice carried through the home as he opened the bathroom door. A grand puff of steam swept into the hallway, bringing with it heady scents of his body wash, shampoo and cologne.

Cruz strode barefoot, in jeans and a gray V-neck T-shirt, toward his living room, smiling at Gina as he pressed the phone to his ear. "I was in the shower. Can't I have ten minutes to myself?" He rolled his eyes, smiling wickedly as he approached his desk. "She's fine. Everything is fine. We're the ones just sitting around waiting for information."

Gina patted the cushion at her side, and Cruz carried his laptop with him to join her.

"Anything new on Tony?" he asked whoever was on the other end of the line.

The sound of her ex's name sent a shiver down her spine.

The look he'd given her through the police station camera returned to her like a punch. There had been something unnatural in his eyes, and she no longer worried he'd fight her for custody of their child. Now she feared neither of them would survive if he had his way.

Cruz reached for her. "You okay?" He set his phone on one leg. The screen was dark, and the call disconnected.

She forced her shoulders back and her chin up. "Yeah. Who was on the phone?"

"Derek." Cruz said the word with a chuckle. "He's tailing Tony and reporting in periodically. So far, there's nothing to report, which means he's bored and checking in to pass his time more than anything."

"Wow," she said with a disbelieving smile. "Has he even had time to go home and shower?" He'd been sound asleep on the couch when Gina and Cruz had left for the police station.

Gone when they'd returned.

"I don't know," Cruz said, "but he's still a little sleep deprived and slaphappy."

Gina gave a soft laugh. "You and your family are pretty amazing. You know that? Actually, you probably hear that a lot, but I can't stop thinking it. So, I figured it was time I said so."

He grinned. "You think I'm pretty amazing?"

"Yeah." She nodded, brows raised. "You took my case, knowing I couldn't pay you, and now I've got five Winchesters in two towns trying to fix my mess. So, absolutely. Never mind the fact that you're letting me stay here, feeding me and acting as my personal chauffeur."

"Lawmen chase bad guys," he said with a smile and a shrug. "It's their job, and I think it's in my family's DNA. I let you stay here so I can keep you close. For safety's sake." He winked, and warmth spread through her body.

"What about you and Derek?" she asked, trying to learn more about his day-to-day when she wasn't there. "Surely you have other, paying cases."

He smiled. "Nothing more pressing than capturing a dangerous stalker and protecting the innocent."

She rolled her eyes, knowing he'd stopped himself short of saying the word *victim*, and she hated being a victim.

"You looked upset a minute ago," Cruz said, catching her gaze with his, then waiting for a response. "You want to talk about it?"

"Not really." She was trapped somewhere between wanting to hash out her extremely complicated feelings for Cruz and not wanting to dwell on what couldn't be changed. She sank back against the cushions with a sigh. "I can't shake the feeling Tony knew I was there yesterday," she said instead. "The way he looked into the camera. The expression he gave. I feel as if something bad is coming," she admitted. "Like there was meaning in that dead-eyed look."

Her phone rang before Cruz could respond, and she stretched to retrieve it from the table. A spark of fear ignited instantly. She'd already spoken to her parents, and they'd agreed to talk again tomorrow. They would only call a second time if something was wrong.

She tensed as she brought the device onto her lap. An unknown number filled the screen.

Cruz frowned. "It's probably a wrong number, but why don't you answer on speaker?"

"You said not to answer unknown numbers," she said, wholly terrified to press the button, which suddenly felt like the switch for an explosive.

Cruz smiled. "I told your folks that. I'm here, and

I'm keeping a list of numbers who call, especially those that aren't automated sales numbers."

Gina nodded, liking the possibility of a telemarketer more than any of the ideas circling her mind. She inhaled, then prepared to make her voice as flat and bland as she could, hoping not to sound too much like herself. "Hello?"

A dark chuckle rose through the speaker in response. "I told you I could find you anywhere," Tony said, a mix of satisfaction and victory in his husky tone. "You can't run forever, baby doll, and your days of hiding are already numbered. Keep it up, and you'll be deeply sorry."

Cruz swiped his phone to life and engaged a recording app, then circled his fingers in the air, indicating she should keep Tony talking.

Gina's mouth dried, and her tongue swelled. "What do you want?" she croaked.

"I want what's mine," he seethed, his voice dripping with venom. "I want to remind you who's in charge here. You belong to me, and I decide when you can leave. I do," he emphasized. "Me. Not you."

"I do not belong to you," she snapped. "I never did, and I will never come back. But I will make sure you pay for all the things you've done." She pressed her lips shut, feeling suddenly more angry than frightened. "That's a promise."

She braced for a cutting, threatening retort, but he only laughed. The low, maniacal sound vibrated through the phone's speaker and chilled her bones.

"You think you're so tough now," he said airily, his voice light and apparently amused. "You hide out for a couple months and think you're untouchable." He laughed again, and Gina's intuition spiked. "Baby, let me make you a promise," he said, tossing her words back at her. "You are touchable. And so is everyone you care about."

Her gaze jumped to Cruz's steady eyes. "Tony?" she asked. "How'd you get this number?"

His returning chuckle sent shards of fear into her heart. "You're not the only one who'll do whatever it takes to get their way," he said. "I'm coming for what's mine. That means you, and it includes my baby you're carrying."

Her face flashed hot and her ears began to ring. "You will never get this baby," she vowed. If she had to leave the state, the country or buy a ticket to the moon, she would do whatever it took to protect her child.

"Well." He blew out a long bored breath, as if the single word was a statement of its own. "We'll see about that," he added. "For now, you're going to have to find a new doctor."

The line went dead, and Gina threw the cell phone onto the coffee table, desperate to get away from Tony's awful threats and everything remotely connected to him.

She wanted to scream, to fight, to vomit, but she was far too shaken to do anything but try not to explode.

Beside her, Cruz tapped wildly on his phone screen, then he stopped suddenly and began to scroll. "What's your doctor's name?"

"Tulane," she said, pressing the heels of her hands against her eyes. A heartbeat later, his question clicked mentally into place. "That's how Tony got this number," she said. "I just updated my contact information with her office yesterday."

Cruz's expression fell as he pumped up the volume on his phone and turned the screen in her direction.

A local news site centered the screen. A beautiful blond reporter stood outside Dr. Tulane's office. Bright red-lettered text scrolled along beneath her, declaring, "Breaking News" and "Local Tragedy."

"According to the Great Falls Sheriff's Department," the reporter began, "local obstetrician Melissa Tulane was stabbed outside her office early this morning when arriving for work. Sources at Falls General Hospital say the thirty-one-year-old doctor is currently in critical condition. No witnesses or details have come to light at this time, making this the third violent attack in our community this week."

Cruz lowered the phone with a curse.

Gina raised a hand to her temple, her mind and body going unexpectedly numb. "I told Dr. Tulane I was hiding from a dangerous man and she agreed to see me, off the record and pro bono, for as long as I was able to remain in town. Her name was on the stolen ultrasound photo," she said. "He used the photo to find her, and her to find my number, then he hurt her to punish me."

"This is not your fault," Cruz said, tapping the screen of his phone again. In the next heartbeat, he reached out to pull Gina near. "We need to let Knox know about the call and that Tulane is your doctor."

Gina accepted his hand, but for the first time in a long time, she didn't want comfort.

She wanted retribution.

Chapter Seventeen

An hour later, Cruz waited with Gina inside Falls General Hospital for information on Dr. Tulane's attack and current medical status. Most of the Winchesters had friends on staff willing to nose around when asked nicely. Unfortunately, none of Cruz's contacts were in the ICU today, which meant Knox had to work his magic instead. And based on how long they'd already waited for his return, Knox's magic was slow.

Gina passed the wide hallway intersection nearest the ICU, jumping each time the doors to the unit opened.

Cruz wasn't faring much better. Cell reception in the hospital was terrible, and Knox wasn't responding to his requests for updates.

To make matters worse, Derek had lost track of Tony after following him into a section of especially dense traffic near the highway headed east. Thankfully, he hadn't been anywhere near the hospital at the time of their separation, but Cruz would feel much better if he and Gina were back at his house, where she was safe and well protected, as soon as possible.

Instead, they were in the busy corridor of a massive public hospital, waiting on Knox.

Gina chewed her lip, then the edge of her thumbnail, looking paler and more on edge than he liked. She hadn't been the same since they'd learned about her doctor's attack, and it worried him. She'd wanted to apologize to her doctor, and the entire Tulane family, for her role as the unintentional link between the doctor and her attacker. He'd reiterated the obvious and known danger in that, and they'd settled on meeting Knox at the hospital, where he would deliver flowers on her behalf. Now she stood around the corner from the ICU waiting room, peeking at men and women with long faces as they ghosted in and out.

Cruz followed her gaze to the small, glass-walled space, only a few feet from the ICU doors.

"I'll bet that's her family," she whispered, eyes trained on a knot of visibly upset people.

A man holding a toddler's hand spoke with an older couple and a deputy. The gray-haired woman carried a baby, and all three adults looked as if they were on the verge of tears.

Gina adjusted her platinum wig, which seemed so incredibly obvious to him. Now that he knew her, the appearance was nearly laughable. His borrowed hoodie hung to her thighs, and the rolled-up sleeves still concealed most of her hands. She probably looked like a child in oversize clothing to everyone else at first glance. "They must be so scared right now," she said, still fixated on the family.

Cruz reached for her hand and gave a reassuring squeeze, then tugged her in his direction.

She buried her face against his chest for a long moment before pushing away once more.

"We'll figure this out," he said softly, hoping the words were true, and beginning to fear they weren't.

Tony Marino had proved to be a much slipperier snake than Cruz had imagined possible.

Typically, he and Derek found their person of interest or gained the information they needed in a ridiculously short amount of time. They were a fast, sharp and effective team. An efficient tool used frequently by everyone from local law enforcement to attorneys and jaded spouses. But this case, arguably Cruz's most important one, was taking far too long to wrap up. And too many people were being hurt in the process.

"We have to stop him," Gina said. "He's completely out of control, and I'm terrified just imagining what he might do next."

"I think that's the point," Cruz said. Terror was Tony's favorite tool and the source of his power. "People in his world fear him and his family—their influence, his abuse. When you left him, you broke the pattern he counted on to maintain control, and he wasn't prepared to feel powerless. Now he's trying to draw you back to him by playing on your goodness. He's counting on you to willingly take the punishment so no one else has to."

She shuddered, then cradled her middle.

He checked his watch, then scanned the corridors in each direction. "I wish I knew what was taking Knox so long. I'm giving him another five minutes before we head out. He can call with updates."

"I'd hoped to hear about Dr. Tulane," Gina said, sounding unusually strained and appearing a little ill. "I wanted to know how she looked when he saw her."

"I know, but the fewer people who see you, the better," he reminded her gently. "As it is, Tony can ask every person in this hospital if they've seen you, and it won't matter as long as they haven't."

She released a heavy breath, then raised a hand to her forehead, where a sheen of sweat had sprouted. Red spots rose high on her cheeks, and the rest of her face appeared uncharacteristically ghostlike.

"What's wrong?" he asked more sharply than he'd intended, his usually unflappable calm completely broken by the possibility Gina wasn't well. "Are you sick? Hurt?"

"I'm pregnant," she said, attempting a joke, but not pulling it off in her current state. "Sometimes, I get woozy. It doesn't happen often anymore, but it can be intense while it lasts. I'll be fine in a few minutes."

"You need to sit," he said, sliding his arm around her back for support and guiding her toward the waiting room. "Do you need a doctor?"

At least they were already at a hospital, Cruz thought, trying to find some kind of silver lining in the new complication. He knew less than nothing about pregnant women, but he knew he needed this particular one to be okay more than he needed air.

"Actually," she said, "I might be sick. If my breakfast makes a reappearance, it has nothing to do with your cooking."

"Funny," he said, attempting to smile back as his heart rate climbed into another bracket. "What can I do for you?"

"I just need to sit a minute," she said. "Cool air and cold water always helps. I think the stress exacerbates everything, but there's not much to be done about that."

Cruz walked her into the small, window-lined waiting room, then to a set of empty chairs situated away from the family and deputy who was still chatting with them. "Here." Cruz lowered her onto an armed chair, then turned anxiously toward the small corner table with a coffeepot. "I'm going to check for water."

"Thank you." She breathed the word, then tipped forward, resting her elbows on her knees and her face in her hands.

Cruz caught the vaguely familiar deputy's eye as he approached the coffee station.

The other man's gaze slid to Gina, then back to Cruz. "She okay?"

"Shaken," Cruz said. "Otherwise, I think she'll be all right."

The knot of people he'd been speaking with drifted away, turning back to themselves for conversation.

"Any chance you've seen my brother around, Stone?" Cruz asked, checking the name on the deputy's badge.

Stone was young and blond with a gangly appearance and general air of inexperience.

"No," he said. "I came straight here from the station when my shift began, and Knox hasn't been around."

Cruz nodded, then turned his attention to the table where a half-filled pot of coffee had gone cold. There weren't any bottles of water, but there was a stack of disposable cups.

He grabbed one, then returned to Gina.

"I'm going to find a fountain and fill this with water. I'll buy a bottle if I see a vending machine, then we're going back to my place, where you can rest. Knox can call and fill us in whenever he figures out we're gone." Cruz strode back to the deputy's side. "Keep an eye on her for a few minutes?" he asked, tipping his head to Gina. "I'm going for more water and a nurse if I can find one. If you see a medical professional of any kind before I get back, have them talk to her."

"Will do," Stone assured him, then he turned his back to Gina and crossed his arms like a long-limbed, baby-faced bodyguard.

"Thanks," Cruz said. He grabbed the empty pitcher, then moved purposefully toward the ICU.

When he saw Knox with a nurse at the end of the hall, Cruz broke into a jog.

GINA OPENED HER eyes to the sounds of subtle chaos. A soft bell registered through the hospital's PA system, followed by the announcement of a Code Blue.

Thankfully, the nausea she'd been experiencing off and on for months was slowly subsiding, and her ability to think of something other than passing out had returned. What she needed to know now was if Dr. Tulane was the patient in need.

Gina straightened in the uncomfortable chair and focused on the sounds of charging feet. A crash team ran past the small waiting room, drawing Gina upright. The people Gina had suspected were her doctor's family spilled into the hall, looking horrified and drifting toward the ICU doors as they closed behind the cluster of men and women dressed in blue scrubs, masks and gowns.

The deputy, who'd been diligently standing guard before Gina, moved to the edge of the room, and beckoned them back. "Y'all need to wait here," he instructed, garnering an array of desperate and angry looks from the adults.

Gina inched closer, wishing she could tell them how sorry she was and knowing now wasn't the time.

A moment later, a doctor in full scrubs and mask darted out from the ICU and ushered the family through the doors, pointing in the direction the team had gone. He was dressed in blue from head to toe, like the others who'd just rushed past. He moved to the deputy next, keeping his voice low and urgent, hands gesturing toward the ICU doors.

Gina crept closer still, heart rate climbing as she tried to make sense of what was happening, and of the awful icy coil in her gut.

The deputy's expression changed, and he looked over his shoulder to Gina.

The doctor followed his gaze, then punched the deputy hard in the abdomen. When he pulled his fist away, the scalpel she hadn't noticed before was crimson with blood.

A scream caught in Gina's throat, choking off her voice and her breaths while cementing her feet to the floor.

Tony's violent gaze was suddenly unmistakable, sandwiched neatly between the protective mask and puffy hair covering. "Hello, baby doll."

"No." She forced her heavy feet to move, then darted backward, into the waiting room.

He snaked one arm out and caught her wrist in a vise of his fingers before she could reach the coffeepot she'd planned to use as a weapon.

"No!" she screamed, finally finding her voice and employing it at maximum capacity.

Tony jerked her painfully to him and tipped the bloody scalpel toward her middle. "Say another word, or fight me, and your baby will pay."

On the floor, the deputy clutched his walkie-talkie with one hand, the other palm pressed tightly against the blooming wound in his gut.

Tony yanked her into the hallway and nearly off her feet.

Tears spilled across her cheeks as she stumbled along at his side, dragged swiftly away from the waiting room.

"Gina!" Cruz's voice echoed in the otherwise quiet hallway, his footfalls beating a steady and increasing rhythm in her direction.

She heard the rumble and bounce of a falling water bottle, and a dozen voices lifting into the air.

"Knox!" he screamed. "He's got her!"

Gina strained to see behind her, to catch sight of her hero one last time.

"Freeze!" Cruz yelled, voice frantic and fervent as he rounded the corner in her direction, closing the distance between them like a track star. He pumped his arms and knees, reaching for the sidearm that wasn't there because he'd locked it in his glove box before they'd left his Jeep. He wasn't permitted to carry it into the hospital.

Gina's heart swelled, and the fear heated to anger inside her. *No more running*, she told herself. *It's time to fight*. "No!" Her feet tangled and her ankles twisted as she grabbed Tony's hand on hers and tried to pry it loose. "Stop!" she screamed. "Help!" And instead of tripping over herself, trying to keep up with him, she dug her sneakers into the ground and forced him to drag her.

Yes, he'd threatened her baby, but whatever he could do to her now, while in a hurry and on the run, would be nothing compared to what would happen if she let him haul her away and take his time.

Tony slammed a shoulder against the stairwell door, and the barrier swung freely open.

"No!" she screamed again, this time throwing her legs out from under her and dropping onto the floor like a 150-pound sack of potatoes. She curled into the fetal position to protect her abdomen.

A string of biting cusses flew from his lips as his forward momentum halted.

He tried to pull her up by her arms, but there wasn't any time, and the cavalry was closing in. His scalpel clattered to the floor and she kicked it away.

"Great Falls Sheriff's Department," Knox bellowed, quickly catching up to his brother's side.

Gina cried out with relief as the stairwell door slammed closed and Tony disappeared behind it.

Chapter Eighteen

Cruz waited impatiently near the back of the emergency room while Gina was seen by a doctor. Her shaky voice mingled with a deeper, more sedate tenor behind a blue privacy curtain.

She'd needed the exam because Cruz had left her in the hands of someone else, and they had both failed her.

He ran through all the possible scenarios, trying to determine a better course of action. One that wouldn't have ended with her nearly abducted, and a deputy in surgery. But he kept coming up short. Maybe Cruz should've insisted the deputy fetch the water. Or called the hospital cafeteria and had water delivered. Something. Anything other than leaving her side, knowing Tony was out there somewhere, waiting to get his hands on her. Cruz had woefully underestimated his opponent's level of determination, and that mistake could've cost Gina's or her baby's life.

Now it was Deputy Stone's family gathered anxiously in a waiting room, desperate for news of his well-being.

Cruz blamed himself for that too.

If there was an upside, in addition to Gina's safety, it was that the crash team had been successful. They'd saved Dr. Tulane, likely after Tony had made a second attempt on her life. Presumably to create a satisfactory distraction and gain access to Gina.

Cruz checked his phone for the tenth time in as many minutes, eager for updates on Deputy Stone, Dr. Tulane or Gina's friend Heather, who still hadn't woken after Tony's attack. Then he double-checked for a missed text from Knox, who was yet again nowhere to be found. He'd last messaged to say he'd lost track of Tony in the stairwell, and was on his way to talk to hospital security about accessing the cameras. But he hadn't returned or texted again, and Cruz was undecided about whether or not to worry. Knox could handle himself in a fair match, even against a sociopath like Tony, but no one was on even footing if they were ambushed.

Cruz prayed his little brother hadn't been ambushed.

He turned back to the blue curtain, longing to yank it aside and know if Gina and the baby were okay. He wanted to be there for her if she was scared, or needed someone to lean on, but he'd been forced outside the flimsy barrier by protocol and manners. He wasn't family, so he wasn't entitled to know anything about her medical condition or care, and he wasn't rude enough to invite himself into the circle. She likely would've agreed for his sake, or from some misguided perception of obligation, but that wasn't the reason he ever wanted to be included.

Instead, he paced the few short steps back and forth, mentally preparing for the worst.

The curtain slid back on his second pass, and Cruz nearly jumped.

A handsome doctor ushered Gina out, a warm smile on his clean-shaven face.

Cruz felt a scowl form. He forced his attention to Gina, who looked unsteady, but less pale than she had before. "How are you?" he asked. "Is the baby okay?"

She nodded quickly, then smiled shyly as she stepped away from the doctor and wrapped her arms around Cruz's middle.

The simple move warmed him and softened the ache in his chest. She and her baby were okay, and Gina wanted his comfort. Not the smiling doctor's. His arms closed protectively, possessively, around her, and he planted a kiss against the top of her head. The move was easy and natural. So much so that it stunned him briefly.

The doctor crossed his arms and nodded smugly. "She and your baby are going to be just fine," he assured him. "Nothing a little rest and hydration won't cure. Maybe a little less excitement moving forward," he suggested. "Over-the-counter meds for pain. Long showers, foot and back rubs for tension and muscle aches. Consult with a counselor in a day or two, just to follow up after the trauma." His expression turned compassionate and deadly serious. "You might feel emotionally fine now, but these things have an uncanny way of sneaking up and taking hold if we ignore them."

Gina nodded, but didn't release Cruz or step out of his embrace.

"For now," the doctor continued, raising his gaze to meet Cruz's, "lavish them both with attention and kindness. That's my prescription for a happy relationship, and it's solid advice. I know because my wife has yet to disagree, and believe me, if I was wrong, she'd let me know."

An incredible feeling rushed through Cruz as he accepted the paperwork passed to him, then watched in stunned silence as the doctor strode away. The concept of Gina being his to care for, and him being the one responsible for lavishing her and her child with love and attention, rattled something loose inside him. And he was instantly certain there wasn't anything he wanted more.

He hadn't known her long, but he loved and appreciated what she was made of, and he saw a kindred spirit in her. She was sweet, but strong, kind and wise. Gina embodied all the things he aspired to be every day. And she loved her family. He knew his family would love her too, if she'd agree to give him a try as more than just her bodyguard, once the danger had passed.

"I'm sorry," she muttered into his shirt, still clinging to him as if he might disappear. "I shouldn't have insisted we come here. I shouldn't have been anywhere near the ICU today."

Cruz pulled back for a look at her face. "You know what I'm going to say about that, right?" He raised one brow and waited for her responding smile, all while imagining how to convince her to date again, when her most recent boyfriend was on a murderous rampage.

"Maybe," she said. "Were you thinking I'm not the boss of you, and you didn't have to listen to me when I asked to come here?"

An unexpected chuckle rose from his chest. "I'm pretty sure you actually are the boss of me," he said, noting a new reverence in his voice and wondering if she heard it too. "But none of this is your fault." He turned her in his arms and set a hand against the curve of her back. "How about we get you home for that shower, a couple pain relievers and some rest?"

She leaned against his side as they made their way

back toward the emergency room exit, where they'd parked his Jeep. "The doctor said there would be pampering," she said.

Cruz's smile brightened. "I believe he said lavishing."

"That sounds spectacular," she returned casually. "He's definitely my favorite adviser now."

Cruz snorted, not bothering to hide his borderline belligerent smile. "I guess he was right. You seem like you're going to be just fine."

"Depends on how the rest of the day goes," she quipped. "I'm quite particular about my lavishing."

Cruz laughed outright, a storm of filthy thoughts pushing into his mind. "We should probably also talk about what happened," he said. "The doctor was right. It helps to talk, and trauma can sneak up on you later if you don't deal with it now. And we should follow up with him for recommendations on counselors, unless you already have one you trust."

Gina slowed, peering up into his face. "Thank you for caring enough to say any of that. I will follow up. I promise. But I really shouldn't have asked you to bring me here," she said, the playful edge in her voice long gone.

"There was no way we could've anticipated Tony would come here," he said. "Not with two towns' worth of law enforcement looking for him, and Derek tailing him in another direction at the time. When I agreed to bring you, I'd assumed the biggest risk was potentially being followed home. I had a dozen alternative routes planned to lose anyone who tried."

"He's really lost it," she said, slowing her pace to a crawl. "His eyes were wild. And I still can't believe he'd come here, knowing the authorities suspect him in all those other crimes. Then he stabbed a deputy. Tried to abduct me in public while posing as a doctor. Tony never would've done anything like that before. He was always so careful about keeping his dark side off the world's radar. It's like he's had some kind of break. I want to ask what could possibly be next, but—"

Cruz's phone rang before Gina could finish her thought, and they froze in unison, while he looked at the screen. "Knox."

She nodded, then stepped aside, pressing her back to the wall at the edge of the emergency room's waiting area.

Cruz moved with her, clearing the way for foot traffic as he answered. "What did you find?" he asked, pressing the phone to his ear.

"Nothing good," Knox said. "You still at the hospital?"

"Yeah, we're in the emergency room waiting area now," he said, turning his attention to Gina, then lowering the phone closer to her ear. "We're getting ready to head out. Where are you?"

The cries of an approaching ambulance registered in stereo, both through the phone line and on the air outside.

Knox released a deep breath. "I'm pulling up now. Don't go anywhere."

Gina frowned, and Cruz felt the wind being pressed from his chest. His brother's voice was tight, and he'd been out of contact too long. Knox had been chasing Tony on foot, then he'd planned to visit hospital security. So, why was he outside and pulling up in his cruiser?

"What happened?" he asked as the black-and-white

rolled into view outside the sliding glass doors, an ambulance hot on its bumper.

"Just..." Knox came up short. "Stay there. I'm on my way in."

Cruz and Gina watched as Knox parked his car, then ran to meet the EMTs at the back of the ambulance.

Gina reached for Cruz, one hand on his arm, the other over her mouth. "Do you think it's Tony?"

"I don't know," Cruz said, knowing in his gut it couldn't be her assailant. If Knox had caught Tony, he would've led with that, but he hadn't. And the names of people Gina cared for tore through his mind like stock cars.

The gurney appeared a moment later, piloted by a pair of EMTs, an IV bag hanging high above the patient's head. A man's head, it seemed, one with dark hair.

Selfishly, Cruz hoped it wasn't someone he cared about, and the possibility Tony had changed his MO momentarily stole his breath. Derek? Blaze or Lucas?

The parade sped past them, drawing every prying eye in the waiting room, and the sight stole Cruz's breath.

The patient's face was nearly unrecognizable, unnaturally swollen and distended from a severe beating, like a boxer who'd gone ten too many rounds. And it wasn't one of Cruz's cousins.

It was Rex, Cruz's friend and informant.

Knox came to a stop as the gurney and its team raced away. "I left the hospital as soon as I got the call," he said. "I thought Rex fit the victim's description, but I wanted to be sure before I told you. When I got there, the EMTs had stabilized him and were loading him for transport. I chaperoned." He lifted, then dropped a hand, looking as helpless as Cruz felt.

"What happened?" Gina asked, forming the words he couldn't. "And when? Tony was here until you chased him away, and he was busy attacking Dr. Tulane this morning."

Cruz braced himself against the wall, mentally tracking the timeline with her and waiting for Knox to speak.

Knox set his fluttering hands on his hips, then pinned Cruz with a determined look, before the words began to flow. "The EMTs think he was likely attacked late last night, based on bruising and the condition of the wound." He stopped short, Adam's apple bobbing. "His assailant left a note, stabbed through his palm with a hunting knife. The medics think he's probably been out cold since then. He's suffered severe blunt force head trauma and lost a lot of blood."

Gina made a small strangled sound.

Cruz forced himself to stand tall, chin up and shoulders squared. It was time to fight for his friend, who couldn't fight for himself. "What did the note say?"

Knox's gaze slid from his brother to Gina, then back. "'How many more people have to get hurt?'"

Chapter Nineteen

Cruz carried a mug of hot tea to where Gina had curled onto his couch. Rex hadn't woken. Neither had Dr. Tulane or Heather. Deputy Stone was awake, but there hadn't been any updates, aside from confirmation of a successful surgery. "I hope you like chamomile," he said. "My aunt brought it here last winter when I caught a cold."

Gina accepted the mug with a soft smile. "It's great. Thank you." Her skin was flushed from a hot shower, and her eyes were bright with the effects of a much-needed nap. Now she was in her pajamas and looking ridiculously cuddly.

"I keep trying to put this day behind me," she said. "But I can't stop dwelling on all of it. I feel so awful for Tony's victims, and I'm terrified by how quickly the number is growing." She inhaled the sweet tendrils of steam from her mug and lifted big dark eyes to Cruz. "I hate it."

"I know." He took a seat, then pulled her feet onto his legs. "This okay?"

She gave a small smile. "Yeah."

Cruz set his palms on her calves and his phone on the cushion beside him. "Knox will call as soon as he learns something new. Until then, we hide out and save our energy. What do you think?"

"Agreed." She sipped her tea, eyes closing for a beat with each small swallow. "I'm really sorry about Rex."

"Me too." Cruz ran a palm absently over the warm skin of her leg, just above a fuzzy pink sock and miles below her plaid cotton sleep shorts. He'd been trying intensely not to think about the sleep shorts. "Rex wanted to help. He came to me, not the other way around, and he went into this understanding the situation. If I'd have tried to stop him, or told him it was too dangerous, he would've told me where to stuff that. I have faith he'll come out of this okay, and when he does, he'll testify against Tony."

Gina took another sip of tea. A frown formed between her dark brows, and Cruz knew she was worrying again.

He dragged his hands down to her socks, getting far too distracted by the feel of her skin beneath his palms. The doctor had recommended foot rubs, and that seemed a safer activity for his wandering mind than caressing her calves. "I think it might be time for us to relocate," Cruz said. He pressed the pads of his thumbs against the soles of her fuzzy-socked feet, and she moaned in response.

He froze. Maybe a foot rub wasn't a great idea. Not if that was how she planned to respond.

"Sorry," she apologized. "That just felt really good, and I wasn't prepared."

Cruz grinned, enjoying the fact that he could bring her enough pleasure to make her moan. He instantly wanted to do it again. "Tony knows about me now," he said. "He saw me at the hospital and heard me calling your name. That couldn't have made him happy. All it takes is a look at the county auditor's website to find my address after he learns my name. Then he'll be on my doorstep. So, how do you feel about spending some time at my family's cabin?"

She frowned again. "I think we should do whatever you think is best. I'm out of my depth, and I trust you."

Her trust was a welcome prize. One he wasn't sure he'd earned, but was incredibly thankful to have. "I hoped you'd say that, because Derek will be calling soon to help me make the arrangements. We can leave in the morning. There should be news from Knox or the hospital by then."

She moaned again as his thumbs worked against the arches and balls of her feet. "Do you regret taking this case yet?" she asked.

"No." His grin widened as her head tipped against the couch.

Their eyes met a moment later, and he stilled, captivated by the unexpected intensity of her gaze. The heat he felt so often in her presence blazed back to life. "I saw you before you walked into my office that day," Cruz said, feeling the urge to tell her exactly how quickly he'd wanted to know her. "I hadn't seen you before, but when I did, I willed you to come inside. My cousins thought I'd lost it."

"What?" She laughed. "You saw me?"

He nodded. "I wanted to meet you the minute you came into view. If you hadn't come inside, I might've gone out to chase you down and ask your name."

Her lips parted, and her expression changed from something like wonder to a hint of disappointment. "You have a thing for blondes."

He laughed. “I love brunettes,” he said. “I thought the only thing that would keep me from losing my mind completely was the fact that you were a blonde.”

Her eyes twinkled with pleasure, and she set her tea aside. “Is that right?”

“Absolutely. I thought you should know.”

She smiled sweetly, her full lips pressed into a tight little grin. “You thought I was pretty.”

“I think you’re beautiful,” he corrected. “I’m glad I’ve gotten to know you, and I want you to know you’re doing an incredible job of holding things together. In case you ever start to doubt that, don’t.”

Her expression softened, and she set her hand on his arm.

“The clock is ticking for Tony. His recent crime spree is evidence he’s losing control. He’s taking bigger chances and acting more frequently. It’s only a matter of time before he’s caught. All we have to do is keep you out of his hands until he’s arrested. Then you’ll be free to make any kind of life for yourself and your baby that you want.”

“Thank you,” she said. “Your continued confidence gives me hope, which is exactly what I need right now.” Gina wet her lips, then lifted her gaze to meet his. “While we’re making confessions and speaking truths,” she began, and Cruz pulled in a slow breath, “I haven’t told you how incredibly patient you’ve been. With me, and with all this…mess.” Her hands fluttered helplessly between them, as if, possibly, to indicate the whole reason they’d met and were hiding out together. “I don’t know anyone else who would’ve opened their home to me the way you have. More than that, you’ve been a friend to me. Now you’re taking care of me. Telling me to rest and bringing me tea." She shook her head. "I don't think you have any idea how much that means."

She pulled her feet away from him and sat up, tucking them beneath her.

Cruz turned, the warm vanilla scent of her shampoo pulling him a little closer. He ached to say more than he could about exactly how much he liked taking care of her, but it wasn't the right time.

"I just want you to know you've become very important to me," she said.

He searched her eyes, as if there might be more hidden there. Something she wasn't ready to say. Could she mean what he hoped she did?

"I had a good life before Tony," she said. "I was raised right, and I never got into trouble. I'd always been the shy girl no one noticed, especially not rich, handsome men." She gave a dark, self-deprecating laugh. "I was incredibly naive, but I also hadn't had any real experience with life or men. I was too trusting. And I liked the attention so much that I let a lot of his initial offenses slide. Then, one day, the things between us weren't little anymore, and I was trapped in a nightmare. Ashamed. Embarrassed. And scared."

Cruz reached for her hand, knowing how much this confession meant to her, and wanting her to understand she could trust him with it.

She turned her palm against his, linking their fingers. Then she forced a tight smile. "I thought you should know how I wound up in this situation. I owe you that much. It's kind of my biggest life failure. My baby is the only good thing that came from any of it. Maybe that makes it all worthwhile." She shrugged. "Either way, you need to know who you're dealing with."

Her cheeks reddened, and she struggled to keep her eyes on his. "Pretty girls aren't always the smartest."

"You are," he said, courage rising in his chest. If she was brave enough to share her story, maybe it was time he shared his as well.

He bit the insides of his cheeks, testing his thoughts and emotional standing. Cruz didn't tell his story often, or without significant cause, but in the name of equality and transparency, it seemed like a right and fair exchange. Gina should know he wouldn't hold back with her. He wasn't hiding a monster or anything other than a lifetime of experiences he tried daily to learn from so he could do better.

"My dad was awful to my mama." He let the words sit between them a moment before going on. "He left years before she got cancer, but while he was with us, he was terrible. He treated her like she was worthless, like she had no value, and it broke her heart. Knox and I were young, but we saw what his words did to her, saw her flinch at the put-downs that never seemed to end. He didn't always come home at night, and she'd sit up and worry. We never had enough money, but he'd blame that on her spending." He shook his head, fighting the unbearable pain in his chest. "One day he hit her. I was in middle school, but nearly as tall as him at the time, and I came for him with my bat." Cruz's jaw locked against the rage and embarrassment he knew were misplaced and pointless. "I didn't hit him, but I wanted to. Mama told me to walk away. I didn't do that either. I told him to get out. He came back the next day for his things, but we never saw him again after that."

"Cruz," Gina whispered. "I'm so sorry. I wish that hadn't happened."

"Knox and I got jobs," he said. "Eventually, so did Mama. I thought she blamed me for a long time because money was a lot tighter without him, especially when she got sick, but she always blamed herself for keeping him around so long." He shook his head, pressing the grief and remorse aside. "I vowed as a small child that I would never intentionally belittle, degrade or devalue someone. I would never be a bully or make someone else cry so I could feel powerful. I've built my life trying to be a better man than the one who raised me. Your case hits home for me in a lot of ways, and you should know that."

The sadness in her eyes stole the wind from his lungs.

"I wish you weren't going through these things," he added, desperation gripping his heart and mind.

"At least I'm not alone anymore," she said. "It's a lot less scary with you here."

The word *scary* brought an awful image into Cruz's mind. "When I saw him with you today," he said, trailing off and struggling for words. "I haven't been that afraid in a long time."

"Really?" she asked. "Because as soon as I saw you, my fear faded, and I felt braver than I ever have."

Her sweet words unwound his remaining tethers, and he leaned carefully in her direction, cocking a knee on the cushion between them and searching her with his gaze.

"Cruz?" she asked, her voice going husky as she glided one hand up his arm, then hooked her fingers over his shoulder. "Is this okay?" She smiled, teasing him with the words he always offered her when they touched.

"Yes," he said, setting his free hand on the curve of her waist. "Are you feeling all right?"

"I feel very well, thank you," she said. "And incredibly safe in your arms." She threaded her fingers into the hair at the back of his head and nudged him gently closer. "But I can't stop wondering how you would feel in my arms." Her sweet breath warmed his face, and his reasons for holding back became as fuzzy as his head.

He closed the remaining space between them and pressed his lips to hers.

The profound perfection of the simple act made him moan with pleasure. He drew her onto his lap, holding her close and gliding his palms against her spine. Their mouths moved together, and like everything else they'd done together, kissing Gina felt as natural as if they'd done it a thousand times.

Cruz's ringing phone forced him out of the delicious, dizzying haze. He stopped to admire her beautiful face before answering the call. Her flushed cheeks and swollen mouth begged him to come back, but if this thing between them could really be everything he wanted it to be, then they didn't need to hurry. Right now, he needed to take Derek's call and make plans to get Gina safely out of town.

Chapter Twenty

"Winchester," Cruz answered, accepting the call quickly, already in a hurry to get back to Gina.

She'd slid off his lap when he took the call, and his arms ached to hold her again.

She pulled her knees to her chest and wrapped her arms around them, setting her chin on top. The shy little smile on her lips provoked another moan from him.

"Cruz?" Derek asked, a fleck of humor in his tone. "Am I interrupting something?"

"No." He grinned. "What's going on? Any news?"

Derek paused, probably hearing the entire untold story in Cruz's tone. Working with a family member he'd also grown up with, and who was a private investigator, made privacy an ongoing challenge, but Cruz wasn't talking. For now, his cousin would have to guess and infer.

He supposed he should feel guilt for shamelessly coveting, then kissing, a client, but he couldn't bring himself to manage it. Now that the line had been crossed, there wasn't any going back, for him anyway. He leaned forward and kissed her forehead, earning another smile.

"I have a little news," Derek said, "but I think your news is better. I'd sure like to hear that, or should I guess?"

Cruz smiled again. Yep. Derek heard everything, even the things folks didn't say. "You first," Cruz said, having no intention to share his news. Because they definitely needed to talk about those kisses.

"I've been sitting outside Tony's home all afternoon, waiting for a sign of him I could report to Knox, so he could come over and arrest him. No one has any idea where Tony went when he left the hospital. His car is here, but there hasn't been any movement inside. No one has come in or gone out. Security lighting came on at dusk. That's it. He had a mask on in all the hospital surveillance footage, and the images of his face are unclear."

"His car was there when you got there?" Cruz asked, his attention fixing on the conversation.

"Yeah. Officers came by and knocked. No answer," Derek said. "Maybe he didn't take his car to the hospital. That would make more sense than giving authorities another way to place him at the crime scene. Not that Knox was able to use that very well before, when his car was on the Riccis' street at the time of their break-in."

"How'd he get to the hospital without his car?" Cruz asked. "It's not the kind of thing he'd call an Uber for. He was taking Gina somewhere. There must've been a getaway plan."

"My questions exactly," Derek agreed. "Normally, I'd say we should look for accomplices, but we know this is personal."

"Does Tony have another vehicle registered in his name?" Cruz asked.

"Nothing the Department of Motor Vehicles is reporting," Derek said.

Cruz turned to Gina for advice. "Can you think of

a vehicle that isn't in Tony's name that he might have access to?" He pressed the speaker button on his phone to include Derek in the conversation with her.

She chewed her lip, eyes sliding up and to the left, searching his ceiling for an answer. When her gaze returned to his, she frowned. "He might've used one of the company SUVs," she said. "They're all identical, black with tinted windows. The company logo is just a big magnet stuck to the side when sales reps go out on business. His dad uses the fleet, without the logos, to arrive at major social events. Put three or more of them in the row, and it gets people talking, like a celebrity is arriving."

Cruz lifted his brows. Dark nondescript vehicles sounded like exactly the kind of ride an undercover killer would love to have access to. "Derek?"

"Already on it," he said. "I'll talk to Knox and see if he can get me plate numbers on the company fleet. Then I'll see if we can place one near the hospital earlier today or in the vicinity of Rex's attack last night."

"Or the doctor's office," Cruz added.

"Will do," Derek said. "Meanwhile, you'd better get packed up and ready to move. I wouldn't put that off until morning. We don't know where this guy is right now, but we know he's mad and motivated."

"Yep." Cruz disconnected the call, and smiled warmly at Gina. "How do you feel about getting on the road tonight?"

She released her knees, then pushed onto her feet. "I'll pack my things."

"Hey," Cruz said, grabbing her hand as she moved to walk away. "We should talk about that kiss before we go. Being alone in the mountains a few days could get awkward otherwise."

Gina's cheeks darkened. She squeezed his hand and locked wide eyes on his. "The kiss was nice," she said. "Doing it again seems like a great way to pass our time alone on a mountain."

Then she flashed him a smile, and headed to her room.

GINA CLOSED HER bedroom door gently, then climbed onto her bed to process. She'd kissed Cruz Winchester, and it had been even hotter than she'd imagined. Which said a lot because she had an excellent imagination.

She plucked the fabric of her shirt away from her overheated skin. Just recalling his touch sent a wave of heat throughout her body. She hadn't been kissed by many men, but her previous experiences had all been somewhat the same, and wholly unremarkable. As a result, she'd never understood other women's fascination with the act, but now she knew. And she wished she didn't have to make time for anything else ever again.

The rumble of his low tenor vibrated outside her door, and she imagined him on his way to his room to pack. Daydreams would have to wait. For now, it was time to clear out and hole up someplace out of town.

She sent out a barrage of silent prayers for the people Tony had hurt, and for those who were on his list now, as she hurriedly packed her things. A year ago, it would've taken hours, maybe days, to decide what to wear or bring. Now she could pack all her earthly possessions into two duffel bags with practiced assurance in under ten minutes. If needed, she could walk out the door with only her purse and never come back. Funny how fear had streamlined her priorities.

When she reemerged from her bedroom, Cruz was in the living room, stacking bags and lidded plastic totes near the front door. His cell phone was pressed to his ear.

"We're headed out now," he told whoever was on the line. "Within the next hour." He smiled when he saw her, then reached for her and winked.

She added her bags to the accumulating pile, then stilled to accept his soft kiss. Goose bumps rose on her arms as he smiled against her mouth, then dropped back into his conversation without missing a beat.

"Ready?" he asked a moment later, sliding the phone back into his pocket.

She nodded, and they were on their way.

The long country road rolled out before them as she dialed the number for the phone Cruz had given her parents.

Her mama answered on the first ring. "Baby? Is everything okay?"

"I'm fine, Mama," she said, smiling despite the circumstances and endlessly thankful for the gift Cruz had given her. She'd missed her folks so much while she'd been on the run. "Cruz is taking me someplace safe while his family hunts for Tony," she said. "I can't tell you much, because it's safer for us both if you don't have details. Just know that I'm safe, and happy, and this is a strategic piece of a careful plan. It won't be long before I can spend all day squeezing you and Dad and eating your manicotti by the pound."

Her mama laughed nervously. "I will make manicotti every night for the rest of my life if that's what you want. Just come home safely."

"I will," she promised. "I'm in good hands."

Cruz seemed to sit taller beside her, a growing grin on his handsome face.

She only hoped he'd still be happy with her when she was nine months pregnant and roughly the size of a barn. "I've got to go," she said. "I wanted you to know I'm okay, just in case the reception is spotty where I'm going. Cruz's family will reach out to you if they need to. Until then, no news is good news, okay?" Gina said her goodbyes, then dropped the phone into an empty cupholder in the console, fighting the sting of rogue tears.

Cruz reached for her hand, then lifted it to his lips. "You okay?" he asked, pressing a kiss against her knuckles.

"I will be," she said, and she hoped that was true.

Above them an inky sky twinkled with the light of a billion stars, and not a single other vehicle shared their road. Fields and forests lined the winding county route, and peace seemed thick upon the earth, if not yet in her heart.

They'd passed the third city limits sign when Derek's name appeared on the Jeep's dashboard display screen.

Cruz answered the call, using a button on his steering wheel. "Hey, we're about an hour outside town now. Hoping to reach the cabin in another ten. What've you got?"

"Update time," Derek said. "Nothing on Tony just yet, but a nurse in Rex's ward just reached out. She says he's awake and speaking with a deputy. She listened. Rex said Tony thought he was a cop and demanded a location on Gina. When he wouldn't give you or her up,

Tony railed on him. He doesn't even remember being stabbed through the hand. Knox is on his way to Falls General now."

Cruz's jaw tightened, but relief washed over his face. "What do the doctors say?" he asked.

"According to the nurse, Rex's healing well and anticipated to make a complete recovery," Derek said. "No lasting trauma from the head injuries, and the knife didn't do any permanent damage."

Gina set her hand on Cruz's leg and offered an encouraging squeeze. Rex was going to be okay. That was the best news they'd gotten from the hospital so far. And she could only hope there would be similar calls about Dr. Tulane, Heather and Deputy Stone soon as well.

Cruz disconnected, then shot her a conflicted expression. "Knox will protect Rex while he heals. He'll build a solid case while we lie low. Meanwhile, all we have to do is stay off the grid and out of Tony's reach."

She nodded, mind racing with hope. If Rex was awake and able to testify, the case against Tony would firm up. She'd spoken to Tony on Heather's phone and again at the hospital. Rex could identify him, and soon, Dr. Tulane and Heather would too. Cruz was right when he said the clock was ticking. It wouldn't be long before Tony was behind bars, and the relief that came with that knowledge was unequivocal.

Gina just hoped Tony didn't realize how close he was to being caught, because she wasn't sure what he would be capable of if he had nothing left to lose.

"Well," she said, forcing her mind back to more-positive thoughts, "we already have a plan in motion, so our job should be easy enough." All they had to do was stay away and let the lawmen work.

Her burner phone rang, and she freed it from the cupholder. "It's my parents," she said, surprised to see their number on her screen again so soon. A bite of terror pinched her chest as she answered. "Hello?"

"Gina!" her mom yelled.

Panic seized Gina's chest. She pressed the speaker button instinctively, then moved the phone between her and Cruz. "I'm here, Mama. What's wrong?"

"She's gone," her mom cried. "No one can find her. No one can reach her. I don't know what to do." Her mama's words broke into sobs, while fear tightened around Gina's neck like a noose.

"Who's gone?" she asked, knowing the answer, but needing to hear it stated plainly before she truly lost her mind as well. "Who can't be found?"

"Your sister."

Chapter Twenty-One

Gina sat with her parents at a conference table inside the West Liberty police station. Cruz's brothers had transformed the space into a war room for finding Kayla, complete with a coffeepot, heavy stack of files and a crime board like the ones she normally saw on movies and prime-time television shows.

Her mother trembled continually from misplaced adrenaline and the threat of shock.

Her father paced the floor.

Gina held her mom's hand and tried to pay attention to the Winchesters' conversations through ringing ears. Lucas, the special victims detective who'd helped coordinate Gina's recent meeting with Kayla, had finally returned from her campus, and she didn't want to miss any details.

The men stood on the opposite side of the table, nearest the crime board featuring Tony's face and an open door. They nodded and traded information as it became available, by phone call or text, occasionally delivered in person by a uniformed officer.

Bottom line—Kayla had been missing for hours, and this too was, at least peripherally, because of Gina. It might not have been Gina's fault, but it had been because she loved her sister. And Tony had told her he could get to everyone she cared about.

Lucas turned to Gina and her folks, then took a seat with an open file, tapping a hand on the tabletop. "We know Kayla called campus security from an emergency phone following a study session with friends," he said, apparently starting from the beginning.

This was information they'd been given upon arrival. Kayla had texted her friends, saying she felt as if she was being followed, but didn't see anyone. The friends had encouraged her to use one of the campus security phones to request an escort.

"A unit responded to her call within two minutes," Lucas said, continuing his story. Kayla hadn't been there when the officer arrived. The phone had been found hanging. "A can of pepper spray was located on the ground nearby," he added.

Gina's dad made a soft choking sound, then turned his back to the group, rubbing both palms over his face.

Her mama stared catatonically, and Cruz offered a thin utilitarian blanket to help with her shivers. When she didn't blink or acknowledge the offering, Gina helped spread the rough material over her legs, and tucked it in along her sides.

Lucas waited for her to finish before moving on. "A team of campus security agents was dispatched to canvass the area and interview students while I was en route to follow up. I spoke with a female living on the second floor of the nearest dormitory, who claims to have seen a large black SUV with tinted glass parked outside when she arrived home. That would've been only a few minutes before Kayla placed her call for an escort. A camera at that location confirmed the presence of the vehicle, and we were able to use additional surveillance footage to track it as it left campus. There wasn't, however, a good image of the driver, passenger or plate."

Blaze moved to his brother's side, coffee in one hand, a deep frown on his face. "Derek is back on reconnaissance duty. He's stationed outside the family home, keeping tabs on the Marinos. At this point, it's going to take more than a good lawyer to distance Tony from his crimes."

Lucas steepled his fingers, elbows anchored on the table. "We've established the family will cover for him, so I've sent officers to question the parents on how they plan to respond to Tony's unraveling. Hopefully, that will spur them into action. If they're hiding him and try to move him, Derek will notify us and follow."

Gina shivered, her stomach tipping and tightening with fear and nausea. She dug her phone from her bag and accessed the internet, then sent a hasty message to Celia. Gina had planned to wait until she'd arrived at the cabin with Cruz, then toil over the exact wording of her request, but time was of the essence, and she no longer cared about finesse. She tapped her thumbs against the screen, providing a rundown of events and asking Celia for any information she had or could get. Then Gina clutched the phone in her hands and waited.

"We're attempting to get a warrant for GPS information on the fleet of Marino company vehicles," Lucas said. "That will tell us everywhere each SUV has been, as well as where they are now. The family's lawyers are doing their best to slow the process, but I feel confident the judge will see our side."

Gina's dad swore, then turned back to face the room with a look of complete desperation.

"Daddy," she whispered, reaching in his direction. "Please. Sit with Mama and me."

He stared, red-faced, either unwilling or unable to move in her direction.

Her heart ached profoundly at the sight of him. Whatever pain Gina felt, knowing her sister was gone, she couldn't imagine what her parents were going through. She'd only been pregnant a few months, and would already do or give anything to protect her child. "Daddy," Gina repeated softly, turning her palm upward and curing her fingers. "Mama needs you."

A tear rolled over her father's cheek as he returned to her mother's side.

Gina mouthed the words, "Thank you," when her mother turned and pressed her cheek to his chest.

His arms went around his wife, and Gina fixed her attention on the Winchesters, hoping they were enough to stop a madman from hurting her little sister.

"What else?" Cruz asked, paging through a file of loose paperwork in his hands. "Tell me there's enough evidence to make a strong case once we get him."

"There is," Lucas said, a small flash of pleasure in his eyes. "Knox was able to identify the knife left in Rex's hand as a brand sold exclusively through the Marino family's outdoor outfitter stores. And it's an exact match for Dr. Tulane's wounds."

Cruz's lips twitched with a flicker of pride and satisfaction. "Good."

"Also," Lucas said, tapping the screen of his phone, "we pulled this image of Tony and his dad on a hunting trip about three months ago off the internet." He turned the screen to face Cruz. "The knife in this picture matches the one in evidence. Add that to the fact that Rex was able to identify Tony as the one who hired, then attacked him, and Gina can name him as her assailant, the case is getting tighter by the minute."

Blaze shifted, widening his stance and shoving his hands into his back pockets. "We've got witnesses confirming Tony's vehicle was in Great Falls on the night the building manager was murdered. A local café worker identified him as well. She said he was handing out missing persons posters of you." His gaze met Gina's and she sucked in a ragged breath.

"I was there," she whispered, the memory returning full force. "I'd given the barista a fake name out of habit. Then I saw him, and I ran." A punch of relief mixed with fear. There were so many witnesses and a load of evidence to prove Tony's crimes. When he went before a judge and jury, there would be more than just her word against his and his family's.

Eventually, the flow of information slowed to a drip, and Gina's parents went home to monitor their landline, in case Tony reached out that way.

Gina folded her arms on the conference table and set her head on top.

The police department was quiet around them. Only a handful of detectives remained, occasionally whisking past the open conference room door.

She woke to the gentle weight of Cruz's hand on her shoulder.

"Breakfast?" he said.

She didn't remember falling asleep, but the scents of fast-food hash browns and croissant sandwiches pulled her eyelids open and caused her stomach to jump with glee. She started to ask for coffee, but Cruz had already set a steaming cup before her, beside a bottle of water, and she longed to hug him for his thoughtfulness.

Lucas yawned and stretched, tired eyes hooked on Cruz. "It's been a long night. If you're not up for a drive to the cabin right now, you can always stay with Mom and Dad, you know. Or at Derek's house. He's got plenty of room, and that place is like Fort Knox."

"I think we'd better stick to the plan," Cruz answered, raising a steamy mug of coffee to his lips.

Gina's phone buzzed, and she pulled it from her pocket, half expecting to find her parents' number on the screen. Instead, she realized it was her personal phone, the burner she'd bought, not the one Cruz had given her, making the noise. And the message was from Celia.

Cruz's expression turned curious, and he moved to stand behind her, reading the screen over her shoulder.

"It's the woman I told you about," Gina explained. "Tony's friend's girlfriend. I reached out to her last night. I didn't want to put it off any longer, and Kayla can't wait."

He grunted. "You used your personal account? Your phone?"

Gina nodded. "The phone's a burner, but yes to using my Facebook account to reach out. Is that okay?"

"Maybe," he said, not sounding as certain as she'd like.

Gina read Celia's message silently, and with quick, hungry eyes.

Oh, my goodness. Are you okay? I've been worried sick about you since you disappeared. I told Ben it was probably Tony's fault. He told me to stay out of it, but I could tell things between you two weren't right. Tony showed up at Ben's house two nights ago, wanting an alibi for something he did earlier this week. He wouldn't say what it was, and when Ben didn't agree right away he threatened him with a gun! Ben agreed so Tony would leave, but he didn't want to do it. I don't understand what's going on. And Tony says you're pregnant?! Is that true? What can I do to help you? Are you somewhere safe? I can pick you up. Find you a place to stay. Maybe a hotel room under an alias?

Cruz moved to face Gina, leaning his backside against the table before her. "This is good. We can work with that. Let her know you're safe, and she should keep this conversation quiet. Don't tell her more than you have to."

Lucas lifted his chin in Cruz's direction. "What's going on?" he asked.

Cruz took a step in his cousin's direction, then turned back. "Ask if she can think of where he might be now, or if her boyfriend can think of someplace Tony would go to disappear."

Gina nodded and her thumbs flew across the screen, energized by the possibility of an inside scoop. She sent a series of short messages in response.

I'm safe. At PD now. Leaving town soon.

Ideas where Tony could've taken Kayla?

Ask Ben?

Celia's response came immediately and was equally brief.

I'm on my way to his place now. I'll ask as soon as I get there.

Gina tucked her phone away, then forced herself to sit and wait.

Nearly an hour later, Celia hadn't responded, and Cruz was visibly on edge.

Blaze rubbed his eyes, looking as exhausted as she felt. "Take my truck," he said, tossing Cruz a set of keys. "If this guy's onto you, he'll be looking for the Jeep. I'll drive that until he's caught."

Cruz snagged the offered keys from the air, then passed the Jeep's keys to his cousin. "Thanks." He glanced at the wall clock, then Gina.

Blaze waved a hand in goodbye as he headed for the hallway. Lucas stayed tight on his heels and tugged the door shut behind them.

Cruz looked at Gina. "Hey," he said. "I know you want to stick around in case there's word on your sister, but the smart move is to get you out of town. Remove you from the game. At the very least, it could buy us some time. Meanwhile, Tony's face is going up on news media across the state, thanks to Rex's ability to identify him. There's nothing more for us to do here. And I'm willing to bet your folks will be glad to know you're out of Tony's reach. You still have your phone if you need it."

Gina's heart plummeted at the thought of leaving town with her sister missing, but Cruz and his family knew what they were doing, and she didn't want to make anything more complicated than it already was. "Okay."

She stretched to her feet, then pulled her personal phone from her pocket. No new messages from Celia. "I should probably leave this with Blaze and Lucas," she said, passing the device to Cruz. "If Celia responds, they can get the message without needing me as the middleman."

Cruz pulled her to his chest and kissed her forehead. "Good idea."

They delivered her phone to Lucas before heading into the bright sunny day.

The streets outside the sheriff's department were dense with traffic and morning commuters.

Cruz lifted his hand, and the lights of a black pickup truck flashed at them. "Blaze loves his big truck," he mused.

Gina smiled at the row of floodlights on top and massive silver grille in the front. "This is a serious ride."

"For a very serious man," Cruz agreed wryly. "Why don't you climb in while I move our things from the Jeep to this behemoth."

"Deal."

He helped Gina climb inside the too tall truck, then smiled at her for one long beat.

"Winchester!" a voice called, turning them back toward the sheriff's department. A uniformed deputy waved a hand overhead, shielding the sun with one hand and beckoning them back with the other. "Your cousin's packing up the rest of this food for the road."

Cruz smiled, obviously thankful for the offer, and likely as relieved as she was that there wasn't more bad news. He swung a questioning gaze to Gina.

She shrugged. "I'm okay. And I could eat." She hadn't taken the time to eat inside, and she regretted it sorely.

Cruz handed her the truck keys, then locked the doors before closing her in the cab and jogging back to the building.

Gina considered sliding behind the wheel. It would be impossible to feel threatened at the helm of Blaze's massive pickup.

A familiar black SUV rolled to a stop at the curb, just outside the police department parking lot, and she froze, telling herself that even Tony wouldn't come for her there.

The back passenger window powered down as she stared, and Kayla came into view. Her dark hair was tangled around a slack face, and thick silver tape ran the width of her mouth.

Gina's heart jerked into a sprint, and her eyes jumped to the building where Cruz had just gone inside.

She fumbled for her phone to text Cruz, but the other vehicle's front passenger window went down too, and Tony became visible behind the wheel. He had a handgun pointed over his seat at her sister.

Gina hastily fumbled for the door while sending the shortest text of her life to Cruz.

911

Then she moved in the SUV's direction, knowing it was her that Tony really wanted, and hoping he would let Kayla go in trade.

Tony's reptilian smile spread across his face as the rear window powered up, removing Kayla from her sight. "Where's your phone?" he called, moving the gun in a circle to indicate she should pick up the pace.

She raised the device into view, and Tony's smile became a sneer.

"Drop the phone and get in," he said. "Now!"

Her heart fell in defeat as she reached for the door.

She wouldn't trade Kayla's life for her own, so she did the only thing she could.

And got in.

Chapter Twenty-Two

Gina fastened her seat belt, then twisted for a look behind her.

Kayla's head rocked on the cushioned headrest, her expression flat.

"What did you do to her?" Gina asked, turning quickly back to keep an eye on her captor, his gun and the road.

"I gave her a choice," he said. "She chose the sleeping pills I swiped from the hospital instead of my more proven method of lights out."

Gina bit her tongue against the urge to lash out. That never ended well for her, and she had her sister and baby to protect this time. Instead, she fixed her gaze through the side window and tried to track their route. "Where are we going?"

Tony checked his rearview mirror, then cut across three lanes of traffic to take an unfamiliar exit. "Don't worry about it," he said. "You and I are going to talk. That's all you need to know."

Gina swallowed a painful lump, terror clutching her chest. She needed an escape plan. Needed a clear head and a way to keep Tony calm. She had to buy the

Winchesters some time to find her, if that would even be possible.

"What did you tell the police?" he demanded. "Whose truck were you in? That wasn't a woman's vehicle. Are you sleeping with that guy now? Going to tell him that's his baby you're carrying?"

Gina pressed her lips tight, refusing to voice the outrage building in her mind. Anger for his ridiculous misogyny. Fury for the implication she fell into bed with someone easily, as if she had time for any of that while running for her life. From him.

Tony swerved around slower-moving traffic, and a cacophony of blaring horns followed. "Well?" he demanded, slapping a hand down on her thigh and digging in with his fingers. "What did you tell the police? Did you cry them a river? Make yourself out to be a victim? Tell them I'm a bad guy?" He used a crybaby voice to ask the final question, then slammed his hand against the steering wheel a half-dozen times.

"You killed my apartment manager," she snapped. "Attacked my friend and my doctor. Stabbed a deputy sheriff, attacked an innocent teenager and abducted my sister. You are a bad guy, Tony, and everyone is going to know it."

The crack of pain across her cheek sent lights dancing through her eyes.

He shook out his hand, as if the slap had hurt him, then flexed his fingers against the steering wheel. "You better not have told them any of those things. That woman was not your friend and that man wasn't your apartment manager. You don't even live there. You live with me!" He screamed the last word, while accelerating through a red light.

Gina's mind and body went numb. The throbbing of her cheek became part of a distant backdrop. She set her hands on her lap and erected the force field she needed to survive whatever was coming. It was time to disconnect. And think.

Lucas was working on a warrant for GPS tracking on the Marino company fleet, which included the SUV she was riding in. The family lawyers could only hold them off for so long, especially after he'd picked her up at the police station parking lot. Surely the department's security feed had captured that.

Meanwhile, she needed to stall Tony's plan, whatever that might be. She couldn't let him lock her up, constrain or injure her to a point that she couldn't run when the opportunity arose. That went for her sister as well.

She stole a glance in the rearview mirror, hoping Kayla showed signs of waking. Her little sister was thin and small, but Gina wasn't strong enough to carry her. Kayla had to wake up before Gina could run.

Slowly, the busier streets of an unfamiliar town bled into a residential neighborhood, thick with uninhabitable homes. Then an industrial park appeared up ahead.

Tony piloted the SUV through an open chain-link fence and into an area lined in warehouses and abandoned buildings.

She recognized the place after a long moment, though she'd never arrived by such a convoluted route. This was the location of his family's largest storage facility, where products for the stores were housed and shipped. It was also the place where Tony often held large, impromptu poker nights with friends, betting everything from stacks of cash to their high-end cars on a single hand.

He rolled the SUV to a stop outside a large bay door, then shifted into Park. "Do anything stupid, and I will shoot your sister," he said, then he climbed out and headed for the building.

Gina tracked him with her eyes and waited until his focus turned to the padlock. "Kayla!" she barked, twisting on her seat to smack her sister's knees. "Wake up! Kayla!"

Slowly, her sister's eyes opened, and a low moan rolled from her lips.

Gina's chest heaved with relief. "We're going to be okay, but you have to wake up."

Kayla tried to speak, the muffled sound barely permeating the silver tape across her lips. Her eyes were unfocused as she scanned the space, probably seeking Gina's face. Whatever Tony had given her was clearly still in control.

Gina faced front and stilled, unwilling to risk Tony seeing her turned around or talking. She covered her face with her hands and did her best to appear as if she was crying when he looked her way.

Outside, he shoved the warehouse door away, then headed back to the SUV.

"Tony's coming," Gina said quickly, behind the cover of her hand. "Pretend you're asleep. We have to make a plan."

The driver's door opened, and Tony climbed behind the wheel once more, then pulled smoothly into the warehouse. "Now, you and I are going to have that talk. You can start by explaining what kind of person would hide her pregnancy, then take a man's baby away from him." He jammed the shifter into Park and scowled.

"What kind of mother are you going to be? Not a fit one, if you'd deny a child access to his father."

Gina scanned the scene beyond the windshield, mentally tallying her options for running or hiding.

"You lied to me, and you embarrassed me," he continued, irrationally outraged and betrayed. "You're going to have to apologize for that, and I'm not sure I can forgive you." He unfastened her seat belt, then jerked her across the console by her arm. "I want to see my baby."

Tony stared hard into her eyes before trailing his gaze down her body and lifting the hem of her shirt to stare at her gently rounded middle.

She gritted her teeth and turned her head away, fighting the weight of a thousand awful emotions.

He set a hot hand on her bare stomach, and she recoiled instinctively.

She tensed for another slap, but Tony shoved her off of him, then climbed out of the vehicle.

He circled the SUV while she scrambled back to her side, tugging her shirt into place. Then he opened the rear passenger door, and reached for her sister.

"Wait." Gina leaped out, eager to help Kayla, and ready to do anything she could to keep Tony's hands off of her. But it was too late.

He tossed Kayla over his shoulder like she was weightless and not even human, then began to move.

Gina rushed after them, down the massive aisles of metal shelving and boxed products meant for the outdoor outfitter stores. Eight-foot stuffed black bears stood beside racks of kayaks and pallets of ammunition. Tents, guns and hunting apparel filled every square inch of cavernous space. A thousand weapons he could use against her. Ten thousand ways he could do his worst.

Kayla's cheek bounced against Tony's back as he strode confidently through the rows of stock. Her eyes flashed open, and her gaze stuck to Gina.

Gina's heart sprinted with hope, and an idea came swiftly to mind. She fished the pepper spray Kayla had given her from her pocket, then passed it into her sister's hand.

"Don't touch her," Tony growled. He stopped and turned to catch Gina's wrist and pull her to his side. "She's off-limits to you. She's collateral."

They stopped at the end of the aisle, where a small living space had been arranged. A tent, a cot, a card table. Pop-up chairs and plastic coolers. He flipped Kayla off him, and she bounced onto the cot with a groan. Her limbs splayed, but there wasn't any sign of the pepper spray.

"Now," Tony said, spinning to face Gina, "I have to live like this because of you. Someone is staking out my house because of you. Watching my office and my folks' place. Because. Of. You. I can't go home. Can't do anything. And it's all your fault." He searched her face with angry eyes and gritted teeth, then his attention fell to her middle. "Show me my baby again."

Gina wet her lips and considered her options, which were few, then took the handful of steps to his side.

"That's right," he said. "Silent and obedient. Now lift your shirt."

Gina stopped short of his personal space, then slowly raised the hem of her shirt, exposing her midriff.

Behind him, red exit signs glowed over endless

shelving. It wouldn't be easy, but she had to get there, and she had to take her sister with her.

Tony's hands snapped out and gripped her waist, then tugged her forward, until their bodies collided and his lips were mashed against hers.

She wrestled against him, and he did his best to keep her in place. Then her hand rose, on instinct, and she slapped his face.

The stillness between them lasted only a moment. Then his hand connected with her face once more.

She fell onto her hands and knees with sudden force and pain. A cry sprang from her lips, and infuriated tears began to fall. How was this happening? Again!

"Get up," he growled. "We're going inside the tent where you can apologize. Now!" He crouched over her, gripping her around the waist and attempting to haul her upright.

"No!" she yelled back, flailing and attempting to connect a foot or elbow somewhere that would count.

The burning scent of pepper spray rose around them, scorching her eyes, nose and throat. Tony yelled out as he released her and stumbled away, cursing violently from the pain.

Kayla grabbed Gina's elbow, and together, they ran.

Chapter Twenty-Three

Cruz had been inside the West Liberty Police Department for less than two minutes when he'd received the simple text.

911

Blaze had met him in the lobby with the to-go bags, bottles of water and a belated offer to help transfer their supplies from the Jeep to the truck.

How had there been enough time for something bad to happen?

Cruz and Blaze had made a run for the truck, until Cruz remembered he'd given the keys to Gina. Thankfully, Blaze had the Jeep keys, and the cousins were on the road inside a minute. But it hadn't mattered. The SUV and Gina were long gone.

Thankfully, Blaze had climbed behind the wheel, because Cruz was slowly losing his mind. Blaze's phone rang before they'd accessed the highway on-ramp, and he passed it to Cruz. "Answer," he said.

Lucas's name was on the screen.

"We're on the highway," Cruz said by way of greeting.

It was the only obvious choice for escape. Traffic was too heavy to get away downtown, and the SUV would be caught for sure on the quieter country roads. The highway, however, could take Tony and his victim anywhere in a matter of minutes.

"Good," Lucas said, his voice rising from the speaker. "We found a phone in the grass between the road and sidewalk. Looks like the one you gave her, Cruz. The photo on the lock screen is the view from your back deck."

Cruz grimaced and pressed one fist against his forehead, longing to chuck the phone out the window or otherwise burn off a burst of frustration any way he could. "What about the surveillance footage?"

"I'm going through that now," Lucas answered. "We've got her on camera leaving Blaze's truck and climbing into the SUV, but until it rolls forward, the vehicle is obstructed by the stone PD sign. It fits the make and model of the Marino company fleet, but I don't have a clear image of the driver or plate."

Blaze glanced at the phone as he navigated the busy highway. "Tell me we have enough to hurry the warrant along now, even without a clear image of the plate or driver."

"I'm working on it," Lucas said.

"Work faster," Cruz snapped. His grip tightened on the small, infuriating device. How much time did he have before Tony hurt her, or worse? Why would she have gone with him like that? He'd left her the keys. She could've driven away or honked the horn. Anything.

Then he realized. Tony had brought Kayla with him. He was sure of it.

Blaze changed lanes and increased his speed. "This is just like when Kayla was taken from her campus," he complained. "No proof Tony was behind the abduction. How can one guy be this slick?"

"I'm sure Kayla was with him in the SUV," Cruz said.

Understanding, then anger, crossed Blaze's features. "He used her as bait."

"He probably didn't even have to ask Gina to get in with him," Cruz said. "If Kayla was there, Gina wouldn't have hesitated."

Blaze activated his turn signal, then eased onto the next exit ramp. "That clears up why she got in," he said. "And how he convinced her to go so quickly. Now we just need an answer to where he took them."

"Hey," Lucas said. "Why don't you circle back, then we can press on the judge together. Get that warrant signed."

"On our way," Blaze said, already reentering the highway in the opposite direction.

"See ya then," Lucas said.

Cruz disconnected the call, his stomach sinking and aching impossibly more. It didn't matter that they hadn't had any specific direction as they'd cruised the highway. At least they'd been doing something, going somewhere. Turning back felt like a massive defeat.

The phone rang again as they merged with the flow of traffic. Derek's name appeared on the screen.

"Yeah," Cruz answered, activating the speaker option so Blaze could listen once more. "What do you have?"

"Me?" Derek asked, a hitch of confusion in his voice. "I thought you had something. I wanted in on it. Wait. Is this Cruz? Why are you on Blaze's phone?"

"I'm here," Blaze said. "We're in the Jeep, but I'm driving."

Silence stretched across the line.

"You're in the Jeep with Cruz," Derek repeated, finally speaking again. "Who's in your truck?"

"My truck's at the precinct," Blaze said. "No one is in it."

"No," Derek said. "Your truck is at the Marino company warehouse," he said. "I thought you'd found Gina and her sister. I'm headed there now, but I'm fifteen minutes out."

Blaze wrinkled his nose at the cell phone, then at Cruz before returning his eyes to the road. "We're in the Jeep. The truck's in the lot."

Cruz's heart leaped as sudden recognition hit. "She's got your keys," he said. "I gave them to her when I ran inside to grab the food. She's got your keys." He repeated the initial statement more slowly, a geyser of hope rising in his chest.

"I put a tracker on those," Derek said, the sound of his car's engine growing louder across the line. "Y'all better get out to the warehouse. And bring backup."

GINA CHOKED AND coughed as she stumbled, almost blindly, through the warehouse, pulled and guided by her sister.

Kayla's strides were awkward and sluggish, but she could see, and that was more than Gina could manage with the burn of pepper spray on her skin and in her lungs.

"I'm so sorry," Kayla whispered repeatedly as she towed Gina over the smooth concrete floor. "I couldn't get him without hitting you."

"It's okay." Gina's throat tightened on the words, and she began to cough again. She wanted to say more, to comfort and praise her sister, but her breaths were hard and shallow. The fire in her eyes, nose and throat was almost too much to handle.

Kayla pulled Gina in a new direction, then pressed

her shoulder to a thick metal pole. "Here," she said, releasing her for the first time since they'd made their escape. "I found the foodstuff section. There's water."

Gina doubled over, rubbing her eyes and willing her lungs to collect more air.

Kayla's hand was on Gina's face a moment later. She pushed Gina's hands away and pried open her right eye. A thick splash of cold water hit her face.

Gina sucked air and blinked, trying not to make more noise than possible in response. Her nose ran and she longed to sob, but feared she'd give away their position. Tony was surely not far behind.

Kayla pressed a bottle into Gina's hand. "Use it. Hurry," she whispered, sounding utterly exhausted. "There's more if you need it, but we have to keep moving, and I'm not sure how long I can stay awake."

Gina followed her sister's instructions, splashing her left eye and wetting her hands to wash her face. Slowly, her vision returned with a blurry, patchy view. The nearest exit sign was a red smear above a door that was still a few aisles away. "Ready," she whispered, then turned to seek her sister.

Kayla leaned heavily against the shelving, her head supported by its metal frame.

"Come on," Gina whispered, wrapping her sister's arm around her shoulder, then willing herself to be strong. "You can't stop now," she said. "We're almost free. I know you can fight it a little longer."

Kayla leaned into Gina's assist with a groan.

A hellacious crash rooted her, temporarily, in place. Around them, the warehouse seemed to quake with the feral yell that followed. "Gina!" Tony's scream raised the hair on her arms and back of her neck to attention. Her heart caught in her already scorching throat, and she forced her feet forward, away from the sounds.

Kayla's head rolled against Gina's shoulder, and her legs twisted uselessly with each small step.

"No," Gina whispered, tugging Kayla's arm and nudging her with her hip. "Wake up."

Kayla moaned and her knees buckled.

Another enormous crash boomed and echoed through the building, like a thousand metal plates or capsizing grills.

Gina tipped slightly forward to accommodate her sister's weight, then began to race toward the exit.

A booming gunshot caused her steps to falter, but she didn't stop. Falling items to her left and right made her think Tony wasn't seeing much more clearly than she was just yet. And that might be what saved her life.

"Gina!" He followed her name with a long string of hate-filled words and vicious, gruesome threats. His heavy footfalls slapped the concrete floor behind her.

The next bullet whizzed past her head, colliding with a sack of feed that exploded and released its contents in a gush.

She gasped and felt the hot, slick tears roll over her stinging cheeks. She couldn't let her life end this way, in a warehouse begging for Tony's mercy. Couldn't be his victim one last time. And she absolutely would not allow her baby sister to die at the hands of her personal monster.

Fresh resolve rushed through her blood and pumped her limbs. Kayla became lighter with the resurgence of will and determination.

Outside, the cry of police sirens launched a spout of hope in her powerful enough to do whatever it took for her to survive.

"Freeze!" a familiar voice bellowed as the sounds of emergency vehicles grew louder. "West Liberty PD," Blaze announced. "Anthony Marino, put the gun down and get your hands up where I can see them. You are under arrest."

Gina's chest heaved with relief as she reached, then pressed her shoulder against the exit door.

"Gina!" Cruz's voice reached her before he came into view. His arms wound around her and Kayla a moment later. "Medic!" he called over her head. "Here!"

"He drugged her," Gina croaked. "She won't wake up."

Cruz pulled Kayla into his arms. "What happened to your face?" he asked Gina, moving swiftly toward an arriving ambulance.

"Pepper spray."

EMTs exited the vehicle and took Kayla from Cruz's arms.

He turned to Gina immediately and pressed her to his chest. "Did he do anything else to you? To your baby?"

Gina sobbed at the memory of Tony's hand on her stomach, of his palm connecting with her face. "I think we're okay," she said, her limbs beginning to tremble. "How'd you find us?"

"Derek tracks us, and you have Blaze's keys," he said, his lips tipping into a small smile. "Also, your friend Celia called the phone you left with Lucas. She said she told her boyfriend about your exchange, and he told Tony. She didn't expect that to happen," he said.

"She called as soon as she could, but we were already on our way."

"Hey." An approaching paramedic raised one hand in greeting. "Did I hear you say pepper spray?"

She squinted against the bright midday light and nodded, her face still on fire.

"Gina," Cruz said. "This is my cousin Isaac. Why don't we ride with him to the hospital. Kayla will be there, and you can make your rounds to visit Dr. Tulane and Heather. We can call your folks on the way."

A bubble of hope rose in Gina's chest as she let the men help her into the ambulance. "Heather and Dr. Tulane are awake?"

He nodded. "We can stop by and bug Rex and Deputy Stone while we're at it."

"Yes," she said. "Please. I have so much to say to all of them."

Isaac pointed to the gurney. "Then why don't you have a seat, and we'll get you checked out."

She agreed easily, then watched as Kayla's ride wound to life and zoomed away.

"She's going to be okay," Cruz said. "So are you."

A few minutes passed as Isaac examined her briefly and flushed her eyes. When he moved away, she watched through open ambulance bay doors as Blaze stuffed Tony into a police cruiser, then patted the roof with one hand. Knox smiled brightly as he piloted the car away from the warehouse.

"You okay?" Cruz asked, pressing a kiss to the side of her head and squeezing her hand in his.

"I am now," she said, moving her attention away from the cruiser and fixing it on the man beside her.

"Thank you for being my hero," she whispered, tugging him down to meet her lips.

"Always."

Chapter Twenty-Four

Gina sighed at the familiar sight of Derek and Allison's house along the river. Spring had come to Kentucky in an explosion of color, and the truth of that could be seen all around their property. The Winchesters were having their weekly dinner, and Gina couldn't wait to see them all again. Cruz had even bought her a new dress, two sizes larger than her prepregnancy clothes, thanks to the baby weight she was still carrying, two months after giving birth. The dress was white eyelet, and he claimed to love the way it looked against her olive skin. She suspected the way it danced around her thighs didn't hurt, but whatever kept his eyes on her was perfect. Not that she'd ever had any trouble holding his attention, even when she'd nearly outgrown her maternity clothes a few months ago. Cruz always thought she looked beautiful, and he told her so often, she even believed it.

A major sign of emotional healing, according to her therapist.

Cruz, on the other hand, had worn a simple black V-neck T-shirt with his usual nicely fitting jeans. He looked like a romance novel cover model.

Gina took a moment to admire the acres of bluegrass, the tidy flower beds and the abundance of baby animals in pens and pastures before climbing out of the Jeep. She had a new appreciation for the mamas with their offspring since she'd joined their ranks in February, with the help of a fully recovered Dr. Tulane. Her daughter, Angelique Marie Ricci, had been born three weeks early, but she was absolutely perfect, and Gina could barely remember life without her.

Cruz unfastened his seat belt and grinned. "Looks like the gang's all here," he said.

"Aren't they always?" she asked, climbing carefully down from the Jeep.

Derek had the most land and interior square footage of all the Winchesters, not to mention animals and an adorable toddler to draw the family to his place every Sunday. This night was no exception. Though there seemed to be more cars than usual.

"Is that my parents' car?" Gina asked.

Cruz pulled the baby carrier from the back seat, then met Gina on the grass with Angelique. "Looks like." He kissed Gina gently before taking her hand and leading her toward the rear deck, where sounds of music, chatter and laughter rose into the twilight. "You sure you don't mind spending another night over here, surrounded by all these Winchesters?" he asked. "We're here every weekend, and I know you're tired. It'd be fine if you'd rather have a nap."

Gina smiled. "I am tired, but you get up at night with Angelique just as often as I do," she said. "And I like seeing your family. They always have such great stories. And food." She linked her arm with his, enjoying the moment and warm evening breeze. "And apparently I get to see my folks too."

Cruz's family had become an extension of her own

last fall, and she'd moved into his house permanently only a few months after Tony had gone to jail. Her relationship with Cruz had grown exponentially and at breakneck speed from there. Moving in with him so soon after what she'd been through with Tony probably seemed like a mistake to some folks, but she'd never doubted her decision. In fact, she still thought about pinching herself most mornings, just to be sure she wasn't dreaming. The only thing she adored as much as her daughter and Cruz was his crazy family and the way they got along with hers. A massive holiday party at her parents' home had confirmed what Cruz had suggested shortly after he'd met Gina. The Winchesters and Riccis made fast friends. They'd mingled for hours, and lasting friendships were forged over tiramisu and eggnog.

She and Cruz turned at the sound of an incoming vehicle, then waited while Lucas and his wife, Gwen, climbed down from their truck.

Gwen met Gina with a hug. "Sorry we're late."

"I'm just glad you're here," Gina said.

Gwen had become like a sister to Gina during the winter, when the pair had bonded over their past traumas and present love of Winchester men. Nowadays, Gina looked forward to seeing her at each family gathering and catching up on anything she'd missed.

Lucas loosened his tie and unbuttoned his dress shirt at the collar. "The judge denied the Marino family's appeals," he said, a small smile blooming on his newly shaven face. "I thought she would, but I went anyway, just in case anyone needed a reminder on the severity of Tony's crimes. They didn't. Judge Hawthorne made it clear Tony will stay behind bars for a very long time. Probably the rest of his life, without parole."

Gina crossed the bit of space between them and hugged Lucas, catching him off guard as usual.

Gwen laughed.

"She's a hugger," Cruz said, the smile evident in his voice.

Lucas patted Gina's back. "We've all got you," he said. "You don't have to worry about anything anymore."

She stepped away with a smile. "I know." She'd spent the past six months in therapy, working through all the issues Tony had caused her, and thanks to all her outside support, she felt stronger every week. "Thank you."

A sharp whistle drew the group's attention to the rear of the home, where Lucas's mom, Cruz's aunt, waved a hand overhead. "Are y'all coming over here? Or do we need to come over there?"

Gwen laughed, then led Lucas in his mama's direction. He swiped the baby carrier from Cruz's hand on his way past. "We've got Angelique," he said. "You two lovebirds take your time."

Gina snuggled against Cruz's side as they walked, reveling in her good fortune and gratitude. She'd been through the unthinkable, but she'd gained a fairy tale, and she wouldn't change it for anything in the world.

An array of bistro lights came into view, strung randomly through the trees and above and around the deck. Several tables had been lined along the perimeter. One of those was packed with food, the rest with people. Winchesters, Riccis and a smattering of cops, detectives and friends.

"What's going on?" Gina asked Cruz softly as the little crowd quieted and smiled at their arrival.

"Baby!" Gina's mom cooed. "Come here." She pulled Gina into a hug, then passed her to her father and sister.

Gina laughed. "I didn't know you guys were coming," she said. "It's so good to see you."

"Well, we weren't about to miss this," Kayla said, looking as if Gina had grown a second head.

Gina smiled, thankful every day for the full recovery her little sister had made from her overdose at Tony's hand. She, too, was still in counseling for the trauma, and Gina enjoyed the occasional session they shared together.

She'd thought her family was close before, but the horrors they'd endured only served to strengthen their already tight bonds.

"Miss what?" she asked, frowning at Kayla's bright smile.

The volume on the stereo lowered, and the song changed to a ballad Cruz had deemed their song on New Year's Eve. That same song had been playing the night he'd first told her he loved her, and on the night she'd officially moved in.

"Cruz?"

She turned to seek his face for an explanation, but he wasn't at her side any longer.

Instead, he knelt on the ground, a small velvet box in his hand. Cruz pinched the lid between his thumb and first finger, then raised it to reveal a simple diamond solitaire. "This was my mama's," Cruz said, his voice cracking slightly on the words. He cleared his throat, then raised the box to her in one hand, wearing his trademark grin. He reached for her fingers with his free hand, then curled them gently in his. "Gina Marie Ricci."

She gasped, and the ragged, emotion-filled breath caused a round of chuckles and giggling from the crowd.

"I know we haven't been together long," Cruz said, "but I've been falling in love with you since the moment we met. I can't imagine living a life without you and Angelique in it. And I'm hoping you'll do me the honor of letting me be your husband."

Gina nodded and laughed as tears pricked, then fell from her eyes.

He stood to wipe the drops from her cheeks. "Marry me?" he asked softly.

And Gina said, "Yes."

* * * * *

ANNIE BURROWS
TAMES
Alison Roberts
The Doctor's Wife
FOR KEEPS
Twin Surprise for the
ITALIAN DOC
MILLS & BOON
BOUGHT
with the
ITALIAN'S RING
50% OFF
YOUR FIRST
PARCEL

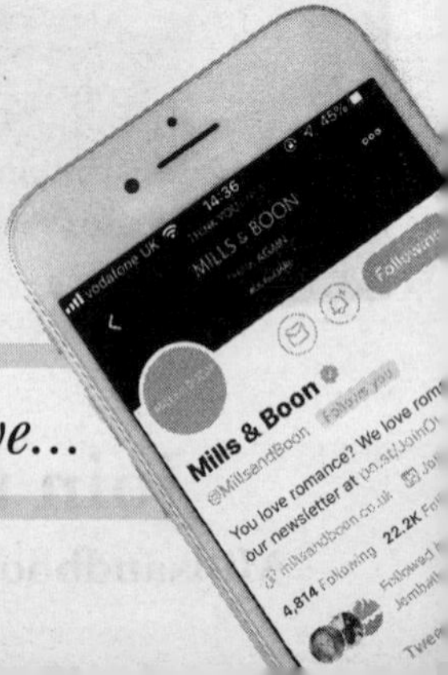

MILLS & BOON
Mills & Boon
@MillsandBoon